Witches Incorporated

He looked up again. 'Do I have to sign right now, or do I get some time to think about it? You know, read the fine pri

Sir Alec [...] enough for cogitation, M[...] ng second thoughts?'

The ghost [...] nal, whispering in his ear. *They're so frightened of you, Gerald, they can hardly spit.*

'No, no, it's not that. I just — well, you know what they say. Never sign a document you haven't read at least twice.'

Sir Alec just looked at him.

Oh, blimey. Gerald stared at the contract again. At his black-and-white future. The years stretched ahead of him, full of danger and duty. Deception and lies. Loneliness. Fear.

Full of doing the right thing. Full of making amends. Full of Lionals who have to be stopped. The dead must be honoured … and you gave them your word.

He signed.

BY K. E. MILLS

Rogue Agent Series

The Accidental Sorcerer

Witches Incorporated

Witches Incorporated

ROGUE AGENT
Book Two

K. E. Mills

www.orbitbooks.net

ORBIT

First published in Australia in 2009 by Voyager,
HarperCollins*Publishers* Australia Pty Limited
First published in Great Britain in 2009 by Orbit
Reprinted 2009

A CIP catalogue record for this book
is available from the British Library.

ISBN 978-1-84149-728-0

Printed in the UK by CPI Mackays, Chatham, ME5 8TD

Papers used by Orbit are natural, renewable and recyclable
products sourced from well-managed forests and certified
in accordance with the rules of the Forest Stewardship Council.

Mixed Sources
Product group from well-managed
forests and other controlled sources
www.fsc.org Cert no. SGS-COC-004081
© 1996 Forest Stewardship Council

Orbit
An imprint of
Little, Brown Book Group
100 Victoria Embankment
London EC4Y 0DY

An Hachette UK Company
www.hachette.co.uk

www.orbitbooks.net

*To the Orbit Sales Team, who work so hard
on their authors' behalf*

CHAPTER ONE

According to Department records, the property was known as Establishment 743-865-928/Entwhistle.

Gathered in smoky mess hall corners, inhaling a quick cig — or a pipe, if they were particular — Sir Alec's senior janitors, his most hard-bitten secret agents, called it 'the haunted house'. Rolling their eyes when they said it. Sort of joking. But mostly not. Never elaborating; why should they? Nobody had warned *them*. Nobody gave *them* a heads-up the day before they faced final assessment. They'd sunk or swum, no half-measures. And no help. What do you reckon, Dunwoody? You reckon you deserve any different, just because someone's told you you're the bee's thaumaturgical knees? Sink or swim, mate. That's how it works. That's how the pretenders get shuffled out of the pack. If you're as good as they say you are, well … you'll be laughing, won't you?

Shrouded in a damp early morning mist, deep in the wilds of rural Ottosland, Gerald wasn't feeling particularly amused. Cold? Yes. Apprehensive? Certainly. Beginning to wonder if he'd made a mistake? Without question. But *really* not in the mood for a giggle.

I wish Reg was here. Or Monk. Melissande, even. At this point I'd probably throw my arms around Rupert, butterflies and all.

But he squashed the thought a heartbeat after it formed. The first rule he'd made for himself upon entering janitorial training was *No pining*. Yes, he missed his friends but he'd see them again sooner or later. He'd already seen Monk once. A work-related visit, to be sure, no social niceties allowed, but still. It proved he wasn't languishing in *permanent* exile.

He just wished the situation with his parents was equally straightforward. Returned at long last from gallivanting around the world, they couldn't understand why he kept putting off a visit and was so *vague* about his new employment and why he'd given up on his last position as a royal court wizard. So prestigious, that had been. What had gone wrong *this* time? And when are we going to *see* you, son?

'*Sorry*,' he kept saying in his letters. He'd phoned them once, but couldn't bear to do that again. His mother's tearful voice was enough to break him. '*I'll tell you all about New Ottosland soon, I promise. Just a bit busy now. You know how it is.*'

Except they didn't know, and they never could. He'd have to lie to them. And once he did that — once he crossed that line — he could never cross back, which meant something precious would be irreparably broken. Too much in his life, in himself, had changed of late. While his parents' backs were turned he'd become some dark, unfathomable stranger ... and he knew he couldn't trust himself not to let them see it. It was still too soon.

They'd have to be lied to eventually, of course. He knew that. He did. Just ... not yet.

Abruptly aware of stinging eyes and ragged breathing, Gerald shook his head sharply. *Enough, Dunnywood.* There was no point working himself into a state over what couldn't be helped. For better or worse he'd chosen this new life. This ... penance. That meant living with the consequences.

Time to focus on the job at hand.

Which right here, right now, was surviving till supper. Because one of Sir Alec's senior janitors, a pale, bruised-looking chap by the name of Dalby — well, this week, anyway — had confided over a mug of stewed tea that the Department property's name-tag designation had a habit of changing. Whenever, rumour whispered, the house claimed a new victim. Today it was tagged Entwhistle. Tomorrow it might be ... well, it might be known as Dunwoody. You never know, eh?

Gerald tucked his cold-nipped fingers into his armpits and bounced on his toes to keep his sluggish blood moving. *That's right. You never know. Life is full of surprises.* And some of them, it turned out, were more palatable than others.

But he wasn't going to think about that, either. What was the point? He'd done what he'd done and he was who he'd become. Regret and remorse could change none of it. If the last tumultuous, exhausting and unexpected six months of his life had taught him nothing else, they'd taught him that one biting, bitter lesson.

Instead, he peered through the impassable, imposing wrought-iron gates before him, up the long straight driveway to the house, trying to make out more than a few haphazard chimney pots and a vague hint of higgledy-piggledy gables. No luck. But whether that was because he was blind in one eye or because the autumnal mist was just too thick or because the house was protected by some kind of deflection incant, he couldn't tell.

Towering oak trees on either side of the gates dripped moisture like a leaking tap, *plink plink plink* on his hatless head and coated shoulders. The water trickled nastily between skin and shirt-collar, all the way down his spine to the waistband of his trousers. Beneath his feet, the gravel was muddy and rutted. Fading into the distance the muffled clip-clop of hooves and the creak of wooden wheels as the cart that had deposited him here returned to the railway station.

Otherwise, the surrounding countryside was quiet. Too quiet. Not a cock-crow, not a bleating lamb. No dog barked. No milch cow lowed. He could hear his heart thudding sullenly against his ribs. That was nerves. Because here he was in far-flung, bucolic Finkley Meadows, and all his hopes, dreams and fears were come down to this.

Testing time.

Tucked beneath his overcoat, in the pocket of his jacket, was a single folded sheet of paper, decorated with precise spiky writing in plain black ink. *Time to pay the piper, Mister Dunwoody. Finkley Meadows. The 8th, at dawn. Someone will meet you on the platform. Sir Alec.* A one-way railway token had accompanied the missive.

He remembered thinking: *So is the Department merely being fiscally responsible, or should I take the hint and give up while I still can?*

But of course he'd accepted the invitation. The challenge. Reg would never forgive him if he tucked his tail between his legs and ran.

So all right. I'm here. I'm ready to be tested.

Except the property's daunting front gates were hexed shut, and he couldn't pin down the incant. Slippery and insubstantial, like melting soap at the bottom of the bathtub, it teased the edges of his awareness. Taunted his newfound, newly-honed expertise. He tried till he sweated but he couldn't lay a finger on it. The gates remained stubbornly, unbelievably closed.

'*Damn!*'

Blowing out a short, frustrated breath he glared at them, and then at the stone wall they were hinged onto. Intimidatingly tall, patchworked with moss and choking ivy, he had no hope of climbing over it. Of course, he could *fly* over the bloody thing if he dared risk a levitation incant on himself. But levitation incants, like the speed-em-up hex, like any kind of thaumaturgy which altered the properties of living tissue, were strictly off limits. If he tried one, and something went wrong, being caught breaking the law would be the least of his worries. Being buried in something no bigger than an egg cup was a far more likely outcome.

So. Scratch that bright idea.

Did whoever was in the house even know he'd arrived? He hadn't a clue. Nor did there seem to be any way of communicating with the distant, fog-shrouded establishment. No crystal ball, not even a boring, ordinary telephone. Of course, he could always shout . . .

Honestly, this was ridiculous.

He blew out another breath. Then, surrendering to temper, he wrapped his fingers around the gates' wrought-iron bars and shook. 'Come on! Let me in! I'm catching pewmonia out here!'

Nothing. The gates' locking incant buzzed fuzzily through his gloves. *Fuzzily* . . .

'Oh!' he exclaimed. 'You *idiot*, Gerald.'

With a fingersnap and a single command he deactivated the anti-etheretic shield that stifled his unique thaumic imprint. Wearing the wretched thing was a bit like enduring faulty earplugs. He wasn't thaumaturgically deaf, not exactly, but he was definitely compromised. No wonder he couldn't get past the hexed gates. He hated the shield, and had said so, forcibly, but nobody would listen. In the end he'd taken his complaints to Sir Alec. Softly-spoken and blandly nondescript, the man lurked in the shadows of every Department conversation. As though he could see through walls and read thoughts from a distance. Even when he was absent, his presence at janitorial headquarters was inescapable. He was the absolute, ultimate authority.

But Sir Alec hadn't had any sympathy either.

'Mister Dunwoody,' he'd said, his pale grey eyes severe, 'stop wasting my time. Your identity must remain obscure and so far that shield is the best method we can contrive. So you'll not put one toe in public without first activating your thaumic obfuscator, is that clear? The last thing we need is anybody noticing you.'

And of course, Sir Alec was right. Janitorial agent Gerald Dunwoody couldn't afford to stand out in any way. Which was also why Monk had devised a nifty little incant that turned his silvered blind eye brown again. The change wasn't permanent; even with Monk's best efforts it wore off after five hours or so, but it was easily reapplied. And with both incants activated he could pass muster as the old Gerald Dunwoody, with two normal-looking eyes and a lousy Third Grade thaumic signature.

The good old days.

With the shield-incant cancelled he could feel his muffled senses coming alive again. Feel the ebb and flow of the ether, fluctuations in the thaumic currents. He could feel his rogue powers, simmering gently beneath his ordinary surface.

Ever since joining Sir Alec's department — whenever he wasn't studying the complicated rules of domestic and foreign thaumaturgic policing and how to apply them without creating fourteen different kinds of international incident — he'd cautiously explored his newfound abilities. So far he'd not met a First Grade incant he couldn't master: something that had him swinging wildly between elation and trepidation. One minute he was awash with heart-pounding apprehension — *nobody should have this much power, not even me* — and the next he was terrified he'd wake up to find it vanished and himself returned to unremarkable mediocrity.

He was still waiting for that pendulum to stop.

And then there was the dizzying parade of mysterious Department experts who came to examine him, who'd smiled vaguely, politely, and said, '*Call me Doc*'. They'd poked him and prodded him, run test after test, pulled faces and gone away again, never bothering to share their findings with their subject. He'd hated it, hotly resenting being kept in the dark. He was the one being poked and prodded, wasn't he? Jumped through hoops like a dog at the circus? He had a right to know exactly who and what he was, didn't he?

No. Apparently he didn't. Not according to Sir Alec, anyway, whose continued lack of sympathy had been chilling ... if not entirely unexpected.

'It's not a question of us wanting to control you, Mister Dunwoody,' Sir Alec said briskly. 'When the time's right we'll tell you everything you need to know.'

'And when will that be?' he'd demanded. 'I don't think you understand what this is like. Knowing what I'm capable of. Knowing what's ticking away inside me. *Not* knowing what I'm — you're — *we're* going to do about it.'

Sir Alec had sat back in his leather armchair then, and shifted his pale grey gaze to stare through his office window at the dreary suburban street outside.

'Well, I rather think that's the crux of the problem, don't you?' he asked, surprisingly mild. 'You *don't* know what you're capable of, any more than we do. The truth is we're still trying to figure you out.'

'Oh,' Gerald said, taken aback. 'So ... what does that mean? Does it mean I can't even be trusted as a janitor? That I'm stuck in this mausoleum for the rest of my life, performing tricks for visiting Department thaumaturgists?'

'No, of course not,' Sir Alec retorted, and leaned forward with his elbows braced on his desk. 'It's not a question of trust. It's a question of making sure we handle this unique situation properly. Mister Dunwoody, I thought your experiences in New Ottosland would've made the danger obvious. King Lional wasn't the only ambitious man in the world. There are other people — entire governments, actually — who, if they knew of your existence, might well go to quite dramatic lengths to get their hands on you.'

It was like being doused with a bucket of ice-water. 'Are you saying I'm some kind of *target*?'

Sighing, Sir Alec sat back again. 'I'm saying this is a game full of hypothetical scenarios. I'm saying one of the things I get paid to do is dream up potential disasters and then concoct ways of preventing — or in the worst case, surviving — them. But the operative word here is *hypothetical*. Really, Mister Dunwoody, you must not be an alarmist.'

'I'll stop if you stop,' he retorted. 'I agreed to join your team so I could do some good in the world, not sit around in basements giving thaumic contabulators hysterics.'

'One step at a time, Mister Dunwoody,' said Sir Alec, infuriatingly bland. 'If we're to teach you how to protect the world and its innocents from nefarious individuals, first we must fully understand what makes you tick. So you need to be patient. Let us complete our investigation. When that's done, we can talk again.'

Investigation. Sir Alec had made him sound like a — a *crime*. Although maybe that wasn't such a poor choice of words. What had happened in New Ottosland ... that had been criminal.

Of course, in the end he'd swallowed his anger and frustration and suffered the Department's endless, ongoing examinations. What other choice did he have? He had nowhere else to go. The government's position had been made perfectly clear: rogue wizards were untidy. They couldn't be left ... lying about.

'There's no point squealing, mate,' Monk told him a week later when he brought the eye-changing incant for testing. 'Sir Alec's the best in the business. He knows what he's doing — *and* he's right. I can name two unfriendly governments and four dubious companies who'd love to bottle what you've got. And that's just off the top of my head. So you stay put here for as long as Sir Alec tells you. Let the boffins run all the tests they want, twice. You'll be safe that way.'

And that had given him a horrible jolt.

Monk was afraid for him? Why? What did he know that Sir Alec wasn't saying?

'There's no need to panic, Gerald,' Monk had added, reading him with unerring accuracy, as usual. 'There's nothing in the wind. Sir Alec's just ... being careful. Don't worry about it.'

So he hadn't. Or at least, not very much. Instead he'd endured the ongoing poking and prodding and rehashing of what had happened in New Ottosland, and put all his leftover energy into his janitorial studies. And he must have done something right because here he was at the front gates of the haunted house, ready to prove without doubt that Gerald Dunwoody was up to the task of being one of Sir Alec's junior janitors. Ready to start paying back the debt he owed his dead.

In which case, Dunnywood, it's past time you got this show on the road.

He tugged off his gloves, shoved them in his pocket, then ran his fingers lightly over the hexed gates' weathered wrought iron. That was better. He could read the incant properly now — and it was a right little sod, too, prickly as a thornbush. Intricately tangled. Deviously devised. Tasting of stinkweed, scented with deception.

Is this one of Monk's hexes? I'll bet it's one of Monk's. I'm sure I can catch a whiff of Monkishness in here ...

But he wasn't only sensing his friend's familiar, anarchic thaumic signature. This incant felt like a joint operation. More than one wizard had helped to create it. So the Department's best were ganging up on him, were they? He grinned.

You want to play, chaps? All right. Let's play.

Except the game swiftly became deadly serious, because as far as thaumaturgic tests went this one was murder. The hex actually *did* test him, which was no mean feat. He was a rogue wizard, after all. Challenges like this were supposed to be *easy*.

At least he thought they were.

Oh, well. If it was easy they wouldn't call it a test, would they?

Sweating, swearing, he dismantled the convoluted hex one brilliant, stubborn strand at a time. Monk and his mates had really pulled out all the stops, doubling and redoubling the bindings, slyly tricking him with feints and misdirections that left his fingers stinging and his hair standing on end. But in the end he was victorious. After nearly half an hour of squinting concentration the incant's final binding snapped and he was rewarded by the gates slowly swinging wide on soundless hinges.

One fist pumped above his head in a restrained exhibition of triumph. 'Ha! *Yes*! Choke on *that*, Mister Markham! You and your fancy Research and Development chums!'

Not that he was taking the hex personally, of course. Chances were that Monk didn't even know who it was being designed for. Sir Alec was a master at keeping secrets, after all. But either way — whether Monk was in on the game or not — there was no denying the deep satisfaction of defeating the best thaumaturgy a team of First Grade wizards could throw at him. Because rightly or wrongly, it was going to take a lot longer than six months to forget what being a despised Third Grade wizard had felt like.

By now the early morning's blanket of mist had almost completely burned away, so the sun was free to gild the hedgerows and grass verges that bordered the country lane. Wild snapdragons and shy bluebells danced among the untidy greenery. Tiny scarlet-faced finches hopped and strutted on spindly legs. Momentarily distracted, Gerald smiled. After so long in grimly tarmacked and cobblestoned Nettleworth, where the only grass to be found was in a painting, Finkley Meadows was a literal breath of fresh air. But there was no time to appreciate its postcard prettiness right now. Right now he had more tests to pass.

Abruptly sober, remembering with a nasty twinge *why* he'd

just unravelled that hex, Gerald took a deep breath, cautiously stepped through the gates, and only jumped an inch or two when they slammed shut behind him. On another deep breath, his heart again banging at his ribs, he started walking towards the Department house's distant front door. More oak trees lined each side of the gravel driveway, their spreading branches and boisterous foliage blotting out the clear blue sky. Beyond their ragged sentinel stand, an unkempt garden swallowed open ground. Lacy shreds of mist tangled amongst the snarled undergrowth, and an ominous chill seeped upwards through the untamed grass, smelling old, and rank, and angry.

He shivered. *So much for picturesque.*

Despite the general theme of 'Don't tell the new chum anything about the establishment', a couple of the younger, more recently recruited agents he'd met in passing at headquarters had let one or two small hints slip. Apparently every trainee agent ended up here at the house, where they faced a test designed specifically for them. If they passed, congratulations. Welcome to one of the most dangerous jobs in the world. Have fun and don't forget to sign your will.

'And if we fail?' he'd asked. 'What happens then?'

No-one knew. Not for certain. But failed trainees were never seen again.

Remembering *that*, Gerald shoved his gloveless hands in his overcoat pockets, scrunched his shoulders round his ears and walked a little faster. Nothing but a hobgoblin story, surely. The government couldn't go around *disappearing* people. That would be illegal. No, the agents had been playing tricks on him. Probably the senior agents had put the juniors up to it. Old dogs geeing up the new pup. Having some fun at his expense.

'That's all it is, Reg,' he said in passing to the wood pigeon staring at him from a nearby low branch. 'Them taking the mickey. I've got nothing to worry about. I'll be *fine*.'

The pigeon, who actually didn't look much like Reg at all, really the only thing they had in common were the feathers, cocked its head to one side and cooed down at him, dimly.

He sighed. 'Right. Yes. Thanks so much for that. Very helpful. Most inspiring.'

Lord, he missed Reg.

It occurred to him then, steadily walking, that the house at the end of the driveway wasn't getting any *closer*. In fact, it seemed to be further away now than when he'd started.

He stopped. Looked behind him. The closed gates seemed the right distance away, given how long he'd been walking. How *strange*. He looked back to the house —

— and nearly fell over, because he was on the other side of the gates again, in the muddy laneway, looking through the wrought-iron bars at misty, haphazard chimney pots and higgledy-piggledy gables.

His jaw dropped. 'Bloody hell!'

This time the hex wasn't the same one he'd so painstakingly unravelled a few minutes ago — but it was just as tricky and demanding. He nearly went cross-eyed dismantling it, but at long last the gates swung open. Practically bolting through, he paid no attention as they slammed shut behind him. Put his head down, sprinted for the house —

— and nearly broke his nose on the closed wrought-iron gates.

'*What*?' he shouted, and jumped up and down a bit. 'This is *ridiculous*! How am I supposed to pass the damned test if I can't even set foot in the house?'

Except, apparently, this *was* the test. Or at least the start of it. Obviously the driveway was hexed, just like the front gates. But why hadn't he sensed it? Worse yet, what else hadn't he sensed? What other nasty surprises were waiting for him? He didn't have a bloody clue. Wonderful. His morning was lurching from bad to worse. All right. *Think, Dunwoody.* Was he supposed to defuse both hexes? No, no, that was too easy. Too obvious. There had to be a different explanation. This was a test devised by Sir Alec, after all. He had to think *sideways*. He had to think *devious*.

What is it I've been training to be? An agent. And what is it agents do? They slide into tricky situations unobtrusively. Hmmm. Nothing terribly unobtrusive about marching through the front gates and up the driveway straight to the front door, is there? So think, you plonker. How else can you get to where you need to go?

Of course he could just blast the establishment's encompassing high stone wall to rubble. Lord knew he had an arsenal of destructive incants at his fingertips these days. Except much of his janitorial training had been about finesse and subtlety.

So. No blasting, either.

Maybe there were some handy little cracks and crevices under the moss and ivy? Finger-and-toe holds that could help him climb up and over?

But when he tried digging handfuls of green stuff off the stonework the most appalling wave of nausea flooded through him, courtesy of a powerful anti-intruder incant. Head reeling, stomach rebelling, he flailed backwards and nearly landed on his rump in the muddy road. Balance recovered, breathing hard, he waited for the awful sickness to subside.

This is embarrassing. I'm a rogue wizard! I turned a cat into a lion. Hell's bells, I made a dragon ... but I can't get myself over a wall?

Apparently not.

So there was no going through the front gates and no climbing over the wall. That meant there had to be another way in. Disgruntled, he switched his shield-incant back on, because he was in public and that was the arrangement, and started tromping.

The moss-and-ivy covered stonework faithfully followed the edges of the country lane, in places so closely he had to leap down from the narrow verge. There was no sign of another gate or any breach in the wall. At this rate he was never going to find his way in. And would that mean some kind of a Department record? Gerald Dunwoody, rogue agent, the first wizard in history to fail janitorial testing by not even making it through the front door?

Bloody hell. I hope not.

Rounding a sharp bend in the lane, without warning he was confronted by an enormous hay wagon heading straight for him. There wasn't time to get across the lane to the hedgerow on the other side, and the only way he wasn't going to get squashed by the dangerously overhanging hay was if he flattened himself against the wall.

Oh no. I am going to be so sick ...

With a despairing groan he closed his eyes and turned his face away. Pushed his shoulder-blades, spine and hamstrings flat to the spongy moss and surrendered to the messy inevitable.

Which didn't happen.

The hay wagon trundled by, its driver oblivious to his discomfort, clearly contemptuous of madcap townie pedestrians who ought to know better than go prancing about the countryside on foot. The wagon's massively hairy carthorse snorted, matching its driver's opinion, soup-plate hooves splashing liquid mud and stones.

Remarkably unflattened and miraculously *not* sick, Gerald gaped at the wall. Then, just to be certain, he leaned his full weight against it. No. Not so much as a quease.

This is absurd. What's going on? What's changed?

Only one thing.

He deactivated the shield-incant and warily touched his fingertips to a bare patch of stonework. A wave of nausea immediately crashed over him. Retching, he slammed the shield in place again and the sickness vanished.

Right. Right. There's a point to this, I know there is. Somewhere here there's a message. I think. What a pity I don't speak fluent Sir Alec . . .

But at least one thing was abundantly clear. With his shield-incant switched on, if push came to shove he could climb the wall. Well. He could climb the wall if he could *climb*. Except climbing had never really been his thing, not even as a small, mildly adventurous boy. Maybe someone had left a handy sheep-hurdle lying about, that he could hex into a wooden flying carpet. This was the countryside after all. *Surely* abandoned sheep-hurdles were as common as dandelions . . .

Except no. They weren't. But there was, it turned out, a tree growing more-or-less close to the wall, further along the lane. It was better than nothing and all he was going to get.

Muddy, splintered, scraped and bruised, Gerald picked himself up out of the quagmire on the other side of the wall. Snapping off the shield-incant again, he held his breath. Then, when nothing terrible happened, he began clearing a path through out-of-control brambles, feral apple trees and hazelnut-thickets taller than he was, making his way back to the waiting Department house.

This is ridiculous. I'm a wizard, not a wilderness explorer.

Branch by thorn by gnarled, tangled root, the jungle surrendered to his careful incants and he slid his way through it, as inconspicuously, as *subtly*, as he could. Getting closer, the haphazard chimney pots and higgledy-piggledy gables of the establishment.

With cautious optimism he pushed through the last of the undergrowth into relatively clear ground. Saw oak trees. Saw the gravel driveway. Saw the house's front door, beckoning. Feeling his face split wide in a smile he tugged his coat free of the last bramble and strode forward.

'Oh, Gerald,' said a petulant voice. 'Why did you have to go and kill me? We made such a grand team. You know, together we could have ruled the world.'

CHAPTER TWO

Gerald spun round, his heart thudding. *Lional*. Not as he'd last seen him, a nightmarish corpse, but exactly as he'd been in his extravagant prime. Dressed in black velvet sewn with seed pearls. Negligently leaning against an accommodating tree trunk. Handsome. Charismatic. Rotten to the core.

It's in the eyes, he realised, staring at New Ottosland's improbably resurrected king. *It always was. Why didn't I see it? How did I let myself get fooled?*

Except he hadn't been fooled. Not really. Yes, Lional was deceptive — the king of deception, as it turned out — but in Gerald Dunwoody he'd had a willing accomplice. He hadn't liked Lional from the moment they met, but the sauce of desperation can make the most revolting meal edible. And there was no getting away from it: after the debacle at Stuttley's he'd been pretty desperate.

As he stood there, staring at impossible Lional, dreadful memories slithered past his mind's eye: *the cavern. The crimson-and-emerald dragon. The dead and dying of New Ottosland and those who'd been left alive, perpetually maimed.*

If this was part of Sir Alec's test he didn't much care for it. He'd prepared himself for metaphysical challenges, not a stagger down potholed memory lane.

Lional looked up from inspecting his beautifully manicured fingernails. 'You haven't answered my question, Gerald,' he said, reproachful. 'I think that's rather rude, don't you?'

He held his ground, just, and with an effort shook off his dismay. 'No. You're not real.'

Lional smiled; a suggestion of crimson scales slid beneath his skin. 'Tell that to your nightmares.'

His nightmares. He shivered. 'You're not real now. You died.'

'Tsk tsk, Gerald,' Lional chided. 'You used to have much prettier manners. Gratitude would be more becoming, you know. After all, I made you. You could at least say "Thank you, Sire".'

Gerald stared at the gravelled driveway. Every muscle and sinew was screaming at him to turn around and walk away. He'd spent the last six months trying to *forget* this bastard. Forget the cave, and what had been done to him there. What he'd done. What Lional had seen. But Sir Alec had to have his reasons for such a charade, so he didn't surrender to the almost overwhelming impulse to retreat. Surrender meant failure.

And I didn't come all this way to fail.

He looked up. Not to look up, not to look at Lional, would've been cowardly. '*Thank you*? I don't think so, Lional. Have you forgotten? You made me a murderer.'

'I made you a thaumaturgical *god*,' retorted Lional. 'Pushed you past your dreary moralities so you could get a glimpse of the infinite realm that was waiting for you.'

'The infinite horrors, you mean.'

Sighing, Lional rolled his eyes. 'Oh, Gerald. Such melodrama. It doesn't become you.' He spread his hands wide, entreating. 'Don't you remember what it was *like*, being a dragon? All right, as dragons go the one you made was pathetic but the principle still holds. You *flew*. You were *invincible*.' Another sigh, sorrowful this time, and his hands dropped. 'And then you threw it all away.'

Gerald let dead Lional's barbed words wash over him. So what was the point of this? Did Sir Alec think he was having second thoughts? Did he want to make sure his newest janitor wasn't regretting the decision to use his outrageous talents for good? Was he somehow listening to this crazy conversation?

Well, if you are, Sir Alec, prick up your ears and listen to this.

'I did what I had to do, Lional,' he said flatly. 'The only thing I could've done and still live with myself.'

Ruby rings flashing in the mellow morning light, Lional clasped his elegant hands before him. 'No, Gerald. You turned your back on brilliance. You chose dancing to mediocrity's dull little tune.' Another smile. More hints of sliding crimson. 'And now tell me you don't regret it. Tell me you don't dream of being a dragon ... and repine.'

As though Lional's words were a summoning, Gerald felt the unnatural forces within him stir. His incandescent *potentia*, these past months kept strictly confined. In his veins the blood warmed. The ether trembled. The glory of the dragon thrummed through his bones.

'All these rules and regulations, Gerald,' said Lional, with spurious sympathy. 'Don't you find them just the tiniest bit *tedious?*'

If I did, I wouldn't tell you. 'Rules are important, Lional. They remind us of our ties to one another. They keep us civilised. You never grasped that, and you paid the price.'

'Yes, I thought you did,' said Lional, looking pleased. 'A wizard like you, as far beyond First Grade as First Grade surpasses a gnat, chained to mundane, mawkish convention. Manacled by *you must* and *you can't* and *under no circumstances shall you*. You are so *grand*, Gerald ... and they are so small. So they have to keep *you* small. It's the only way they can control you.'

He felt a prickle of temper. 'No-one's controlling me, Lional. I'm in the Department of my own free will.'

Lional's eyebrows lifted. 'Really? All right, Gerald. If you say so. But what if you wake up tomorrow and choose another path? What then?'

'I won't.'

'Perhaps not,' said Lional, watching his rubies flash and sparkle in the sun. 'But that wasn't the question, was it?'

Gerald shoved his hands in his pockets and stared at the sky. Once upon a time he'd been twinned with a dragon. Had flown untrammelled in the wild, warm air. Sometimes, in his dreaming, he was that dragon again. A creature of myth and magic, bound only by his will. Born because he wanted it. Brought to life because he could.

No, said a sharp, scolding voice in his head. *Because Lional was about to commit wholesale slaughter. So you took a small innocent life, because it was there and you needed it. And then you warped it, tortured it and in the end destroyed it to fix the mess you made. Nothing glorious about that, sunshine.*

Frowning, he scuffed his shoe-heel in the gravel.

'Would you like to know what *I* think, Gerald?' said Lional. His eyes were glittering. 'I think you *do* repine. I think you repine *daily*. I think if we could turn back time you'd choose differently. You'd join me. You'd *run* to me.'

He stepped back. 'No, Lional. I wouldn't.'

Lional laughed, softly mocking. 'The true test of honesty is what a man says to himself when no-one else can hear the words. Remember the cave? I *know* you, Gerald. Better than any man alive. Or dead.'

The cave. He took another step back. 'You don't know anything. You're not *real.*'

'I'm real enough to know you resent that ridiculous etheretic shield,' said Lional, with a nonchalant shrug. 'I know you're tired of being restrained. After all, what's the point of having power if you never get to use it? And they won't let you use it, you know. Sir Alec and his minions. They're so frightened of you, Gerald, they can hardly spit.'

'That's not true.'

Lional smiled. 'Isn't it?'

Sickened, Gerald stared at him ... forced at last to confront what he'd been trying for weeks now to deny. Lional was right. They *were* afraid of him. All that poking and prodding. All those tests. All those questions. Always someone watching when he ran through his selected, approved repertoire of incants. Watching. Measuring. Taking careful notes. As though they didn't trust him. As though they thought that if they turned their backs he'd do something crazy ... like make another dragon. Or turn them all into stoats.

'The real question, Gerald,' said Lional, 'is what are you going to do about it?'

'Nothing,' he retorted. 'They've got good reason to fear.'

I've got good reason. I need to be watched.

'Do you know what I think, Gerald?' said Lional, considering him carefully. '*I* think you've let them bamboozle you. You've let them turn you inside out and upside down. Got you convinced there's something *wrong* with who you are. *What* you are.'

Gerald folded his arms. 'And what am I, Lional?'

'Whatever you desire to be, of course.'

'Which makes you what — my conscience?' He snorted. 'Thanks, but I've already got one of those. Her name's Reg. And one is more than enough.'

Lional laughed, mocking again. 'One is one too many, Gerald. No man can fly with a millstone round his neck. Genius requires freedom. Morality is for the weak. Compassion is —'

'If you think that argument's going to convince me I made a mistake when I killed you, I'm afraid you're doomed to disappointment.'

Lional's cerulean eyes opened wide. 'Oh, no, Gerald. I know you don't regret killing me. I know you think you did the world a favour. I'm merely stating *my* position, that's all.'

He shook his head. 'Then *why* —'

'Because I want you to believe me,' said Lional, simply. 'I want you to believe yourself. I want you to be perfectly clear on the facts. You're *convinced* you did the right thing in New Ottosland. You *do* repine. You *know* they're afraid of you ... and even while a part of you shares that fear, another part — a much bigger part than you're willing to admit — resents them for holding you back.'

Gerald stared at him, silenced. *This isn't fair. Murderous madmen who tortured you to the brink of insanity aren't supposed to tell the truth.*

Lional yawned. 'Was there anything you wanted to add?'

'Just this,' he said quietly. *Are you listening, Sir Alec?* 'I do know I did the right thing, Lional. But when you claim I don't regret it ... *that's* where you're wrong. I regret I wasn't able to save you.'

'Oh, Gerald, Gerald,' said Lional, and wagged a roguish finger. 'Such an arrogant young man. Whatever makes you think I wanted to be saved?'

He shrugged. 'I never said you wanted it. I only know you needed it.'

Lional laughed again, a soft, shivering sound. 'Well, well. Fancy that. It seems, my dear Gerald, there's hope for you yet.'

Okay. That's it. Enough is enough. If I wanted mental therapy I'd have kept my second appointment with the Department's brain boffin.

'Look,' he said. 'It's getting late and I have a test to pass. Whatever game this is, I'm tired of playing it.' He turned on his heel and started walking. 'Goodbye, Lional. Or whoever you are.'

'Oh, you know who I am, Gerald,' Lional called after him. 'And you know where to find me. I'm never far away.'

Right. Fine. Gerald hunched his shoulders, feeling the gravel scrunch under his feet. Feeling his belly churn. What the hell was Sir Alec playing at? They'd already talked about Lional. Spent days and days dredging through the sorry escapade in New Ottosland. There was nothing new for Sir Alec to learn. Lional was dead. Literally and metaphorically. And the dead should stay buried.

He stopped walking, struck by a horrible thought.

Unless, of course, this has nothing to do with Sir Alec. Unless it's not even happening. What if I'm still in bed, back in Nettleworth, dreaming this is my final test? Because this is impossible. The hexed gates, the wall, Lional. It's crazy, all of it, just like a dream.

Profoundly unsettled, he swung about. The driveway behind him was empty. Lional had gone.

Yes, but was he ever there? Am I here? Or am I going to wake up in the next five minutes with my alarm clock dinging and drool on my chin?

Feeling like an idiot he slapped his own face, hard. *Ow.* The stinging in his cheek and palm seemed to suggest that yes, he was here.

But does that mean I've spent the last twenty minutes talking to myself? Because if I have there's a good chance I've gone mad. On the other hand, if Lional really was here that means I've been talking to a ghost and that means, hello, there's a good chance I've gone mad.

'Bloody hell, Reg,' he said to the empty sky. 'Why aren't you ever around when I need you?'

He spun on his heel again and stamped the rest of the way up to the house.

It was an old place, two storeyed and rambling, built from weathered yellow sandstone. Thick green ivy crept up the walls in search of a better life. There were five timber-framed windows, all crooked, all with sun-bleached curtains blocking the glass. A long time ago the front door had been painted fire-engine red. Now it was faded, its brass gargoyle knocker and round doorknob desperate for attention. An ivy-covered archway protected anyone forced to bang on it in the rain.

Gerald hesitated, just for a moment, then marched right up, rapped the gargoyle knocker emphatically, twice, and waited.

No answer.

He pressed his hand flat to the door's dulled red paint, expecting to feel some kind of incant or hex. Nothing. He banged the gargoyle knocker again, hearing a faint suggestion of hollow echoes deep within the house. Still no answer.

'Well, bugger this for a boatload of monkeys,' he said at last, grabbed the doorknob and turned it. The door opened without protest, a conservative inch. So he took a deep breath, pushed it wide, and stepped over the threshold . . .

. . . into Sir Alec's austere office at Department headquarters, Nettleworth.

Seated behind his polished teak desk, neat and tidy as always, Sir Alec made a note in an open file then looked up. His unremarkable face was expressionless, but in his cool eyes lurked the merest hint of approval.

'At last, Mister Dunwoody,' he said. 'I was beginning to wonder if we'd see you again.' He nodded at the discouraging wooden visitor's chair. 'Have a seat. Just a few formalities, then we can discuss your first assignment.'

Stunned, Gerald sat. 'My first — you mean — that's *it*? That was the test? And I *passed*?'

Sir Alec was the least *casual* man he'd ever met. Sir Alec never slouched. He never slumped. He never leaned against anything. And if he was weary he never ever showed it. There was nothing whatsoever *restful* about him. His wintry smile appeared, briefly.

'Mister Dunwoody, the testing of your janitorial suitability started from the moment you arrived here. Surely you knew that? Or at least suspected it?'

'No. Well. Sort of. Maybe. At least — I thought — I

wondered —' He slewed round in the wooden chair and stared at the office door. 'Ah — Sir Alec — if you don't mind me asking — um — how did I get here? I mean, was that a portal? The door at the haunt — the establishment? Because it didn't feel like a portal. At least not like any portal I've ever travelled through.'

'Really, Mister Dunwoody,' said Sir Alec. Now he sounded irritated. 'We are a secret government Department. Did you think we *wouldn't* have a few surprises up our sleeve?'

He swallowed, hard. 'No, of course not. So who invented that one? Not Monk, by any chance?'

Instead of answering, Sir Alec reached for another file from the pile on his desk, opened it and extracted a sheet of heavy, official looking paper, embossed in five places with enormous crimson wax seals. The black ink printing looked equally official and impressive.

Gerald read his name on it, upside down, and felt his heart thud heavily.

This is it. I've done it. I'm a real live janitor.

He wasn't ready. He didn't know nearly enough. The international law, the restricted incants, the seventeen volumes of case files that didn't even scratch the surface of the Department's work over the past ten years. He'd barely absorbed any of it. All was chaos in his head, facts and figures tumbling like leaves in a windstorm. He didn't know enough yet to be let loose on the world.

Sir Alec was holding out a pen and a second sheet of paper. 'Mister Dunwoody?'

Still dazed, he took them. 'What am I signing?'

'Your permanent contract.'

'Oh.' He looked down. The words swam on the paper. *Insofar as ... wherefore the agent aforementioned ... duty and diligence ... penalties under the Act ... utmost secrecy ... blah blah blah blah ...*

He looked up again. 'Do I have to sign right now, or do I get some time to think about it? And, you know, read the fine print.'

Sir Alec frowned. 'Six months isn't long enough for cogitation, Mister Dunwoody? Or are you having second thoughts?'

The ghost of Lional, whispering in his ear. *They're so frightened of you, Gerald, they can hardly spit.*

'No, no, it's not that. I just — well, you know what they say. Never sign a document you haven't read at least twice.'

Sir Alec just looked at him.

Oh, blimey. Gerald stared at the contract again. At his black-and-white future. The years stretched ahead of him, full of danger and duty. Deception and lies. Loneliness. Fear.

Full of doing the right thing. Full of making amends. Full of Lionals who have to be stopped. The dead must be honoured ... and you gave them your word.

He signed.

'Excellent,' said Sir Alec, and stood. 'Now come with me.'

Gerald followed him out of the office, along the dingy corridor, down five flights of stairs to the underground complex beneath the unremarkable premises in Nettleworth, where he'd spent so much of his time lately being poked and prodded and investigated, like a crime.

But instead of going to the laboratory, which had become his second, reluctant home, Sir Alec led him to a small, featureless room with two doors, one chair and a table in it. On the table, in a black cradle, sat a lump of pale yellow scrying crystal.

'Have a look,' Sir Alec invited. 'Then tell me what you see.'

Bending over the table, Gerald stared into the crystal. 'A man,' he said. 'He looks ... frightened.'

'As well he should,' said Sir Alec grimly. 'The fool's been caught with the wrong secrets in his pocket. Now it's our job to find out precisely how much more he knows, that he shouldn't, and to which of our enemies he's passed — or intends to pass — his pilfered information.'

'I see,' said Gerald, and gazed again into the scrying crystal.

Slightly distorted by etheretic vibrations, the man sat on a wooden chair rather like the one in Sir Alec's office, his right arm pressed against his middle as though he had a pain, agitatedly chewing the fingernails of his left hand. He was thin and sallow ... or maybe that was just the scrying crystal's influence. He didn't much look like a thief of secrets. A traitor to his nation. Or not the way Gerald imagined a man like that would look. If you took away the fear and the fingernail-chewing he appeared earnest and prosperous. Like many of the men he'd worked with when he was a Probationary Compliance Officer.

'Is he a wizard?' he asked, straightening.

Sir Alec nodded. 'A Second Grader in the Department of Industry. The perfect target for subornment, Mister Dunwoody. Likes the ladies a little too much. Enjoys one tipple too many at his local club. Tends to bet just that fraction more than he can afford at the races.' He made a small sound of contempt. 'And then thinks he can save himself by betting more the next time.'

'Ah,' said Gerald. 'I have a second-cousin like that.' Morley, who'd never met a broken-down racehorse he wasn't convinced would win the Five Furlong Dash. 'So this man — this wizard — ah —'

Sir Alec smiled. 'His name's not important.'

Oh. 'So ... let me guess. This wizard got into debt, and couldn't get out of it, and did something stupid to try and save himself. Is that right?' Oh yes. *Just* like Morley.

'You consider him a victim, do you, Mister Dunwoody?' Sir Alec asked softly. 'A hapless, harmless ne'er-do-well who's just made a silly little mistake? Committed a small error of judgement?'

Surprised by the sudden chill in Sir Alec's voice, Gerald frowned. 'Well, no, not exactly. I mean, if he's been selling proprietary government information, well, obviously that's wrong. But —'

'But because he's not spilled blood, because he's not a murderer, because, really, how much trouble can you get into with a dull set of chaps like the Department of Industry, you don't think I should be taking this quite so seriously?'

Sir Alec's voice was so cold icicles were practically forming in the air.

'No, sir,' he said, close to shivering. 'I didn't say that, either.'

'Shall I tell you the consequences of this traitor's actions should we fail to uncover the extent of his perfidy and the identity of every last foreign agent in receipt of his stolen information?'

'Yes. Please.'

'You've been out of the way here, Mister Dunwoody,' Sir Alec said, his voice clipped. Still chilly. 'And fairly well occupied, so it's not unreasonable you're a trifle behind the times. Allow me, therefore, to bring you up to speed. There's been a breakthrough in the application of artificially agitated thaumicals to certain non-thaumically sensitive items. It's early days still, but should preliminary tests prove out, the patents will be worth a fortune. And before you ask, no, Mister Markham is not involved. I realise you're a great champion of his talents but he has only eight fingers and two thumbs and we — the government — have a few more pies to dabble in than that.'

Gerald managed, barely, to keep his face straight. 'Yes, sir. Of course, sir. Can you tell me any more about this breakthrough?'

'Once the process has been sufficiently refined and is applied,' Sir Alec continued, 'it will have a significant impact on various sectors of the economy. Enormous benefits will accrue to both government and selected private enterprise — at the

expense of several nations currently enjoying certain ...
monopolies. And that is as specific as I'm prepared to be. The
point, Mister Dunwoody, is that should these nations be warned
ahead of time as to our progress, or be given access to research
on the patents, they could either attempt to usurp the process or
take pre-emptive and punitive action that will severely damage
our economy.'

Gerald thought about that. 'But aren't we trying to damage
their economies?'

'*Trying?*' Sir Alec raised an eyebrow. 'Certainly not. We are
striving to benefit our nation, the primary duty of any good
government. I admit there will be some inevitable realignments
in some foreign revenues. An adjustment to income for the
nations in question. But that is the nature of international trade.
Swings and roundabouts, Mister Dunwoody. A loss here, a gain
there, and it all comes out in the wash. Eventually.'

Gerald nodded. 'I see.' *And I'm getting a headache.* 'So this is
about money.'

'It is about sovereignty and security,' Sir Alec snapped. 'And
preventing a war.'

'*War?* How did we get to war? I thought we were talking
about trade?'

'Trade is war,' said Sir Alec. 'Or at least a close relative. Mister
Dunwoody, you are not a stupid man. Ottosland has long been
the envy of lesser thaumaturgically-gifted nations. To allow the
envious to use our own gifts against us would be to encourage
their predations. To give the impression that we are an easy
target, disinclined to stand our ground. And as history so amply
demonstrates, to give that impression to one's enemies never
leads to a happy ending. In short we must nip this matter in the
bud. Before it comes to *real* war, and people start dying.'

'I can see that it's necessary,' said Gerald, slowly. 'But where
do I fit in?'

Sir Alec's wintry smile appeared again, brief as ever. 'You, Mister Dunwoody, are my pruning shears.'

Pruning shears? 'I'm sorry. I don't understand.'

'The wizard in question has proven himself remarkably ... stubborn,' said Sir Alec. 'Not only does he steadfastly decline to willingly co-operate with our investigation, he has managed to acquire for himself a shadbolt, to ensure his lack of assistance.'

What? Gerald stared, disbelieving. 'Is he mad?'

'Better say desperate,' said Sir Alec. 'Or greedy beyond any reason.'

'But not even the thaumaturgical black market deals in shadbolts. Does it?'

Sir Alec sighed. 'It deals in everything, Mister Dunwoody. No matter how ill-advised, distasteful or patently illegal. If one can pay, one can purchase.'

'Yes, but a *shadbolt*?'

'Clearly our friend next door gambled that his rewards would compensate for any ... personal inconvenience.'

'Next door? You mean he's —'

'Through there. Yes,' said Sir Alec, nodding at the small room's other exit. 'Waiting for you.'

Gerald felt his skin crawl. 'For me?'

'Indeed.' Sir Alec frowned. 'We can't break his hex, Mister Dunwoody. Whoever designed this particular shadbolt used some ... regrettable ... incants. After due consideration it's been decided that we need *your* particular and peculiar talents to loosen our man's tongue.'

Oh. 'I see.'

'So in you go. I'll be here, watching through the scryer. Ready to lend a hand should assistance be required.'

'Yes, sir,' he said. 'Ah ... Sir Alec? I'm only guessing because I've never done this before, but — forcibly breaking a shadbolt. That's not going to be pleasant.'

'Not for our treacherous friend, no,' Sir Alec agreed. 'But I'm inclined to feel he should've thought of that before he betrayed his country.'

'Yes. Only, was he thinking about betraying his country? Or was he just thinking about the money. Getting himself out of debt.'

Sir Alec raised an eyebrow. 'I don't know. Is it relevant?'

'Well ... yes. I think it is.'

'Mister Dunwoody, you are an agent of the Ottosland government,' said Sir Alec, impatient. 'Committed to its service and the defence of the nation's sovereignty. You just signed a contract to that effect. And now you're being asked to honour that contract. Are you telling me you're not able to fulfil your obligation?'

'No,' said Gerald. His hands were sweaty. 'No, I'm not.'

'Then fulfil it,' said Sir Alec. 'The clock is ticking, Mister Dunwoody. Lives are depending on what you do next.'

Dizzy, he nodded. 'Yes, sir.'

The nameless Second Grade wizard jumped as the door into his small room opened.

'Hello,' said Gerald, closing it behind him. 'I'm Gerald.'

The wizard looked at him, uncertain. 'William.'

'Hello, William.'

William frowned. 'So, what are you? My lawyer?'

'Lawyer?' he said, feeling ill. 'No, I'm a wizard. Like you.'

'Ha. If you can turn around and walk out of here, you're not like me,' sneered William.

There was a second chair in this room. Gerald sat down and pressed his hands between his knees. 'Look. William. They've sent me in here to break your shadbolt.'

'Then you're wasting your time,' said William, dismissive. Beneath the bravado he stank of fear. 'My shadbolt's the best a small fortune can buy. Guaranteed to make me unbreakable.'

Gerald looked at him. *Let me out, let me out. I don't want to be here.* 'No-one's unbreakable, William.'

Arms folded across his chest, William sat back. 'I am.'

'No, you're not. Trust me.'

'All right. Fine. Go on, then, *Gerald*,' said William, shrugging. 'Give it your best shot. The others failed. You will too.'

Deeply apprehensive, Gerald closed his eyes and let his senses unfurl. He felt the shadbolt straight away, saw it in his mind's eye as a series of chains and padlocks looped and secured around William's etheretic aura. It was ingenious. Complicated. Diabolically strong. But so was he — and he could sense how to break it. In fact he could break it quite easily, in one fell swoop, if he didn't mind sending William insane. Or killing him.

He opened his eyes. 'William, you need to listen to me. Deactivate the shadbolt and tell Sir Alec whatever he needs to know. Because I really, *really* don't want to hurt you.'

William snickered, even as his fingers crept towards his mouth. 'You won't. You can't.'

Gerald stared at his hands, pressed almost bloodless now between his knees. 'Sir Alec,' he said, just loudly enough for the scrying crystal to pick up. 'I don't want to do this.'

'*He's not an innocent casualty, Mister Dunwoody,*' said Sir Alec, seemingly out of thin air. '*He's a willing accomplice. The kind of man who creates innocent casualties. Your compassion should be reserved for them.*'

'Even so ...'

'*I told you once this was not a job for the faint-hearted. I told you there were times when you'd have to be a scalpel. This, Mister Dunwoody, is one of those times.*'

A scalpel. Pruning shears. A dustpan and brush. How many euphemisms were there for what he'd become?

'*Please*, William,' he said, not caring that Sir Alec could hear his desperation. 'Tell us what you did. All of it. And after that we can work things out.'

William's eyes were the colour of dirty dishwater. Filled with unease now, his gaze jittered from side to side. His fingernails were so badly bitten they'd started to bleed. 'Can't. Can't. No talking. That's the deal.'

'*Mister Dunwoody.*'

Gerald flinched. Sighed. 'I'm sorry, William.' Looking with his mind's etheretically-tuned eye, he reached for the first strand of the shadbolt ... and snapped it.

William howled like a dog run over by a carriage.

Fighting a wave of nausea, he leaned forward. 'William, please, I'm *begging* you. Save yourself. *Talk.*'

William sobbed, and shook his head.

He snapped another strand of the shadbolt. William toppled sideways off his chair to the floor, blubbering, all bravado burned away in white-hot flames of pain. Gerald stared down at him ... and remembered the cave.

I can't do this. I'm not Lional.

'I can't do this,' he said out loud, to Sir Alec. 'If that means I'm in breach of contract then fine. Sue me. But I can't — I *won't* — do this.'

Without waiting for a reply he got off the uncomfortable wooden chair and walked to the small room's other door, the door that would let him get out of this place. He turned the handle, pulled it open ...

... and found himself outside the wrought-iron gates of the haunted house. The morning mist was heavy. Fading into the distance, the muffled clip-clop of hooves and the creak of wooden wheels as the cart that had deposited him here returned to the railway station.

And as he stared at the gates, numbed beyond any thought or feeling, they swung wide and soundless, inviting him to enter.

Cold despite his overcoat, gloved hands thrust deep in its pockets, he walked unhindered up the gravel driveway to the mist-shrouded, ivy-covered house. Banged the gargoyle doorknocker. Nodded to the very proper butler who answered the door.

'I'm Gerald Dunwoody. I believe I'm expected.'

'Certainly sir,' said the butler. 'Sir Alec is in the parlour. Please, follow me.'

And yes, Sir Alec was in the parlour, a buttercup yellow and fresh dairy-cream room. Seated in a blue-and-white striped wingback armchair and conservatively, nondescriptly dressed in a grey pinstripe suit, he was sipping tea from an elegant porcelain cup. He looked up as the butler announced his visitor.

'Ah. Mister Dunwoody,' he said, unnervingly expansive and genial. 'So good of you to join me. Come in. Sit down. Would you care for some refreshment?'

Standing just inside the doorway, Gerald shook his head. 'No, thank you,' he said, struggling not to sound as dazed as he felt. 'Sir Alec, what was that? Lional ... the hexed gates ... that wizard, William? What just happened?'

Sir Alec considered him over the rim of the teacup. 'What do you think happened?'

'I don't know, I — I thought it was real, then I thought I was dreaming, and then —' He shook his head again. 'I don't know. I'm assuming it was ... all part of the test?'

Sir Alec nodded. 'Correct.'

'And I passed?'

Not even this warm, cosy room could thaw Sir Alec's smile. 'Well ... let's just say you didn't fail.'

Oh. Well. That was good ... wasn't it?

'Do sit down, Mister Dunwoody,' added Sir Alec, much less genially. 'I'm not fond of repeating myself.'

He dropped onto the parlour's couch. 'Sorry, sir. So, if I've passed, and I'm a janitor, then what happens now?'

'Now, Mister Dunwoody?' Sir Alec put down the cup. 'Now I have a job for you.'

'A job?' he repeated. He still felt not quite real. 'Already?'

'Certainly,' said Sir Alec. 'The government's not in the habit of paying agents to loll about. It's time, Mister Dunwoody, for you to get your feet slightly damp.'

CHAPTER THREE

'*Anyway*,' said Monk, bounding back through the dining room doorway, slightly out of breath and looking ever-so-slightly flustered, 'it's going to be a while before I can fix the place up. I mean, Great-uncle Throgmorton may have left me the house but unfortunately his bequest didn't include the dosh for repairs and modernisation and so forth.'

'Huh,' said Emmerabiblia, as Monk slid into his seat at the table. 'At least Great-uncle Throgmorton remembered you exist. You *and* Aylesbury. He didn't leave *me* so much as a copper penny, the female-hating old miser. I hardly call *that* fair.'

Swallowing a groan, Melissande reached for her half-nibbled bread roll. She was fond of Monk's sister, she really was, but for the last three weeks all Bibbie could talk about was the gross unfairness of Great-uncle Throgmorton's will. And really, once you'd agreed fifty or sixty times about the unspeakable rottenness of mingy old men who were stuck in the middle of last century, what else was there to say? Apart from *Oh for the love of Saint Snodgrass, do shut up!* and that would only lead to unpleasantness ... which wasn't a good idea. They had enough on their plates without adding hurt feelings to the menu.

'I know, I know, it's not fair,' said Monk, impatiently sympathetic. Then he turned. 'The thing is, Mel, Great-uncle

Throgmorton was a die-hard old fogie. Women as Decorative Objects, Seen but Seldom Heard, that kind of thing. Not to be trusted with money or property or anything remotely smelling of business.'

'Yes,' she replied, with heroic restraint. 'Bibbie has mentioned that, in passing. Very outdated of him.'

'Still,' he added, 'you're welcome to come and live here with me, Bibbie. I already told you that. It's a big house, we could rattle around in it together and never bump into each other from one week to the next.'

Bibbie pulled a face. 'No, thank you very much. If you want someone to pick up your discarded socks and cook your meals and dust cobwebs off the ceilings then you can blasted well pay for the privilege, Monk. I have *no* intention of being your housekeeper.'

'What?' Monk adopted an air of wounded disbelief. 'Bibs, how can you even suggest it? *I'm* not Aylesbury, *I'd* never treat you like that! I'm the *nice* brother, remember?'

Even though she was still cross, Bibbie smiled, a little. 'Well. Nicer than Aylesbury, anyway,' she conceded. 'But I'm still not moving in. You spend most of your time staggering about in a thaumaturgical haze. I'd have to start cooking and cleaning and picking up your socks out of self-preservation and I have *much* better things to do with myself.'

'That's it, ducky,' said Reg, chortling on the back of the fourth dining chair. 'You tell him.'

Now Monk was looking put out. 'What better things?' he muttered. 'It's not like you're solving the great metaphysical mysteries of our time, are you?'

Which was *exactly* the wrong thing to say. Melissande, wincing, debated pitching the remains of her dinner roll at him. Bibbie didn't bother debating, she just went ahead and threw her untouched bread, hard.

'Hey!' said Monk indignantly as the missile whizzed past his head to explode in a shower of crumbs against the peeling-papered wall behind him. 'Don't do that!'

'I'll do it if I want!' Bibbie retorted. 'Every time you say something horrible I'll throw something at you, I swear. Starting with bread rolls and working my way up to — to *elephants*! You're just like Aylesbury, Monk. You're as bad as Great-uncle Throggie, and if you think I'm going to sit here and —'

'Deary, deary me,' said Reg, sidling closer along the back of her chair. 'I suppose this brings back fond family memories, does it?'

Melissande spared her a sharp glance. 'No.'

But of course it did. Well. Memories, anyway. Most of them ... difficult. Dinner in New Ottosland's palace with Lional and Rupert, so often a volatile affair. Of course, then it had been Lional doing the throwing and the shouting with Rupert ducking and herself cast in the thankless role of peacemaker. Usually with very little success.

She felt her insides squeeze tight. *Lional*.

Enough time had gone by now that she could get through two or three whole days at a stretch without once thinking of him. Guilt and regret ambushed her less frequently. But the pain was still there, buried deep and lingering. She thought it might never completely go away. She wasn't sure if she wanted it to. If the pain went away it might take Lional with it.

And whatever else he was ... whatever he became ... he was my brother and part of me still loves him. Still wants to love him.

Which was, perhaps, the hardest thing of all to reconcile.

Bibbie and Monk were still spatting, dredging up nursery-tales of cross and double-cross, of who got the biggest scone at tea-time and who was *never* allowed to stay up late on Fireworks Night and who *really* put the fizzing incant in Nanny's sugar bowl which led to *everyone* getting spanked.

It was all so very *silly*.

Melissande picked up her nibbled dinner roll, pulled it in half and took aim at her business partner and her business partner's brother, who was also her young man. At the moment. More or less. Sometimes, it seemed, far less than more. His Research and Development work for Ottosland's government tended to swallow Monk alive, and hardly ever spat him out again. And even when they did spend time together, a part of his attention was always ... somewhere else. Off in the ether. Reg called it the peril of being involved with a genius. For herself, she preferred to call it tactless.

She tossed the bread.

As one, brother and sister turned on her. 'Don't do that!' they chorused, and even though Bibbie was magnificently fair-haired and Monk was dashingly dark, they were in that moment of unified outrage as alike as two peas in a dilapidated pod.

'Why not?' she demanded. 'You're carrying on like five-year-olds, the pair of you, so why should I be left out? What are you fighting over, anyway? Monk's already got a housekeeper, Bibbie.' She looked at him. 'Haven't you? You must have a housekeeper. I mean, you've got a butler. And obviously someone's cooked dinner.' She waved a hand at the table, littered with their emptied bowls of mock turtle soup. 'And I'm pretty sure I didn't imagine the footman who helped serve the first course. So obviously you've got hordes of servants catering to your every whim.'

'And huddling in corners making fun of you,' Reg added. 'Don't forget that. Better than a circus you are, sunshine.'

Monk gave her a dirty look then cleared his throat. 'Yes. Well. The servants. The thing is ...'

'They don't belong to Monk,' said Bibbie. 'Not this lot, at any rate.'

Melissande frowned. 'What do you mean?'

'I mean they aren't the servants he inherited from Great-uncle Throgmorton. They're on loan, every last one of them.'

'On *loan*?' she said blankly. 'What are you talking about? Servants aren't — aren't *library books*. You don't just *borrow* them.'

'Not usually, no,' said Monk, harassed. 'It was an emergency.'

'So where did they come from?'

'Mother,' said Bibbie, and giggled.

'You borrowed your mother's butler?' she said, incredulous. 'And her footman? What about her cook?'

Monk hunched into his dinner jacket. 'Yes, the cook too. Actually, the under-cook. I didn't leave Mother to *starve*, if that's what you're thinking.'

'But *why*? Honestly, Monk, you're starting to sound like Gerald. What's going on? What happened to the staff who came with the house?'

Reg hooted. 'I'll tell you what happened, madam. He scared them away, butler to boot boy, with his experiments and his smelly smoke.'

'Is that true, Monk?' Melissande demanded. *I don't believe it, I don't believe it.* Except that she did. This was Monk, after all. 'Is that why every one of your great-uncle's servants gave notice? Are you *experimenting* again?'

Now Monk was looking distinctly evasive. 'Well —'

'You *are*!' she said, and leaned sideways to poke a finger in his shoulder. '*That's* why you keep dashing out of the room, isn't it? You've got one of your madcap inventions percolating somewhere in this house, haven't you?'

Monk's expression shifted from evasive to bolshy. 'So what if I have? It's what I *do*, Mel. I *invent* things.'

'Things that get you into a lot of trouble!'

'Things that save lives!' he retorted. 'And expand our knowledge of the etheretic plane!'

'Things that aren't sanctioned by the Department!' she

groaned. 'Things that get you hauled over the coals, put on probation and rapped over the knuckles till you can't hold a pen! Monk, you raving *idiot*, are you out of your *mind*?'

'Of course he is,' said Reg. 'Every last genius I ever met was both oars short of a rowboat. And even then you can't trust them to paddle. Don't see why your young man should be an exception.'

Melissande turned to Bibbie. 'Did you know about this?'

Bibbie shrugged. 'Of course.'

'And you didn't try to *stop* him?'

'Stop him?' echoed Bibbie, eyebrows raised. 'Why would I stop him? You heard him, Melissande. Inventing is what Monk does.'

Very carefully, Melissande folded her hands and rested them on the dingy white tablecloth. *Saint Snodgrass, I beg you, give me strength* ... 'Monk, as a recent beneficiary of your illegal inventing I suppose I shouldn't criticise, but *honestly*. I do wish you'd think *first* and invent *later*. The stink from what happened in New Ottosland has barely evaporated. You've only just been released from probation. So *why* would you risk running foul of the Department again so soon after —'

'I'm not risking anything!' said Monk, defensive. His untidy black hair flopped over his eyes. As a rule she found it appealing, but now it annoyed her. He was hiding. 'Because I *am* off probation, and that means I'm free to —'

'Frighten a bunch of servants with your thaumaturgical shenanigans!'

'Mel, I'm *telling* you, the domestic staff quitting has nothing to do with me!' said Monk. 'It's Great-uncle Throgmorton's fault. He won't leave.'

Bibbie sat back, staring. 'What do you mean, he won't leave? He's dead, Monk. He left weeks ago.'

'Huh,' said Monk. 'That's what *you* think.'

Melissande exchanged a look with Reg. The wretched bird dropped one eyelid in a rollicking wink, clearly prepared to take her entertainment where she could find it.

Much help you are, Reg. Thanks ever so.

She turned back to her perplexing and frequently infuriating young man. 'Are you saying the house is *haunted*, Monk?'

Monk slumped. 'I think so. Yes. It's the only explanation I can come up with.'

'But that's silly,' said Bibbie. 'There's no such thing as ghosts, every wizard worth his staff knows that.'

'Well, someone forgot to tell Great-uncle Throgmorton,' said Monk morosely. 'Because the boot boy swore blind the old geezer kicked him down the scullery stairs. Cook claimed he flattened five soufflés in a row. And both the parlour-maids were certain he pushed them out of bed. Twice! Sadie said he pushed her into the *chamber pot* — which she *hadn't* got around to emptying. So everyone quit, which is why I had to ask Mother to lend me some of her people. But she can't spare them for more than a few days because Father's invited the High Hantofeermi of Tetin to stay with us after next week's international symposium. And even if she hadn't, and I could keep them, there's *already* been muttering and they only got here this morning. I very much doubt this lot will stay the night. Oh, Bibbie —' He turned to his sister, beseeching. 'I do wish you'd move in. You know how Great-uncle Throgmorton felt about *gels*. He'd run away screaming if he thought he'd have to share the house with you.'

'Well, Monk, flattered as I am by your generous offer,' said Bibbie, pink with crossness, 'I'll have to decline.'

'Decline?' Monk was almost wailing. 'But *why*? I mean, you could have your own work room here, Bibs. You know you miss having your own work room. And I wouldn't keep coming in telling you how you're doing it all wrong, like Father always does. Why *wouldn't* you want to move in?'

'Why?' Bibbie echoed. 'I swear, Monk, for a genius you can be *such* an idiot. Because I've only just moved out of one family home, that's why, and I'm not the least bit inclined to move into another. I like being on my own, thank you very much.'

'But you're not on your own,' Monk objected. 'You're sardined in that boarding house with a bunch of other girls. Every time you turn around you're tripping over one of them, you said so yourself.'

'Maybe I am,' said Bibbie, her colour still heightened, 'but the point is, Monk, that not one of them is related to me and that's as good as being on my own.'

Reg chuckled. 'That's the way, ducky. Twist the knife. The only good brother is a squirming brother.'

'And another thing,' said Bibbie, with a pleased nod at Reg. 'Great-uncle Throgmorton left you *two* houses — this one and the terrace in Pilkington Mews. But I don't seem to recall you asking me if I'd like to live there. If you're so worried about me turning into a sardine, why not hand over its front door key right now?'

Monk was gaping. 'How can I, Bibbie? You know the terms of the old fogie's bequest! *Gels cannot be permitted to set up their own establishments.* I might not agree with him, in fact you know I don't, but I'm stuck with his instructions.'

'Why? The houses belong to you now,' said Bibbie. 'Surely you can do whatever you like with them.'

Monk dragged ink-stained fingers through his floppy hair. 'Only up to a point! And I'm sorry, call me selfish if you like, but that point stops short of me breaking the terms of the will and seeing both places given to Aylesbury.'

'Well,' said Reg, head cocked towards Bibbie. 'He's got you there, ducky.'

'I know,' sighed Bibbie, and pulled another face. 'But it's still not fair.'

'Not fair?' Reg rattled her tail feathers. 'Don't you talk to *me* about *not fair*, madam. I'm the queen of *not fair*, not to mention Lalapinda.'

'Lalapinda doesn't count,' said Bibbie, wrinkling her nose.

'It certainly does!' Reg snapped. 'I was *usurped*, ducky. That throne still belongs to me!'

'You were usurped more than four centuries ago, Reg. The moment, as they say, has passed.'

'It's done nothing of the sort. I'm still alive, which means I'm still the queen. I'm queen-in-exile, that's what I am. Lalapinda's current throne-sitter's bum is polishing stolen property!'

Overcome by an excess of feelings, Reg launched herself off the chair-back and flapped around the dining room, swearing under her breath.

Melissande looked at Bibbie. 'You had to do it, didn't you? You had to bring up Lalapinda.'

'I didn't bring it up,' Bibbie protested. 'She did. She brings it up every chance she gets and I'm telling you, Mel, I'm pretty bored by the subject. Do you know how tedious it can be, hearing someone banging on and on and on about something that was over and done with four hundred years ago and can't be changed?'

Melissande looked at her. 'Give me a moment. Let me think ...'

'*Ha!*' said Reg, skidding along the table top. She collided with the salt cellar and came to a spectacular halt in a shower of condiment. 'That's telling her, Princess Pushy!'

'How many times do I have to say it, Reg, *don't call me that!*' said Melissande, and seized the dreadful bird by her legs so she could hang herself upside down and flap all the seasoning from her drab brown plumage.

'Now who's being told?' said Bibbie, still rankled.

Melissande plopped a saltless Reg back on her chair and

sighed. 'I'm sorry, Bibbie, I don't mean to be nasty, but honestly, you have been —'

'Well, it's all right for you, isn't it?' said Bibbie, eyes swimming with angry tears. 'You're a royal highness, you've got a palace to go home to, haven't you? Any time you get sick of pretending to be an ordinary person you can swan off back to New Ottosland and prance about in a carriage all day waving at your adoring subjects. You don't have a stinking rich Great-uncle Throgmorton who says gels are good for nothing but marriage and doesn't leave you so much as a *teapot* in his will. How would you like it if you knew you were as gifted as your genius brothers but couldn't amount to anything because the world of thaumaturgics is run by stodgy old *wizards*.'

Too shocked to be stung by Bibbie's cheap shot, Melissande stared. 'I'm sorry,' she said gently. 'I had no idea you were this upset about it.'

Bibbie folded her arms. 'Yes. Well. Now you do.' She scowled at Monk, who was just as nonplussed. 'You both do.'

'But — but Bibs,' he said, uncertainly, 'there's the agency. Nobody's stopped you and Melissande from opening the agency.'

'They didn't have to, did they?' said Bibbie. 'Opening the agency was the easy part. But *keeping* it open? *That's* the trick!'

'Don't you stare at me in that tone of voice,' said Melissande as Monk regarded her reproachfully. 'You know things are a bit slow at the moment.'

'I get the feeling it's worse than *a bit slow*. You should have told me, Mel.'

'When? You've been working around the clock for weeks!' she retorted. 'This is the first meal we've sat down to at the same time in the same place since the fourth of last month.'

'Well, what about the other night, at the opera? We saw each other then.'

'Only because of Department politics and anyway, who could talk over all that caterwauling? Besides —' She shot Bibbie a quelling look. 'It's nothing to worry about. We're fine.'

'Doesn't sound like you're fine,' said Monk, unconvinced. 'It sounds like —'

'Like Bibbie in a bad mood because of Great-uncle Throgmorton,' she said firmly. 'Forget it. Honestly, Monk, you've only just winkled your way back into the Department's good graces. You need to focus on keeping your nose clean, not worry about the agency's teething troubles. Which *won't* last much longer, I have *no* doubt,' she added, with another stern glance at Bibbie.

'Yes, but still,' said Monk, sounding hurt. 'You could've mentioned it in passing. I know I can get a bit wrapped up in my work but I do care, you know.'

Yes, he did care. Even when he was consumed by the fires of thaumaturgical invention, Monk Markham cared. It was only one of the many reasons why she was so fond of him.

Smiling, she reached over the salt-scattered tablecloth and rested her hand on his. 'And I appreciate it.'

'Oh *please*,' said Reg, gagging. 'I'd be sick, if I'd eaten anything yet. Are we getting to the second course any time soon, by the way, or should I just start on my toes?'

'Sorry, Reg,' said Monk. 'Second course coming up.'

He tugged on the servant's bell rope ... and it came loose in his hand amidst a gentle snowstorm of plaster.

'Oh,' he said. 'Y'know, I'm really starting to resent whoever it was made the rule about wizards not being able to use their powers for personal gain. The Department doesn't pay its scientists a fraction of what it's going to cost me to repair this mouldering pile!'

'Actually,' said Bibbie, dusting plaster off her shoulders, 'it was Great-great-great grandfather Thackeray who thought up that one, Monk. Yet another blithering dunderhead who should've been pruned off the family tree.'

'Excuse me,' said Monk, and pushed back his chair. Returning to the doorway, shedding bits of plaster like dandruff, the bell rope dangling from his hand like a murdered snake, he stuck his head into the corridor. 'Dodsworth! Dodsworth? We'd like the second course now, please!'

Eventually the roast beef and dumplings and various vegetable side dishes arrived, only slightly shrivelled. After the meal was served, Dodsworth cleared his throat and looked down his nose at Monk.

'Cook's apologies, sir, but there'll be no strawberry syllabub dessert this evening.'

'No?' said Monk, torn between apprehension and crushing disappointment. 'Ah — why not?'

'Because, sir,' said Dodsworth, rigidly disapproving, 'Cook is wearing it.'

Monk blinked. 'Oh. I see. Well. I'm sorry about that.'

'So is Cook,' said Dodsworth. 'I regret to say, sir, that pink is not her colour.'

The butler and the footman withdrew.

'Great-uncle Throgmorton?' said Melissande, surveying her laden plate with suspicion. If the old fogy really was haunting the place and his views on *gels* hadn't been exaggerated, Saint Snodgrass knew what he'd done to the gravy.

Monk nodded dismally. 'Great-uncle Throgmorton.' With an effort, he summoned a smile. 'Silly old bugger. Let's forget about him, eh? Let's have a toast instead.' He raised his glass, which Dodsworth had three-quarters filled with a robust red wine. 'To absent friends. Well, friend. To Gerald, wherever he is and whatever he's doing!'

Melissande stopped her own glass halfway to her lips. 'You mean you don't know?'

'Haven't a clue,' said Monk, shrugging. 'Haven't laid eyes on him since that one visit to Nettleworth. Sir Alec's lot play their cards very close to their chests. Not even Uncle Ralph knows what he's up to. Believe me, I asked.'

Bibbie looked up from poking her fork through her spinach. Clearly she too was untrusting of her ghostly great-uncle. 'Maybe he just didn't want to tell you, Monk. You may be off probation with the Department but Uncle Ralph holds a grudge for years. He still hasn't forgiven me for the time I turned his beard grass-green, and I was three.'

'True,' said Monk. 'But I'm pretty sure he really doesn't know. When he *does* know something and won't tell, he gets this kind of smug twinkle in his eye. And when I saw him yesterday, he wasn't twinkling.'

'Well, wherever Gerald is, he must be all right,' said Melissande. 'We'd have heard if he wasn't all right, wouldn't we?'

'Probably,' said Monk, risking a mouthful of roast potato.

Reg looked up from dubiously inspecting her saucerful of minced raw beef. 'Probably? What do you mean *probably*, sunshine? What kind of a Department are you people running? Wait, don't tell me, I already know. You're so busy impressing each other with your big bad secrets you let the little people fall through the cracks. Or worse yet, you treat them like cogs in the machine that can be replaced if they get broken! Well, my Gerald's not a *cog*, young man, he's my Gerald, and if you think you and your Sir Alec can —'

'Hey, hey, hey!' Monk protested, hands upraised. 'For a start he's not *my* Sir Alec. To be honest, I don't think he's *anyone's* Sir Alec. As far as I can work out, Sir Alec calls his own tune and too bad if his masters don't like it. Cards close to the chest, remember?'

'I don't give a fat rat's bum about tunes or cards or anything except Gerald!' said Reg, eyes flashing. 'What's more, I think it's past time I checked up on that boy. Saint Snodgrass only knows the kind of trouble he'll get himself into if I'm not around to steer him right. For all we know he's been tossed arse over teakettle into his first assignment, and how's he going to cope with it if I'm not there to —'

'Reg, don't,' sighed Melissande. 'You'll give yourself indigestion. I'm sure Gerald's fine. If he was in trouble someone would've told us. Anyway, it's far too soon for them to send him out on assignment.' She turned. 'Isn't that right, Monk?'

'Mmm,' said Monk, hair flopping over his face, and attacked another roast potato.

Bibbie frowned. '*Mmm?* What's that supposed to mean? Is it too soon or isn't it?'

'Good question,' said Reg. 'Now answer it, sunshine, before I forget I'm a lady.'

Monk put down his knife and fork. 'It means that given his … special talents … they put him on some kind of accelerated training program.'

'Accelerated training program?' Melissande exchanged an alarmed look with Reg. 'What do you mean, *accelerated training program?* Are you saying they *would* send him off on assignment so soon?'

'I'm saying I don't know,' said Monk. 'Haven't you been listening? Sir Alec is *secretive*. When I tried a little discreet question-asking I nearly got my head bitten off.'

'Well, that's just not *good* enough!' Reg flapped her wings and rattled her tail feathers. 'I've been patient, Saint Snodgrass knows I've been patient, but if Gerald's out on his first assignment I want to know about it. So just you forget about finishing your dinner until you've found Gerald with a seeking incant so I can —'

'*Reg!*' Monk pushed his plate to one side and leaned over the table, his expression a muddle of exasperation and earnestness.

'Don't you think I would if I could? Don't you think I'm worried about him, too? He's my best friend!'

Bibbie drummed her fingertips on the tablecloth. 'You've already tried to find him, haven't you, Monk? But you can't.'

He took a deep, affronted breath, ready to bluster ... then blew it out noisily. 'They've got him muffled or screened or something,' he muttered. 'I can't pinpoint his location.'

'And if you can't,' said Bibbie, deflating, 'then nobody can.'

'Which means he *could* be in trouble!' said Reg. 'Or even — even —'.

'No, Reg, he's not dead,' Monk said hastily. 'I do know that much.'

'How can you be sure?' she demanded, chattering her beak. Her dark eyes were suspiciously bright.

Melissande rounded on her. '*Stop* it, Reg. You're being ridiculously melodramatic.'

'Melodramatic?' screeched Reg. '*Melodramatic?* Have you developed spontaneous amnesia, madam? Who was it knew your deranged brother tried to kill Gerald in the woods? *Me.* And would anybody listen? *No.* And was I right? *Yes.* So if you don't mind we'll have a little less "You're being melodramatic" and a little more "Gracious Reg, you're amazing, you can see trouble coming a hundred miles away with both eyes tied behind your back." I think we should kidnap that sneering Sir Alec and —'

'Reg, we're not kidnapping *anyone*,' said Monk. '*Especially* not Sir Alec. For the last time, Gerald's not dead. I was able to get that much out of Uncle Ralph before he swatted me like a mosquito. Now can we please eat our dinner before it's completely stone cold? If the plates go back to the kitchen untouched Cook will complain to Mother and I'll never be allowed to borrow the servants again.'

So they ate dinner, Reg grumbling under her breath the whole time. When they were finished, Monk took them on a guided tour of the old house. It was long on dust, cobwebs and hidden passages, and short on pretty much everything else, including curtains and doorknobs.

'I'm afraid Great-uncle Throgmorton was a bit *peculiar* towards the end,' Monk explained, as he opened the door to the huge attic that occupied all the space beneath the roof.

'And does peculiar run in the family?' said Reg, perched on Melissande's shoulder. 'Because if it does, and you're thinking of popping the question to madam here any time soon, you might want to think twice. There are the children to consider, after all.'

Melissande felt embarrassed heat wash through her. '*Reg!*'

'Well, somebody's got to say it,' said Reg, unrepentant. 'We both know you'll be thinking it.'

'No, Reg,' she said grimly. 'Only you would think — or say — something like that.'

'*Anyway,*' said Monk, pushing the attic door wide. 'Here's where I'm experimenting. See? Nothing sinister, nothing dangerous, nothing to worry the Department at *all*.'

'Provided they never get wind of it,' said his sister, peering in at the bubbling test tubes, the thaumic agitators, the etheretic quantifiers and the multi-dimensional wavelength gauges. 'Honestly, Monk. No wonder you're too skint to pay for servants and doorknobs. All this equipment! It must have cost you a *fortune!*'

Monk mumbled something and pulled the door shut. 'So anyway, that's the house,' he said, shepherding them back down the creaking stairs. 'A bit decrepit, but with possibilities.'

'Provided you don't blow the roof to matchsticks,' said Reg. 'Because just between you, me and the cobwebs, sunshine, one of those thaumic agitators didn't look entirely stable.'

'What?' He frowned. 'Are you sure? Because I've realigned the wretched thing four times tonight! I don't understand what's going on, it won't hold its settings, but I could've *sworn* I —'

Bibbie rolled her eyes. 'Just check it again, Monk, or else you will blow the roof to matchsticks and we'll never hear the end of it.'

'Right,' said Monk, backing up the staircase. 'Right. Yes. Ah — look — this might take a while. I'll have Dodsworth drive you home, shall I? Yes. Just give him a shout, Bibs, and he'll bring round the jalopy. Thanks for coming, girls. I'll see you both soon.'

'On second thoughts, madam,' said Reg, as Monk disappeared round the first bend in the staircase, 'at the rate you two are progressing there's absolutely no need at all to worry about the children.'

Melissande, staring after him, swallowed a sigh. *Not even a chaste little peck on the cheek. Trust Reg to notice that. Sometimes I wonder, I really do wonder, if he remembers I'm Bibbie's friend and not her sister.*

'Come on,' she said. 'Let's go home, shall we?'

CHAPTER FOUR

Morning. Melissande groped for her glasses, slid them on, then rolled back onto her pillow.

After growing up as a princess in a palace, complete with courtiers, servants, extensively manicured gardens and frequent public outings to fulfil her 'being ogled' duties, there was something deeply *satisfying* about living in a tiny bedsit in a tiny rented office on the top floor of an elderly four-storey building in a nook-and-cranny corner of a large and crowded city. It offered the kind of freedom she had never expected to experience, what with being a princess and then a prime minister, crushed beneath the burden of an entire kingdom's welfare. Until Gerald hurtled into her orbit she'd more or less resigned herself to a life of duty, of obligation, of walking on eggshells around unpredictable, kingly Lional.

But Gerald ... and Lional's insanity ... had topsy-turvied all her glum expectations and suddenly she'd found herself bereft of duty and obligation, given the chance to spread her wings, so to speak, and fly into a different future.

She'd snatched it with both hands and hadn't looked back.

Here in Ottosland's sprawling, cosmopolitan capital she was practically anonymous. She could walk the streets day or night and nobody stopped to point and stare. Or if they did it wasn't because she was the local Royal Highness. The novelty of *that* was yet to wear off.

She'd definitely made the right decision ... even if things weren't *entirely* working out the way she'd planned.

As the city's post-dawn symphony sounded beyond the bedsit's single open window — chugging motor cars and clopping horse-drawn drays, optimistic street-sellers and barrow-girls and shrill messenger boys, barking dogs and rattling milk cans — she stretched beneath her blankets, luxuriating in the ongoing deliciousness of being plain Miss Melissande Cadwallader.

'Oy,' said Reg, gliding in between the faded curtains to land neatly on the bedsit's single bookcase. 'How much longer are you going to glorm about in bed, madam? The sun's up, in case you hadn't noticed, and witching agencies don't run themselves. You're not a pampered princess anymore, you're one of the downtrodden working class, that's what you are. So it's time to rise and shine and think of how we're going to keep the office door open when we haven't had a single nibble of a client in over three weeks!'

Of course, nothing was ever perfect ...

Melissande sat up, looking for Boris, but he'd let himself out through the open window already. At first she'd worried about him, wandering about in a brand new city, but it seemed Boris was a cat blessed with a multitude of lives. He always came home no matter how creatively Reg insulted him.

'Your hair's a rat's-nest, by the way,' the bird added helpfully. 'You should sleep with it in a nightcap. I always did.'

'And good morning to you too, Reg,' she muttered, and fell back against her lumpy pillow. 'Now go away.'

Reg sniffed. 'So much for the royal work ethic. Come along, madam, you've got to rally to the cause, you've got to spit the world in the eye, you've got to hunt us up some clients before I starve to death! You can't just lie there dreaming about that Markham boy. He's probably blown himself to smithereens by now anyway.'

Monk, and his unsanctioned, brilliant, mysterious experiments. Heart thumping, Melissande leapt out of bed. 'I know you think you're being funny, Reg, but you might actually be right for once. God alone knows what he's getting up to in that stupid attic of his. You've got to fly over there, quick, and —'

'I'm way ahead of you, ducky,' said Reg, sounding smug. 'Great-uncle Throgmorton's legacy is still standing and that Markham boy is in one piece … but he won't be for much longer if those old fogies in the Department find out what he's been up to.'

Chilly in bare feet and a sensible nightdress, Melissande snatched her green flannel dressing gown from the battered bedpost and hauled it on. 'What do you mean? What's he working on?'

Once, Reg would have used the question as an excuse to make pointed remarks about the manifest inadequacies of Madam Rinky Tinky and her correspondence witching course. Since the humiliations of Madam Olliphant's exclusive Academie of Witchcraft, however, the bird had been mercifully — not to mention uncharacteristically — restrained.

Oddly, the restraint hurt worse than the pointed remarks.

'Well,' said Reg, scratching the back of her head. 'It's a bit hard to say, really. But I'll tell you this much, ducky: you wouldn't catch *me* getting cosy with thaumic generators, etheretic quantifiers and multi-dimensional wavelength gauges. Not all together under the same roof, at any rate.'

Feeling faint, Melissande dropped to the edge of her bed and pulled the dressing gown more tightly round her ribs. 'Yes, but you're not Monk. He's a thaumaturgical genius.'

'He's a thaumaturgical genius today,' said Reg, looking down her beak. 'By this time tomorrow he could be a nasty stain on the carpet.'

'Oh, *Reg.*' If there'd been a slipper handy she would've thrown it. 'Do *stop* being so *melodramatic.*'

'Only if you get dressed,' said Reg. 'You'll catch your death sitting about the place half-naked and if you think *I'm* going to be mopping your fevered brow you've sadly misread the situation.'

'Oh, all *right,*' she groaned, and hunted up some clean tweed trews and a not-too-wrinkled white shirt, her everyday attire of choice. Even in modern Ottosland such a masculine outfit raised eyebrows, but she was loath to abandon it for skirts and dresses. Baggy trousers were comfortable. During her hard-fought campaign to avoid a royal marriage of convenience she'd first grown accustomed to having the shape of her legs more-or-less on show, and then positively attached to the habit of walking fast without tripping over flounces.

And the ruder Reg got about princesses who couldn't tell if they were Martha or Arthur the more determined she became never to dress like a girl again.

Ignoring the wretched bird's eloquent stare and heavy sighs, she swapped nightwear for daywear, wrestled her rat's-nest hair into submission with a brush and tidied it into a long plait. Then she made her way down the four flights of rickety stairs to the outside convenience in the building's rear courtyard, checked for spiders, twice, washed her hands afterwards under the recalcitrant water pump — Saint Snodgrass, how she missed the palace's plumbing — and trudged all the way back upstairs to face a breakfast of two cold hard-boiled eggs left over from last night's supper. Without salt or pepper, because she'd used up the dregs yesterday.

Of course if she'd followed Bibbie's example and taken a room at Mistress Mossop's Boarding House for Refined Young

Ladies, she'd be eating a hot breakfast in style right about now. Fresh eggs scrambled in butter, juicy fat sausages, toast and marmalade, sweet, creamy coffee . . .

But she couldn't do it. Partly because of the money — she was determined not to be a drain on Rupert's strained royal purse — and partly because she wasn't certain she could face hordes of Refined Young Ladies, even if one of them *was* Emmerabiblia Markham . . . the first real friend of the female persuasion she'd ever made.

Reg didn't count.

'So, what's the plan for today, then?' the bird enquired, perched on the bedrail. 'Seeing as how we've got no clients there's an awful lot of time to fill between now and sunset.'

Melissande looked up from sweeping bits of eggshell into the bedsit's tiny rubbish pail. 'And you think I need reminding of that yet *again* because . . .'

'No point getting snippy with me, ducky,' said Reg, shrugging. 'We're floundering and that's all there is to it.'

'We are not *floundering*,' she retorted. 'We are experiencing a temporary dearth of clients. It's not the same thing at all.'

'Well, if you'd just make more of the fact that *you're* a princess and your brother's a *king*, madam, we'd have so many clients we'd be beating them off with a stick!'

'How many times do I have to say it, Reg?' Melissande demanded, glaring. 'I left New Ottosland so I could *stop* being a princess. I'm *not* going to — to *flaunt* myself in Ottish society just so we can —'

Reg rattled her tail feathers. 'Flaunt? Flaunt? Who said anything about flaunt? *I* never said you should *flaunt*. But you could wear a regal dress and your mother's tiara, couldn't you, and let the local snobs draw their own conclusions? Drop them a hint, where's the harm in that?'

'Oh, *Reg*!'

'Don't you *Oh, Reg* me!' said Reg crossly. 'Because you know that I know the piggy bank's pretty much run out of oink!'

Yes, she knew it. She wished she didn't. She wished — well, she wished a lot of things. But wishing wouldn't change the facts. Reg was right, drat her. They were facing dire financial straits, and without some kind of miracle the agency's doors wouldn't stay open much longer than another week. Maybe two, if they were lucky.

I don't understand. It wasn't supposed to be this difficult.

'It's one thing for that Markham boy's sister not to use her family's connections,' Reg continued, relentless. 'She doesn't turn twenty-one for two more years so they've still got *some* say over what she does. But what's your excuse? Cutting off all our noses to spite your freckled face, that's what *you're* doing, madam, and I for one don't approve!'

'Really?' she replied. 'I had no idea, Reg. You'll have to stop being so subtle.' She shoved her hands in her pockets. 'Look, I know you think I'm being contrary. I know you'd give anything to get your old life back. You *liked* being royal, which is fine, but I'm not you. I'm me. And I want to find out who I am. The *real* me, not the me who's spent her life being a — a — *title*. A *function*. Just one more portrait in a long line of portraits. Is that so unreasonable?'

'Weeeeell ...' Reg let out a grudging sigh. 'No, I suppose not, when you put it that way.'

'Besides, things will improve around here,' she said. 'Every new venture takes a little time to find its feet. It's not like we haven't had *any* clients. We just haven't had enough. But they'll come. And in the meantime we'll just have to economise.'

Reg looked around the tiny room, which had started life as a smaller second office. 'Ducky, this place is worse than Gerald's bedsit in the Wizard's Club and that's not something I ever thought I'd hear myself say. The only way you're going to get more economical is by moving into the outdoors convenience.' She sniffed. 'Or you could try tapping that Markham boy on the shoulder. He's got plenty of empty rooms going spare in that new house of his, I'm sure.'

Melissande turned away so Reg wouldn't see the tell-tale flush of colour in her cheeks. 'Don't be ridiculous, Reg. I might wear trousers but I'm not completely *abandoned*. Bibbie could move in with him, she's his sister. I'm not.'

The truth is I'm not sure what I am to him. Honestly, things were much less complicated when we were in the middle of an international crisis.

Another sniff. 'All right, all right. Untwist your knickers, ducky. It was only a thought.'

But not the kind of thought she wanted to be thinking. Besides, she had far more immediate concerns. 'Well, those kinds of thoughts are best kept to yourself,' she said briskly. 'Anyway, I've already come up with one way for us to pinch our pennies. I'm going to brew up a fresh batch of tamper-proof ink. I might not be a patch on Miss Markham when it comes to proper witchcraft but I'm a dab hand at brewing tamper-proof ink. I went through gallons of the stuff once Lional —'

And there he was, tripping her up again, curse him. Ottosland's wizards were wrong. There really were such things as ghosts.

I wonder if it's like this for Gerald, too? Wherever he is. Whatever he's doing. I wonder if he thinks of Lional every time he remembers he's only got one good eye.

'Good idea,' said Reg, breaking the difficult silence. 'That'll keep you out of mischief. And I'll help. *I* was brewing tamper-proof ink five minutes after ink was invented.'

Melissande groaned. 'Of course you were.'

It was still too early to go shopping for regular ink that she could gussy up with a dash of her limited thaumaturgy, so she trudged back downstairs to see if the morning paper had arrived. Yes, it was there on the building's front doorstep beside the agency's daily half-pint of milk, which they had delivered in the frail hope that prospective clients would arrive parched and desperate for a rallying cup of tea. Sadly, Boris had been the main beneficiary of that little plan.

Of course it could be argued the newspaper was another pointless extravagance, except there was always the hope — possibly forlorn, but a hope nonetheless — that a client might be found by perusing the crime section. Or the social pages. According to Reg they were usually one and the same. And even though Bibbie was forbidden from actively exploiting her family connections, she still knew a great many people in the upper strata of Ottosland society. Inside information would never go astray.

The clunk of the stoppered milk jug against the steps brought Boris out of hiding from the shadows next door. Green eyes gleaming, black tail flicking suggestively, he wound himself endearingly around Melissande's tweed ankles.

'Forget it,' she told him. 'Prospective clients come first.'

Boris twitched his whiskers in disgust and leapt back into the shadows. Arms full of newspaper and milk jug, Melissande looked up and down the narrow street, searching for signs of life, but it was empty. Daffydown Lane wasn't what anyone could call a bustling thoroughfare. Unfortunately, the rent for premises on bustling thoroughfares was daylight robbery. Daffydown Lane was the best they could afford.

She turned to go back inside ... and was confronted by the tenant roll attached to her building's brickwork beside its slightly warped door frame. Amid the faded listings for Briscowe's Best Bootlaces, Argent Exports and Dashforth's Superior Comestibles, one entry stood out.

Witches Inc. No thaumaturgical task too large or too small. Reasonable rates, discretion guaranteed.

The bold, black-edged gold lettering leapt starkly to the eye, still so brand-new and hopeful compared with the faded announcements of the building's other occupants. Without warning she felt a flutter of fear in the pit of her stomach, as delicate as one of Rupert's butterflies.

Please, Saint Snodgrass. Don't let us fail.

Subdued, she trudged upstairs to the office and made herself comfortable with the paper in the overstuffed, high-backed client armchair. She wasn't supposed to, because the client armchair was the only newish piece of furniture they possessed and was meant for Special People, otherwise known as clients, but it seemed a pity to let it go to waste.

Ignoring violent partnerly opposition, Reg had insisted on keeping her revolting old ram skull on top of the office's sole filing cabinet. Ensconced there now, she looked down her beak.

'Well? Find anything interesting?

The paper's front page was decorated with a splendid photograph of Rupert, diplomatically losing a camel race to his next-door neighbour Sultan Zazoor. She felt her heart skip and quickly flicked the paper open. Homesickness was like a scab: not nearly so painful if you didn't pick at it.

'Interesting?' She scanned the various stories of the day. 'Well, the last injured travellers from the most recent portal accident have been released from hospital, poor things. Still no official announcement of what went wrong this time. Five accidents in four months? It's unprecedented.'

'What went wrong is some fool of a government inspector fell asleep on the job,' said Reg, scornful. 'Portal travel might be convenient but it's only been around for five minutes. Mucking about with that kind of metaphysics is no romp in the park. What else?'

Melissande turned another page. 'Not much. Lots of nattering about this upcoming symposium. The usual blowhards blustering in Letters to the Editor. Oh, and the Potentate of Aframbigi's lodged a formal complaint about his sanctions.'

'Never mind him,' said Reg. 'He'll need a sight more help than the likes of us can provide, the silly old fogey. Try the social pages. With any luck one of our Miss Markham's old school chums has lost an expensive bracelet and needs us to —'

'Don't be ridiculous,' she said, turning to the back section of the paper. 'Why would one of Bibbie's friends need us? Any graduate of Madam Olliphant's would be perfectly capable of — oh *no!*'

'What?' said Reg, and flapped from her ram skull to the arm of the client chair. 'What's wrong?'

Mortified, Melissande stared at the photograph in the paper's breathlessly overwritten social section. 'What do you think?'

'I think that bustle was a big mistake,' said Reg, peering at the offending picture. 'You've got more than enough bum to be going on with, madam. No need to go *enhancing* it.'

Melissande gritted her teeth. 'Yes, so you said at the time, Reg. But —'

'*Her Royal Highness Princess Melissande of New Ottosland,*' Reg said aloud, reading the photograph's caption, '*only sister to the King of New Ottosland and co-proprietor of Witches Inc., the capital's newest thaumaturgical agency, escorted by Monk Markham, Esquire, younger son of celebrated thaumaturgist Wolfgang Markham, attending a performance of "The Shepherd's Revenge" at the Opera House.* What's wrong with that? That's free advertising, that is. Even if most of you that isn't bustle is hidden behind that Markham boy.' She chuckled. 'Although he does scrub up quite nicely, doesn't he?'

Yes, he did, very nicely, but that wasn't the point. 'I could've *sworn* I managed to fritz that wretched man's camera!' Melissande fretted. 'He's always lurking around public events hoping to photograph me. Next time I'll get Monk to fritz his camera. Better yet I'll get Monk to fritz *him.*'

'Oh, no you won't, madam!' said Reg. 'Not when he's giving us free advertising, you won't!'

She threw the paper on the floor and shoved out of the armchair. 'I don't *care* about the free advertising. I care about Rupert seeing this and thinking I'm exploiting him for my personal gain! He's been so wonderful about what happened at Madam Olliphant's, and me starting up the agency even though it's got the potential to embarrass him. They're still wittering about it back home, you know, all those fuddy-duddy aristocrats. Lord Billingsley and the rest. I'm flying in the face of Tradition, Reg, and they're not impressed. But Rupert's standing firm. The *last* thing I want is for him to think I'm taking him for granted. *Using* him.'

'If you think he thinks that, ducky,' said Reg, surprisingly gentle, 'you're daft. That brother of yours adores you. In his short-sighted eyes you can do no wrong.'

Which was precisely the problem. Rupert's loyalty was limitless, so she had to place the limits for him. Otherwise he could get himself into trouble. She'd have to write him a letter, and bother the expense of postage home. If his feelings were hurt he'd never tell her. He'd just brood and look sad ...

Oh, Rupes. I'm sorry. Maybe coming to New Ottosland was a mistake after all.

'Mister Cripps will be at his shop by now,' she said abruptly, glancing at the tinnily ticking clock on the wall. 'I'm going out to buy that ink. In the unlikely event a client should turn up while I'm gone don't do anything, just let them fill out the enquiry card and pop it through the door-slot and I'll deal with it when I get back.'

Reg immediately looked outraged. 'Do you mind? I'm perfectly capable of —'

'Pretending to be an etheretic answering machine, getting into an argument with a client and sending them away in a huff?'

she interrupted. 'Yes, Reg, I know. Last week's demonstration was flawless. You could give tutorials. Which is why I'm saying *don't do anything.*'

And on that trenchant note she picked up her slightly faded velvet reticule and swept out of the office, banging the door firmly closed in Reg's offended face.

It took her not quite three-quarters of an hour to walk to Mister Cripps's Office Supply Emporium, which was nowhere near as grand as its title suggested, make a purchase of his cheapest black ink, convince him she was perfectly capable of carrying the tin back to her office unassisted, and do so.

Reg, determined to remain offended, pretended to be asleep on her ram skull. Knowing perfectly well the dreadful bird was just aching to be appeased, Melissande pointedly ignored her. After setting up her test tube, conductive tubing, large beaker and etheretic condenser on Bibbie's desk, since Monk's sister wasn't there to object, she started the process of tamper-proofing the first batch of ink.

Task completed, she returned to the client armchair with a book about the impact of cosmic rays on the etheretic field, which she'd borrowed from Monk. Her practical skills might leave a lot to be desired but there was no reason why she couldn't be a theoretical expert. And who knew? Maybe if she read enough of his books some of his genius would rub off. A forlorn thought, most likely ...

But there's no law against dreaming.

Twenty minutes later the percolating ink on Bibbie's desk hissed then evaporated in a belching of noxious orange smoke.

Melissande stared at it. 'What? How did that happen?'

Reg sniggered.

'Huh,' she said, still ignoring the bird, and started the tamper-proofing process again with a fresh lot of ink.

Fifteen minutes after that, just as she staggered to the end of chapter five, the ink fizzed, turned bright yellow and condensed into a scum of froth around the lips of both test tube and beaker.

She let Monk's book drop into her lap. 'Oh, please. I know it's Mister Cripps's cheapest ink but this is *ridiculous*.' Muttering under her breath, she cleaned the test tube and beaker again, replaced the conductive tubing, triple-checked the etheretic condenser, poured her third batch of ink — good job she hadn't succumbed to the temptation of a more expensive brand — and settled back into the armchair.

Seven laborious minutes into chapter six, the third batch of ink erupted into bubbles. Incredulous, Melissande looked up, saw the ink morph in a flash from black to emerald and made a frantic dive for test tube and beaker.

Too late. With a last despairing fizzle the ink expired in a cloud of damp green mist. She sneezed, then broke a cardinal rule and threw Monk's book to the floor.

'Oh — oh, *buttocks*!'

The cry roused Reg from her pretend doze on the ram skull. '*Language*, madam.'

'Language yourself,' she retorted, tugging off her glasses so she could clean the green mankiness off them. 'You've said much worse, I've heard you.' Having ruined the tail of her blouse, she shoved the glasses back on and turned. 'Buttocks, buttocks, buttocks, so there.'

Instead of scolding, Reg stared into the distance, a reminiscent gleam in her dark eyes. 'I had buttocks once,' she said dreamily. With a ruffle of feathers she hopped from the ram skull to the open window, because the drifting green mist smelled like a men's locker room whose cleaners had gone on a workers' picnic. 'They were lovely. All tight and firm and round like a fresh young peach.' Another remembering sigh, and then a considering glance at Melissande's trouser-clad behind. 'I could show you some exercises if you like.'

'I really wouldn't,' she said, teeth gritted.

'Well, you should,' said Reg. 'Tight buttocks can take a girl a lot further than you'd think.'

She closed her eyes. *Count to ten, count to ten, get to ten and keep on counting* . . . 'Look,' she said, snatching up her glass potion stirrer and waving it for emphasis, 'why don't you make yourself useful for once and help me work out what's gone wrong with the stupid stuff *this* time.' Gingerly she poked the rod into the beaker and stirred the teaspoon-worth of green sludge at the bottom; the end of the rod promptly melted.

'Whoops,' said Reg, with another snigger.

'Oh *bu* — ugger it!' she shouted, one wary eye on Reg, and stamped about the tiny office to relieve her feelings. Thanks to the wretched bird she was aware of a slight but definite wobbling sensation in regions she had no intention of mentioning ever again. 'It just doesn't make sense,' she fumed, still stamping. 'I followed the incant exactly. Every time!'

'Then you must've misremembered it,' said Reg.

'Nonsense. I've tamper-proofed so much ink in the last two years I could do it in my *sleep*.'

Reg tut-tutted. 'Then I blame that Madame Rinky Tinky and her cut-rate under-the-counter flim-flam of a correspondence witching course. That's who taught you the technique, isn't it?'

Melissande groaned. So much for Reg's newfound restraint. *I should've known it was too good to last.* 'There's nothing wrong with studying metaphysics by mail. Gerald studied metaphysics by mail and look where he is now — a super special secret agent in a government Department that's so hush-hush they're not allowed to tell *themselves* they exist!'

'True,' Reg conceded, then looked pointedly down her beak. 'But Gerald had *me*.'

Slumping against the filing cabinet, she glared at the test tube and beaker. 'It's got to be the ink. I'm going straight back to see Mister Cripps and give him a piece of my mind. He's got no business selling substandard ink to unsuspecting customers. It may be his most economical brand but that's *no excuse* for —'

'Now, now,' said Reg. 'Only a bad worker blames her tools.' Staring at the residual mess in the test tube and beaker, she shook her head. 'Deary deary dear. You really have cocked it up this time, haven't you? Good lord, madam, what were you thinking? *Gerald* never —' And then she squawked as a pointed finger was jabbed between her eyes.

'I swear, Reg,' breathed Melissande, 'on my honour as a princess, finish that sentence and I will shove your beak where the sun doth not shine!'

Reg sniffed. 'You know what your problem is, don't you, ducky? You can't take a little constructive criticism, that's your problem. You may be Her Royal Highness Princess Melissande in disguise but you don't have the authority to shove my beak anywhere. And even if you *weren't* in disguise and you owned up to being an HRH instead of prancing about calling yourself *Miss Cadwallader* and you *did* have that kind of authority, *I'm* a queen and therefore outrank you.'

'Once upon a time you were a queen, Reg,' she snapped. 'Now you're just a bird of no fixed parentage. And disguise or no disguise, if you think I'm going to be dictated to by an ambulatory feather duster with delusions of grandeur you can bloody well think again!'

From outside the open window a coolly amused voice said, 'Now now, girls. How about a little decorum?'

CHAPTER FIVE

With a startled squawk Reg fell off the windowsill to land beak-first on the elderly cabbage-rose carpet. With an equally startled cry of '*Reg!*' Melissande leapt forward and scooped her up to make sure she was all right.

'Izz by deak brogen?' mumbled Reg, eyes rolling. 'Id veels brogen!'

'No, no, it's not broken,' she soothed, straightening Reg's mussed feathers and sitting her gently on the seat of the client armchair. Then she whipped around and glared at the face in the window. 'Bibbie! For the love of Saint Snodgrass, what are you *doing*? If anyone catches you levitating yourself we could lose —'

'Oh, relax,' said Bibbie, waving one hand. 'I hexed a dustbin lid, not me.'

'Well *don't*. Now *get down*! Or get inside! Quick, hurry, before someone notices!'

Monk's appalling sister grinned, folded her arms along the windowsill and rested her elegant chin on her wrists. 'Come on, Mel. Don't be a spoilsport.'

'I am *not* a spoilsport, I'm trying to save our hides. If the landladies walk in and see you hovering out there they'll have *conniptions*. You *know* what they said about Peculiar Goings On.

We're already up to our fifth official warning and we've only been here three and a half months. One more incident and we'll be out in the street!'

Bibbie sighed. 'Mel, *relax*. Our landladies aren't going to see me up here, the old dears are as blind as a herd of bats. But even if they do see me they'll just think I'm a well-dressed weather balloon. Or a novelty kite.' She frowned. 'I wonder ... *is* there such a thing as a herd of bats? Maybe it's a flock. Or a gaggle. Or possibly a school ...'

'Trust me when I say I neither know nor care,' said Melissande grimly. 'But if there were more than one of you, for which I thank Saint Snodgrass daily there isn't, you'd be known as a Headache of Emmerabiblias! And *don't* call me Mel!'

Bibbie pretended to pout. 'Monk calls you Mel.'

'You're not Monk!'

'Sorry,' said unrepentant Bibbie, back to grinning.

She took a deep and goaded breath. 'This is *not funny*! You just about frightened the life out of poor Reg! Now would you *please* be serious for five consecutive minutes and come inside? It's well after half-past nine, which means you're horribly late.'

'Sorry,' said Bibbie, still unrepentant. 'I overslept. After I got back to the boarding house Demelza Sopwith and I ended up in an argument about the accurate measuring of etheretic fluxes and it went on for *hours*. Oooh, she's *such* an ignorant hag. She says you need to take five readings to be certain of the thaumic variations but *I* say you only need three, provided you —'

'Yes, yes, yes,' she said impatiently. 'That's fascinating, Bibbie, and I'd love to hear all about it, honestly, only *not now*. Now you need to come inside before I drag you inside. I want your help.'

'Help?' Bibbie looked pleased. 'With what?'

She felt her chin tilt. 'Nothing much. Hardly anything at all, actually. Just —'

'She's forgotten how to make tamper-proof ink,' said Reg. 'So if you're quite finished impersonating a deranged bumblebee, ducky, perhaps you'd care to join us and earn your keep.'

When it came to Reg, Bibbie had a hide like a rhinoceros. Instead of arguing, she just nodded and smiled. 'Not a problem, girls. Don't go away.' And with a jaunty little wave she dropped out of sight, plummeting like a hydraulic lift with its cables cut.

'*Bibbie*!' Melissande threw herself precariously across the windowsill, sure that Monk's mad sister would end up smashed to pieces on the ground. But no — she was touching down on the cobbles quite safely with a gentle clatter of hexed dustbin lid. 'And don't forget to check the mailbox on your way upstairs!' she shouted.

Another jaunty wave was the only reply.

Sighing, she hauled herself back into the office. 'It doesn't matter how many times I remind her, she always forgets to fetch the first post.'

Reg snorted. 'Too busy levitating. She's as bad as her brother, that girl, and that's saying something.'

Despite her aggravation Melissande smiled as she picked up the scattered bits and pieces of the discarded *Ottosland Times*.

'Well, I suppose it's to be expected. They are related, after all. And really there's no harm in her. She's just young and high spirited. I expect I'd be the same if Lional —' She cleared her throat. 'Well. If he hadn't turned into a homicidal maniac.'

'You'd be young and high spirited if you had tighter buttocks,' said Reg. 'I'm telling you, ducky, flab is not your friend.'

The bird was saved only by Bibbie's arrival. Witnesses to murder were so inconvenient.

Melissande swallowed a bubble of unbecoming envy as Monk's sister sauntered into the office, the morning mail tucked under one arm. Every so often — like right this moment, for example, probably thanks to the spirit-crushing debacle of the exploding tamper-proof ink — she found herself struck speechless by the girl.

Simply put, Emmerabiblia Markham looked like a princess. Well, the way people imagined a princess should look, anyway. And despite being the genuine royal article, Melissande Cadwallader regrettably didn't. Not even when she went to the trouble of sprucing herself up.

Slender and shapely in watered green silk, with the kind of complexion oft-compared to strawberries and cream, Bibbie also enjoyed luxuriously waving hair the obligatory colour of a sun-ripened wheat field, cherry-red lips, eyes like blazing sapphires and so on and so forth ad absolutely nauseum and sometimes — galling as it might be to admit — it was hard to feel anything but inferior. Especially since Bibbie was also a phenomenally gifted witch.

Beautiful *and* talented: it was a daunting combination.

But at least there was one tiny glimmer of salvation: talented, beautiful Bibbie was practically bereft of common sense. Without Captain Melissande's pragmatic hand on the tiller, the good ship Emmerabiblia would have capsized some time in the first week of the agency's operation. In her weaker moments, like this one for example, Melissande hugged that comforting knowledge tight.

'Well, that was fun,' said Bibbie, nudging the office door closed, her face alight with mischievous amusement. 'One of the boys from Briscowe's Bootlaces pulled a shell game with all our postboxes. Nobody's letters were where they're supposed to be and there was so much squawking the foyer sounded like a poulterers' convention run amok.'

'But this is our mail?' said Melissande, snatching it from her and perching on the arm of the client's chair. 'You're sure? Because that Mister Davenport swore blind he was posting us payment and there's the milk account due tomorrow and —'

'Of course it's our mail,' said Bibbie, waving a negligent hand. 'A simple *locati locatorum* and hey presto, confusion resolved. It was so simple I did one for everybody.'

She groaned. 'For *free*? Emmera*bib*lia! *What* did we say about handing out free samples!'

Bibbie heaved a theatrical sigh. '*We* didn't say anything. *You* said don't, *I* said yes sir and I think Reg was eating a mouse at the time so *she* just burped.'

'Exactly! I said *don't*!' Melissande tugged at her stubbornly unluxurious rust-red plait. '*Honestly*, Bibbie, how can we expect to make ends meet if you keep on handing out free samples?'

Bibbie patted her on the shoulder in passing, then stopped in front of her desk to stare down at the woeful results of the tamper-proof ink experiment.

'Oh, stop fussing. Think of it as free —'

'*Don't* say it,' she snarled. 'I've heard more than enough about free advertising for one day.' She took a deep breath and shoved her temper aside. Quarrelling wasn't going to find them new clients. 'Oh well. What's done is done. And since you can't very well go back downstairs and take back the *locati locatorum* we'll call it your very last charitable act of the year and leave it at that. Agreed?'

Bibbie shrugged. 'Sure, Mel. Whatever you say.'

'And *don't* call me Mel!'

'Bullseye,' said Bibbie, grinning.

Ignoring Reg's snickering, taking refuge in dignified silence, Melissande retreated to her own desk and started to sort the morning's post. 'Bill — circular — bill —' she muttered, flicking through the envelopes.

'What does a circular Bill look like, I wonder?' mused Bibbie, still staring at the forlorn test tube and beaker on her desk. 'Positively rotund or just pleasantly plump? What do you think?'

'I think I'm going to smack you if you don't work out why that ink won't take a tamper-proof incant,' said Melissande, still mail-sorting. There was absolutely no sign of payment from Mister Davenport. Saint Snodgrass preserve them, if they didn't make some money soon ...

Bibbie picked up the test tube. 'So what happened?'

'I don't know. It just went kablooey. Three times.'

'Kablooey?' Bibbie raised one impeccable eyebrow. 'That's a technical term, is it?'

Melissande glowered. 'It is now.'

Holding the test tube up to the light from the window, Bibbie inspected it from every angle, her lips pursed in concentration. Then she waved it under her nose and inhaled the lingering stink like a wine taster at a festival. Finally she clasped the test tube gently between her palms and with her eyes closed hummed a strange harmonic under her breath. A stiff breeze sprang up out of nowhere, and Melissande had to clutch at her pile of bills to stop them blowing straight through the open window.

'Oy! Do you mind?' Reg protested as her plumage tried to turn itself inside out.

Bibbie opened her eyes and frowned at the test tube. 'You're right, Mel. This ink is well and truly kablooeyfied.'

'*Yes*, Bibbie, I *know*.' Honestly, much more of this and she'd grind her teeth down to stumps and then there'd be dental expenses on top of everything else. 'The question is *why*?'

'Sorry,' said Bibbie, shrugging. 'Haven't a clue. All I can tell you is the inherent thaumaturgical substructure of the incant has somehow been degraded and deconstructed then retranslated from an eighth dimensional transvibration to a sixteenth.'

Melissande blinked. 'And that's bad, is it?' she asked eventually.

'Well, I don't know about *bad*, precisely, but it's certainly interesting,' said Bibbie. 'How in the name of all things metaphysical did you manage it? I don't think even *Monk's* pulled off something as outlandish as this.'

'I don't have the foggiest idea,' she said glumly. 'I was hoping you would.'

Another shrug. 'Sorry.'

'Don't look at me,' said Reg. 'I was catching up on my beauty sleep. At my age I need all the help I can get.' When nobody contradicted her, she subsided into offended silence.

'I suppose we could ask Monk to test what's left of the ink in one of his Department's labs,' said Bibbie. 'He'll be able to —' Breaking off as the phone on her desk rang, she reached for the heavy black receiver and answered it. 'Witches Incorporated, No Job Too — Monk! Fancy that, we were just talking about you. Were your ears burning? — They were? Not literally, I hope. — Well, all right, but with what you get up to down in your Department basement, let alone in your attic, I never really know for sure. And there was that time in the nursery when you —'

As Bibbie squabbled with her brother, Melissande started filing the bills in their concertina folder. Where did they all come from? And why did it seem that life was easier when she was juggling the finances of an entire kingdom? How could it be that keeping the doors open to one insignificant little witching agency was proving to be a thousand times harder than keeping New Ottosland solvent?

She snuck a surreptitious glance around the shabby office. It wasn't much, true, but it was theirs, and if after so much hope and effort the agency didn't work out … humiliatingly, she felt her eyes burn and her nose start to run. She had to accidentally-on-purpose knock the bills to the floor so she could dive under the desk before the other two noticed she was cry— very upse— having an allergy attack.

'— argue about it any more,' Bibbie finished. 'One more

word out of you and we won't come. Fine. Good.' She hung up the phone. 'That was Monk. He needs to see us. Urgently.'

Melissande scuttled backwards out from under the desk and hauled herself to her feet. 'Why? What's happened? Has Great-uncle Throgmorton struck again? Or is this something to do with one of his wretched experiments?' She turned to Reg, staring accusingly. 'I thought you said the house was still in one piece!'

'Eh?' said Reg, startled. 'It is! Or it was first thing this morning. Whatever he's gone and done now, ducky, he did it after I left so don't you go giving me the mouldy eyeball.'

She turned back to Bibbie. 'So what's wrong? What's *happened*?'

Bibbie pulled a face. 'He wouldn't tell me. All he'd say was that he wants to see us urgently in the Botanical Gardens. The Tropical Glasshouse, to be exact.'

'Oh, Saint Snodgrass's bunions,' said Melissande, and banged the office window shut. 'You should've let me talk to him.'

'You don't suppose it's Gerald, do you?' said Reg. Her voice wasn't quite steady. 'You don't suppose something's happened to my Gerald?'

Melissande exchanged a nervous look with Bibbie then picked Reg up off the client chair and settled her onto one shoulder. 'No. I don't suppose anything of the sort,' she said firmly, collecting her reticule. 'Monk's probably got another staffing crisis on his hands, that's all. Probably he wants to talk us into pretending to be housemaids.'

'Yes, that'll be it,' said Bibbie. 'Something totally ridiculous like that. Bags I hit him first.'

Another exchange of nervous looks, then Melissande cleared her throat. 'Well, there's only one way to find out what he wants. Let's go!'

*   *   *

The world-famous Ottosland Botanical Gardens stood in the exact centre of the city, and at a quarter to eleven in the morning of a working weekday the squirrels outnumbered the people five to one. Melissande, Reg and Bibbie hurried along the neatly tended paths, between immaculate flower beds and meticulously nurtured trees, to the Tropical Glasshouse on the Gardens' west lawn, directly across the street from the looming Department of Thaumaturgy building.

'Urrggh,' said Melissande as they went inside. Four steps through the entrance and sweat was already trickling down her face. She didn't need a mirror to know her cheeks were swiftly turning beetroot. 'Why does he want us to meet him in *here*? This place is worse than a steam bath, honestly!'

The overheated air contained within the Glasshouse was heavy and wet, soaked in a melange of ripely exotic perfumes. An international cornucopia of tropical trees and flowers and vines and creepers flourished in profusion, brilliant greens, vivid scarlets, oranges and yellows, bright blues and shameless pinks, nature at its exhibitionist best.

Monk was waiting for them at the end of the tamed jungle's main path, anxiously pacing back and forth in front of a towering Lanruvian Palm. Dressed in a sober blue suit, his hair ruthlessly combed into submission and his permanently potion-stained fingers hidden in his pockets, he looked like a banker. All he needed was the bowler hat.

Melissande mopped her face with an inadequate hanky. *A pity he's not a banker, really. He could've given us a loan.* As usual her heart skipped a half-beat, seeing him, but she schooled her expression. This wasn't the time or place for being girlishly coy.

'Ha!' said Reg, her claws clutching tighter. 'There he is.' She took to her wings and hurtled ahead of them down the path. Melissande looked at Bibbie, sighed, and broke into a reluctant, unladylike jog to catch up.

Luckily it seemed they were alone in the Glasshouse, because Reg — having reached Monk first — was making no effort to be discreet. 'Well? Well?' she demanded loudly. 'Is he all right? Has there been another international incident? Does he need rescuing again?'

Monk looked confused. 'What? Who?'

'*Who?*' Outraged, wings flapping, Reg hovered in his face. 'Who do you *think*, you thaumaturgical tosser? *Gerald!* Your best friend! Skinny fellow, brown hair, one silver eye, good with incants, works as a spy. Am I ringing any bells yet?'

'Reg, what are you going on about?' said Monk. 'Gerald's fine. I told you that last night.'

'Then what are we doing here, you raving nitwit?'

'Good question,' said Melissande, joining them, and offering Reg an arm to perch on before she flapped herself into asphyxiation. Acutely aware that she must appear absolutely hideous — even Bibbie looked less than exquisite for once — she scowled at her young man. 'I don't suppose you've got a good answer, have you?'

'He'd better,' said Bibbie, folding her arms. 'Because romping around this steam bath was not on my list of Things To Do This Morning and there must be at least a dozen places to hide a body in here. I'll just bet the tropics are full of flesh-eating beetles.'

Monk took a hasty step back. 'Okay. Look. I'm sorry to drag you out here like this but I had to speak to you.'

'You were speaking to us, Monk,' said Bibbie. 'That funny contraption you were talking into is called *the telephone.*'

Flinching, Monk darted a quick look around them. They were still alone. 'This isn't a telephone kind of conversation, Bibbie! Telephone calls can be monitored!'

'Then why not use the crystal ball?' Bibbie demanded. 'Why make us huff and puff all the way —'

'Because I couldn't trust that, either!'

Melissande transferred Reg from her arm to her shoulder. The urge to display girlish coyness was rapidly fading. 'This is ridiculous. I thought Gerald was the one playing cloak-and-dagger games. Whatever you want to tell us, Monk, just spit it out so we can get back to the office. For all we know clients are lining up three deep in the corridor!'

'Heh,' said Reg under her breath. 'Chance'd be a fine thing. But she's got a point, sunshine,' she added to Monk, at full disapproving volume. 'Flap your lips or get on your bike, boy. We're busy women and we don't have all day.'

Monk cast another anxiously furtive look around the Glasshouse's moist interior, then stepped closer again. 'I just need to know if you've noticed anything ... peculiar ... since last night.'

'That rather depends on how you define "peculiar," doesn't it?' said Bibbie. 'I mean —'

'Put a sock in it, ducky,' said Reg, and fixed Monk with a beady glare. 'All right, Mister Clever Clogs. I know that look, so out with it and no more messing about. What have you gone and done this time?'

A rising tide of embarrassment flushed Monk's face pink. 'Er ... well ...'

'Oh, Saint Snodgrass preserve us,' said Melissande, her stomach sinking. 'You've invented something else, haven't you? And we accidentally ate it at dinner last night, didn't we? So any minute now we're going to — to — sneeze ourselves into an alternate reality, aren't we!'

'Close,' said Monk apologetically, 'but alas, no cigar.'

Bibbie grabbed his right earlobe between thumb and forefinger and twisted. Monk yelped. 'Just tell us what's happened, brother dear,' she growled, 'or you'll be sorry.'

With some difficulty Monk wrested his earlobe free. 'All right,' he said, dropping his voice to a near-whisper and beckoning them even closer. 'What's happened is I've managed to invent an interdimensional portal opener.'

'Of course you have,' Melissande breathed. 'Isn't everybody these days?'

Monk winced. 'I hope not. If they are the Department'll go spare.'

Taking a deep breath, she reached for the iron forbearance that had stood her in such good stead back home. 'And did you invent it on purpose or was it an accident?'

'An accident,' said Monk, as though he were admitting to some terrible wizardly crime. Then he brightened. 'But you know what they say.' Lurking beneath his anxiety was a reprehensible flicker of glee. 'Genius will out.'

'So will blood,' said Reg. 'After I've punched you in the nose.'

'Reg, you're a bird,' he sighed. 'You can't punch anyone.'

'I'm talking theoretically,' said Reg, leering. 'It's called punching by proxy. Why do you think I keep these two bruisers around?'

'Can we *please* not get sidetracked?' said Bibbie, stamping one foot. 'Monk —'

'Yes, yes, I know,' he said. 'Mel, do you remember the portable portal I invented?'

'Of course,' she said impatiently. 'But what's that got to do with anything?'

Monk shoved his hands back in his pockets. 'Well, a couple of nights ago I was at home, in the library, having a good hard think about a Department project I'm not allowed to discuss, and I was kind of ... fiddling with it. The portal, I mean. Running the baseline etheretic harmonics through my back brain while my front brain was focused on this other project, you know, kind of like doodling, and I sort of tweaked the portal's matrix. Not a lot. But just enough.'

Melissande looked at him. *He can't be serious.* 'I thought the Department made you surrender the portable portal,' she said, amazed that she sounded so eminently reasonable. Politely disinterested, even. She wanted to hit him. *Really* make him yelp.

'They did,' said Monk. 'And I did. At least … I surrendered the final version, the one I used to get us to and from New Ottosland. And the prototype Mark A.'

'Don't tell me, let me guess,' said Reg, sweet as a song bird. 'You kept the prototype Mark B all for your little self, didn't you, you gold-plated twaddle-brained gormless unsanctified *git!*'

Monk's expression turned mulish and his voice rose defensively. 'Well, why shouldn't I? The portal was mine, wasn't it? I bloody well invented it! Why shouldn't I keep a copy of my own inventions?'

Bibbie took a step sideways, leaned on the trunk of the Lanruvian Palm and banged her forehead against its purple bark. 'I'd like to point out,' she announced to the world at large, 'that any resemblance between me and the unmitigated moron on my left is purely coincidental and in no way implies that we are actually *related!*'

'Hey!' Monk protested. 'You're supposed to be on my side!'

'And I would be if your side didn't give me a headache,' retorted Bibbie. '*I* got read the riot act after New Ottosland too, remember, and *I* wasn't even involved! *You* kept me out of that little adventure just like I was a *gel*.'

As Monk and Bibbie exchanged ferocious grimaces, Reg snickered. 'Your superiors at the Department can't know you very well, Mister Markham, if they don't know you always work with parallel prototypes.'

Monk immediately looked cagey. 'I … might have forgotten to mention it.'

'We can discuss your amnesia another time,' said Melissande. 'Right now let's stick to this crisis, shall we? Why should we care that you accidentally invented an interdimensional portal? It's not as if —' And then the penny dropped. 'Oh, for the love of —

don't tell me, let me guess. You used it, didn't you? You opened the portal to another *dimension*.'

'Of course he did,' said Bibbie with a scornful, inelegant snort. 'Haven't you worked it out yet? My genius brother never met a door he wasn't willing to wrench so wide that it falls off its hinges!'

'Oh, look who's talking!' retorted Monk. 'The girl who souped up Father's etheretic distillation modulator so all the clocks ran backwards and the cat lost its —'

'If we could please just *focus*!' said Melissande loudly. 'Or I swear by all things metaphysical there *will* be a great deal of punching by proxy!'

'Something's come through, hasn't it?' said Bibbie, arms folded again. 'That's what this panic is all about.'

'I don't know,' Monk muttered. He had the grace to look abashed. 'Not for certain.'

Reg rattled her tail feathers. 'In other words, yes.'

'What was it?' said Bibbie. 'I mean, what dimension did the portal open onto, Monk? And what kind of things live in it? Are we talking microscopic creepy crawlies? Slimy tentacles? Alternate versions of ourselves? What?'

'Actually,' said Monk, brightening again, 'it turns out that I've made an important discovery. In *fact* it looks like I've debunked another popular misconception.'

'Of course you have,' said Bibbie, rolling her eyes. 'And which one have you debunked this time?'

Monk was all lit up now, his thaumaturgical enthusiasm burning like a fever. 'I've discovered that when you open a portal between dimensions it's not as simple as stepping from one to the other. It's not like — like going from the dining room to the parlour, say.'

Bibbie frowned. 'It's not? Are you sure? Because Hepplewight's Theorem *distinctly* postulates —'

'Oh, bollocks to old Hepplewight,' Monk said airily, waving an excited hand. 'What would that old fossil know? He's not had an original thought for twenty-seven years, not since he worked out how to splice a thaum and they made him a Grand Master on the strength of it. No, no, no, I'm telling you, Bibs, there's a kind of empty space between the dimensions. A passageway. A conduit. I managed to get a reading, not much, just a few seconds' worth. But it was enough to prove Hepplewight wrong.'

Irritation forgotten, Bibbie's face lit up just like her mad brother's. 'You *didn't*! Monk, that's fantastic! That's — that's *phenomenal*!'

'I know!' he said, grinning like a loon. 'I could hardly believe it! If I could sneak the results into the Department I'd be able to work out exactly what that means but I don't dare risk it, I'll have to —'

Melissande, having heard more than enough, turned her head till she was nose-to-beak with Reg. 'Shall I take the first swing, Your Majesty, or would you care for the honour?'

'You take it, ducky,' said Reg, eyes gleaming. 'I'll follow it up with a one-two jab to their skinny arses!'

Monk and Bibbie stopped enthusing about his latest discovery and gave them another patented Markham peas-in-a-pod stare.

'Eh?' said Monk. 'What? No — wait —'

'I don't want to wait,' said Melissande, advancing on him with both sweaty hands clenched to fists. 'I want to conduct myself in a thoroughly unladylike fashion and pummel you to a whimpering pulp, Monk Markham! I want seventeen generations of New Ottosland princesses to stand up in their graves and *cheer* as I abandon every last shred of royal tradition and knock you into the middle of next week! I want —'

'To calm down!' said Monk, retreating with both hands raised. 'That's what you want to do, Mel. Just — just — calm down so we can —'

'*Don't call me Mel!*'

Monk's shoulder blades collided with a Botchaki Silk Tree. 'Okay. All right. I get it. You're upset. I don't blame you. I'm upset too.'

'Really? Because it looked to me like you were congratulating yourself. It looked to me like you were patting yourself on the back so hard it's a wonder you haven't dislocated your shoulder.'

'Well, all right, fair enough, I'm excited about my new invention,' he confessed, 'but I *am* sorry it's causing this slight difficulty. And I swear I had *no idea* that there was anything living in the spaces between dimensions. I mean, how could I? I had no idea there *were* spaces between dimensions. I had no idea —'

'So you admit you're mucking about with things you don't understand?' Melissande demanded. 'Just — just — plotzing about tra-la, tra-la, not having the first wretched *clue* of what might —'

'Plotzing? Plotzing? I'm not *plotzing*!' said Monk, offended. 'You seem to be forgetting that I'm a research thaumaturgist, Mel — issande. This is what I *do*. I reveal hidden metaphysical truths, I chart uncharted mysteries, I —'

'Need your bloody head examined!' she shouted at him. '*What's come through that door you opened?*'

Monk shoved a finger between his shirt collar and his throat and wiggled it, hard. 'Um ... well ... I'm not sure, exactly. I haven't seen it. As far as I can tell it's most likely invisible, due to the incompatibility of the comparative dimensional vibrations.'

Melissande exchanged another look with Reg. 'How delightful.' Only her intimate acquaintance with homicidal maniacs and rampaging dragons kept her voice steady. 'And where do you think our invisible friend might be right now?'

Monk swallowed convulsively. 'Ah. Yes. Well, I'm not *entirely* sure ... but I think you've got it.'

CHAPTER SIX

Once the shouting and squawking had died down, and Monk had picked himself up and brushed the leaf mould off his sober blue suit and rubbed the bits that Reg had poked with her beak, Melissande clapped her hands for order.

'All right,' she said sharply. 'If everyone can just calm down? Good. Now, Monk. Do you have *any* idea what it is you think we've got?'

'Well,' said Monk, frowning, 'after a lot of careful consideration and by a comprehensive process of elimination I'm pretty sure it's a concatetanic conglomeration of uber-parallel-dimensional anti-etheretic particles supercharged with extraneous thaumaturgical emissions on a scale of seventeen to the eleventh power, cubed.'

Melissande blinked at him. 'I see,' she said, after a pause. 'Ah — let me put that another way. Would you have any idea what it was if you weren't a thaumaturgical genius working in a secret government Research and Development facility?'

'Of course,' said Monk, as though surprised she'd even ask. 'It's a sprite.'

'A *sprite*?' Bibbie's eyes lit up yet again. The wretched girl really was as bad as her equally wretched brother. 'Really, Monk? You're positive? Because according to Herbert and Lowe —'

'Sprites are just another postulation of theoretical

thaumaturgical metaphysics,' said Monk eagerly. 'I know, I *know*. But now I'm not so sure!'

Melissande groaned. 'Well, *I'm* sure. I'm sure I don't understand a word the two of you are saying. Now start talking Ottish or I swear I'll walk away and let Reg do her worst!'

'Sorry,' Monk said, sheepish. 'Basically, what it means is I seem to have proven the actual existence of a theoretical construct, which when you think about it is pretty bloody exciting, really, even if it's proving a trifle inconvenient, because —'

Melissande grabbed him by both ears and pulled his face towards hers until their noses were touching. 'Dearest Monk, I don't care if it's the most exciting thing since the invention of expanding corsets. As far as *I'm* concerned this sprite of yours is nothing more than a pain in the bu —' She glanced at Reg, who'd perched herself on a handy low-slung palm branch, and smoothly changed tracks. 'Nothing more than a huge inconvenience. Incidentally, is it alive?'

With enormous care, Monk disengaged her fingers from his ears then inched himself away from the Botchaki Silk Tree. 'I suppose that depends on how you define "alive".'

'Does it have thoughts? Feelings? Can it communicate?'

'Mel, I don't know,' he said. 'Honestly. It exists, I know that much. But until I can study it that's all I'm prepared to say.'

'And how is it you're so sure *we've* got it?'

'*Oh*!' said Bibbie suddenly, and danced a little on the spot. 'Of *course*! Great-uncle Throgmorton's ghost! The sprite's incompatible with our dimension's etheretic vibrations so it's causing physical manifestations on our plane. The housemaids being tossed out of bed and the exploding strawberry syllabub and —'

Monk nodded vigorously. 'Exactly!'

'And the *ink*, Mel,' Bibbie added, still dancing. 'This explains your debacle with the tamper-proof ink!'

'What debacle with the tamper-proof ink?' said Monk.

Melissande sighed. 'I tried to brew up some tamper-proof ink this morning,' she muttered, cheeks heating. 'And it went kablooey. Three times.'

'But now we know it wasn't your fault!' said Bibbie.

'Perhaps if you could manage *not* to sound quite so surprised?' she said, teeth gritted again. 'That would be nice.'

'Heh,' said Reg, flapping back to her shoulder. 'Fat chance of that, ducky.'

Bibbie ignored both of them. 'It's the only explanation that makes sense. Assuming a sprite *is* an agitation of super-charged inverse etheretic particles with a cohesive substructure in direct reverse proportion to our dimension's thaumaturgical vibrations. Monk?'

'That's the idea, more or less,' he said, nodding.

Bibbie slitted her eyes. 'Can you come up with a *better* definition?'

'Ah ...' He shook his head. 'No.'

'*Right*, then,' said Bibbie, and dusted her hands. 'That means the sprite's likely to have a *particularly* deleterious effect on any ambient thaumaturgic processes. In other words — the ink!'

'So I was right,' said Monk, vastly relieved. 'I *knew* you had the rotten thing because it's not in the house any more and it's not at work, either, and when I called Mother nothing untoward was happening there so it didn't go home with Dodsworth and the others.'

'But why would it have left with us?' said Melissande.

'Well, if my theory on the nature of interdimensional sprites is correct, they're attracted to the corporeal essence of something substantial in their immediate vicinity.'

Reg snorted. 'Are you quite sure you don't want me to show you those buttock-reducing exercises, ducky?'

'*Amazing*, Monk,' said Bibbie, forestalling an imminent

outbreak of hostilities. Her eyes were burning with a resurgence of thaumaturgical fervour. 'And it's all because you accidentally shifted the polarities of your portable portal prototype.'

'*Precisely!*'

Bibbie threw her arms around her brother and kissed him enthusiastically on both cheeks. '*Monk*, you're a *genius!*'

He hugged her back, laughing. 'Yeah, well, I dunno —'

'You are, you are! This'll be your second article in *The Golden Staff*. Oh, I'm so *proud* of you!'

'*Proud* of him?' Reg snorted, and gave her tail feathers a peevish rattle. 'He's a menace to society, that's what *he* is.' More rattling of tail feathers, and a pointed glare. 'And only *you* could fall arse over teakettle for him, Princess Pushy. I'm starting to think you should've fallen for Gerald after all.'

Melissande heaved another sigh. There was no point holding a grudge against the horrible bird: Reg made a warthog look thin-skinned. Besides, she had a point. Not about falling for Gerald, but about Monk.

I care for him a great deal, I truly do, but . . .

'It does sound as though you're playing with fire, you know,' she told him. 'You really ought to be more careful.'

Sometimes he reminded her of a helium-filled balloon: impossible to repress for longer than a few moments. 'Mel, trust me, it's *perfectly* safe,' he insisted. 'We're not in a skerrick of danger. Not from the sprite, and not from the portal opener. I *promise.*'

How could she doubt him? He was a thaumaturgical genius, after all. 'Fine. If you say so.'

'I say so,' he said, that anarchic grin lighting up his face.

'Yes, well,' she muttered, trying in vain to smother her own answering smile. 'Only the thing is, aren't you talking theoretically? I mean, I don't suppose you can actually *prove* any of it, can you? Because if you're right and this sprite creature did leave your place with us last night, I'd like to know for sure.'

'And so would I,' Bibbie added. 'Because I've got some hexes to put together and I don't want them going kablooey.'

'As a matter of fact I *can* prove it,' said Monk. 'Hold on.' He rummaged in the nearby lush tropical undergrowth and pulled out a large, shabby carpetbag. 'I threw this together over breakfast. It's a bit rough and ready but I'm pretty sure it'll do the trick.'

Melissande frowned as he opened the bag and took out an eye-boggling contraption consisting of a metal rod wrapped in copper wire and attached to some kind of needle-and-gauge arrangement.

'What is it?' she said, suspicious.

His eyebrows shot up. 'A portable etheretic sprite detector, of course.'

Which he'd invented while eating scrambled eggs and bacon. *Of course.* She shook her head. 'How does it work?'

Monk opened his mouth to answer, then closed it again. 'Ah ... do you really want me to explain or should I just show you?'

She sniffed. 'Good point.'

Flicking a switch, he passed the wire-wrapped rod down his front. Nothing happened. 'See?' he said, grinning again. So ridiculously pleased with himself. Take away his inventions and Monk would go into a decline, she was sure. Just like a baby deprived of its rattle. 'No reaction. That means no sprite activity for the last ten hours at least.'

Bibbie clapped her hands like a child at a party. 'Ooooh, test me, test me!'

Her brother obliged. The needle flickered a couple of times, and the gauge emitted a squeak.

'Ha!' he said. 'Contact ... but only minimally. You've been in the vicinity of a sprite recently but you haven't had a significant encounter.'

'All right then,' said Melissande, bracing herself. 'Test me.'

As Monk ran the sprite detector over her the gauge screeched like a long-tailed cat in a roomful of rocking chairs. Reg let out a shriek and erupted into the humid air, shedding feathers and curses in equal measure.

'Bullseye!' Monk said, practically chortling with satisfaction. 'That's excellent. It's always nice to see a theory proven out. You, Melissande, are *covered* in etheretic spores.'

She took a step back. '*Etheretic spores*? What do you mean *etheretic spores?* What are *etheretic spores?*'

'Oh, you know,' he said vaguely, checking the readings on the gauge. 'Randomly excreted thaumaturgical particles.'

Still squawking, Reg landed on a branch of the Botchaki Silk Tree and started a complicated little foot-wiping dance on its pale yellow bark. Horrified, Melissande stared at her outstretched hands.

'Monk, I don't like this!' she said, mortified to hear a quaver in her voice. 'I don't like this at —'

'Oh, don't worry,' he said blithely, glancing up from his equipment. 'I'm pretty sure the spores are harmless.'

'*Pretty sure*? Monk, you raving lunatic, you irresponsible bird brain, you —'

'Oy!' said Reg. 'Mind who you're calling a bird brain, madam!'

Monk looked up, surprised. 'You're fine, Mel. Really.'

'Says *you*,' she retorted. 'Forgive me if I'd like a second opinion. After all, you're the one who thought sprites were *mythical*!'

His face split in another wide grin. 'And now we know they're not! Isn't it great? I had no idea that humming three bars of descending cyclonic harmonics in B-flat minor while holding the portal key would get me into other dimensions! If I had I would've gone looking for the one with the voluptuous can-can girls!'

If she'd had a parasol handy she would have poked him in the buttocks with it. 'Monk Markham, I swear, either you start taking this seriously or —'

'I am taking this seriously!' he protested. 'This is a major thaumaturgical breakthrough, Mel, and they don't come along every day. It's *fantastic!*'

'*Fantastic?*' Breathless with outrage, she came perilously close to snatching up the carpetbag and throwing it at him. 'It's not fantastic, you — you *turnip*, it's *disgusting*! I'm covered in interdimensional *sprite shit!* Where's the nearest tap? Has anybody got a clean hanky? How much of the stuff is on me, I can't see a bloody thing!'

Monk stared at her, bemused. 'Of course you can't. We're dealing with a basic visual incompatibility between dimensional vibrations, remember?'

'No, not really!' she shouted. 'I'm a bit too busy being covered in interdimensional *sprite shit!* Where's the wretched thing now, Monk? Is it in my hair?' She began frantically patting her head. 'Oh, Saint Snodgress preserve me, don't let there be a sprite in my *hair!*'

He ran the sprite detector over her again. This time the volume was appreciably lower, more beeping than screeching. 'It's okay, it's okay, it's not in your hair, Mel,' he said, trying to appease. 'It's not anywhere. You're one hundred percent sprite-free, I promise.'

'And yet still covered in sprite shit, yes?' she demanded.

'Um ... well ... yes. Sorry about that. But the rate of decay is accelerating,' he added encouragingly. 'That's good, isn't it?'

She goggled at him. '*Decay*? You mean I'm covered in *decomposing* sprite shit? *How is that good, Monk?*'

'It's all right, Mel,' said Bibbie, trying to be helpful. 'We'll get you cleaned up somehow.'

'We certainly will,' said Reg from her safely distant tree

branch. 'The Department's bound to have a decontamination chamber they can spare for a week or two. In the meantime, Mad Miss Markham and I can mind the agency. She'll even remember to collect the mail without being reminded, won't you, ducky?'

'Absolutely,' Bibbie agreed. 'I promise.'

Breathing heavily, Melissande glared at the pair of them. 'Strange as it may seem, I don't consider that particularly comforting. In fact I won't be comfortable until we track down this inconvenient creature and send it back where it belongs!' She rounded on Monk. 'So if it's not stuck on me, where is it?'

'Still at the agency,' said Bibbie. 'It must be.'

Raising her eyebrows, Melissande flicked a glance at Monk's unhelpful sister. 'Must it? How do we know it's not rampaging around town even as we speak?'

'Because there's nothing registering on the Department's monitors,' said Monk. 'Believe me, I've checked. Besides, if the sprite was loose in town we'd have heard about it by now. Exploding tamper-proof ink would be the least of our worries.'

'Then what are you waiting for?' she demanded. 'Let's get back to the office so you can catch the little bugger and send it packing!'

He winced. 'Sorry. I'd love to, only I can't. I've got a secret briefing with Uncle Ralph. But after I invented the portable sprite detector I invented a sprite trap to catch it in. See?'

She stared as he opened the carpetbag again and pulled out what looked like a birdcage for a stunted canary. 'It's not very big.'

He shrugged. 'Neither's the sprite.'

'How do you know, Monk? The sprite's invisible!'

'I know,' he insisted. 'I'm a thaumaturgist, remember?' When she didn't say anything, he adopted a wounded expression. 'What? Don't you trust me?'

She gave him an incendiary look. *And to think he nagged Gerald for turning Tavistock into a lion* ... 'Of course I do, Monk. When it comes to inventing new ways of getting into trouble I trust you implicitly.'

Reg sniggered. 'You tell him, ducky.'

'And speaking of invisible,' she added, 'since we can't see this wretched sprite, how exactly are we supposed to catch it?'

'Easy,' said Monk, so effortlessly confident. So completely unmoved by her righteous indignation. He was the most *infuriating* man ... 'There's an etheretic normaliser built into the trap. You activate it with this switch here, see?' He pointed. 'If the sprite's within range the multi-phase thaumaturgic agitation will render it visible.'

'For how long?'

'Long enough, I promise.'

'And how do you define "within range"?'

'A few feet.'

'Is that all?' she said, dismayed. 'Monk —'

'I know, I know,' he said, carelessly apologetic. Infuriating? He was *impossible*. 'Sorry, Mel. What can I say? It was a rush job.'

As solutions went it was far from perfect, but with time and circumstances against them it would have to do. 'Fine. And what happens once we've caught our uninvited guest?'

'You can leave me a message at the Department and I'll drop by the agency and pick it up,' said Monk. 'Better yet, come to dinner tonight and bring it with you.'

She stared at him. He was serious. He was actually, deadly, serious. *If I wasn't in lo — quite fond of him, I really would punch him in the nose.* 'Monk —'

'Oh, save your breath, ducky,' said Reg, and flapped down from the tree branch to take up her favoured shoulder-perch. 'Let's just take care of this, shall we? I don't know about you but I want a bath!'

'*One* bath?' Melissande stared down at her invisible-sprite-shit-covered self. 'I won't be getting out of the tub for a *week*! I don't care how many times I have to tramp up and down those stairs with kettlefuls of hot water!'

'Does that mean you'll do it?' her infuriating, impossible young man asked hopefully.

Yes, indeed. She *so* wanted to punch him. 'Do I have a choice?'

Beaming, Monk kissed her swiftly and chastely on the cheek. 'Terrific!' He shoved the sprite detector and sprite trap into the carpetbag then thrust the bag at her. 'Knew I could count on you, Mel.'

'And me,' said Bibbie, offended.

'Yes, yes, you too,' he added hastily.

'Oh? And what am I, then?' demanded Reg. 'A bowl of chopped chicken liver?'

'Of *course* not!' said Monk. 'I can count on *all* of you.' He fished out his fob watch and flicked it open. 'Only I'm going to have to count on you from afar, because —'

'Not so fast!' said Melissande. 'You have to show us how this sprite trap works.'

'I wrote down some instructions,' he said. 'They're in the bag. Honestly, Mel, you'll be fine.'

'You hope,' she retorted. 'I mean, what if your precious sprite does have a mind of its own and doesn't want to be caught? What if it fights back? What if —'

'It won't. I doubt it's aware of what's going on. To be honest, Mel, I don't even think it's intelligent.'

'Well, that makes two of you,' she snapped. And to think that an hour ago she'd thought the darkest clouds in her sky were shaped like sagging buttocks. 'Honestly, Monk. Why does *your* problem have to become *my* problem?'

He winced. 'I am sorry. Truly.'

And he was, she didn't doubt it. The trouble was, being sorry this time wouldn't stop him next time. When metaphysical madness struck again, and it would, he'd not be strong enough to resist it. Asking Monk to turn his back on a new discovery was as futile as expecting Reg to be ladylike.

The only question is am I strong enough to endure the consequences? Because any moth fluttering around Monk Markham's flame is going to get its wings singed, sooner or later.

The thought must have shown on her face, because Monk took an alarmed step towards her. 'Melissande? I mean it. You're not in any danger. I wouldn't put you in harm's way. Not *any* of you.'

She let out a gusty sigh. 'Not on purpose, no.'

'Not *ever*,' he insisted. 'Look — if you don't want to do this —'

'No, no, I'll do it,' she said. She glanced at Bibbie and Reg. '*We'll* do it. But you owe us a tin of tamper-proof ink.'

'A *big* tin,' added Bibbie.

Reg snorted. '*Three* big tins.'

'Three big tins of tamper-proof ink,' said Monk, a relieved smile lighting his face. 'Absolutely. I'll make it myself.'

'All right then, girls,' said Melissande, watching Monk beat a hasty retreat. 'Let's go catch ourselves an invisible sight-seeing interdimensional sprite, shall we?'

As they hurried back to the agency, still on foot unfortunately, given the parlous state of their finances, she could only hope the stares they attracted were the usual ones on account of the tweed trousers, and had nothing to do with the invisible sprite shit becoming inconveniently visible.

Clustered with Bibbie and Reg in the dingy corridor outside their office — Saint Snodgrass be praised the other two offices on their floor were empty — she stared at the agency's locked door. 'So . . . how do we know the sprite's still in there?'

Bibbie shrugged. 'There's only one way to find out.' She grabbed her brother's carpetbag and took out the portable sprite detector. 'Stand back,' she added, turning it on. 'This could get interesting.'

Melissande flattened herself against the corridor's far wall and watched Bibbie pass the sprite detector's copper wire-wrapped rod over their recently painted door.

'Does that answer your question?' Bibbie shouted above the detector's hysterical shrieking.

Melissande nodded, hands clapped over her ears. 'Yes! Yes! Now turn it off before we have everyone in the building up here asking inconvenient questions and calling the landladies!'

Bibbie turned off the detector then unhexed the agency door's lock. Not that it needed hexing *and* a key. It barely needed the key, since there wasn't anything in there worth stealing. But they were a witching locum agency. It was a matter of professional pride.

'Right,' said Bibbie, as the hum from the unhexing faded. 'Got your key, Mel? I left mine at the boarding house.'

Of course she did. When it came to 'scatty', Bibbie was a dictionary listing all by herself. She fished out her key, unlocked the door — then hesitated. 'Wait. We need a plan first.'

'We've got a plan,' said Reg. 'Find the sprite, catch the sprite, make that Markham boy eat the sprite for dinner, without mustard. That's the plan.'

Melissande frowned. 'That's not a very specific plan, Reg. For starters I think that before we go charging in there we'd better make sure we know how to work Monk's sprite trap.'

'Oh, well, if you're going to insist on being all *sensible* about things,' said Bibbie, grinning.

'I don't know,' she said, suddenly uncertain, while Bibbie read Monk's hastily scrawled operating instructions. 'Perhaps we should wait until Monk's finished his meeting at the

Department. I mean, this isn't ordinary thaumaturgy we're dealing with, is it, it's uncharted territory, and —'

'Bollocks to that,' said Reg, nipping her on the ear. 'Since when do we need a man to do our dirty work? We're Witches Incorporated, ducky, and it'll take more than some cheeky sod of a sprite on an interdimensional sightseeing safari to get the better of us! *Perhaps we should wait for Monk.*' She snorted. 'I'm surprised at you, madam. And not in a good way!'

'All right, all right,' she muttered. 'It was just a suggestion.'

In truth, she was a little surprised at herself. It seemed her confidence had taken more of a battering lately than she'd been willing to admit, even in the privacy of her own thoughts.

Get a grip, woman. You're a royal princess and a former prime minister. This is no time to be going to pieces.

She turned to Bibbie. 'Well? What do you think? Will Monk's sprite trap work?'

'It ought to,' said Bibbie, thoughtfully. 'I mean, his theory's sound enough — as far as I can tell.' Then she rolled her eyes with sisterly scorn. 'Although if he'd bothered to ask me I'd have told him you get much better etheretic cohesion if you use *two* parts powdered shloss-root to one part dried dragon-tongue, not three. But did he ask? Of course not. Just because he works for the Department he think he knows every —'

'*Excellent*,' she said briskly. 'So let's get this over with, shall we? When I open the door, Reg, you fly left. I'll dart right. And Bibbie, you forge straight ahead with the trap activated. As soon as we spot the sprite, Reg, you play sheepdog and herd it into a corner so Bibbie can get it into the trap.'

'And what are you going to do?' said Reg.

'Take notes for the post-mortem.' She took hold of the door handle. 'Right, girls. On three. One — two —'

There was a click and a brief, high-pitched buzz as Bibbie activated Monk's invention.

'*Three!*'

She flung the door wide and they charged into the office like a very small herd of maddened wildebeest.

'There it is!' shouted Bibbie, as the sprite trap's flux capacitor illuminated the sprite. 'Oh look — it's so *pretty!*'

Kicking the door shut behind them, Melissande stared at the creature. Bibbie was right, drat her. The sprite *was* pretty, beautiful even, all dancing blue etheretic particles. Not much bigger than one of Rupert's late lamented butterflies, it shimmered with an incandescent brilliance as it perched on the test tube of ruined tamper-proof ink. And floating deep within the blue sparkles, a face. Or something that maybe, possibly, looked like a face ...

No. No. It's my imagination. And I am not about to get attached or feel sorry for it just because it's a long way from home.

'Ha!' she said. 'A pretty big pain in the arse, you mean.' Abandoning her plan, she snatched the sprite trap from Bibbie and advanced. 'Come here, you horrible little creature! I'll teach you to cover *me* in interdimensional sprite shit!'

'No! Wait!' chorused Reg and Bibbie, for once in perfect harmony. 'Don't do that, you'll fri —'

Too late. Temporarily brought into dimensional phase by Monk's sprite trap, the startled sprite emitted a shrill squeak and launched itself into the air.

'After it, Reg!' cried Bibbie. 'Melissande, you raving nutter, give me the trap!'

Shamed by her loss of control, Melissande surrendered the sprite trap and stood back as Reg and Bibbie ran and flew to and fro beneath the agitated blue sprite. Cries of '*Go left — watch out for the armchair — go right — higher — mind the umbrella stand — lower — it's on the curtain rail — no, no, now it's behind the curtain — yes, ducky, I can see it. I'm old and ensorcelled but I'm not blind yet!*' bounced from window to wall and back again as they pursued the agitated escapee from the dimension-next-door.

'Yes! Yes!' shouted Bibbie as Reg, panting like an antiquated racehorse, chased the sprite into the drooping embrace of the potted Weeping Fireblossom Monk had given them as an office-warming present.

With a shout of triumph Bibbie leapt at the sprite, the trap's door open wide to swallow the creature. '*Gotcha!*'

Too late, Melissande realised she was standing in precisely the wrong place. Bibbie's spectacular leap carried her clear over the potted Fireblossom and —

'*Ow!*' she cried as Bibbie sent her sprawling. 'Get off me, get *off* me!'

'Shut the trap door, shut the trap door!' shrieked Reg, hovering above them. 'I'm too old for all this excitement!'

As Melissande and Bibbie both dived for the trap their heads collided with a resounding *thwack*.

'*Ow!*' said Melissande. 'Bibbie, you *idiot!*'

'*I'm* not the idiot,' moaned Bibbie, clutching her forehead. '*You're* the idiot, you idiot!'

'Oh, Saint Snodgrass preserve me!' said Reg. 'It's getting away!'

On a string of colourful curses Melissande threw herself over Bibbie and slammed the trap's door shut just as the sprite made a swoop for freedom. 'Oh no, you don't!' she snarled. 'You *stay* in there, you disgusting little horror!'

'Oh do get *off* me you *lump!*' said Bibbie, sounding squashed.

Melissande shoved Bibbie sideways. '*Lump*? Who do you think you're calling a —'

'I'm sorry,' said a clipped and disapproving voice above them. 'Have we come at a bad time?'

'Bugger,' said Reg, under her breath, and strategically retreated to her ram skull.

Gasping for air, red-faced from more than exertion, Melissande staggered to her feet. Standing in the open office doorway were two astonished middle-aged ladies. One was short and comfortably plump, her walking-dress an eye-searing combination of mandarin and peacock blue. Her flat-brimmed bonnet was also blue, adorned with a bedraggled mandarin-dyed feather. Her companion, unfashionably tall and uncomfortably spare, was swathed in deepest black silk; a high-brimmed black hat with a sheer half-veil completed her mourning ensemble. Decorating each woman's buttressed breast was a brightly enamelled pin shaped like a chocolate éclair. The thin woman's pin was edged with gold.

Clients? *Botheration.* 'Bad time, ladies?' she echoed, painfully aware of her tousled appearance. 'Ah. No. Not as such. We were just — ah —'

'Concluding a very important assignment,' said Bibbie, on her feet again. Naturally, though she'd been rolling on the floor with equal abandon, she looked immaculate even while clutching Monk's doctored birdcage in front of her. Unfortunately she hadn't thought to deactivate the sprite-revealer, so the blue buzzing creature was in plain, inconvenient sight.

The plump woman squeaked and pointed. 'Gracious me, what's *that*?'

Bibbie dropped sprite trap and sprite on the desk, neatly flicking the off-switch. There was a high-pitched hum and the sprite promptly vanished. 'I'm sorry? What's what?'

'That, in there,' said the plump woman, quaking. 'It looked positively *unnatural.*' She squinted. 'But how strange … it seems to have disappeared.'

Bibbie smiled her most dazzling smile. 'I'm afraid I don't quite follow you. As you can see, the cage is empty. Must've been a trick of the light.'

'No, I don't think so,' said the plump woman. 'I *definitely* saw —'

Melissande cleared her throat. Time to nip this in the bud. 'I'm so sorry, but we're not at liberty to discuss it. Strict orders from the Department of Thaumaturgy, actually.'

'That's right,' chimed in Bibbie with a dazzling smile. 'They trust us implicitly. We have the closest relationship, you've no idea. But ... top secret, hush-hush, you know how it is.'

'No,' said the tall, thin lady — she of the clipped and disapproving voice. Despite being attired for a longstanding bereavement, everything about her suggested wealth. The cameo pinned beside the gold-trimmed éclair pin was just that little bit larger than her companion's. The stones in her tasteful gold necklace were real rubies, not garnets. An aura of old money surrounded her, impervious to youthful, upstart charm. 'I'm afraid we don't.'

'You don't?' said Bibbie, taken aback. 'Oh. Well, I'm sorry to hear that. I'd explain, you know, except — hush-hush — top secret —'

'And, as my colleague has pointed out, concluded!' Melissande added firmly, because Saint Snodgrass knew she wasn't about to let these women or their money get away without a fight. 'So ... how might we assist you, madam?'

Their unimpressed visitor looked down her high-arched nose. Clearly she was too well-bred to comment on the trousers, but her expression was as eloquent as a politician's speech. 'Young ... lady, I doubt very much that you can. In fact, it would appear we have come to the wrong establishment. So if you'll excuse us —'

'Which establishment were you looking for?' said Bibbie gamely, still trying to dazzle them with her best smile.

'Witches Incorporated,' said their plump visitor, before her disapproving friend could speak.

'Then you're in the right place!' said Bibbie. 'That's us. Witches Inc. I'm Miss Markham and these are my colleagues Miss Cadwallader and Reg. Reg is the one with the feathers.'

The haughty spokeswoman silenced her companion with a severe look then smiled at Bibbie, not at all dazzlingly. In fact her expression was positively unpleasant. 'You have a bird for a colleague? How ... quaint.' Her voice could have stripped paint.

'Actually, she's more of a pet,' said Bibbie, doughtily undaunted. 'But we like to humour her. It saves hurt feelings.'

As Reg made a noise like an exploding tea kettle, the disapproving woman looked Bibbie up and down. 'I'm sure. However, as I said, we appear to have the wrong —'

'Oh please, Permelia, no!' said the other lady anxiously, plump fingers plucking at her friend's leg-of-mutton sleeve. 'Please, can't we at least explain what we need? I mean, we *can't* leave. We've nowhere else to turn and there's no more time!'

'*Hush*, Eudora,' her companion snapped. 'Kindly restrain yourself. I hardly think we're so desperate we must throw ourselves upon the mercy of *these* two hoydens.'

The chastened Eudora shrank. 'Of course not, Permelia,' she whispered. 'Only —'

'*No*, Eudora. There is no "*only*",' said Permelia, magnificently magisterial. 'Obviously the *Times* has made a grave error. You can be assured I shall have Ambrose speak to its editor in the strongest possible terms. Now I suggest that we withdraw immediately and —'

'Excuse me,' said Melissande, heart sinking. *Reg is never going to let me hear the end of this.* 'I'm sorry, I don't wish to be impolite, or — or unbecomingly forward, but by any chance are you referring to this morning's edition of the *Ottosland Times*?'

Before the formidable Permelia could speak, her companion stepped forward with a puppyish eagerness. 'That's right, Miss Cadwallader! In the society pages. There was a photograph — and a mention of your agency —'

'Which is *clearly* a case of misrepresentation!' said icily unimpressed Permelia. 'Now hold your tongue, Eudora Telford! I will *not* have the sterling reputation of our organisation tarnished by an unfortunate —'

'Oh, I'm sorry, I'm sorry, Permelia!' Eudora Telford exclaimed, pinkly penitent. 'It's dreadful of me to contradict you, I know, but I simply *can't* stay silent, not when such an injustice is being perpetrated upon you!'

'Forgive me, ladies,' said Melissande, very carefully not looking at Reg. 'I *really* don't mean to be rude, truly, but —' She picked up the agency's copy of the *Times* from the rickety occasional table where she'd earlier dropped it, and opened it to the despised social gossip pages. '— did you mean *this* photograph?'

Courageously ignoring the irate Permelia, Eudora joined her. 'Why, yes! That's the one! Her Royal Highness Princess Melissande of New Ottosland, proprietor of Witches Inc., attending the opera.' She peered at the newspaper, then frowned sideways. 'Oh. Dear. My gracious. I'm sorry, Miss Cadwallader, are you *quite* sure — I mean to say —'

'Of course,' said Bibbie, with a grin as lunatic as her mad brother's, 'when I introduce my esteemed colleague as *Miss Cadwallader*, really that's just her name of convenience. *Really* she's Her Royal Highness Princess Melissande of New Ottosland. Don't let the tweed trousers fool you. Go on, Mel. Don't be shy. Show 'em your tiara.'

It was almost worth Reg's evil chuckling to see the look of unbearable snobbery congeal on the awful Permelia woman's face.

'Her Royal Highness?' Permelia said in a strangled voice. 'Princess Melissande?'

'Well, yes,' said Melissande. 'I'm afraid so.'

'I see,' said Permelia faintly. 'Of course. Well. Do forgive me, it appears I — I didn't recognise you without your bustle.'

'Oh, Your Highness!' cried Eudora, snatching up Melissande's hand and hanging onto it like a life preserver. 'Oh, please, please, you have to *help* us! *Please*. It's ever so important! In fact it's a matter of life and death!'

CHAPTER SEVEN

'Life and death?' said Melissande, discreetly attempting to retrieve her hand from Eudora Telford's fervent clutches. 'Really? How very alarming. Well, of course we'll help you, if we can. And for a very reasonable fee.'

'Oh thank you, *thank* you,' the woman said, breathless all over again. 'I *knew* we were right to come to you, I knew —'

'Eudora Telford,' said her disapproving friend. 'Do stop *fawning*. It's most unattractive in a woman of your age. Especially as you and the princess have not been formally introduced.'

Eudora Telford blushed bright red. 'Oh — oh, how *awful* of me!' she choked. 'How embarrassing. Such a social solecism. I'm quite beyond the pale.'

Finally released from the poor woman's desperate adoration, Melissande cleared her throat, uncomfortable. 'Oh no, truly, it's —'

'Eudora being Eudora,' said Permelia Wycliffe bitingly. 'Alas.' Lips pinched in additional, silent criticism, she advanced like a warship under full sail. 'Allow me to introduce myself, Your Highness. Miss Permelia Wycliffe. Of the Ravenscroft Wycliffes. *Not* to be confused with the Lormley Wycliffes, who now find themselves genealogically extinct.' There was no 'alas' this time. The addendum *And serve them right* wasn't spoken aloud but nevertheless, the words hovered in the air.

Melissande looked at Permelia Wycliffe's gloved and outstretched hand.

I could be wrong, but I thought I was the one meant to make the first move. And isn't she supposed to be curtseying or something? I am a princess, after all ...

Except Ottosland had long since shrugged off the oppressive shackles of monarchy — Monk's words, not hers — and now took a positive delight in putting visiting royalty in its place. Although apparently no-one had thought to mention that to Eudora Telford. Banished to the back seat of this encounter, she was bobbing up and down like a cork in a stream.

The part of Melissande that was related to Lional prickled in the face of Permelia Wycliffe's overbearing condescension. But with penury looming this was no time to indulge offended feelings.

'Miss Wycliffe, it's a pleasure,' she said, decorously shaking the woman's hand.

'Likewise,' said Permelia Wycliffe. 'Doubtless you have heard of my brother, Mister Ambrose Wycliffe. He heads the Wycliffe family firm. The Wycliffe Airship Company, established fifty-two years ago by my distinguished, world-famous late father Mister Orville Wycliffe.' Her disciplined eyebrows lifted, inviting a response.

'The Wycliffe Airship Company,' Melissande murmured, playing for time. No, she'd never heard of it. Her acquaintance with airships was severely limited, since New Ottosland had never gone in for newfangled contraptions. Installing their own portal had practically caused a revolution. 'Ah —'

'Her Highness hasn't long been among us in Ottosland, Permelia,' said Eudora, as her daunting companion's thin face froze with disapproval. 'And when at home in New Ottosland she travels by royal carriage, of course. But now that she's here among us, living *incognito* — so romantic! — doubtless she wishes to maintain her anonymity, which she couldn't do if she travelled with the best of the best on a Wycliffe airship.'

'Ah,' said Permelia Wycliffe, barely thawing. 'Incognito. Yes. Although there is the matter of that photograph in the *Times* ...'

'A mistake,' said Melissande grimly. 'Believe me.'

'Incognito,' Permelia Wycliffe repeated. 'I see. Doubtless that accounts for Your Highness's ... unorthodox ... attire. Unless ... perhaps you dress yourself in the costume of your native land? New Ottosland is a colony, after all. I believe colonials can be ... eccentric.'

On her ram skull, Reg was wheezing with half-strangled laughter. And Bibbie was clearly biting the insides of her cheeks. They were far too easily amused, both of them.

Melissande fought to keep her expression welcoming. *Eccentric? Trousers aren't eccentric, you silly woman. Eccentric is my brother turning himself into a dragon.*

'Actually, I prefer the term "practical". You should give trousers a try, Miss Wycliffe. They might give you a whole new outlook on life.'

Permelia Wycliffe's haughty expression congealed. 'Indeed. What a quaint suggestion.'

'Oh yes, that's our Mel,' said Bibbie cheerfully. 'Quaint as anything.'

Melissande shot her a quelling look then returned her attention to Permelia. 'And your charming associate, Miss Wycliffe? Since we seem to be making our formal introductions?'

'Yes. Of course,' said Permelia Wycliffe, reluctantly co-operative. 'This is Miss Eudora Telford. My secretary.'

'And bosom friend,' Eudora Telford added, bobbing up and down some more. 'Such an honour. Such a pleasure. So regal. So distinguished.'

'Regal and distinguished, exactly!' said Bibbie, outrageously beaming. 'That's our Princess Melissande to a T. Just like her brother King Rupert the First! Of course you *must've* heard of him.' She snatched the *Times* from Melissande's hand and waved the front page under Permelia Wycliffe's nose. 'He's regal and distinguished, too. And handsome. Don't you agree he's a handsome king?'

'Oh *yes*,' breathed Eudora, before Permelia could speak. 'Terribly handsome *and* distinguished! A positive *jewel* of a monarch. I've read all about him in the *Times* and the *Ladies' Almanac*.'

Melissande frowned. While she unashamedly adored Rupert, only a woman with a bag over her head could honestly call him handsome. So this appeared to be yet another case of unrequited adoration from afar. Poor Rupert. Ever since ascending New Ottosland's throne he'd been inundated by passionate expressions of affection from all over the world. It seemed a crown was the most potent yet indiscriminate aphrodisiac ever discovered.

'I'm sure he'd be moved by such beautiful compliments, Miss Telford,' she said. 'Now, you mentioned something about a matter of life and death ...?'

Eudora rallied. 'Oh *yes*, Your Highness. Of *course*. Please, *do* forgive me. Such a rattletrap, I am, and a regular fusty gossip. So sorry. So very sorry.'

Really, she was the most horribly *damp* woman. Perhaps it wasn't surprising that overbearing Permelia Wycliffe squashed her at every opportunity. Perhaps it was even understandable. Anyone spending any length of time in Eudora Telford's company must surely end up wringing wet.

'Oh, there's no need to apologise, Miss Telford. I appreciate it's not always easy to discuss personal problems.'

'We have not come here to discuss Eudora's personal problems,' said Permelia. 'We have come in response to a *disgraceful* situation in the Guild. A situation that must be remedied before untold damage is done to the sterling international reputation I have worked so long and hard to build.'

Guild? International reputation? What was the dreadful woman going on about? But before she could betray her woeful ignorance Bibbie stepped forward, her expression suspiciously earnest.

'Then you must tell us all about it, Miss Wycliffe,' she said, her voice hushed. 'We can't have trouble in Ottosland's world famous Baking and Pastry Guild. Indeed, Witches Inc. is *honoured* that its president would bring the Guild's problems to us.'

Baking and Pastry Guild? President? What? How did Bibbie know that? Melissande looked at Reg, who seemed just as surprised, then back at Permelia Wycliffe. The woman was perilously close to letting her jaw drop in shock.

'So you are familiar with the Baking and Pastry Guild, Miss Markham?' she said, eyebrows raised disbelievingly. 'I must confess to some surprise. I don't believe we've had the pleasure of seeing you at one of our … at our … at … *oh*.' She cleared her throat. '*Markham*? Surely you're not — am I correct in surmising — do you mean to tell me that *you* are —'

'Yes, Miss Wycliffe,' said Bibbie, a wicked gleam in her eyes. 'I *am* related to Antigone Markham. She was my great-aunt, as a matter of fact.'

'In*deed*,' said Permelia, her nostrils pinching as she plumbed new depths of disapproval. Beside her, Eudora Telford was making little squeaking sounds. 'And how can it be that you have *failed* to follow in her illustrious footsteps? Surely the great-niece of Antigone Markham is sensible of her obligations to the noblest calling to which any woman of breeding may aspire!'

'Oh I am, I am,' said Bibbie, adopting an air of martyred tragedy. She'd even managed to put a sob in her voice. 'And it's *because* I am sensible to them that you've not seen me in your hallowed Guild's halls, Miss Wycliffe. Alas, I am bereft of Aunt Antigone's talent for shortcrust. I felt I would've been betraying her if I'd asked you to overlook my lack of aptitude just because of my familial connections.' Another small, artistic sob. 'Please, Miss Wycliffe. Don't ask me to explain further. As I'm sure you can imagine, it's a painful subject.'

Permelia Wycliffe was transformed into a monument to sympathy. '*Poor child.* You have my *sincere* condolences *and* my heartfelt admiration. That you would so revere your great-aunt's legacy as to not sully the memory of her magnificence — I am *speechless* with approbation.'

On her ram skull, Reg was back to chortling like a kettle. Eudora Telford seemed close to tears of worshipful joy. With nothing useful to contribute, Melissande warily let Bibbie have the floor. Tiny alarm bells were ringing in the back of her mind. Monk's sister might have Permelia Wycliffe eating from the palm of her hand now ... but in her experience, the Permelias of the world were fickle in their approval. One injudiciously uttered sentiment, one expressed opinion that deviated from the acceptable, and the air would swiftly freeze solid again.

And then of course I'll be the one picking up the agency's pieces.

She tried to semaphore as much to Bibbie with her eyebrows, but Bibbie was resolutely paying no attention.

'Thank you, Miss Wycliffe,' she said, one hand pressed to her heart. 'I can't begin to tell you how that makes me feel.'

'You see, Permelia?' quavered Eudora Telford. 'It was *meant* that we should come here for assistance. Her Royal Highness and sainted Antigone Markham's great-niece will save the day!'

'Yes indeed,' said Bibbie robustly. 'There's nothing we'd like better. Isn't that right, Miss Cadwallader?'

Willing Reg to stop snickering, Melissande crossed her fingers behind her back. 'Absolutely, Miss Markham. Saving the day is what we live for.'

'So, Miss Wycliffe — forgive me, *Madam President*,' said Bibbie. 'How exactly does the day need saving? What is it you'd like Witches Inc. to do for the Guild?'

Permelia Wycliffe lifted her chin as though she'd just received a challenge. 'Miss Markham, you can unmask a villain!'

'Happy to,' said Bibbie. 'Does this villain have a name?'

'Millicent Grimwade,' said Permelia, through tightly pinched lips. 'The most sly, underhanded, dishonest, deceitful and third-rate cook the Guild has ever known!'

'Really?' said Bibbie. 'She's that bad? Then — if I might be so bold as to ask — how is it she was admitted to the ranks of the illustrious sisterhood?'

Two bright spots of colour burned hotly in Permelia Wycliffe's thin cheeks. 'Allow me to assure you, Miss Markham, that had *I* been Guild President when her application was submitted she would have been summarily refused the honour! Unfortunately my predecessor lacked the acumen essential to the august position of Guild President.'

'It's an absolute tragedy, Miss Markham,' added Eudora Telford, when it appeared Permelia Wycliffe was momentarily overcome. 'Because Millicent's been cheating. *Brazenly* cheating. And if we don't put a stop to it she'll win this year's Golden Whisk uncontested.'

'The honour of the Guild is at stake,' said a recovered Permelia, eyes glittering. 'It is *unthinkable* that the likes of Millicent Grimwade should receive our highest accolade.'

'It certainly is,' said Eudora, choking with emotion. 'Why, Permelia's won the Whisk for the last sixteen years, ever since she became our president. *Everybody* knows she's the best cook in the Guild. Why, her Chocolate Rum Tart is renowned throughout Ottosland. When it failed to win its division in this year's first county fair, *well*, we *knew* something dreadful was going on. And it's *still* going on, because Permelia's been defeated by Millicent at *every* county fair this year. It's — it's *unheard* of!'

Melissande exchanged a glance with Reg, who rolled her eyes, then cleared her throat. Time for her to rejoin the conversation before Bibbie enthusiastically committed them to a case they couldn't possibly solve. To a case that wasn't even a case, but simply a matter of sour grapes.

'Ah ... that sounds very ... disheartening, Miss Wycliffe,' she said with care. 'But I'm obliged to point out to you that any understandable disappointment over your recent defeats isn't proof of illegal behaviour. How is it you're so sure that Millicent Grimwade is cheating? I mean, do you have any proof?'

Permelia Wycliffe looked at her as though she were an idiot. 'Of course I have proof,' she said, witheringly. 'The *proof* is that I've yet to win a single baking contest. You may rest assured, Miss Cadwallader, that Millicent Grimwade is using some kind of thaumaturgical charm to influence the judges or enhance the quality of her cakes or *something* equally nefarious. It's the only explanation for her unprecedented success.'

Melissande stared. The *only* explanation? Was Permelia Wycliffe serious?

The woman is obsessed. Most likely delusional. And when we can't prove there's been cheating of any kind by this Millicent Grimwade — because who would cheat at baking cakes? The idea's ridiculous! — this appalling Wycliffe woman is going to sue us for inadequate representation. Or at the very least tell every one she meets not to touch Witches Incorporated with a forty-foot barge pole. And then we really will go out of business.

No matter how long it took she was going to find that wretched photographer from the *Times*, and when she found him she was going to stuff Monk's sprite down the front of his unmentionables.

Strangely, Bibbie didn't seem at all disconcerted or

disbelieving. Instead she was frowning. 'I must apologise for my colleague, Miss Wycliffe. Not being of the Guild, she doesn't understand. It goes without saying that if *you're* convinced Millicent Grimwade is cheating then she is. After all, they don't appoint just anybody as president of the Guild, do they?'

'Well, not usually,' said Eudora Telford loyally. 'Although our last president was a sad disappointment. But of course since we've had *Permelia* at the helm we've surged from strength to strength. Seven times Best Cake in Show at the International Baking Symposium.' She beamed at the object of her uncritical adoration. 'Which is why this has been so particularly distressing, Miss Markham. It's even been suggested that Permelia is motivated by — by — oh, I can scarcely bring myself to say it.' Her eyes brimmed with tears. 'By *jealousy*.'

Bibbie patted the silly woman's arm, like someone comforting the bereaved. 'Please don't weep, Miss Telford. That would be giving Millicent Grimwade the victory.'

'Oh, Miss Markham,' whispered Eudora Telford. 'You're so wonderfully sympathetic. It really has been awful, you know.'

'Eudora, I can imagine,' said Bibbie, so earnestly that even Melissande believed her. 'The petty tyrannies of the mediocre are endless. But you must buck up, really you must. Witches Inc. is here to help. Now I take it you've approached other thaumaturgical experts regarding this wicked state of affairs?'

'We have,' said Permelia Wycliffe mordantly. 'We have availed ourselves of the services of several highly recommended witches and wizards, Miss Markham ... all to no good purpose. They've come along to this county fair or that one, taken our money and then told us we're imagining things. One wizard even had the effrontery to suggest I stop imbibing so generously of my Rum Tart's prime ingredient!'

'How *shocking*!' said Bibbie, shooting Melissande and Reg a repressive look. 'Please, Miss Wycliffe, allow me to apologise again, this time on behalf of my misguided fellow-thaumaturgical practitioners. Clearly they have failed to grasp the gravity of your situation. Why, thanks to Millicent Grimwade the Guild's integrity now hangs by the proverbial thread. The lustre of the Golden Whisk is about to be irretrievably tarnished!'

Permelia Wycliffe's clasped hands tightened. 'The Guild be praised. You really *do* understand!'

'Of course she does, Permelia,' said Eudora Telford, fresh tears trembling on her lashes. 'Is she not the great-niece of Antigone Markham?'

'I am,' said Bibbie. 'And I promise you, in my great-aunt's illustrious name, we *will* unmask this dastardly Millicent Grimwade. The final bake-off's tomorrow, isn't it? In the Town Hall?'

'That's correct,' said Permelia Wycliffe. 'Commencing at eleven o'clock sharp. I take it we can count on you to be there in time?'

'Have no fear, Miss Wycliffe,' said Bibbie grandly. 'My colleagues and I will be there in *plenty* of time to prevent a grave miscarriage of culinary justice ... and see that Millicent Grimwade receives her comeuppance.'

Incredibly, it seemed that Permelia Wycliffe was on the brink of losing her intimidating composure. 'Please, Miss Markham. Call me Permelia.'

'Of course, Permelia ... if you'll agree to calling me Emmerabiblia.'

'It would be an honour,' said Permelia Wycliffe, very nearly smiling. She extended her gloved hand. 'Until tomorrow, Emmerabiblia.'

Bibbie shook the woman's hand. 'Until tomorrow, Permelia,' she said gravely.

'Come, Eudora,' said Permelia Wycliffe. 'We still have the bake-off's preparations to oversee.'

Eudora bobbed a curtsey to Melissande, and nearly to Bibbie. 'Your Highness — Miss Markham — so pleased — so gratified —'

'Come *along*, Eudora!'

'Coming, Permelia, coming!'

With a last frosty nod at Melissande, and a thoughtful glance at the apparently empty birdcage on the desk, Permelia Wycliffe sailed towards the door with Eudora bobbing in her wake like a dinghy. But at the doorway, she hesitated then turned back. 'I'm sorry. Did I hear you say your colleagues — *plural* — would be at the Town Hall tomorrow?'

Bibbie nodded. 'That's right.'

Permelia's gaze shifted to Reg. 'Do you mean to say you'll be bringing ...'

'Reg?' Bibbie grinned cheerfully. 'Of course. She feels left out if we don't bring her along. Especially since she's the National Bird of New Ottosland and figures prominently on the kingdom's coat of arms. Doesn't she, Miss Cadwallader?'

Melissande scorched her with a look. 'If you say so, Miss Markham.'

'I see,' said Permelia Wycliffe, after a precarious moment. 'Well, I'm sure the great-niece of Antigone Markham knows best.'

And on that note, the door closed emphatically behind the two women from the Baking and Pastry Guild.

'*Gosh*!' said Bibbie, and sagged on the desk. 'Wasn't that a stroke of luck, the president of the Baking and Pastry Guild needing our help! And to think I never thought batty old Great-aunt Antigone would ever come in handy.'

'Luck? *Luck*?' said Melissande, free to stamp about the office in an excess of temper. 'Luck's not the first word that comes to *my* mind, you raving nutter!'

'*Why*?' said Bibbie, amazed. 'What have I done wrong *now*?'

'You know perfectly well what you've done wrong!' she retorted. 'Promising those two nitwits we could solve this ridiculous case? And all that guff about Rupert! Reg on the royal coat of arms! *Honestly*, Bibbie, you *know* I hate using that royalty claptrap to impress strangers. It's crude and it's common and it's —'

'Going to help us pay the bills!' said Bibbie. 'Just like me being related to the saintly Antigone Markham saved us from your *stupid* insistence on wearing those *ghastly* tweed trousers! The least you could do is wear velvet, Melissande, at least velvet's got some class! But no, *you* have to —'

'*Shut up!*' roared Reg, rattling her tail feathers so hard she nearly fell off the ram skull. 'The pair of you!'

Shocked silent, they looked at her.

'Mad Miss Markham's right,' Reg continued severely. 'We can't afford to tiptoe on our principles. Not if we want to avoid landing on our penniless arses in the alley.' She bestowed upon Bibbie an approving nod. 'Nice work spotting the Guild pins, ducky.'

Bibbie dropped an ironical curtsey. 'Thank you, Reg.'

'But don't you see?' said Melissande, despairing. 'That dreadful Eudora Telford's going to run around telling everyone I've got a tiara stuffed up my blouse!'

Reg snorted. 'Down the back of your trousers, more like it.'

As Melissande advanced, Bibbie leapt between her and Reg's ram skull. 'Ignore her, Mel. You know she only does it to get a reaction.'

'And anyway, madam here didn't flap the *Times* under that silly woman's nose!' Reg added, hopping from the ram skull to Bibbie's shoulder. 'That was *you*, ducky.'

'Look, Mel, you need to focus on the big picture,' said Bibbie, impatient. 'Which is that the Baking and Pastry Guild is a really, *really* big deal. I'm talking about an upper-crust sisterhood full of women of affluence and influence. Women with excellent connections — and *money*. Once we've solved the mystery of Millicent Grimwade's cheating, trust me: we'll have more work coming in than we know what to do with.'

Melissande stared at her. '*Once we've solved* — Bibbie, are you saying you think that dreadful Wycliffe woman's got a case against this Millicent Grimwade?'

'Of course.'

'Emmerabiblia Markham, are you telling me that a grown woman would stoop to dishonesty — if not downright illegality — just to win some cheap statue of a *cooking utensil*?'

'Mel, Mel, Mel,' sighed Bibbie, shaking her head. 'Don't you have a Baking and Pastry Guild in New Ottosland?'

'Probably,' she said. 'I know I used to get served up some pretty awful jam rolls when I was out and about on official duty. But I was never a *member*. I had better things to do!'

'Don't you let Permelia Wycliffe hear you say that,' said Bibbie. 'And stop being such a snob. I'll have you know the internecine warfare of the Baking and Pastry Guild makes international politics look like a kiddie's afternoon tea party. Trust me. Millicent Grimwade is up to no good.'

'Why? Because she's won a few cooking contests?'

Bibbie wagged a finger. 'Not a few, Mel. *All* of them. And all of them over the reigning Guild president. Trust me, it's just not possible. Not without some unorthodox assistance.'

Melissande blinked. It sounded utterly potty. But Bibbie seemed convinced, and she was the one with the presidential great-aunt.

I suppose I'd be mad to discount her expertise and experience. It just all sounds so dreadfully silly . . .

'Fine,' she sighed. 'So there's a legitimate case. But Bibbie, even if Millicent Grimwade *is* cheating, how are we supposed to prove it? I mean if a tribe of other witches and wizards have failed to uncover even the tiniest hint of thaumaturgic interference, what makes you think we'll fare any better?'

'*Because*,' said Bibbie, eyes shining, 'Witches Inc. has a secret weapon!'

With a flourish she reactivated the sprite trap's etheretic field. In its small cage, the newly visible sprite buzzed and hummed.

Melissande stared at it, then at Bibbie, with a dawning horror. 'Oh, no. Emmerabiblia Markham, you *cannot* be serious!'

Bibbie picked up the cage and made coochie-coochie faces at the sprite, which sparkled and buzzed back at her.

'I can, you know,' she said. 'I've never been *more* serious. We've already established that this thing disrupts thaumaturgic vibrations. All we have to do is smuggle it into the bake-off tomorrow morning and let interdimensional nature take its course!'

'But what about Monk?'

She shrugged. 'What about him?'

'Bibbie, he needs to send this sprite back to where it came from! *We* need him to send the horrible thing home, it's a menace!'

'And he will send it back, Mel. Once we've used it to save the agency,' said Bibbie. 'Come on. Monk owes us. What's three tins of tamper-proof ink? We can buy that ourselves ... or at least, we could if we had any money. But this sprite is priceless. This sprite is going to put Witches Inc. on the map, I can feel it in my bones. It's not going back to Monk until it's made us the heroines of Ottosland's internationally celebrated Baking and Pastry Guild.'

Melissande gnawed the edge of her thumb. 'I don't know. I don't like this, Bibbie. I've had enough unnatural creatures to last me a lifetime.'

'Really?' said Reg, staring down her beak. 'Well, thank you very much, I'm sure.'

Distracted, she smiled at the bird. 'Don't be silly, Reg. You're not unnatural, you're just irritating.'

'And so are you,' snapped Bibbie. '*Honestly*, Mel. How can you be so short-sighted? Don't you see this sprite is a *gift*?'

A curse, more like it. But either she was going to trust Bibbie, or she wasn't. 'All right. Fine. But if this blows up in our faces — which is hideously likely — then I give you fair warning: I will swear with my hand on my heart that I don't know you from a hole in the ground.'

Bibbie put the sprite trap back on the desk and leaned over for the phone. 'And when my plan works brilliantly — *which* it will — *I* am going to take all the credit.' Picking up the receiver she dialled, then waited. 'Hello, Monk? It's me. — Yes, we've got your stupid sprite but you can't have it back until tomorrow. — Because I say so, that's why. — Because something's come up. — All right, because if you don't stop yelling at me the next person I telephone will be Uncle Ralph. — Well, actually, I *can*. But I won't. Not unless you — Good. I didn't think so. — You're welcome. See you tomorrow night, for dinner.'

Melissande sighed. 'Don't tell me, let me guess. He's not happy.'

'Who cares?' said Reg. 'Bibbie's right. This is about saving the agency. So, Miss Markham. About this crazy plan of yours …'

'It's mad,' said Melissande much later, getting ready for bed. 'And *I'm* mad for agreeing to it. Honestly, Reg, if something goes wrong …'

Reg swallowed the last of her supper mouse, burped genteely then fluffed out her feathers. 'Most likely it won't. But *if* it does we'll deal with it, ducky. Now put a sock in it and turn out the light. I'm not the only one around here who needs her beauty sleep.'

Melissande concentrated on doing up her nightdress buttons. The trick with Reg was to just … *not react*. No matter what she said, no matter how rude she was, reacting only made things worse.

Besides. It only hurts because she tells the unvarnished truth.

Swathed in sensible pink flannel she padded across to the sprite trap on her lone bookcase, lifted up the blouse covering it then flicked on the activation switch. Metaphysically revealed, the doleful sprite moped in the corner of the modified birdcage, its blue brightness dimmed.

She frowned. 'It doesn't look very happy, Reg.'

'Well, don't you go trying to cheer it up,' Reg replied, cosily settled on the bedsit's sole rickety chair. 'No joyful ditties, for example. I'm still emotionally scarred from the last time I heard you sing.'

The last time she sang she'd been three-quarters full of Orpington whiskey, which was totally understandable given the dire prevailing circumstances. She glowered at the bird. 'That's not very nice, Reg.'

'Neither is your singing, ducky.'

Ah — ah — ah! No reacting, remember?

With teeth-gritted forbearance she turned off the sprite-revealer, dropped her blouse back over the cage and retreated to bed. 'I still say this is a bad idea,' she said, putting her glasses on the bedside table then turning down the oil lamp's wick until the bedsit was plunged into darkness.

'Only because you didn't think of it,' said Reg. 'That Markham girl may be scatty but she's also inventive. And she's not scared to give things a go.'

Melissande sat upright. 'And you're saying I am?'

Reg fluffed her feathers again, the soft sound loud in the late night silence. 'I'm saying it's easy to let yourself get timid when life's not behaving itself.'

Stung, she felt her fingers tangle in the blankets. 'I am not *timid*, Reg. I'm *cautious*.'

Reg sniffed. 'If you say so.'

'I *do* say so! *Somebody's* got to be. Between them, Monk and Bibbie are reckless enough to tip the whole world upside down and then shake its pockets so a few more bright ideas can fall out.'

'It's perfectly understandable,' said Reg, ignoring that. 'Being timid. You had your whole life planned, didn't you? Thanks to that charlatan Rinky Tinky woman, you thought you were a genuine witch-in-the-making. You thought Bibbie's Madam Olliphant was going to proclaim you a star. But that's what these Rinky Tinky hussies do, ducky. They tell you what you want to hear so you'll give them money, and so long as you keep on paying they'll keep on fertilising your false hopes.'

Slowly, she lowered herself back to the mattress. *Do I want to talk about this? Let me think* ... 'Yes, well, my beauty sleep beckons. Night-night, Reg, I'll see you in the morning.'

'No need to be ashamed,' said Reg, oblivious. 'You were bamboozled by a line of hokum, madam, but that's not a crime. You're not the first and you won't be the last.'

'It seems to be about the only thing I've got a talent for,' she muttered. 'Getting bamboozled. I've been hoodwinked twice now. By Madam Ravatinka ... and by Lional.'

'You can't go blaming yourself for Lional,' said Reg, gruffly. 'Nobody can help being related to an insane thaumaturgical criminal. I mean, it's not as though you *weren't* related and fell in love with him, is it? And it's not as though he was some bugger you met and fell in love with, and married, even though everyone was telling.'

Melissande blinked in the bedsit's faintly illuminated gloom. 'Is that how you ended up an immortal bird?'

'I'm not immortal,' said Reg, with another sniff. 'Not exactly. I can get run over, shot, stabbed, starved or beheaded like the next careless clot. But provided I don't do anything silly, the only way I'll die is if someone tries to lift the hex my hus — that got put on me.'

'That's good to know,' she said, after a moment. 'But it's not what I asked.'

'Yes, Melissande,' said Reg, so quietly. 'That's how I ended up an immortal bird.'

There was *such* a wealth of sadness in Reg's funny, scratchy little voice that Melissande felt her eyes prickle. '*Anyway*,' she said, clearing her throat and blinking hard at the hazy ceiling. 'I'm *not* being timid. I'm simply expressing a perfectly reasonable concern about Bibbie's plan.'

Another soft rustling sound as Reg fluffed out her feathers yet again. 'Then think of another one if you're so convinced hers is going to go kablooey.'

She felt her face scrunch into another frown. 'I can't.'

'I suppose we could have a word with Mister Clever Clogs,' said Reg idly. 'He must know all there is to know about black market thaumaturgy. Maybe —'

'*No*, Reg,' she said. 'This is none of Monk's business. This is Witches Inc. business and we're going to solve the case without his help.'

Reg snorted. 'Except for the sprite, you mean.'

'The sprite doesn't count.'

'If you say so, ducky.'

Well, it *didn't* count. It was an accident. A case of serendipity. It wasn't as if they'd *asked* Monk to give them an interdimensional sprite.

Besides. He owes me. I'm still not sure I scrubbed off all the sprite shit.

'You know, Reg,' she said, snuggling beneath her blankets, 'this whole affair is so hard to believe. And all those stories Bibbie told us ... pastry brushes at forty paces and the rest of it. Grown women! They ought to be ashamed of themselves.'

'Ah well,' said Reg, around a yawn. 'Everyone needs a hobby. Besides. Do you really want to tell that Wycliffe woman to bugger off back to her cake tins and take her money with her?'

'Of course I don't,' she murmured, eyes drifting closed. 'I just hope we're not biting off more than we can chew.'

'Ha,' said Reg, stifling another yawn. 'From the size of your buttocks, ducky, I'd say there's nothing you can't chew through.'

If she hadn't needed her pillow, Melissande would've thrown it at the wretched bird.

She and Reg met Bibbie outside the Town Hall at half-past ten the following morning. From the number of well-to-do ladies crowding the footpath and jostling their way up the Town Hall steps to go inside, the annual Golden Whisk competition was something of a highlight on Ottosland's social calendar.

'Blimey!' said Bibbie, staggering back a few paces. 'Do my eyes deceive me, Mel, or are you wearing a *dress*?'

Melissande glowered at her. 'No, actually. I'm wearing a blouse-waist and a walking skirt.'

'Never mind the pettifogging details,' said Bibbie, waving them away with a flick of her fingers. 'The salient point is that you're not wearing *trousers*.'

'Oh, shut up. Your brother's carpetbag didn't go with my tweeds.'

'It doesn't go with the blouse-waist and walking skirt, either,' said Reg, under her breath in case a passer-by was listening. 'But let's not try to run before we can crawl.'

'And you can shut up too,' said Melissande, twitching her shoulder. She still hadn't quite forgiven that last crack about butt — muscles one sits on. 'Now, are we going to get this done or would you two prefer to stand out here critiquing my sartorial efforts while Millicent Grimwade gets away with metaphorical murder?'

Bibbie was still grinning at the change of attire. 'Really, a princess dress would've been more appropriate, Mel.'

'A princess dress is what they'll bury you in, Bibbie, if you don't shut up so we can get this over with!'

Bibbie rolled her eyes. 'Tetchy, isn't she?' she asked Reg, conversationally. 'Did you remember the sprite?'

'No,' said Melissande. 'I just brought the carpetbag as a fashion accessory.'

'Where you're concerned, Mel, anything is possible,' said Bibbie, then hastily raised her hands. 'All right, all right. Truce. Let's go inside shall we, girls, and save the day.'

The Town Hall chamber set aside for the Baking and Pastry Guild's prestigious annual Golden Whisk competition was crowded with women of varying shapes, sizes, ages, wealth and rabid intensity. Silks and muslins whispered and rustled, sweeping the richly parqueted floor ... or flirted above it as some daring young ladies risked censure by lifting their hems dangerously towards their mid-calves. The warm trapped air beneath the convolutedly decorated ceiling was redolent of lavender, patchouli, rosewater, musk, attar of roses and lily of the valley, combined into a heady perfume soup.

'Blimey,' Reg muttered, wheezing. 'We've come to the asphyxia convention by mistake. I hope these cake-obsessed biddies have got first-aid officers standing by.'

Melissande twitched her shoulder again. 'If you don't shut up,' she muttered under her breath, 'I'm going to find a hat and pin you to it.'

'Oh no you won't,' said Reg. 'Last thing you want to do is make yourself conspicuous.'

'Given there's a woman in the corner wearing a stuffed monkey on her head, I doubt anyone would turn a hair. Now be quiet and pretend you're an exotic shoulder ornament just like we agreed, Reg, *please*.'

'Look,' said Bibbie, pointing over the hats and bonnets of the women crowding round them. 'There's Permelia.'

And indeed, there she was. Permelia Wycliffe, faithful Eudora Telford in tow, stood ramrod-stiff at her display table, which was cordoned off from the hoi polloi behind a scarlet rope. All in all it appeared there were twelve finalists vying for the Golden Whisk. The grand prize itself stood in the centre of the room on a pedestal, protected by a glass case and its own scarlet cordon. Shafts of sunlight struck golden sparks from the coveted kitchen implement.

Melissande shook her head. *Surely these women have something better to do with their time than sweat blood and shed tears over baking the perfect date scone?*

Except clearly they didn't. Clearly they believed that winning a stupid egg beater meant they'd reached some lofty pinnacle of success. What was the *point*? It wasn't as if they could *use* the wretched Golden Whisk — all the gold would peel off in the omelette and give the dinner guests heavy-metal poisoning.

But practicality, or the lack thereof, didn't seem to bother Permelia Wycliffe or the other eleven women standing guard over their culinary offerings. If they weren't darting furious glances at each other's Rum Balls they were feasting their avaricious gazes on the prize. It was a wonder the organisers hadn't provided silver drool-salvers.

'Wait a minute,' Melissande said, frowning. 'Why is Permelia a finalist? Didn't she say she hadn't won a single regional contest thanks to Millicent Grimwade?'

Bibbie grinned. 'Perks of the presidency,' she whispered. 'But don't tell her I told you.'

Permelia was pulling extraordinary faces, eyebrows shooting up and down, nose twitching, head minutely jerking sideways.

'Don't look now,' said Reg, 'but I think the pressure's finally got to her. Any moment she'll start foaming at the mouth.'

'I *think*,' said Bibbie, 'she's trying to tell us which one's Millicent Grimwade.' She nodded at a woman third from the end along the row of wound-up, waiting contestants. 'There. *Her.*'

'Right,' said Melissande. 'Then let's prove she's a rotten cheater and get out of here, shall we? Because if I have to stay in this room for much longer I'll never be able to look a cake in the face and smile again.'

'Not a bad idea, ducky,' Reg muttered. 'Your buttocks'll thank you for it, believe me.'

Ignoring that, Melissande hefted Monk's carpetbag and got to work.

CHAPTER EIGHT

They fought their way through the growing crowd, past the other contestants' cake and pastry-laden tables, until they found themselves standing in front of Permelia Wycliffe's nemesis, usefully camouflaged by two shifting rows of gossiping spectators.

Glimpsed between feather-crowned hats and silk-shawled shoulders, Millicent Grimwade lived up to her name. She was a tall, thin, hatchet-faced woman dressed head-to-toe in deep purple silk and basking in a premature aura of victory. A delicate lace cloth covered her display table right down to floor level, pinned in place by a cream-slathered gooseberry sponge, a primrose-yellow iced pound cake and a seductively glistening chocolate log.

Melissande considered the offerings, then sidled a little closer to Bibbie. 'I'm sorry,' she murmured, mindful of eavesdroppers. 'But I don't see what's so terrible about those cakes. They look like cakes you'd buy in a shop. In fact, they make Per —' She darted a glance around the jostling crowd. '*You-know-who* look like a sore loser. Which means we're in grave danger of making *ourselves* look like idiots if we start throwing about unsubstantiated accusations.'

'What? Are you blind?' said Bibbie, in a disbelieving undertone. 'Those cakes are *terrible*, Mel. They've got no business being in the Golden Whisk finals. The cream on the sponge is over-whipped, there's too much yellow in the pound cake's icing *and* she's used the wrong kind of chocolate for the chocolate log. I can only *imagine* what they taste like.' She shuddered. 'Sawdust, probably. I can hear Great-aunt Antigone's ashes now, whirling in their urn.'

Close around them the scented crowd swirled and shared its unfettered opinions. Everyone was praising Millicent Grimwade's entries. Melissande considered the apparently ghastly cakes for a moment. No, she still couldn't see what had woken Bibbie's scathing contempt.

'Are you sure?'

Bibbie glowered. 'Of course I'm sure.'

'Reg?' she whispered. 'What do you think?'

'I think it's a long time since I ate cake,' Reg whispered back, mournful.

'That's very helpful, thank you.' She chewed her lip. 'The thing is, Bibbie, how is it you can tell they're so awful when nobody else can? If they have been incanted surely you'd be singing their praises too.'

Bibbie's cheeks turned pink. 'Oh. Um. That. Well, I zapped myself with one of Monk's classified anti-hex hexes. It — ah — it only works if you're thaumaturgically sensitive. Sorry.'

Ouch. Thrusting aside the sting of that, Melissande glanced again at Permelia Wycliffe's smug opponent, who was presiding over her entries like a queen receiving homage. 'So you're saying there is definitely black market thaumaturgy in play?'

'After one look at those cakes?' Bibbie snorted. 'I'd stake my First-Class diploma on it. Only it's some of the slickest incanting I've ever met.' She opened her neatly gloved fingers, revealing a small green crystal. 'This thing is supposed to turn black in the presence of an obfuscation or enhancement hex. Kindly note, girls, its conspicuous greeniosity. Whoever designed Millicent's judge-fuddling incant is *good*. I mean, they're bad, they're *very* bad, but —'

'Yes, yes, we get it,' Melissande snapped. 'All right. Let's see if we can put an end to this farce, shall we? I'd like to leave with at least the dregs of my self-respect intact.'

Ignoring the molten glances and mutterings from their fellow spectators, they shoved and insinuated their way through the crowd until they were pressed against the scarlet cordon-ropes separating the public from the Guild's illustrious competitors. Trying to remain inconspicuous, Melissande wafted Monk's carpetbag to and fro before the table of suspect cakes. Any second now, surely, *if* Bibbie was right, the sprite's interdimensional nature would disrupt whatever thaumaturgic influences had been placed on Millicent Grimwade's entries and this ridiculous expedition could be successfully concluded.

The gooseberry sponge, the pound cake and the chocolate log refused to co-operate. Not a single culinary crime went kablooey.

'Psst!' she hissed into Bibbie's ear. 'Your brilliant plan doesn't seem to be working. Don't suppose you thought of an alternative, did you?'

'We're a good twelve feet from Millicent's abominations,' Bibbie hissed back. 'I think you'll have to take Monk's little friend out of the carpetbag.'

'Oh, that's a bright idea!' she whispered, staring. 'I'll just wave the interdimensional sprite around for all and sundry to see, shall I? I'm sure nobody will blink twice at the sight of a bright blue buzzing thing in a birdcage!'

'They won't if you don't activate the etheretic normaliser,' Bibbie retorted. 'There's no need for anyone to see anything except Millicent Grimwade being unmasked!'

'So you're saying they'll completely ignore the mad woman waving the empty birdcage about?'

Bibbie groaned. 'No, Mel, I'm saying —'

'Oy,' said Reg, speaking out of the side of her beak. 'Don't look now, duckies, but we're attracting the wrong kind of attention.'

Sure enough, Millicent Grimwade was staring at them in a less than friendly fashion. Her gimlet gaze raked them up and down, then darted suspiciously to Eudora Telford, who was doing her very best to ruin everything, it seemed: smiling and nodding at them, and wagging a finger at Millicent while Permelia was distracted by a question from the crowd.

Bibbie cursed under her breath. 'Strategic withdrawal, girls, quick, before the Grimwade crone screams for a Guild Invigilator.'

'A what?' said Melissande, as they hurriedly retreated to the nearest stretch of empty wall.

'A who, not a what. Over there,' said Bibbie, jerking her chin. 'There's one. See her? The Guild appoints six of them altogether and trust me, we do *not* want them taking an interest in us. Guaranteed to cramp our style, that is, *and* get us tossed out on our well-padded posteriors.'

Safely withdrawn from Millicent Grimwade's line of fire, Melissande stared over the heads of the milling spectators and saw an official-looking woman prowling the edges of the chattering crowd. Dressed in a severely plain blue gown covered in a capacious and crisply spotless white apron, and carrying a wooden spoon of office, she looked imposing enough to tame a ravening horde single-handed.

'Blimey,' said Reg. 'Let her get near the cream and it'll be clotted whether you want it clotted or not!'

'Oh, don't be mean,' said Bibbie. 'She's just doing her job. Believe me, it's a thankless task. Great-aunt Antigone got her start as an Invigilator so I know all about it.'

Holding their breaths, they waited to make sure the dreaded

Guild Invigilator's attention was focused elsewhere then went into a huddle.

'All right,' said Melissande. 'What do we do now? We've been here nearly half an hour, the judging must be about to start and we're no closer to proving Millicent Grimwade is a cheating cheater who cheats than we were this time yesterday. Suggestions?'

'What I already said,' said Bibbie, impatiently. 'We've got to get the sprite in a direct line of sight with Millicent's cakes. Which means like it or not, Mel, it's got to come out of the carpetbag.'

'And then what, Bibbie? I'm telling you, the minute I start waving an apparently empty birdcage around the place those Guild Invigilators are going to —'

'What if it's not empty? What if we put Reg in there?'

'Over my dead body, madam!' Reg almost shrieked. 'Are you out of your tiny mind? Shove me in a cage with an interdimensional sprite, would you? I'll bloody shove you, ducky, I'll —'

Melissande pinched the wretched bird's beak shut before someone noticed that her exotic shoulder ornament was having a fit. 'She's too big to squish into the cage, Bibbie. Besides, it says quite clearly on the door: No Pets Allowed.'

'Good point,' Bibbie admitted, and lapsed into furious thought. 'All right,' she said after a moment. 'How about this?'

'How about what?' said Melissande suspiciously, watching as Bibbie removed the velvet choker from around her neck and carefully unthreaded the exquisite cameo dangling from it. 'Bibbie, what are you doing?'

Bibbie dropped the cameo into her reticule then held out her hand. 'Give me the birdcage, Mel, quick.'

Baffled, she took the cage out of Monk's carpetbag, handed it over and watched as Bibbie threaded the velvet choker through its handle. Then, in a blinding bolt of horrified comprehension, she realised what Monk's mad sister was doing.

'Oh, no. *No*, Bibbie. You *cannot* be *serious*!'

'I can, you know,' said Bibbie, testing the weight of the cage as it dangled from her velvet choker.

'It's out of the question! You can't wear a birdcage around your neck, it's far too conspicuous!'

Bibbie glanced up. 'Well, no, of course *I* can't. But *you* can.'

'*Me?*'

'Yes, Mel. You.' Bibbie rolled her eyes. 'I know this might come as a shock but women wear jewellery all the time.'

'Jewellery, *yes*. But since when is a birdcage a fashion statement, you raving madwoman?'

'Since Her Royal Highness Princess Melissande of New Ottosland makes it one,' said Bibbie, with her most anarchic grin. 'Royalty always sets the trend in fashion, didn't you know? After today, Mel, I'll guarantee you that an empty birdcage around the neck will be the must-have accessory of the season! Or the week, at any rate. Even a day will do, provided it's today.' She looked around the crowded room. 'I wonder if that photographer from the *Times* is here ...'

Melissande tried to ignore Reg's strangled laughter. 'I hope so!' she hissed, glowering. 'I'll bet he'd just love to photograph a woman swallowing a birdcage whole!'

'Now, now, you two,' Reg chided, her voice still choked. 'We don't have time for girlish romps.'

'But —'

Reg tightened her claws, warningly. 'Like it or not she's right, ducky. We've got to get that sprite close to Millicent Grimwade's tricked-up nosh, and hanging it round your neck is our best bet.'

'But it'll never work!' she protested, even as the clammy waters of inevitability closed over her head. 'I'll be a laughing-stock! One of the Invigilators will throw me out!'

'I doubt it,' said Reg with a derisive snort. 'Not if they let that woman wearing the stuffed monkey stay. Now hurry up, because unless I'm mistaken those three fat men coming in now are the judges.'

'What? Where?' Melissande spun round. 'How can you tell?'

'Well, for a start, it says "Judge" in six-inch high letters on their chests.'

Botheration, the bird was right. They were indeed the judges, solemn and sober in their black morning coats and boiled shirt-fronts, diagonally bifurcated by their gaudy crimson sashes of office, guarded by the Guild Invigilators as though they were visiting royalty.

The richly dressed and enthusiastically scented spectators broke into enthusiastic applause as the judges made their way from the doorway to the special 'Judges Only' section of the chamber, which was also cordoned off by ropes.

'Quick, Mel,' said Bibbie. 'Get this on while nobody's paying us any attention.'

Depressed, Melissande stared at the birdcage dangling from Bibbie's velvet choker. Then, with a surreptitious glance around the judge-absorbed crowd, she flicked on the etheretic normaliser.

'Ah — is it my imagination, or does the sprite look sickly?' she whispered, staring through the cage's bars at the unlikely creature. Its bright blueness had definitely faded since yesterday, and even its odd, not quite certain little face looked forlorn.

'It's fine,' said Reg, hopping over to Bibbie's shoulder. 'You're imagining things. Now let's get this over with! I'm about ready for my morning tea.'

Get this over with. Easy for Reg to say. Reg didn't have to make a fool of herself by dangling a birdcage round her neck. Honestly, if she'd ever once thought that she'd be brought this low she'd never have approached Bibbie with the idea of opening Witches Inc. She'd have applied for a position as a governess first, even though other people's children appalled her.

'Come on, come *on*,' whispered Bibbie, quivering with anxiety. 'Before it's too late!'

It was already too late. *But I don't have a choice, now. I'm committed ... or I will be, once this madness is over.* She gave the sprite one last worried look, switched off the etheretic normaliser and donned her lovely new necklace. The cage balanced precariously on her front, drawing embarrassing attention to her bosom. It was so in the way she was forced to rest her chin on it.

'Excellent!' said Bibbie. 'Now, let's get into position, quickly, before the judges start their perambulations.'

With ruthless courtesy, sublimely oblivious to glares and complaints, they pinched and pushed and weaselled their way back through the crowd of perfumed spectators until they'd reclaimed their prime ogling position directly in front of Millicent Grimwade's table. Upon spying their return to the fray, Eudora Telford immediately began flapping her hands and pulling alarming faces. Even Permelia lost a little of her iron-clad composure and began to lock and unlock her fingers in a nervous rhythm. Fortunately, before Millicent Grimwade or one of the prowling Invigilators could notice, they were both distracted by the polite yet insistent ringing of a tea bell.

'Ladies! Ladies!' cried a fluting, excessively modulated voice. 'The annual Golden Whisk competition now commences to be adjudicated! Resounding applause, if you please, for this year's revered, respected judges, Ottosland's Mister Huffington-Smythe and Mister Pertpeach, and our very special overseas guest adjudicator, Mister Grilliski from Blonkken.'

Under cover of the obedient response, scores and scores of gloved hands patting each other with such restrained, ladylike enthusiasm it sounded as though a velvet-clad thunderstorm had struck, Melissande inched forward until she was pressed as hard against the scarlet boundary rope as she dared. In its cage round her neck the invisible sprite whined ... but there was no reaction from Millicent Grimwade's allegedly illegal cakes.

'Get closer!' hissed Bibbie, handily muffled by the continued applause.

Melissande glared at her. 'I can't,' she muttered. 'Not without making a scene.'

The judges were already inspecting the first simpering contestant's offerings. Ceremoniously they sliced into an oozing jam roll with a large silver knife supplied for the purpose, popped bite-size portions into their eager mouths and masticated solemnly, like judicial cows. There followed a great deal of nodding and eyebrow-waggling, and the furtive recording of notes in official notebooks. Next they partook of cherry tart, and after that blueberry scones. Judging concluded, they proceeded to the next contestant and began assessing the relative merits of a custard flan.

'This is no good, Mel. We're running out of time,' whispered Bibbie, as the crowd commented and tittered and passed judgement on the cakes they were never going to taste for themselves. 'I'm going to create a diversion.'

Alarmed, Melissande shook her head. She didn't dare remonstrate aloud because the ladies crowded beside and behind them, many of whose silk-covered chests were decorated with enamelled chocolate éclair pins, were clearly irritated by the non-cake based conversation and were muttering and frowning and threatening an all-out protest.

Naturally, Bibbie paid no attention to that. Instead she closed her eyes, wiggled her fingers, and waited.

Nothing happened.

'Damn, my thaumics are fritzed,' she whispered. 'It's the sprite. Unlike Millicent's cakes I'm too close to the little darling.'

'Then what are we going to do?' Melissande whispered back. She darted a glance along the row of tables. The judges, having finished with the second contestant's offerings, were now sampling the third contestant's vividly-hued pumpkin cheesecake. 'Permelia looks ready to burst into flames.'

Bibbie flapped her hands, heedless of the annoyed 'hushes' and 'well, reallys' and 'disgracefuls' being uttered all around them. '*I* don't know, Mel! *You're* the organised one, *you* think of something!'

Think of something? Think of *what*? What could she *possibly* think of that would save them from this horrendous debacle? This was all Bibbie's fault, volunteering the agency's aid without consultation, practically promising that awful Permelia Wycliffe they'd save her from Millicent Grimwade's unhinged machinations.

I never should've agreed to this. I should've known it'd go arse over teakettle.

'Blimey,' said Reg, rattling her tail feathers. 'So it's up to me to save the day again, is it? That'd be right. Fine, you two. Listen to me. As soon as I've got everyone's attention, *someone* shove that bloody birdcage under Millicent Grimwade's table, right? That should get our invisible friend close enough to trigger the hex in the cakes. *If* there's a hex in the cakes, that is. And if there isn't . . . *run*.'

Before Melissande could stop her Reg uttered a piercing shriek and launched herself off Bibbie's shoulder to fly in manic circles beneath the chamber's ceiling. Still shrieking, she flapped round and round at speed, eliciting ladylike cries of fear and alarm from the startled contestants and spectators below.

'Quick!' said Bibbie. 'While the old cat's not looking at us!'

With a helpful shove from Monk's mad sister, Melissande ducked awkwardly under the scarlet cordon-rope, one hand tugging at the birdcage round her neck. The velvet choker gave way and she thrust the sprite beneath the long lace cloth covering Millicent Grimwade's table.

Mission accomplished, she staggered back under the cordon-rope and looked up. 'Done!' she shouted, hoping Reg could hear her over the increasingly agitated cries from the crowd.

With one last piercing shriek Reg stopped imitating a crazed falcon and instead dived through the nearest open window. Three determined strokes of her wings and she was gone from sight, lost among the city's prosperous rooftops.

'Gosh,' said Bibbie, eyes wide with repressed hilarity. 'She's better than a circus, isn't she?'

'Never mind Reg,' said Melissande, staring at Millicent Grimwade's cakes. 'Just cross your fingers that this actually works!'

Even as she spoke, the lace cloth rippled as though a breeze had sprung up beneath it. On the table's top, the three cake-laden plates jittered. Millicent Grimwade leapt back with a startled cry.

The plates began to dance in earnest. Squeals of surprise and consternation went up as spectator after spectator noticed blobs of over-whipped cream fly into the air, primrose-yellow icing turn an embarrassed vermilion and all the chocolate smothering the chocolate log begin to curdle. One of the Invigilators marched along the row of staring, whispering contestants to investigate, wooden spoon at the ready.

'What is this?' she demanded, goggling at the metamorphosing cakes as they shimmied back and forth across the lace tablecloth. 'Miss Grimwade, please explain!'

'I — I can't!' said ashen-faced Millicent Grimwade. 'It's a trick — it's foul play — it's — it's —' Staring wildly about her, she caught sight of Permelia Wycliffe's expression of undisguised triumph. 'It's *sabotage*!' she cried and pointed an unsteady finger. '*That woman* has sabotaged me! She's pea-green with envy because I've beaten her at every turn and now she's trying to steal the grand prize. But the Golden Whisk is mine, I tell you! *Mine*!'

Uproar as Permelia advanced upon Millicent Grimwade with dreadful solemnity, Eudora Telford bleating loyally in her wake. The judges scattered like lawn bowls before her barely-restrained wrath. Helpless, because Permelia Wycliffe was Guild president and no-one in her right mind smacked the president with a wooden spoon, not if they wanted to keep their prestigious position, the Invigilators dithered on the fringes of the fray. And all around them the spectators gasped and wittered and repeated the dreadful accusations until the Town Hall chamber sounded like a henhouse routed by a fox.

Now the transformed cakes were leaping up and down as though they'd been imbued with unnatural, frantic life.

'Stop it! *Stop* it!' sobbed Millicent Grimwade. 'Permelia Wycliffe, I demand that you stop this sabotage *at once*!'

'And *I* demand that you confess you've been *cheating*, Millicent Grimwade!' cried Permelia Wycliffe, majestic in her triumph. 'You've hexed your cakes so they'll win the Golden Whisk!'

Millicent Grimwade's hatchet face flushed as vermilion as her pound cake. 'How *dare* you? I have done *no such thing*! How could I? *I'm* not a *witch*.'

'Then you hired a witch to do it for you!' Permelia retorted. 'Or a wizard. It's plain for all to see, so don't go trying to split hairs now you — you *termagant*!'

Highly entertained, Melissande felt a sharp elbow-nudge in her ribs and looked at Bibbie. 'Don't do that, this is just getting interesting.'

'I'll say,' said Bibbie, her sharkish grin on full display, and unfolded her fingers. In the palm of her hand the green hex-detecting crystal pulsed a deep and vibrant black. 'Looks like we've got her, Miss Cadwallader.'

'Indeed it does, Miss Markham,' she replied, feeling an equally sharkish smile spread across her own face. 'Don't look now, but I think that's your cue.'

'I say that you *have* done this dreadful thing!' Permelia Wycliffe continued in her vindicated glory. 'And not just today. You've been cheating all year! *You*, Millicent Grimwade, have single-handedly brought the Baking and Pastry Guild into dire disrepute! By the power vested in me as president I demand that you hand over your Guild badge *at once*! You are a *disgrace* to the chocolate éclair!'

'I'll do no such thing!' cried Millicent Grimwade. She was practically panting. 'You can't prove I've cheated, Permelia Wycliffe. You can't prove a *thing*!'

'*She* might not be able to, Miss Grimwade,' said Bibbie, ducking under the scarlet cordon-rope. 'But *I* can. And I *will*.' She held up the black crystal in full sight of the crowd. 'Do you see this?' she demanded in a loud and carrying voice, brandishing the crystal overhead. The closest of the deliciously shocked spectators craned their necks for a closer look. 'It's a hexometer, ladies. Designed to register thaumaturgic activity. If there isn't any in the immediate vicinity it's a pleasant pale green. But if there *is* it turns black. And as you can see, this crystal is *indeed* black.' She spun round to face a shocked and gibbering Millicent Grimwade. 'As black as the heart of a woman who'd stoop to illegal thaumaturgy to win the Golden Whisk!'

A fresh outcry, as the direness of Bibbie's claims registered with every Guild member in the room.

Despite the desperately dancing plates on her table, which was starting an alarming shimmy in counterpoint, Millicent Grimwade managed to rally. 'And who are you, pray tell? Some hussy Permelia's dragged in off the street?'

'*Hussy*?' said Bibbie, milking her moment. 'How *dare* you, madam? *I* am Miss Emmerabiblia Markham, one third of Witches Incorporated, the new witching locum agency recently opened in town. No task too large or too small, reasonable rates, absolute discretion guaranteed. Unmasking thaumaturgical villainy is our business and you, Millicent Grimwade, may consider yourself *unmasked!*'

Still Millicent Grimwade stood her ground. 'Poppycock!' she retorted. 'Do you think we're going to take one look at your silly little crystal and believe that a woman of *my* social stature would stoop to cheating? That my Guild sisters would take your word over mine, some upstart young person who dares to show her ankles in public? *Do you?*'

As Bibbie stared, momentarily silenced, Melissande shoved under the scarlet cordon-rope and ranged herself at Bibbie's side.

'*Yes!*' she said, in a loud, commanding voice. 'Because those ankles belong to none other than the great-niece of former Guild President *Antigone Markham!*'

Outright chaos ensued. The judges shouted, the shrieking Invigilators waved their wooden spoons, Eudora Telford bleated her support, Permelia Wycliffe demanded Millicent Grimwade's confession and Millicent Grimwade demanded her presidential resignation in return. Not a single woman in the chamber kept her opinion to herself. The noise was so loud the windows started to vibrate.

And at the height of the uproar ... Millicent Grimwade's hexed cakes exploded.

'Well,' said Bibbie into the ringing silence, flicking a blob of chocolate log off the end of her nose. 'I suppose that's one way of winning the argument.'

Everyone within twenty feet of Millicent's table was now wearing a sticky souvenir from the most exciting Golden Whisk competition in the Baking and Pastry Guild's long and chequered history.

'Urrrgghhh ...' said Millicent Grimwade, dripping gooseberry sponge, and fainted theatrically onto the floor.

Which was a signal for the room to erupt into fresh cacophony. Ignoring the outcry, Permelia Wycliffe stepped over

Millicent Grimwade's prostrate body to snatch Bibbie's chocolate-daubed hands in a convulsive clasp. Incredibly, she seemed on the verge of tears. It made her all of a sudden more human. Less dislikeable.

'Oh, thank you, Miss Markham. *Thank you.*'

Reprehensible Bibbie grinned. 'You're welcome, Miss Wycliffe. We guardians of the Baking and Pastry Guild have to stick together, after all.'

Permelia Wycliffe leaned close, still clutching, her black silk-clad bosom painted with sloppy vermilion icing. 'I must speak to you on another matter, Miss Markham,' she said, eyes narrowed with purpose. 'Now that I know I can trust you *implicitly*. The Wycliffe honour is at stake and I feel you might be my only hope.'

Smeared with cream and bits of gooseberry, Melissande turned away from incoherently gushing Eudora Telford, determined to step in before Bibbie had the bright idea of volunteering their unpaid services in the name of Baking and Pastry Guild sisterhood.

'I'm sure it sounds most serious, Miss Wycliffe,' she said briskly. 'And of course Witches Inc. would be only too pleased to undertake any commission on your behalf. Perhaps we might discuss the particulars tomorrow morning, at ten?' She fished in her reticule for the account she'd prepared last night, and held it out. 'When you come by the office to settle today's successfully concluded assignment?'

Permelia Wycliffe stared at her blankly for a moment, then nodded and took the sealed envelope. 'Why, er, yes. Yes, certainly.' She turned. 'You will be in attendance, won't you, Miss Markham?'

'We'll both be there, Miss Wycliffe,' said Melissande firmly. 'The agency is our joint endeavour.'

Permelia Wycliffe drew breath to say something blighting, but before things could go from wonderful to woeful she was swept away by a gaggle of voluble Invigilators and various other agitated Guild members.

Melissande felt a plucking at her stained sleeve, and turned. *Oh, dear.* 'Yes, Miss Telford?'

'I must go, Your Highness. Permelia will need me,' Eudora Telford whispered. Tears sparkled in her faded brown eyes. 'I just wanted to thank you, again. This was so important to her . . . and I couldn't help.'

Honestly, she really was the *soggiest* woman. 'It was my pleasure, Miss Telford.'

'Gosh,' said Bibbie, emerging from under Millicent Grimwade's table with the sprite trap as Eudora scuttled after her friend. 'So that's another job for Witches Inc., eh? Hmmm, didn't someone recently say that using Monk's interdimensional escapee to solve the Case of the Cheating Cake Cook might well work out to our advantage? Who could that have been, I wonder?'

Melissande sighed. 'Yes, yes, rub it in, why don't you?'

'Don't worry, I will,' said Bibbie, grinning, the sprite trap dangling on the end of one careless finger. 'I'm going to rub it in until —'

'I say! I say!' an excited voice called out. 'Can you look this way?'

'What?' said Melissande, turning. 'I know that voice! It's —'

And then she was blinded by a flash of thaumically-enhanced light as the appalling photographer from the *Times* assaulted her yet again with his camera.

A tide of red and righteous wrath rose within her. '*You!* What are *you* doing here? *Give* me that camera, you *revolting* little man!'

The photographer yelped and ran. Hurdling the still-prostrate Millicent Grimwade, scattering spectators like skittles, she chased the mingy weasel out of the chamber, down the Town Hall steps and into the busy carriage-filled street.

'That's right, you little rodent!' she bellowed after him. 'Run, go on! And just you *keep* on running, you hear? Keep on running and *don't look back!*'

'Now, now,' said Reg, landing on her shoulder in a fluttering of brown-and-black feathers. 'That's not very nice of you, ducky. I mean, in a roundabout way he did get us this job.'

Hotly aware of the stares and imprecations she was collecting from various shocked pedestrians and carriage-drivers, Melissande leapt back onto the sidewalk and lifted her chin, refusing to be embarrassed. 'I don't care. It's an invasion of privacy, that's what it is. He's a weasel and a toad and I've half a mind to slap Millicent Grimwade silly with a soggy cooked noodle until she gives up the name of the witch or wizard who devised that hex of hers. Could be I might have some business for them. There's a certain camera I need to futz with.'

'No, don't do that,' said Monk, behind her. 'Black market thaumaturgy is kept strictly hush-hush. If you stick your nose in I'll have to report you to the Department and that could get a bit awkward. And speaking of awkward, Mel, what have you done with my sprite?'

Melissande spun on her heel. 'Monk? What are you doing here?'

'Reg came and got me,' he said, his eyes warm, his expression guarded. 'Now can I have my sprite back, please? We're up to our armpits in a controlled thaumic inversion back in the lab, and Macklewhite won't cover my absent arse forever.'

'The wretched thing's inside,' she said, desperately attempting to recover her poise. If only she wasn't wearing *quite* so much whipped cream ...

'Inside?' Monk repeated, horrified. 'What do you mean, inside? You mean inside the *Town Hall*? Where people can *see* it? Mel, what were you *thinking*?'

'I wasn't!' she said hotly. 'This was all your mad sister's idea! So if you want to shout at someone I strongly suggest you shout at *her*!'

Monk scrubbed a distracted hand over his face. 'Mmm. Yes. That never turns out well for me.'

'And you think *this* conversation is destined for a happy ending?'

'Quit while you're ahead, sunshine,' said Reg, snickering. 'Want me to go and fetch Mad Miss Markham?'

They stared at her in mutual dismay. '*Absolutely not!*'

Reg sniffed. 'Suit yourselves.'

Melissande watched her flap away, then sighed. 'Wait here, Monk. I'll fetch Bibbie and your precious sprite.'

But there was no need, for as she turned to trudge back into the Town Hall Bibbie came out with the deactivated sprite trap.

'*There* you are!' said Monk, wrathfully advancing. 'Bibbie, are you completely *cracked*?'

Ignoring the question, his sibling thrust the seemingly-empty birdcage at him. 'Here's your sprite, Monk. Lucky for you it came in handy or I might've had to devise a truly awful payback hex. As things stand, we'll call us even.'

'*Even*?' he said, flicking on the etheretic normaliser. 'Not bloody likely!'

'Honestly, it's *in* there, Monk,' said Bibbie, with unrestrained sisterly scorn. 'Do you really think I'd — oh.'

Oh was right. The interdimensional sprite was puddled on the bottom of the birdcage, its only sign of life a faint, pulsating blue twitch.

Melissande stared at it, aghast. 'Oh yes? My imagination, was it? I *said* the thing didn't look very well, didn't I say that? But no-one *ever* listens to me. Just because *I'm* not a thaumaturgical genius I get *ignored*!'

It was true. Bibbie was ignoring her now. 'You'd better do something, Monk. If the stupid thing dies it'll be your fault.'

'*My* fault?' He looked in danger of falling to the pavement in an apoplectic fit. 'Bugger that, Bibbie! If you'd done what I asked in the first place and brought me the damned sprite as soon as you caught it —'

'*Not here!*' said Melissande, acutely aware of the unfortunate attention they were attracting from the public-at-large. She grabbed brother and sister by an elbow each. 'Let's find somewhere to discuss this in private, shall we?'

Monk wrenched himself free. 'There's no time. Can't you see the rotten thing's *dying*? And if it dies in this dimension I have no idea what the thaumaturgic fallout might be. And I *really* don't want to find out the hard way! Do you?' Clutching the birdcage with its ailing occupant close to his chest, he made a dash for the pool of shadows cast by the Town Hall's wide, imposing front steps.

'What are you doing?' said Melissande, following him, with Bibbie at her heels.

'What does it look like I'm doing?' he retorted, harassed. 'I'm sending this bloody sprite back where it came from!'

'Here? This minute?' said Bibbie. 'Monk, you can't! There are too many people around, what if —'

Now it was Monk's turn to do the ignoring. Deeply frowning, he pulled a rock out of his pocket and hummed complicatedly and untunefully under his breath, then held it above the sprite trap he'd so casually invented. Melissande recognised the rock as a relative of the portable portal he'd used in New Ottosland.

'Oooh!' said Bibbie, twitching. 'Feel that!'

Melissande stared at her. 'What? Feel what?'

'*That,*' said Bibbie. 'Ewww, it's like a thousand caterpillars crawling over my skin! Can't you *feel* it?'

No. She couldn't. Because she wasn't a real witch. But that didn't bother her *at all*.

Monk was grinning now, and Bibbie was grinning back at him, their nursery-squabbling forgotten. 'Any second,' he murmured. 'Wait for it ... wait for it ...'

The air surrounding the ailing sprite shivered. Sparkled in an impossible whirlpool of silver and gold. The sprite emitted a tiny, surprised squeak. Then, as though an invisible hand had reached out to grab it by the scruff of the neck, or what passed for its neck, it was sucked into the sparkling whirlpool ... and vanished.

'*Excellent!*' said Monk briskly and returned the rock to his pocket. 'Now I'd best be on my way. Oh, and there's no need for you to worry about Millicent Grimwade. Reg filled me in on her shenanigans, and I've passed along the particulars to the relevant Department. In fact —' He nodded as an official-looking black car pulled up in front of the Town Hall. 'Here comes justice now.' He grinned as two stern-faced men spilled onto the pavement and started marching up the Town Hall steps. 'So that's the cake cheat and her black market chum taken care of. She'll spill every last bean, I'll bet, to make things easier for herself.' Still grinning, he shoved the birdcage at Bibbie.

'And what am I supposed to do with this?' she said, bemused.

'Hang onto it until the next time we have dinner?' he suggested, walking backwards. 'Thanks!'

They stared after him, open-mouthed, until he was lost to sight amongst the city's teeming pedestrians.

Then Bibbie laughed. 'Never mind. All's well that ends well.' She linked her arm through Melissande's. 'Now I want tea. *Lots* of tea. And scones with lashings of blackcurrant jam and cream.'

Melissande shook her head. The Markhams were totally incorrigible and utterly impossible. 'Bibbie, no. We can't *afford* —'

'Oh, pishwash!' scoffed Bibbie. 'We just solved the greatest crime in Baking and Pastry Guild history, sent a sightseeing interdimensional sprite home to its mother *and* put a black market thaumaturgist out of business! If that's not an excuse to celebrate then I don't know what is! Do you?'

'Well . . . no,' said Melissande, reluctantly. 'Only we mustn't go overboard, Bibbie. *One* celebratory scone each and a teapot between us. That's it. And then we go back to the office and make sure we're ready for round two with Permelia Wycliffe. Because if you're right, and this ridiculous cake fiasco is the start of something big, then I want to be ready for it. Agreed?'

'Agreed,' said Bibbie, rolling her eyes. 'Now come on, do. It's time for some *fun!*'

CHAPTER NINE

The story appeared on page twelve of the next morning's paper. *This Year's Golden Whisk Award Anything But A Cake Walk!* the *Times'* headline snickered. The accompanying photograph was of Bibbie, looking effortlessly beautiful even while covered in sprite-exploded chocolate log and holding a stupid birdcage.

'Ha!' said Reg, perched on the back of the client's armchair and peering over Melissande's shoulder. 'What were you saying about the evils of free advertising?'

Trust Reg to remember that. 'Nothing,' she muttered. 'Shut up. I'm trying to read.'

But instead of reading she stared at Bibbie's picture, her attention transfixed. It was petty, no, it was *smaller* than petty, to feel her throat close up and her eyes burn hot. It wasn't Bibbie's fault she'd still look glorious dipped head to toe in mud. That even under such kerfuffled circumstances as yesterday's she could emerge at the end of the fracas looking cool, calm, unruffled and glamorous.

I really thought that horrible little man was photographing me. With Bibbie standing there? How silly could I get ...

'So?' said Reg, and tugged on a stray, escaped lock of hair. 'Well? What does it say about us?'

'What?' she said, blinking hard. 'Oh. I don't know. I haven't finished reading.'

'Then finish,' said Reg. 'I don't know, young people these days, no application, no discipline . . .'

With a concerted effort she banished treacherous self-pity and focused on the brief article about the previous day's eventful Golden Whisk competition.

'It doesn't say very much,' she said after swiftly perusing the two short paragraphs. 'Only that some hanky-panky — unspecified — was thwarted at the Guild's annual baking contest. And there's a quote from Permelia Wycliffe about the organisation's unsullied international reputation and dedication to transparent cooking practices.'

'You mean we're not *mentioned*?' said Reg, scandalised. 'And that Wycliffe woman didn't give us due credit?'

'No. Which I admit is a little disappointing.' She frowned, thinking about that. 'Although I wonder . . .'

'*Wonder*? What's to *wonder*, madam? We've been *gypped*!' Reg retorted, vibrating with outrage. 'We saved the day, ducky, we rescued the Guild's bacon from the fires of a public roasting and now we've been filleted, we've been fricasseed, we've been —'

'Oh, Reg, do calm down and *think* for a moment.'

'There's nothing to think about!' Reg screeched. 'We was *robbed*!'

She sighed. 'No, Reg, we were gazumped.'

'*Gazumped*? What's that? That's not even a word!'

'It's a government thing,' she said, and tapped the newspaper. 'I'll bet you a week's supply of mice that the whole story was kept vague because someone important had a word with the editor. Don't forget, Reg, in the end this case boiled down to black market thaumaturgy. That's not the kind of thing Monk's Uncle Ralph wants splashed across the *Times*'s front pages. From the little Monk's told me, the less people know about the thaumaturgical black market the better off we'll all be.'

But Reg was in no mood to be placated by anything so humdrum as reasonable common sense and sober government responsibility. Taking to the air, she flapped about the office in a rage.

'I don't give a tinker's cuss about your young man's uncle! If that Sir Ralph's so worried about black market thaumaturgy, *I* say let him knock it on the head *without* trampling all over *our* moment in the sun!'

Melissande shook her head. 'Well, yes, Reg, it would've been nice if we'd been mentioned by name but —'

'*Nice?*' Panting, Reg thumped onto her ram skull. '*Nice* would be you *not* taking the bureaucrat's side, ducky! You know what *your* problem is, don't you? *You* still think you're a bloody prime minister!'

What? 'Oh, that's rich coming from someone who's been a bird for the last four centuries and still wants everyone to treat her like a queen!' Ignoring Reg's sharp, offended gasp, she turned back to the *Times*. 'Now if you don't mind, I'd like to —'

'Girls! Girls! Did you see?' cried Bibbie, frothy in pink muslin and dancing into the office brandishing another copy of the *Times*. 'We're *famous*!'

'Famous? We're not famous!' Reg retorted. 'We're *ignored* is what we are. And madam here can't see it's a disaster! *She's* too busy applauding a government cover-up!'

Surprised, Bibbie stopped dancing and stared at them. 'Ignored? What are you talking about, Reg? There's an article *and* a photograph.' She shook the paper again. 'Haven't you seen it?'

Melissande lifted her own copy of the *Times*. 'We saw,' she said, then glanced at the clock. Ten to nine: an early morning record for Bibbie. 'Reg is upset because the agency didn't get a mention. I've been *trying* to explain that —'

'But we did get a mention,' said Bibbie. 'Didn't you read the caption on the photo?'

Caption? No. She hadn't wanted to look at the picture that closely.

With an impatient sigh, Bibbie lifted her paper. '*Miss Emmerabiblia Markham, co-proprietor of Witches Inc.,*' she read aloud, '*after successfully unmasking the Golden Whisk cheat.*' She looked up. 'See? It's all there in black and white. So there's no need for Reg to be in a flap. Just you wait, the phone will be ringing off its hook after this.'

Feather by feather, Reg let her ruffled plumage settle. 'Oh. Well. That's more like it. Of course it's not the same as being mentioned in the actual article, but it's better than a slap in the face with a stunned mullet.'

Bibbie dropped a swift kiss on the top of Reg's head then perched on the edge of her desk. 'It's a lot more than that,' she said. 'It's utterly fantabulous. We could never have afforded this kind of publicity.'

Melissande sat back in the client's armchair and brooded at the photo.

The little cogs and wheels of her imagination were clicking, stirring up a definite sense of unease.

'Oh-oh,' said Bibbie, noticing. 'I know that look. Come on, Mel. Out with it. What's wrong now?'

She tapped a finger on the picture of Monk's triumphantly smiling sister. 'What's wrong is I'm not entirely certain this kind of attention really is going to do us any favours.'

'Whatever do you mean?' said Bibbie, astonished. 'We're going to be run off our feet after this. Saving the Baking and Pastry Guild's day is going to put us on the map!'

She shook her head. 'I don't have a problem with the agency appearing on a map. I'm just not convinced that us being turned into topographical features is a good idea.'

Bibbie stared at page twelve in her own copy of the *Times*. 'Being photographed, you mean? But Mel, it was your picture with Monk at the opera that got us the Guild job. How can that be a bad thing?'

'It wasn't,' she admitted. 'But Bibs, really, think about it. Ottish society's already forgotten that photo of me. *You*, on the other hand, are an entirely different boatload of monkeys.'

'Oh, please, don't start on that,' Bibbie muttered, squirming. 'You know I hate it when —'

'Too bad,' she said firmly. 'Like it or not, Bibbie, the fact is that *you* don't have a forgettable face.'

Bibbie scuffed the carpet with the toe of her pink kidskin slipper. 'Possibly,' she said grudgingly. 'But I fail to see what that's got to do with anything.'

'Oh, come now. You *must*. I mean, we were successful yesterday because Millicent Grimwade didn't have a clue who we were. But how successful are we going to be next time, do you think, if we need to be inconspicuous and you've been turned into a walking advertisement for the agency?'

Bibbie tossed aside her paper and slid off her desk. 'That's not fair, Melissande! I didn't *ask* for my picture to be taken.'

She held up one placating hand. 'I'm sorry, Bibbie. Of course you didn't. This isn't your fault. I just think we need to be careful, that's all. The last thing we can afford to do is limit the kind of jobs we can accept. We need to *grow* Witches Inc., not prune it while it's still practically a seedling.'

'Mel, honestly, you worry too much,' said Bibbie, pouting. 'Why are you always looking for the silver cloud's dark lining?'

Reg rattled her tail feathers. 'Now, now, ducky. Madam's got a point. Being famous is all very well for five minutes. After that it tends to get inconvenient.'

Astonished, Melissande swivelled round in the client's

armchair. 'You're *agreeing* with me now? You know, Reg, I do wish you'd make up your mind.'

'She must be sickening for something,' said Bibbie, with a teasing smile. 'Take her temperature, quick.'

'Yes, yes, very amusing,' said Reg, rolling her eyes. 'But you mark my words, Mad Miss Markham. There are far worse things in this world than being anonymous.' She sniffed. 'Trust me, I speak from personal experience.'

Now it was Bibbie's turn to roll her eyes. 'And nobody's had as much personal experience as you, we know.'

'Well, nobody has,' Reg snapped. 'And you'd do well to remember that instead of —'

Reg's familiar scolding refrain was interrupted by the telephone, ringing. Bibbie picked up the receiver. 'Good morning, this is Witches Inc. No thaumaturgical task too large or too — I'm sorry? — Yes, this is Miss Markham. — Yes, that's me in the *Times*. — Why yes, I am Aylesbury Markham's sister. — Distinguished? Well, that's one word for him. — Really? How very distressing for you, Miss Martin. Perhaps you'd care to stop by the agency so we can discuss your situation in person? Just a moment and I'll look in our appointment book ...'

'Reg,' said Melissande, keeping her voice down, 'tell me not to get my hopes up, would you? Remind me that it's still very early days. Lecture me on not counting my chickens while the eggs are still being laid.'

Reg's dark eyes gleamed. 'I don't need to, ducky. You're far from perfect but you're a sensible girl ... and a little bit of dreaming never hurt anyone.'

'*Well!*' said Bibbie, grinning, as she hung up the phone. 'Whoever would have thought Aylesbury could come in handy? Wonders will never cease.'

Melissande took a deep breath, trying to steady her unsteady heart. 'A new client?'

'Prospectively,' said Bibbie. 'The Honourable Miss Letitia Martin. She saw the story in the paper *and* she knows Aylesbury. Thinks he's charming, what's more, which means either she's a noddycock or she can't have known him very long.'

'When is she coming in?'

'After lunch.'

'And what's her problem?'

Two dimples danced in Bibbie's cheeks. 'Aside from the fact she thinks Aylesbury's charming? She's lost some valuable jewellery and wants us to find it. Tactfully. No public hue and cry.'

'Oh? Well. That doesn't sound too hard.'

'Not hard at all,' said Bibbie, openly grinning again. 'It'll be money for jam. We'll be rolling in dosh soon, just you wait and see!'

'At this point, madam, allow me to remind you about unhatched chickens,' Reg said severely. 'One new client does not a bursting bank account make.'

Bibbie groaned. 'You're such a spoilsport, Reg. Why don't you go catch a mouse or something so Mel and I can celebrate in peace?'

'I might just do that,' Reg retorted. 'Because for all your overconfidence, ducky, a mouse might be the only thing standing between the three of us and starvation before long!'

'*Honestly*, Bibbie,' Melissande sighed, watching Reg flap across next door's rooftop in high dudgeon. 'You know she's only trying to help.'

'Trying to burst my balloon, you mean,' Bibbie grumbled. 'Just *once* you'd think she could be encouraging.'

Yes. Well. Probably it was time to change the subject. 'Look at the time!' she said brightly. 'Permelia Wycliffe will be here soon. We should spruce up the office, I think.'

But instead of sprucing, Bibbie slumped against her desk, arms mutinously folded, her brow scrunched in another scowl.

'Reg should stop treating me like a — a peahen. I mean, you're not the only one who's been losing sleep lately, Mel. This place is all I have that's *me*. If it doesn't work out I'll have to go back to being a *gel*. It's all right for you. You might not much like being a princess but at least it means nobody dares tell you what to do.'

'Ha,' said Melissande. 'That's what you think. There's an entire herd of lords back home who do nothing but witter on about my frivolity and make formal demands that I come home and be decorative.'

'Yes, but you don't have to pay attention to them,' said Bibbie, impatient. 'You can tell them to shut up and they have to listen because you're the king's sister and they're not.'

Bibbie really did look unhappy. 'What's going on, Bibs?' she said, pushing out of the client's armchair to perch beside her on the edge of the desk. 'Who's been filling your head full of rainclouds? Not Monk?'

'No, of course not Monk,' said Bibbie. 'He's the only one who really understands.' She shrugged. 'But everyone else seems to think that all I should care about is making a brilliant marriage. Even Father, and he's forever boasting about me to his wizard chums. I tell you, Mel, you may get away with wearing trousers in public but the world is still full of Great-uncle Throgmortons. I don't care if I *never* get married. I want a *large* life. A life that has *purpose*. I mean, truly, what's the point of being a thaumaturgical prodigy if I never get to be prodigious?'

Melissande cleared her throat. 'Yes, well. Not that I'd know anything about being a prodigy, of course, but —'

'Oh, Mel, I'm sorry,' said Bibbie quickly. 'I didn't mean to — I wasn't thinking.'

She bumped Bibbie with her shoulder. 'Never apologise for speaking the truth. You *are* a prodigy, just like Monk. Almost like Gerald. And I'm not.'

'No, you're not. Far from it,' said Bibbie, with more honesty than tact. 'But you're a genius at being practical and organised and that's nothing to sneeze at.'

Possibly not, but it hardly compared. Still. No point pining after the impossible. 'The thing is, Bibbie,' she said firmly, 'that I *do* wear trousers and I *don't* get hauled off the street. Slowly but surely things are changing. So you're not to lose heart, do you hear me? Married or not you *will* have a large life *full* of purpose. In fact it's my belief you're going to take life by the scruff of the neck and shake it into trembling submission. We *both* are. Starting with Witches Inc., which is going to be the most successful witching agency in the history of Ottosland. *Agreed*?'

Bibbie straightened out her slump. 'Yes. All right. *Agreed.*'

The phone rang eight more times while they were dusting and rearranging and getting ready for Permelia Wycliffe's arrival. Three of the callers were eager young men pretending to require assistance from Miss Markham. They were given short shrift. But the other five were genuine enquiries for agency help, and were duly noted in the appointment book. Bibbie managed to restrain herself from saying 'I told you so', but her eyes shone like blue stars and her lips remained curved in the faintest of smug smiles.

Melissande didn't begrudge her. *The more clients the merrier. And it's always possible I'm making grapefruits out of lemons. Bibbie's right: I am a worrier by nature . . . and Lional only made things worse. Perhaps I need to start looking on the bright side first instead of last.*

At precisely ten o'clock Permelia Wycliffe arrived, this time without Eudora Telford in tow. 'Good morning, Emmerabiblia,' she said grandly, sweeping into the office like a duchess on a goodwill tour. Her costly mourning attire was elegantly restrained, as before, her discreet sapphire necklace quietly expensive. 'Miss Cadwallader,' she added, almost as an afterthought.

So . . . in the absence of Miss Telford's staunch royalism she'd been emphatically demoted. Hiding her amusement, Melissande nodded. 'Miss Wycliffe,' she murmured, and indicated the freshly plumped client's armchair. 'Please, do have a seat. Might I offer you some refreshment?'

Permelia Wycliffe thawed the merest fraction. 'Thank you. Yes.'

Further relegated to the role of maidservant — a good thing Reg hadn't come back or she'd be blue-faced on the floor with suppressed laughter, feathers and all — Melissande busied herself with brewing a pot of tea and setting out some freshly bought macaroons on their only unchipped plate. While she toiled, Bibbie and Miss Wycliffe exchanged animated reminiscences about late lamented Great-aunt Antigone. Clearly, as far as Permelia Wycliffe was concerned, Melissande Cadwallader didn't exist.

But that doesn't matter, Melissande reminded herself. *It's her money I'm after, not her undying friendship.* An unflatteringly mercenary attitude, to be sure, but hearts-and-flowers didn't pay the rent.

Once the tea and cakes had been served and consumed it was time to get down to business. Permelia Wycliffe withdrew from her gold-embroidered reticule a sealed envelope and gave it to Bibbie. 'Payment for services rendered, Emmerabiblia, as agreed. Your performance yesterday on the Guild's behalf was most impressive. *So* impressive that I have no qualms at all in entrusting to you an even more serious and sacred task.'

More sacred than the honour of the Baking and Pastry Guild? This was going to be something.

'It was our pleasure to be of service, Miss Wycliffe,' said Melissande, neatly plucking the envelope from Bibbie's grasp. 'And we're gratified that you wish to trust us again.'

Permelia Wycliffe looked down her nose. 'As you should be, Miss Cadwallader.' She turned again to Bibbie. 'What I'm about to divulge to you, dear Emmerabiblia, is highly sensitive information. I must ask that you not repeat it to another soul.'

Seated on her own desk chair, pulled out for the occasion, Bibbie leaned forward and daringly patted Permelia Wycliffe's gloved hand. 'You have our solemn promise, Permelia. Client confidentiality is the Witches Inc. watchword.'

Permelia Wycliffe drew in a deep breath through pinched nostrils, her fingers fiercely interlaced in her lap. 'Emmerabiblia ... the Wycliffe Airship Company is nursing a *viper* in its bosom.' Incredibly, her voice broke on the last word, and her eyes glittered with emotion. 'One of my gels is — is a *thief.*'

As Permelia groped in her reticule for a handkerchief, Melissande slid the envelope she'd given them into her desk drawer and exchanged a raised-eyebrow look with Bibbie, who pulled a face. *Don't just sit there, say something!* She wasn't very good with emotional crises, not her own or anyone else's.

Pulling a face back at her, Melissande cleared her throat. 'I'm very sorry to hear that, Miss Wycliffe. Can I offer you another cup of tea?'

With a shuddering effort, Permelia Wycliffe banished all unseemly hints of distress. 'Oh. Yes,' she said, and thrust the hanky back in her reticule. 'Thank you, Miss Cadwallader. Forgive me. That was most inappropriate.'

'Um ... when you say your *gels*, Permelia,' said Bibbie. 'Who exactly do you mean?'

'My gels,' said Permelia, as though everyone should know. 'The gels who work in the Wycliffe Airship Company office. My busy little worker bees, industriously toiling to keep our beautiful airships afloat. Orders. Queries. Paperwork. The throbbing lifeblood of the business.'

'Ah,' said Bibbie. 'I see. *Those* gels.' Her dimples appeared and disappeared, swiftly. 'Witches Inc. has one of those, too. We call her Miss Cadwallader.'

Melissande looked up from filling a fresh teacup with fragrant Sweet Tangtang and frowned, but Bibbie wasn't paying attention.

'So, you're convinced one of the Wycliffe office staff has sticky fingers,' she said. 'What is it that's being stolen, Permelia? Money?'

'Oh *no*,' said Permelia Wycliffe, accepting the fresh cup of tea from Melissande. 'I keep no money in the office, naturally. That would be *far* too great a temptation.' She sipped. 'The gels, you understand, aren't from Ottosland's first families. Some of them aren't from the city at all. Quite rustic, many of them. It would be unkind to keep money within their reach. After all, as this current crisis demonstrates, one can make a mistake in the hiring of staff. Why, just the other day I was forced to dismiss a gel.'

Standing by Bibbie's desk, Melissande felt her fingernails dig into her palms and had to make a conscious effort to unclench her fingers. 'Really? On what grounds?' *Too rustic, was she?*

Permelia Wycliffe's lips thinned with distaste. 'She cut off her hair, Miss Cadwallader. A bob, I believe it's called. *So* unfeminine. Despite their unfortunate social position the gels who work for Wycliffe's are young ladies — broadly speaking. I couldn't have such a precedent set in *my* office.' Her gaze dropped to Melissande's trousered legs. 'We have the highest standards and I insist they are maintained.'

'Yes, yes, Permelia,' Bibbie said hastily. 'We quite understand. So if it's not money going missing . . .?'

'Biscuits,' said Permelia Wycliffe. 'Pencils. Pencil sharpeners. Sugar. Various and sundry other office supplies. It was Miss Petterly who brought the matter to my attention, some three weeks ago. Miss Petterly is my office supervisor. Naturally, as a Wycliffe, I am in charge of the company's administration but I'm far too busy to be bogged down in the day-to-day supervision of our gels.'

'Oh, naturally,' said Melissande. 'We quite understand.' *So many cakes to bake, so little time to care for your employees or your company.*

'Miss Petterly agrees with me that one of the gels is our culprit,' said Permelia Wycliffe. 'She and I have done our best to uncover for ourselves the identity of this ungrateful miscreant — laid many and various cunning little traps — but alas, we have failed. Whoever is doing this has even managed to infiltrate my private office, which is where the expensive biscuits are kept. Under lock and key, I might add! Which is why I am here today making public this dreadful state of affairs.' Her lower lip quivered, just for a moment. 'I hope you appreciate how difficult it is.'

Melissande nodded. 'Of course. Your courage is admirable, Miss Wycliffe. So if I can just clarify the situation: you want to hire us to find a *biscuit thief*?'

'And why not, Melissande?' said Bibbie swiftly. 'I'm sure the last thing Miss Wycliffe wants is a formal police investigation. So insensitive. So — so *not private*.'

'Precisely, Emmerabiblia!' said Permelia Wycliffe, her lower lip quivering again. 'To think of our shame being made known to the world — I can't bear it. It is *imperative* that this matter be handled with the utmost discretion, which is why I have come to you.'

'Well, we certainly appreciate your patronage, Miss Wycliffe,' said Melissande. 'And your confidence. Tell me, as well as laying many and various cunning traps, have you tried confronting the ge — your staff — with the facts of this regrettable affair?'

'No,' said Permelia Wycliffe, taken aback. 'I couldn't possibly trust the innocent not to gossip about our crisis with undesirable persons. Miss Cadwallader, I thought I'd made myself understood: this dreadful business *cannot* become public knowledge. *Nothing* is more important than the protection of our good name.'

'Oh, we do understand, Permelia,' Bibbie said hastily. 'I think what my colleague means is that sometimes, when a miscreant is caught off-guard, they can reveal themselves. You know. A guilty thing surprised?'

Permelia Wycliffe shook her head emphatically. 'No. I won't hear of it. The risk is simply too great. Besides. While I'm sure all but one of my gels is not a thief, I don't wish to give any of them *ideas*.'

Ideas? Melissande choked back her outrage. *Honestly, this bloody woman makes Lord Billingsly look like a champion of workers' rights.* 'And you are absolutely certain your thief is one of Wycliffe's office staff?'

Permelia Wycliffe looked at her as though she were a particularly dim-witted servant. 'Who else could it be, Miss Cadwallader? The young men who work in the Wycliffe Research and Development laboratory have no business upstairs in the office. They are the purview of my brother Ambrose, and rarely set foot out of his domain. I'm sure I couldn't tell you even one of their names.'

Bibbie nodded understandingly. 'And why would you, Permelia? Really, Melissande,' she added, with a look, 'I do think we must trust that Miss Wycliffe knows her situation.'

Oh, doubtless she did, as thoroughly as she knew how to be an unbearable snob. 'Of course. I'm sorry, I didn't mean to imply otherwise,' she replied. 'And what you've told us is very useful information, Miss Wycliffe. Armed with your insights, no doubt we'll crack the case in a trice.'

'So you'll seek out this miscreant for me, my dear Emmerabiblia?' said Permelia Wycliffe. She sounded ever so slightly breathless, as though that banished emotion was still close at hand. 'You'll apprehend this dread viper in my — that is to say, the Wycliffe Airship Company's bosom?'

Bibbie nodded soothingly. 'Absolutely, Permelia. You can rest assured that Witches Inc. will leave no stone unturned to —'

'No, no, not Witches Inc., Emmerabiblia,' said Permelia Wycliffe. 'You. I want you to handle this matter personally. I've already given it a great deal of thought. Since I currently have a staff vacancy you could join my little family and investigate this travesty on site.'

Bibbie blinked. 'Work in the office, you mean? As a gel?'

'Yes! Precisely!' said Permelia Wycliffe. 'I think it's the perfect solution, don't you? For this is so important, Emmerabiblia — and you are the great-niece of the incomparable Antigone Markham. Greatness flows unhampered through your veins!' Her gaze flicked sideways, doubtful and disparaging. 'Of course, I'm sure Miss Cadwallader is perfectly competent, but —'

The phone rang again. Melissande, who was closest to it, snatched up the receiver. 'Good morning, this is Witches Inc. No thauma—' The male voice on the other end of the conversation buzzed in her ear. 'No, I'm sorry, Miss Markham is currently unavai—' More buzzing, a little agitated this time. Her heart sank, and she shot a dire look at Bibbie. 'Yes, indeed, sir, she did save the Golden Whisk. But as I say, she —' Buzz buzz buzz. My, this one was persistent. 'Perhaps, sir, if you'd care to explain your difficulty I could —' Buzz buzz buzz buzz. 'Oh, really! Go away, you silly man!'

She slammed down the receiver and glowered at Monk's troublesome sister.

'That was another one of your would-be admirers. I told you your photo in the paper would be trouble.'

'And you were right,' said Bibbie, suspiciously contrite. Turning to Permelia Wycliffe, she clasped the horrible woman's hand. 'I'm so sorry, Permelia. It appears I've been plunged into a whirlwind of notoriety, thanks to that dastardly photographer from the Times. I'm afraid I don't dare show my face at your office for fear I'd be recognised and my purpose there discovered. However, all is not lost. Miss Cadwallader remains incognito. And I give you my word, as Antigone Markham's great-niece, she's an absolute demon for paperwork. Seriously. She used to be a prime minister, you know.'

Permelia Wycliffe was looking bewildered. 'But — but —'

'And of course I'll be here at Witches Inc. headquarters, slaving away on your behalf, following up on all the leads that she is bound to discover.' Bending, Bibbie gently but inexorably drew Permelia Wycliffe to her feet. 'I'm as heartbroken as you, Permelia, honestly, but we must put aside our personal feelings — for the good of the Wycliffe Airship Company.'

'Oh ... well, yes,' said Permelia Wycliffe faintly. 'Of course. Undoubtedly. The Company must always come first. No sacrifice can be too great.'

'*Exactly*, Permelia!' said Bibbie. 'I knew you'd understand.' She turned. 'Isn't she wonderful, Melissande?'

Melissande summoned a smile. 'Inspirational.'

'We'll start work on your case tomorrow, Permelia,' said Bibbie. 'What time would you like Melissande to report for duty?'

With a visible effort, Permelia Wycliffe thrust aside the lingering remnants of her disappointment. 'You should present yourself to Miss Petterly at a quarter to eight, Miss Cadwallader.'

Oh, joy. That meant rising at the crack of dawn knowing that Bibbie was still tucked up warm and comfortable in her bed. 'Certainly, Miss Wycliffe,' she said, forcing a smile.

Permelia Wycliffe looked her up and down. 'I would point out, Miss Cadwallader, that Wycliffe gels are the very embodiment of sartorial discretion. They wear black from head to toe. Skirts and blouses, naturally. Not ... male attire.'

Of course they did. 'That won't be a problem, Miss Wycliffe.'

'Then I shall see you in the morning, Miss Cadwallader.' A thin, unenthusiastic smile. 'In the hope that our goal might be swiftly reached.'

'Why don't we make that Carstairs?' she suggested. 'I realise I'm eminently forgettable, especially when I'm not wearing my bustle, but as my photograph also appeared in the *Times*, to be on the safe side I think I need a different name. Molly Carstairs. That's got a nice rustic ring to it, I think. Don't you?'

'Lovely!' said Bibbie, brightly. 'Perfect. Didn't I tell you she's a marvel, Permelia? She thinks of *everything*.'

'Including the contract,' added Melissande. She returned to her desk, opened a drawer and pulled out one of the boiler-plate contracts she'd had drawn up. 'If you'd care to read this, Miss Wycliffe, and affix to it your signature?'

'I shall take it with me,' said Permelia Wycliffe, holding out her hand. 'For a leisurely perusal. One should never sign a binding legal document in haste.'

Ha. So, even with all the cake and biscuit nonsense, Permelia Wycliffe wasn't a fool. 'In which case,' she replied, 'perhaps you'd care to call when it's ready to be collected. We'll send a messenger. And if you could be so kind as to include with it the agreed retainer, as specified, and a complete list of your company's employees? They should be independently investigated. References, sadly, can be forged.'

'Indeed,' said Miss Wycliffe. 'But I shall only pay in advance *half* your retainer. My late father placed great faith in financial incentives.'

No, she most definitely wasn't a fool. Melissande swallowed. 'Half. Yes. All right. But only this once.'

'Excellent,' said Permelia Wycliffe, and allowed Bibbie to shepherd her to the door.

'*Emmerabiblia Markham*!' said Melissande, as Bibbie closed it behind their client.

'What?' said Bibbie, with spurious innocence.

'You know perfectly well *what*!' she retorted, and

advanced, pointed finger jabbing. 'You're a sneaky, conniving, opportunistic —'

'Oh, come on, Mel,' said Bibbie. 'Do I look like a Wycliffe gel to you?'

'I'll tell you what you look like! You look like a sneaky, conniving, opportunistic —'

'Put a sock in it, ducky,' said Reg, hopping onto the open office window's sill. 'Unless you want to explain all that half our retainer nonsense. Mad Miss Markham's outfoxed you, and that's all there is to it.' She flapped herself across to the back of the client's armchair and tilted her head. 'Very neatly, too. Nice work. Well done.'

She spun round. 'You were listening?'

Reg fluffed out her feathers. 'Of course.'

'And you're *defending* her? *Reg*!'

'Now, now, don't you start *Regging* me,' said the bird. 'Facts are facts. She's no more credible as a Wycliffe gel than I am and you know it. Besides, we'll need her on the outside pulling the thaumaturgical strings. And taking care of any other business that comes our way.'

Because it, too, might require the talents of a *real* witch. Feeling her eyes prickle, Melissande blinked hard. 'Fine. Wonderful. I'm a Wycliffe gel. I get it.'

'Sorry, Mel,' said Bibbie, trying to look apologetic. Unfortunately a grin kept breaking through. 'But I'd be hopeless, you know I would. You, on the other hand, will be perfectly *wonderful*.'

'In a black skirt and blouse,' she muttered. 'Oh, yes. I can hardly wait.' She heaved a sigh. 'Fine. And now, if you've quite finished being sneaky, conniving and opportunistic, perhaps we can get ready for our next appointment!'

CHAPTER TEN

'And here,' said Miss Petterly, 'is your cubicle, Miss Carstairs.'
Melissande looked. Cubicle? More like a shoebox.
Designed to house a shoe for a very small dwarf. If she sneezed
in here she'd give herself concussion against the dull grey wall.

'Wycliffe's is a very particular firm, Miss Carstairs,' said Miss
Petterly, a desiccated old stick with a voice like a disapproving
nanny-goat. 'Miss Wycliffe insists upon the gels keeping their
workplaces neat, tidy and unobtrusive. That means no personal
mementoes, cards, photographs, knick-knacks, paraphernalia or
frivolous nosegays from bold young men.'

Beyond the wall of her shoebox — cubicle — someone
snorted. Miss Petterly's narrow nostrils flared. 'I heard that,
Delphinia Thatcher. I shall tell Miss Wycliffe if I hear it again.'

'Sorry, Miss Petterly,' said an unrepentant voice. 'I swallowed
a fly.'

'There are no flies in Wycliffe's, Delphinia Thatcher.
Wycliffe's is a very hygienic firm.'

'Yes, Miss Petterly,' said the unseen Delphinia Thatcher.

Miss Petterly plucked a sharpened pencil from the breast-
pocket of her high-necked black blouse and used it as a pointer.
'Your desk, Miss Carstairs, and your chair. They are not to be
moved for any reason. Your typewriter, Miss Carstairs. There is a
daily allowance of blank order sheets and paper, which has been

carefully determined by me. If you exceed that allowance the cost of the extra *shall* be deducted from your weekly wage. There are your pens, pencils and ink, Miss Carstairs. You have been supplied with enough to last you a month. Should you remain with us that long, and exceed that supply, the cost of the extra *shall* be deducted from your weekly wage. Here is your abacus, Miss Carstairs, for swift and accurate mathematical calculations. Should you exceed a rate of one error per transaction a penalty *shall* be deducted from your weekly wage. Here is your in-tray, Miss Carstairs, which periodically shall be filled with customer orders. This must be emptied at least twice every hour into your out-tray *there*, Miss Carstairs. Failure to do so shall also incur a penalty which *shall* be deducted —'

'From my weekly wage, yes,' said Melissande. 'I think I'm getting the picture, Miss Petterly.'

And the next time I see that wretched photographer I'm going to kidnap him. And then I'm going to steal Monk's interdimensional portal opener and send that photographer on a one-way holiday to sprite-land!

Miss Petterly's nostrils flared again. 'Miss Carstairs! Wycliffe's gels are renowned for their courtesy. I shall overlook your interruption this time, but should you interrupt me again —' Miss Petterly smiled, revealing small, even teeth. 'I shall have you shown the door. Is that perfectly clear?'

Melissande hooked a finger between the high-necked collar of her own hideous, brand-new black blouse and eased the material away from her throat. Slow strangulation, what a way to die.

'Yes, Miss Petterly.'

'Excellent,' said Miss Petterly, with another fierce smile. 'Once your workday commences, Miss Carstairs, you do not arise from your desk for any reason other than your ten minute morning tea-break and your thirty minute lunchbreak. The office-boy —'

'Ah —' She raised an apologetic finger. 'Sorry. I don't mean to interrupt, Miss Petterly, but what if — that's to say — is it permissible to leave one's cubicle if — you know — one is required to answer a call of nature?'

Miss Petterly's sallow cheeks tinged with pink. 'What a singularly indelicate question, Miss Carstairs. I do hope Miss Wycliffe hasn't —' On a deep breath, she regained her self-control. 'Unauthorised absences from your desk will not be tolerated. At the first infraction a deduction *shall* be made from your weekly wage. A second infraction shall result in immediate dismissal.'

Melissande blinked. *In which case I'd best start imitating one of Zazoor's camels.* 'I see, Miss Petterly.'

'The office boy,' Miss Petterly continued, still pink-cheeked, 'is responsible for bringing you your fresh orders, and taking away such paperwork as has been correctly completed. As you can see —' She pointed her pencil at the pile of papers overflowing the in-tray. '— your first orders are awaiting your attention. A list of instructions as to how they are processed is pinned there.' Another pencil stab, this time at a sheet of paper tacked to the wall. 'Should you require assistance you shall call for *me*.' Her pencil tapped a little silver handbell which had been fixed to the cubicle wall above the desk. 'You shall not engage in gossip with any other Wycliffe gel, nor ask for their assistance, nor render assistance if it is asked of you. In theory, Miss Carstairs, your workday ends at six, but naturally no Wycliffe gel would dream of departing before every last order or query is dealt with. Wycliffe gels are dedicated and true.'

Well, all except one, apparently. 'Yes, Miss Petterly,' said Melissande, dulcetly obedient. *If Monk could hear her now he'd have a fit.*

Miss Petterly consulted the fob-watch pinned to her lacklustre bosom. 'Miss Wycliffe will see you in precisely ten minutes, Miss Carstairs. Do not be late. Wycliffe gels are always punctual.'

Melissande stared after the woman as she stalked away, her long black skirt sweeping the office floor. *Blimey*, as Reg would say. What an old misery-guts.

Still. At least I don't have to endure her for long, not like the other girls in this horrible place. Lord. I didn't treat my palace staff like this, did I?

Appalled by the notion, she slid into her cubicle's wooden chair and snatched up the top sheet of paper from her in-tray. It was an order for replacement machine parts. Perusing it she frowned, attention suddenly focused. *Velocipede* spokes? Whatever was Wycliffe's doing selling veloci —

'Hello,' said a cheerful voice, hushed to a whisper. 'I'm Delphinia Thatcher, prisoner number twenty-two. Welcome to Wycliffe's, prisoner twenty-three.'

Turning, Melissande saw a plump and freckled girl grinning at her from round the side of her cubicle. 'Molly Carstairs,' she replied, keeping her own voice low. 'Pleased to meet you. What do you mean, prisoner twenty-three?'

'This place,' said Delphinia, wrinkling her nose. 'And its twenty-five cubicles. Little prison cells, they are, each one containing a *gel*, slaving away for the fading glory of Wycliffe's. How they manage to keep on paying everyone's wages I'll never know.'

Melissande flicked a glance in Miss Petterly's direction but the ghastly woman had returned to her desk and was bent over a ledger. Hiding behind her own cubicle's wall, she leaned a little closer to Delphinia Thatcher and softened her voice to the merest breath.

'I'm sorry, are you saying that Wycliffe's is — ah —'

The girl pressed a finger to her lips. 'I'm not saying anything, Miss Carstairs.'

'Oh, please, call me Molly.'

'I'd love to,' said Delphinia, 'only Wycliffe gels are *never* familiar. If I get caught it's a fine and I've had so many wage deductions already this week I'm going to end up owing the company money.' She smiled, derisive. 'Probably that's how they can afford to keep paying us.'

So the company was struggling? Well, this was interesting. This was something Bibbie would need to look into. 'That's . . . a little alarming.'

'Miss Carstairs, you have no idea,' said Delphinia, and returned to her work before someone noticed she was chatting illegally.

Killing time before her interview with Permelia Wycliffe, Melissande hunted through the in-tray. How puzzling: most of the orders were for velocipede and car parts. Hardly any were for airships. How could that be, if this was an airship company? Something odd was happening here. But she'd have to think about it later, because her ten minutes were up and it was time to chat with Permelia.

Standing, she patted her pocket to make sure her secret weapon was safe then made her way through the crowded ranks of identical cubicles to the far end of the room. Her not-quite-floor-length black serge skirt dragged at her, annoyingly, threatening to tangle around her legs and trip her face-first to the floor.

Little steps, little steps, mince, don't stride. You're a Wycliffe gel now, Melissande, remember?

She came to a polite halt before Miss Petterly's knick-knack and memento-cluttered desk, which sat like a sentry box before Permelia Wycliffe's closed office door.

'Hmmph,' said Miss Petterly, by way of greeting, and put down her pen.

Melissande waited while the dreadful woman got up from

her chair, tapped on Permelia Wycliffe's door, cracked it open and engaged in a low-voiced conversation then stepped back.

'Miss Wycliffe will see you now,' Miss Petterly said grudgingly, as though the idea of sharing Permelia was more than she could bear.

Another Eudora Telford? *Please no, I couldn't bear it.* 'Thank you, Miss Petterly,' she said, squeezed past her into Permelia's office and closed its door emphatically in the ghastly woman's offended face.

Permelia Wycliffe finished shoving something into her desk drawer, banged it shut and looked up. 'Miss Cadwallader,' she said, eyebrows lifted. 'Do have a seat.'

'Thank you, Miss Wycliffe,' she said, but took her time getting settled in the visitor's chair so she could have a good look around at her client's well-guarded domain.

The first thing she noticed was the enormous painting on the pale yellow wall behind Permelia's imposing mahogany desk. It featured a daunting, dignified and prosperous gentleman wearing a sober black three-piece suit, top hat and extravagant ginger whiskers. Age and family resemblance suggested its subject was her father; the notion was confirmed by the large brass plaque attached to the heavy timber frame.

Orville Wycliffe, Esquire.

Melissande, considering the portrait, felt the smallest unwelcome twinge of sympathy for Permelia. Just like her own father, Orville didn't strike her as the *cuddly* kind of Papa.

The office's left-hand wall was plastered with sketches and blueprints of airships, each and every one the pride and joy of the Wycliffe Airship Company, while the right-hand wall was almost completely covered in framed photographs. A pity she wasn't close enough to snoop at them. The section of wall not crowded with photographs was filled by a large, immaculately dusted bookcase crammed with the seventeen Golden Whisks Permelia had won down the years. They might be ridiculous, pointless trophies but still — they were an impressive sight. A testament to Permelia Wycliffe's dogged pursuit of excellence in the culinary arts.

'Well?' said Permelia, hands folded neatly on her desk's blotter. 'What are your first impressions of Wycliffe's, Miss Cadwallader?'

'Well, I'm not really sure,' she said incautiously, as she sat. 'I've only been here an hour. Of course —' she added, with haste, noticing the ominous flush mounting in Permelia Wycliffe's cheeks, 'it doesn't take long to see you've created a fine family establishment, Miss Wycliffe. The office is just *full* of hardworking, dedicated Wycliffe gels. And I'm sure I'll find the same kind of dedication in the laboratory and the —'

'It won't be necessary for you to go further than the office, Miss Cadwallader,' said Permelia Wycliffe. 'As I indicated yesterday, you should focus your attention upon the gels.'

'Is that why you only sent us their details for checking?'

'Correct.'

'Um ...' Melissande smoothed her horrible serge skirt over her knees. 'Forgive me, but I don't think I can put this politely. Miss Wycliffe, I'm afraid you don't know what you're talking about. If I understood Miss Petterly correctly, most of the company's Research and Development staff are *wizards*. And when it comes to wizards even a half-witted Third Grader would have no trouble thieving from anywhere on the premises — even this office. In fact, now that I've seen how your department operates, it seems less and less likely that one of the gels *could* be responsible. Or if she is, she's most likely in cahoots with someone. Which means that if you're serious about stopping this theft I need complete access to everywhere in Wycliffe's. No department can be off limits.'

'I see,' said Permelia Wycliffe, lips pinched. 'And isn't that likely to prove disruptive?'

'It might,' she admitted. 'Of course I'd try my best not to be a distraction but in the end that could prove unavoidable.'

Permelia Wycliffe bridled. 'I find your answer unacceptable, Miss Cadwallader. You've been hired to take care of an administrative matter, not set the cat among my brother's wizardly pigeons.'

Melissande considered her, eyes narrowed. What was she not saying? The woman was hiding something … *ha.* 'You haven't told him, have you? Your brother, I mean. He has no idea one or more of your employees is a thief.'

'Mister Wycliffe and I have quite clearly delineated duties,' said Permelia Wycliffe, her cheeks flushing again as she fiddled with her elaborately carved jet hairpins. 'There is no need to bother him with trivial office affairs.'

So, this mystery thief was *trivial* now? Or was it just that Permelia was afraid to admit the problem to her brother? And what did that mean? Was Ambrose Wycliffe a bully …?

Rats. If that's the case I am going to start sympathising with her and I really don't want to. The woman's a cow.

'Really, Miss Cadwallader,' Permelia Wycliffe continued, aggrieved, 'I thought you'd be able to resolve this problem as swiftly as you took care of Millicent Grimwade. I anticipated that you and Miss Markham would be able to — to whip up some kind of truth-compulsion incant that would have the culprit confessing her guilt within moments.'

That had been Bibbie's inevitable thought too, last night. And of course, being Monk's sister, she was perfectly capable of fudging together some kind of hex that would do the trick. Of course the fact they'd be breaking quite a few iron-clad rules along the way didn't perturb her. Just like Monk, she had a … flexible … approach to authority. There'd been quite an argument about it in the end. But with Reg weighing in, making it two against one, the hair-raising idea had finally been discarded.

Of course, trust Permelia to come up with the same plan. Basted with the same pastry brush, the pair of them.

Forever mindful that she was the plain, freckled face of Witches Inc., Melissande offered up a sympathetic smile. 'I wish it were that easy, Miss Wycliffe, but the kind of incant you're talking about is highly restricted. Government use only. And the penalties for unsanctioned thaumaturgical activities are extremely severe … as Millicent Grimwade is currently learning first-hand.'

Permelia Wycliffe stiffened. 'Obviously I cannot be associated with anything *illegal*, Miss Cadwallader. That would hardly be appropriate for a firm of our prestigious reputation.'

'I agree,' she agreed promptly. 'And it goes without saying that Witches Inc. is *perfectly* capable of resolving your dilemma without resorting to questionable tactics. Only without our clients' full co-operation, well … success is likely to prove elusive.'

Permelia Wycliffe stared down her nose. 'Are you implying I would be anything less than —'

Rats. 'No, no, not at all. It's just … there's no way around it, Miss Wycliffe. In order to solve your problem I need my freedom. I can't be restricted to my cubicle from eight till six every day.'

Not and stay sane, anyway, never mind cracking the case.

'You're convinced of this?'

'Absolutely,' said Melissande. 'I'm sorry. In this instance you need to trust *my* expertise.'

Permelia Wycliffe frowned at her clasped hands. 'Naturally, Miss Cadwallader, I don't presume to do your job for you. I am, after all, paying a handsome fee for your services.' She looked up, her gaze penetrating. 'And you think it ridiculous that I'd do so, don't you? You think this a lot of nonsense. So much fuss over something so petty as … missing biscuits.'

Caught out, Melissande felt herself blush. 'No, of course not. Anyway, it's none of my business.'

'Perhaps you're right. Perhaps it is silly,' said Permelia, shrugging. 'But as I said yesterday, *nothing* is more important to me than protecting this company. Even if that means I must look a trifle foolish pursuing the theft of a few lead pencils and shortbread creams.'

Shifting in her chair, she stared reverently at her father's portrait.

'My dear Papa dreamed that one day Wycliffe's would be the premier airship company of the world. He loved airships, you know. Their grace. Their beauty. The way they glide through the sky like giant silver swans. He died a year ago, before seeing his dream realised, and on his deathbed I vowed to carry on his legacy. Since that dreadful day I have kept my word in the face of many difficulties and crushing disappointments. So surely you see, Miss Cadwallader, that I cannot stand by and allow some — some *biscuit-pincher* to tarnish his life's work! To jeopardise the reputation of the company Papa lived for!'

There was no doubting the woman's passionate sincerity. Melissande, watching Permelia closely, felt that inconvenient tug of sympathy strengthen. The woman's loyalty to Orville and his company ... her own loyalty to Rupert and the kingdom of New Ottosland ... she and Permelia Wycliffe stood on common ground there, united by the need to protect from all harm what they loved the most.

Rats.

'I understand, Miss Wycliffe,' she said with a sigh. 'And you mustn't fret. Miss Markham and I will do whatever it takes to keep your father's legacy safe.'

Permelia Wycliffe turned, her expression easing towards hope. 'Truly, Miss Cadwallader?'

'My word as a Royal Highness,' she replied. 'Oh — except I'm not one, remember? And I'm not Miss Cadwallader either. I'm Molly Carstairs.'

'Yes, yes, of course,' said Permelia Wycliffe. 'Although, if I might ask, why are you so determined not to be a Royal Highness? I'd have thought it would be something of an advantage in your line of work.' Her high-arched nose wrinkled. 'The world is full of Eudora Telfords.'

It was none of the wretched woman's business, but ... 'Because I love my brother, Miss Wycliffe,' Melissande said quietly. 'And while His Majesty fully supports my desire to be an independent woman of means, his enlightened attitude isn't shared by all his subjects. So while I forge my way in the world I try to remain inconspicuous, for his sake.'

Permelia Wycliffe smiled. 'I understand. And let me say how much I admire you for taking such a bold stance in the face of what must be daunting opposition.'

Melissande felt herself smiling back, for the first time liking Permelia Wycliffe ... which came as a surprise. 'It would only be daunting if I gave a turnip what the old tossers thought,' she said. 'But since I don't ...'

'Oh dear,' said Permelia Wycliffe, her lips twitching. 'You mustn't make me laugh. Miss Petterly will think I'm having a spasm.' She took a moment to rearrange her pens and pencils, then looked up. 'Very well, Miss — Carstairs. As soon as I can contrive it I'll see that you set foot beyond the office. In the meantime I presume you'll continue to search for this thief among the gels.'

It was her cue to leave, so Melissande stood. 'That seems like an excellent plan, Miss Wycliffe. And of course I shall keep you discreetly apprised of the investigation's progress.'

Miss Petterly gave her a gimlet stare as she left Permelia Wycliffe's office. 'Your in-tray is full, Miss Carstairs. Did I mention that should it not be emptied in a timely fashion a penalty *shall* be deducted from your weekly wage?'

Melissande bobbed a curtsy in passing. *I swear, before this is over I'm going to deduct you, Miss Petterly.* 'Yes, Miss Petterly. I'll get right to it, Miss Petterly. Thank you, Miss Petterly.'

She minced back to her horrible little grey cubicle, passing all the other horrible little cubicles where gels clad head-to-toe in sober black bent over their abacuses and their typewriters and their paperwork, striving not to earn a deduction from their weekly wage. Not a single gel looked up as she passed, and the air beneath the high ceiling smelled ever so faintly of an anxious tedium. Clack-clack-clack went all those typewriter keys. Click-click-click went the wooden abacus counters. The office boy dragged his little cart up and down the aisles between the cubicles, its wheels creaking a protest. He never once looked up or smiled.

Probably there's a penalty for smiling.

Even though this was fieldwork, even though this was a job, one that might well lead to other jobs and the saving of Witches Inc., Melissande shuddered.

Is this what it's going to be like, then? From the ridiculous to the depressing? Exploding cakes one day, a grim office the next? Sliding in and out of other people's lives, in and out of their unhappiness and stifled dreams and stunted ambitions, knowing that when I'm done I can leave but they can't?

Maybe. But that came with the territory, didn't it? No job was perfect. She just had to remember she'd opened the agency for a reason, to help people who needed helping. All right, so this assignment promised to be dreary. But dreary or not, she was helping Permelia Wycliffe protect her family's business from a person — or people — who didn't care who they hurt just so long as they got whatever they wanted. Yes, all right, *biscuits* ... but even so. The principle was noble. This was a calling of which she could be proud. That was worth a little boredom and discomfort.

And let's face it, Melissande. Life can't all be interdimensional sprites and exploding chocolate logs.

As promised, her in-tray was now full to the point of overflowing. Swallowing a sigh she slid into her chair, selected a pencil, lined up her abacus and got to work.

Melissande returned to the agency after seven that evening, tired and hungry.

'Well?' Reg demanded from her ram skull. 'What happened? Who's guilty? How soon do we get paid?'

With a groan, still clutching her carpetbag, she dropped into the client armchair. 'Too much paperwork, I don't know yet, and just as soon as I do.'

'Was it awful?' said Bibbie, sympathetically, glamorous as ever behind her desk.

'Yes.'

'And what did you find out?'

She grimaced. 'Not much.'

'You don't even have an *inkling* of who might be the thief?' said Bibbie, patently disappointed.

'I told you. No. I didn't have a chance to do any actual investigating. I was too busy processing orders for jalopy door-handles and velocipede tyres.'

'What?' said Bibbie, astonished. 'But I thought —'

'It seems Wycliffe's is diversifying,' she said, and swallowed a yawn. 'Where's Boris?'

'Who knows? Who cares?' said Reg, sniffing. Then she stared down her beak. 'You look like a crow in that getup, madam. I almost think I prefer the bustle.'

With another groan Melissande levered herself out of the client chair, took the cat's dinner out of her carpetbag and staggered towards her adjoining bedsit. 'Yes. Thank you, Reg. That's what I need after today — one of your trenchant fashion critiques.'

'Honestly, Reg,' said Bibbie. 'That's not very nice. The least you could say is that she looks like a *royal* crow.'

Melissande slammed the bedsit door behind her.

After stripping out of the hideous black blouse and skirt and carefully hanging them up so she could look like a royal crow again tomorrow, she pulled on her beloved tweed trousers and a pale pink blouse then hung out of the tiny window calling for the cat.

Just as she was beginning to despair, Boris leapt lightly through the open bedsit window, all long lean nonchalance, tail flicking, whiskers bristling, and butted her under the chin once or twice to say he was sorry. She unwrapped his fresh fish and put it on the floor, using the waxed wrapping paper as a plate. Then she returned to the office where Reg was sulking on her ram skull and Bibbie was making her share of the office paperclips dance like silver butterflies above the desk.

'I don't know, Mel,' she said, looking up. 'Maybe I should've taken the chance and gone to Wycliffe's. I'd have tracked down the thief by lunchtime. Betcha.'

Melissande dropped again into the client armchair. 'No, you would've tried to turn the office supervisor into a nanny-goat, which is just what she sounds like and richly deserves.'

Bibbie grinned. 'Oooh! Can I?'

'No.'

'Have I ever mentioned you're a spoilsport, Mel?' said Bibbie, pretending to pout. With a snap of her fingers she dropped the floating paperclips back in their tin dish. 'All right, so you were too busy to snoop. What about the hex detector? Did it locate any incriminating sleight-of-hand incants by any chance?'

Drat. Melissande got out of the chair, trudged back to the bedsit, fished the hex detector out of her skirt pocket, trudged back to the office and dropped it onto Bibbie's desk. 'None. Thanks to Wycliffe's Research and Development laboratory there's so much ambient thaumaturgical energy in that place your hex detector whimpered and gave up.'

'Hmm,' said Bibbie, staring at the murky orange crystal. 'That's disappointing. What a shame you didn't stumble across one of the gels shoving packets of biscuits down her knickers.'

She stared. 'Yes, I was just thinking that. Oh well. There's always tomorrow.'

'The answer's obvious, ducky,' said Reg on her ram skull, rousing from her sulk. 'We need a better hex detector. *And* something thaumaturgical to help us identify our thief. Which is right up Mad Miss Markham's alley.'

'I was thinking that, too,' said Melissande, nodding. 'What about it, Bibbie? Can you come up with something strong enough to swamp Wycliffe's etheretic atmosphere?'

'You have to ask?' said Bibbie, mildly offended. 'Just leave it to me.'

'Gladly. And speaking of leaving things to you, how did you go checking up on the office staff?'

'I left a message with Monk to call me pronto. He knows people who know everything about everyone.'

'Oh,' she said, frowning. 'You know, Bibbie, I'm not entirely certain I'm comfortable with that.'

'Relax, Mel,' said Bibbie. 'It's called exploiting our resources. Besides, he'd come running to us fast enough if he needed to know something about witches.'

'Well, possibly,' she admitted reluctantly. 'Only —'

'Only nothing. *Trust* me, Mel,' said Bibbie, offended again. 'I know what I'm doing.'

'Pleased to hear it. So that's you taken care of. And

tomorrow I'm going to see if I can make friends with some of the gels and find out who the wizards are at Wycliffe's. Which just leaves Reg.'

Reg fluffed out her feathers. 'I can take care of myself, madam, thank you very much.'

'Nobody said you couldn't, Reg,' she retorted. 'But it's going to take all three of us to solve this case and *I'm* the one of us on the inside so *if* you don't mind? Wycliffe's has an employee garden. Everybody except Permelia and her brother use it for lunch and sometimes tea break. It's the perfect place for you to eavesdrop. You never know what might be let slip while people are gossiping, especially if — as I suspect — we're dealing with more than one thief.'

'What, me sit in a tree all day?' said Reg, staring down her beak.

'Well, yes. That's what birds do, isn't it? Sit in trees?'

'*Birds*, yes,' said Reg. 'But I'm not —'

'Going to say *one more word*,' she said, glaring. 'Because unless *you* can type thirty words a minute, do mathematics on an abacus *and* fill out purchase orders in triplicate you *are* going to sit in that garden until your tail feathers fall out, if that's what it takes to solve this case.'

'Oh dear,' said Bibbie. 'I think somebody needs to go nighty-night.'

Melissande rubbed her eyes. 'Sorry. I can still hear the typewriters.' Then she looked at Reg. 'I know it won't be much fun sitting there all day, but the employee garden's the only place you can go where you won't be conspicuous *and* there's a chance to learn something useful from everyone.'

'Everyone except the Wycliffes,' Reg pointed out.

'Yes, except the Wycliffes, but since our clients aren't paying us to investigate *them* let's not get into an argument about that.'

'Agreed,' said Bibbie, before Reg could answer. 'And now that we've got that settled, don't you want to know what *I've* been up to while you were slaving over a hot abacus?'

'Oh,' she said, feeling guilty. 'Sorry, Bibbie. Yes. Of course I do.'

Bibbie looked at Reg and grinned. Reg couldn't grin exactly but her eyes went shiny, a sure sign she was pleased.

'Well, for a start I found Letitia Martin's jewellery.'

'Oh, well done!'

'And I cast three progressive horoscopes, booked in four more consultations and helped two clients who walked in off the street. The first one wanted to know if her young man was stepping out on her. So I looked and he was, the cad. Poor girl cried a river.'

Alarmed, Melissande sat up. 'Yes, but did she pay? I mean, you didn't feel sorry for her and give her the answer for *free*, did you?'

'She wanted to,' said Reg, before Bibbie could answer. 'So I looked at her and she changed her mind.'

Bibbie threw a paperclip at her. 'Traitor.'

'No, she's a lifesaver,' said Melissande, sagging. 'What about the other client?'

'She's a Guild Invigilator,' said Bibbie, still glowering at Reg. 'Her daughter's about to have a baby and she wants me to put up some hexes in the nursery. You know, a lullaby incant so the baby sleeps through the night, something to help it smile a lot and not get colic.' Mercurial as ever, she laughed. 'I hate to say it, Mel, but I think we're going to have to send that *Times* photographer a box of chocolates.'

'Only if they've been laced with a laxative,' she muttered. Then she pulled a face. 'Um ... is it my imagination or is this *frippery* work, Bibbie? Millicent Grimwade. Permelia Wycliffe's purloined biscuits. Babies and horoscopes and cheating young men.'

'Mel, we're *witches*,' Bibbie sighed. 'Females. *Not wizards*. As far as the wider world is concerned frippery is what we *are*, let alone what we're supposed to do.'

'But doesn't that bother you? Because I'll tell you, Bibs, it bothers me.'

'Are you kidding?' said Bibbie. 'It *kills* me. But babies and cads and horoscopes are good bread-and-butter money.'

'Which pays the rent,' Reg added. 'And that's nothing to sneeze at.'

'Yes, I suppose so.' She stifled an enormous yawn. 'Saint Snodgrass, I'm tired. Time for supper and bed, I think.' She rummaged again in the carpetbag and this time pulled out what was now a lukewarm pork pie, wrapped in more waxed paper.

Bibbie looked horrified. 'What's that?'

'I told you. Supper. I bought it from a barrow girl on the way home.'

'It looks *revolting*!'

'Maybe, but it's cheap. And it's doing my part for barrow girls.'

'Monk would feed you,' said Bibbie, fanning herself. 'There's no need to be a martyr.'

Melissande felt a blush creep over her cheeks. 'Monk hardly ever remembers to feed himself, even when someone puts the meal on the table in front of him. I'm fine. You should head home. Good work today. But tomorrow make sure you find out *something* about the gels. I don't want to be stuck in that place a minute longer than is necessary.'

After Bibbie departed, Melissande ate her pork pie — more pastry than pork, but it could've been worse — then spent an hour carefully writing up the day's events for the Wycliffe case file. By then she could hardly keep her eyes open.

'Right. Now I am going to bed,' she announced. 'What about you, Reg?'

'I'm off hunting,' said Reg.

Melissande held out her arm for Reg to hop on, then returned to the bedsit and stood by the open window. 'Have fun. Be careful. I'll see you in the morning. Don't let me oversleep.'

'Hmmph,' said Reg, sleeking all her feathers. 'I make no promises, madam. I'm a queen, not an alarm clock.'

With a snap of her wings, she flew into the night.

Melissande changed into her nightgown and crawled into bed. 'And I'm a princess, not a gel. But we do what we must in this cold, cruel world.'

On which thought, as Boris draped himself over her knees, she promptly fell asleep.

The next morning, as she trudged through more grim piles of paperwork and resisted the urge to throw her abacus across the room, she jumped to find Permelia Wycliffe standing beside her cubicle.

'Miss Wycliffe!'

'Miss Carstairs,' said Permelia Wycliffe, her tone indifferent. 'As Miss Petterly has stepped away from her desk I wish you to take these files down to Mister Ambrose Wycliffe in Research and Development.' She held out a sheaf of buff-coloured folders. 'Each one must be perused and initialled and returned to me, in person.'

Clever. Very clever. Wait for Petterly's morning tea break and pounce. She took the folders. 'Yes, Miss Wycliffe. At once, Miss Wycliffe.'

'Cor, aren't you lucky!' whispered Delphinia Thatcher, as soon as Permelia Wycliffe was safely out of earshot. 'Getting to go downstairs, Molly. All those handsome wizards. Have fun!'

Melissande swallowed a smile, just in case one of the other gels was watching. She did *like* Delphinia. The young woman was a bit like Bibbie — relentlessly cheerful. Determined not to let life squash her.

Blimey, I hope she's not the thief. That would be awful.

'What's the matter?' said Delphinia. 'You're not interested in handsome wizards?'

Melissande took a moment to make sure her blouse was tucked in and her hair tidy in its horrible bun. 'Oh. Well. I wouldn't say *that*,' she murmured, and left the office quickly before Miss Petterly returned.

CHAPTER ELEVEN

'Well, Dunwoody? Are we set?'

Gerald looked up from the gauges on the etheretic quantifier and nodded. 'Yes, Mister Methven. Gauges are reading at zero.'

Robert Methven, First Grade wizard, thirty-six years of age, graduate of Tenlowe's Private School of Thaumaturgics, no criminal record, no question marks in his Department file, second most senior wizard at Wycliffe's, turned back to the model prototype Ambrose Airship Mark VI and raised his hand.

'Very well then, Dunwoody. On three. One — two — *three*!'

As Methven pressed his thumb to the remote control for the prototype airship, Gerald flicked the switch on the etheretic quantifier. As he watched, the model quivered and began to gently bump up and down in its cradle. A moment later the needles on the quantifier began to flicker, reflecting the thaumic resonance within the prototype's experimental engine chamber.

'Readings, Dunwoody!'

'Four thaums, Mister Methven. Five — eight — thirteen — oh, dear.' He looked up. 'Twenty thaums, Mister Methven. Perhaps we ought to —'

'No, no,' said Methven, impatiently. 'We're still within the tolerances. There's no point pussyfooting around, man. This is a test, not a tickle.'

Third Grade wizards did not argue with their betters. Third Grade wizards were the equivalent of — of *clerks*, at Wycliffe's. They twiddled knobs and filed reports and fetched mugs of coffee for their superiors. They didn't, if they wanted to keep their job, contradict a senior wizard. Not even when that wizard was making a very big mistake.

And especially not when they're only pretending to be a Third Grade wizard and shouldn't be able to sense the thaumic imbalance in the experimental engine's central chamber.

Gerald held his breath and closed his eyes. Any second now. Any second. Three ... two ... one ...

'*Damn!*' cried Methven, as the lovingly constructed prototype of the Ambrose Airship Mark VI lurched free of its confining cradle and shot up to the rafters of the laboratory like a bullet.

'Yes, Mister Methven,' said Gerald, staring at what surely was about to become a very expensive pile of useless spare parts. 'Ah — is it supposed to be spinning like that, Mister Methven?'

The prototype Mark VI, all twelve shiny feet of it, had begun to revolve, bow chasing its stern, and was picking up speed even as they gaped.

'No,' said Robert Methven, slowly. 'No, I don't believe it is, Dunwoody.'

The shiny silver airship was glowing like a lantern now, the thaumic emissions from the experimental engine spilling into its empty interior.

Gerald felt his skin crawling. The wretched thing was going to blow. It was going to spectacularly explode and take half the roof with it, and possibly half the laboratory as well. Which meant all of Gerald Dunwoody and Robert Methven, probably. Unless they made a run for it right now, or said Gerald Dunwoody dropped his etheretic shield and obliterated his carefully manufactured cover with a spectacular display of thaumaturgic skill not —

'Bloody hell, Dunnywood! What have you done now?'

For the first time in his life Gerald was pleased to see Errol Haythwaite.

'Nothing, sir, nothing,' he said, taking the opportunity to grab Robert Methven by the arm and drag him to the very back of the lab, which was as far as they could get from the Airship Mark VI without actually leaving. 'I was only —'

'Looking to repeat your demolition of Stuttley's!' said Errol, flicking him a contemptuous glance. He was holding his gold-filigreed First Grade staff tightly against its jittery reaction to the airship engine's overcharged thaumic particles. 'You bloody cretin. Methven, what did I tell you about letting this imbecile within fifty feet of *anything* important?'

Methven pulled his arm free, and took a prudent step sideways. 'Ah — well — I needed someone to —'

'Bugger up the test? Well, good job, Robert. You picked the perfect man!'

'Sorry, Haythwaite,' muttered Methven, and took another step sideways.

'That's *Mister* Haythwaite to you, Methven,' snarled Errol, glaring up at the wildly spinning model airship. 'Now shut your trap while I save the day.'

Gerald and Methven watched, hardly daring to blink, as Errol pointed his staff towards the madly gyrating airship.

'Good lord, what's he doing?' muttered Methven.

'Trying to siphon off the excess tetrathaumicles created as a by-product of the engine's overheating,' said Gerald, without thinking. And when Methven goggled at him added, weakly, 'Um. Isn't he?'

'Yes … yes, of course,' said Methven. He was sweating, great damp patches staining the armpits of his white lab coat, beads of moisture rolling down his blanched face. He had a receding chin, and it was trembling. 'That's exactly what he's trying to do. Yes.'

And in fact not only trying, but succeeding. Amazing. There was so much randomly generated thaumic energy inside the airship now it was glowing like a brazier, angry and bright red. The gold filigree on Errol's staff was glowing too, hotter and hotter. It had to be almost too hot to hold, it had to be on the point of scorching him, surely, and he wasn't wearing gloves, but Errol didn't let go. Instead he was using an incredibly complicated and hard-to-balance etheretic-reversal incant to suck the excess thaumic energy out of the airship and into the staff where it could be stored temporarily.

Gerald shook his head. Errol was loathsome, an arrogant, insufferable, nasty piece of work ... but there was no denying it. He was also a bloody brilliant wizard.

The experimental airship's spinning slowed. Slowed further. Its furious colour began to fade. Now sweat was pouring down Errol's face, which was twisting with the pain of his efforts and his blistering hand.

'I say, Errol!' shouted Methven, entirely forgetting his manners. 'You ought to stop now, that staff is going to implode!'

'It's fine,' Errol grunted, his chiselled jaw clenched. 'I know what I'm doing. And that's *Mister Haythwaite* to you, pillock!'

Gerald held his breath again. Methven was right, not even the kind of First Grade staff the likes of Errol could afford was strong enough to absorb much more raw thaumic energy. Remembering what had happened at Stuttley's, remembering the catastrophic devastation caused by those overcharged First Grade staffs, he stepped forward and tentatively touched Errol on the sleeve.

'Errol — Mister Haythwaite — it can't take any more.'

Errol wrenched his head round to glare at him with bloodshot eyes. 'Did I ask for your opinion, you little maggot?'

'No, but that doesn't mean I'm wrong. The airship's stabilised, sir. Now get that staff out of here before it overloads!'

Cursing, Errol looked up at the vanquished Ambrose Mark VI prototype then stared at his staff. Its filigree was starting to melt, an ominous blue haze rising above the tracery.

'Damn you, Dunwoody,' said Errol, and ran.

Methven bolted after him, and Gerald, first hastily deactivating the prototype altogether and leaving it to plunge willy-nilly to the laboratory floor, hustled in their wake.

Wycliffe's lofty-ceilinged Research and Development laboratory was laid out like a horse-barn, two long rows of individual labs separated by a wide aisle, which was crammed full of desks and chairs and benches and sinks. At one end of the building was Mister Ambrose Wycliffe's office, and at its opposite end was the Emergency Pit, where thaumaturgically compromised articles were thrown for later, carefully supervised disposal.

Shouting at the top of his lungs Errol ran full pelt for the Pit, blue-hazed staff raised above his head.

'Get out of my way — shift your bloody arse, you fool — move — move — move — *move*! Don't just *stand* there, get the Pit open, *now*!'

Startled wizards scattered before him. Someone made a dive for the Pit's double doors and hauled them open. Errol turned sideways as he ran ... adopted the lanky, long-legged lope of a javelin thrower ... threw back his head on a roar of pain ... and speared his staff down into the Pit.

'Shut the bloody doors, you fool!' he bellowed at the helpful wizard — Monaghan, one of Wycliffe's Second Graders.

Monaghan obeyed. As the doors slammed shut Errol triggered their protective shielding hex then staggered to a halt.

'Good job, I say, good job,' Methven was panting, shoving his way through the stunned crowd of wizards. 'Well done, Err — Mister Haythwaite! Are you all right, old ch — sir?'

Gerald, his heart stuttering, prudently hung back. Errol had dropped to his knees, the fingers of his left hand gripping his right wrist very tightly, his pale, sweaty face a grimacing mask of fury. He held up his right hand, and the other wizards gasped to see the livid, blood-filled blisters on its palm and fingers.

'Do I look all right to you, Methven?' he snarled. 'Where the *hell* is Dunnywood, I'm going to —'

And then the floor heaved under their feet and the Pit's hexed doors buckled and the air beneath the high roof of the R&D division shivered, as Errol's caged First Grade staff surrendered to metaphysical inevitability and exploded.

'*Where is he?*' shouted Errol, lurching to his feet. 'Show your bloody face, Dunwoody, if you dare!'

Reluctantly abandoning the shelter of his muttering, whispering colleagues, Gerald shuffled into view. *Oh dear. Oh no. I don't think this is what Sir Alec meant by keeping a low profile.*

'I'm here, Mister Haythwaite.'

'And why is that, Dunwoody?' Errol ground out, his eyes slitted. '*Why* are you here? Why are you *anywhere*? First you blow up Stuttley's. *Then* your new employer breaks his neck hunting. And *now* here you are trying to wreck Wycliffe's. You're a *menace*! You're a one-man walking disaster! *Everything* you touch turns to *shit*!'

'Ah — actually, Mister Haythwaite, that's not quite —' Methven started to say.

'Did I ask *you*, Robert, you — you *turtle*?' said Errol, turning on him. 'Did I invite *you* to express your ignorant opinion? Did I —'

'What in the name of all things thaumaturgical is going *on* here?' demanded an unimpressed baritone voice from the back of the crowd. 'Would someone kindly *explain* this fracas?'

Mister Ambrose Wycliffe, lured out of his den by all the excitement.

Gerald and his colleagues turned towards the man Sir Alec had characterised as *decent enough, but not a patch on his father* —

and nearly fell over. Because hovering behind Mister Ambrose Wycliffe, the very image of sober prosperity in his black three-piece worsted morning suit, was — was —

Melissande?

What? What? What was *she* doing here?

Melissande seemed just as shocked to see him as he was to see her. Mouth dropped, she slid her prim glasses down her nose and stared at him over their rims, dumbfounded. Clutched to her black-bloused chest — lord, that was an ugly outfit! — was a pile of buff-coloured folders.

Then her expression changed to a warning, which gave him just enough time to duck aside as Errol Haythwaite thrust his way past to confront Mister Ambrose Wycliffe.

'What's going on, sir, is that you've hired the most useless, incompetent and downright dangerous Third Grade idiot in the country ... if not the entire world. If you'll accept my recommendation, sir, you'll get rid of him. Right now.'

Ambrose Wycliffe frowned, making his untrimmed bushy gingery grey eyebrows bristle. He looked a lot like a middle-aged basset-hound: sagging jowls, a wrinkled brow, and deeply dark brown, mournful eyes. 'What? Who? Who are you talking about, Haythwaite?'

Gerald exchanged looks with Melissande, sighed, and raised his hand. 'He's talking about me, sir,' he said, as his colleagues prudently retreated from the direct line of fire. 'Gerald Dunwoody.'

Ambrose Wycliffe squinted. 'Never heard of you. Never laid eyes on you before, have I? How long have you been here?'

'Three weeks, sir. I was sent by Truscott's, sir.'

'The locum agency?' Ambrose Wycliffe chewed at his lip. 'They sent you?'

'Yes, sir.'

Ambrose looked at Errol. 'You must be mistaken, Mister Haythwaite. He can't be *that* bad. Not if Truscott's sent him.'

Errol seemed nonplussed. 'You use a locum agency, Mister Wycliffe?'

'For the unimportant staff, yes,' said Ambrose Wycliffe. 'I only hand-pick the important people, like you. Don't have time to waste on functionaries. Leave that to Truscott's.'

'Oh,' said Errol. 'Well, sir, did Truscott's happen to mention that *this* functionary is the man who blew up Stuttley's last year?'

Ambrose Wycliffe blinked, then took a step forward, squinting again. His extravagant ginger muttonchop whiskers quivered. '*What*? That was *you*, Mister Dunwoody?'

Gerald managed not to look at Errol. Managed to keep his lowly Third Grade obsequiousness intact. Just. *Damn, Sir Alec. I told you this would happen.*

'The investigation did exonerate me, Mister Wycliffe,' he murmured humbly. 'Mister Harold Stuttley was found culpable on a number of regulatory violations. The official government conclusion was that the unfortunate destruction of the factory wasn't my fault.'

'I see,' said Ambrose Wycliffe. He laced his pudgy fingers over his substantial belly and frowned more deeply, rocking slightly on his heels. 'Still. That doesn't explain what's going on now. And what *is* going on now? I'm still waiting for someone to tell me. What the *devil* was that explosion?'

'*That*,' said Errol, teeth glittering in a sabre smile, 'was Mister Dunwoody destroying yet another of my First Grade staffs. He seems to think I have an unlimited supply. And I can I assure him that I don't. Not of staffs ... and not of patience, or tolerance for unmitigated incompetence. I'm sorry to have to tell you this, Mister Wycliffe, but he's managed to wreck the latest Ambrose Mark VI prototype as well.'

A cry of dismay went up from their audience of goggling wizards. The Mark VI was their latest, greatest project. A great many hopes and dreams — not to mention jobs — were pinned to its experimental fuselage and propulsion design.

Ambrose Wycliffe's florid face paled, dramatically. 'Is that true, Mister Dunwoody? Have you wrecked the Mark VI prototype?'

'No, he hasn't, Mister Wycliffe,' said Robert Methven. 'I'm sorry, Mister Haythwaite,' he added, coming forward. 'I don't mean to disrespect you or contradict you or interfere in any way. It's just that Mister Dunwoody wasn't working on the Mark VI. I was, as per Mister Haythwaite's request. I just asked Mister Dunwoody to step in and read off the gauges on the etheretic quantifier while I fired the new engine up for a burst. That's all. I swear, he didn't lay so much as a finger on the airship prototype.'

'Maybe not,' muttered Errol. 'But he looked at it. And that's more than enough where Dunnywood's concerned.'

'Now, now, Mister Haythwaite,' said Ambrose Wycliffe, indulgently. 'I can see that what we have here is an unfortunate clash of personalities. But since it's been proven by an official government investigation that Mister Dunwoody here *didn't* blow up Stuttley's, and our Mister Methven has manfully owned up to his part in this unfortunate business and exculpated Mister Dunwoody, I don't think it's fair to sack the chap. Not when he comes with a Truscott guarantee and I won't get a refund on my deposit.'

'It's your decision, sir, of course,' said Errol, his voice dangerously clipped. He turned on Methven. 'So you're saying I'm responsible? The Mark VI is my ship. I designed it. I invented the new thaumic conversion matrix. So if there *is* a problem with the engine the fault is mine? Is that what you're saying?'

Gerald cleared his throat. 'No, Mister Haythwaite, I think what Mister Meth—'

Errol seared him with *such* a look he actually stepped back. '*Shut up*, Dunwoody,' Errol hissed. 'Didn't you get the memo? Third Grade wizards should be seen and not heard.'

A ripple of unease ran through the gaggle of watching wizards, and as though Errol's vicious retort was some kind of signal — or warning — they began to drift away to their desks and benches and labs.

Ambrose Wycliffe unlaced his fingers from his belly and stepped to Errol's side. Sliding an arm around his shoulders he harumphed, understandingly. 'Mister Haythwaite, your distress does you credit. We all know how dedicated you are to the success of the Ambrose Mark VI. But you must not allow yourself to become overturned. We are still in the experimental stages, are we not? These little setbacks are bound to happen.'

'That's very generous of you, sir,' said Errol, stiffly. 'I appreciate your understanding.'

Ambrose Wycliffe shook his head. 'Not at all, not at all. Why, I could tell you stories of prototype disasters in my late father's day that make this look like a mere peccadillo. Don't forget, Mister Haythwaite, that this grand laboratory was my childhood playpen. I grew up with airships and I can assure you, when it comes to design teething troubles there is nothing new under the sun.'

Errol grimaced. 'Keep Dunwoody around, sir, and I promise you'll see it.'

'Ah, you're a witty man, Mister Haythwaite!' said Ambrose Wycliffe, jowls jiggling. 'And I do so enjoy the company of witty men. But I'm bound to remind you, sir, that I lost the Ambroses Marks II through V long before Mister Dunwoody arrived on the scene.'

'Yes, sir,' said Errol. 'Which is why you hired me, and why I'm determined we'll not lose the Mark VI as well. The future of Wycliffe's is riding on this airship and I'll do whatever I must to makes sure it succeeds.'

Ambrose Wycliffe's basset-hound eyes went moist. 'Dear boy,' he said, his voice choked with emotion. 'Come. Let's inspect the prototype, shall we, and see what's to be done about salvaging it.

And then you'd better have some ointment put on those blisters. Very nasty. Mister Methven —'

Robert Methven, who'd been hovering uncertainly on the sidelines, jumped. 'Mister Wycliffe?'

'You'd best accompany us. Perhaps you can shed some light on precisely what happened, and how we can avoid an encore performance.'

Swallowing convulsively, Methven shoved his hands in his lab coat pockets. 'Yes, Mister Wycliffe,' he whispered.

As Ambrose Wycliffe and Errol took a step towards the Mark VI lab, Melissande squeaked. 'Ah, sir?'

He swung round. 'Eh? What? Oh, it's you. Permelia's gel. What did you want?'

Gerald wondered if Ambrose Wycliffe knew how close he was to having his toes stamped on. 'Miss Wycliffe requests that you read and authorise these purchase orders, Mister Wycliffe,' she said in the most alarmingly and uncharacteristic self-effacing murmur.

'What?' said Ambrose Wycliffe and held out his hand. Melissande passed him the first folder, which he flipped open. 'What's the woman fussing at me now for?' He snapped his fingers impatiently. 'Pen!'

Robert Methven snatched up a pen and inkpot from a nearby bench. 'Here you are, sir.'

Without even bothering to read what he was authorising, Ambrose Wycliffe dashed his signature at the bottom of all seven purchase orders.

'There you are, gel,' he said, vaguely staring past Melissande's left ear. 'And tell Permelia not to send you back here again. If she wants me to sign things, tell her to send that office-boy. She knows I don't allow gels in the lab. They interfere with the thaumaturgical ether. I expect when we look into it we'll find it's *your* presence that caused the Mark VI prototype to fail. Oh yes — and tell Permelia I'll not be in for dinner tonight. I'm dining with Calthrop at the Club.'

Melissande thawed just enough to nod. 'Yes, Mister Wycliffe. I shall do that, Mister Wycliffe. Thank you, Mister Wycliffe.'

As Ambrose Wycliffe swept a still icily furious Errol away to the other end of the building, Robert Methven took a moment to replace the inkpot and pen on the bench. Gerald waggled his eyebrows at Melissande then touched the First Grade wizard's elbow, very deferential.

'Ah, sir? Thank you for speaking up on my behalf.'

Methven gave him a distracted look of intense dislike. 'Wasn't personal, Dunwoody. I'd sack you too, for damned cheek. But it's not good form to blame an inferior who can't defend himself. Now get back to work. Find some filing or something. Don't touch *anything* remotely thaumaturgical, is that clear?'

He nodded. 'Yes, Mister Methven.'

'*Pssst!*' said Melissande, crept up behind him. 'Gerald, what the —'

'No, no, not here,' he muttered, keeping an eye on the other wizards who'd returned to their own tasks. They hadn't noticed anything but that wouldn't last long. Robert Methven, scuttling to catch up with Errol and Ambrose Wycliffe, was looking back over his shoulder, his expression still unfriendly. 'Employee garden. Lunch at one.'

'But my lunch is at —'

'Then change it. Goodbye.'

And he hurried off before Melissande could try arguing with him. Because she would, he just knew it. He was convinced the first word she ever spoke was 'but'.

He spent the next two and half hours trying not to speculate on the reason for Melissande's presence at Wycliffe's, and collecting test result sheets from the other labs and the wizards working on various projects at their benches, and filing them.

Well, surreptitiously reading them and *then* filing them, making mental notes of anything that might even remotely have to do with his reason for being undercover at Wycliffe's in the first place.

He paid particular attention to Errol's results. Errol, who'd joined Wycliffe's not quite a month after the Stuttley's debacle. Who'd taken one look at him, his first day at the firm, and simply ... erased him from the landscape. It had actually been a little frightening: the contempt. The desire for him to disappear. To not exist. Today had been the first time Errol had acknowledged his presence.

Which is fine. It's quite suited me, really, all things considered. Only — why did his bloody staff have to explode?

Monaghan and another Second Grader — Phipps — were cleaning out the Pit now, decontaminating it and neutralising the overcharged thaumic particles. He sighed. It was a shame he'd not get the chance to inspect what was left of Errol's staff, or the stricken experimental Ambrose Mark VI. He'd rather like to know why the prototype engine had exploded. From what he could tell it was sound ... and ingenious. No two ways about it, Errol had a definite flair. And then the clock struck one and he stopped filing. He'd have to think some more about that later. Now it was time to meet Melissande for lunch.

Doing his best to appear nonchalant, he entered the employee garden and found an empty bench to sit on, located a convenient distance from the other dozen or so staff who'd been allotted a one o'clock lunch. Luckily there was a goodly amount of conversation going on that would cover nicely anything he and Melissande had to say to each other. Pretending interest in his packed lunch of fish-paste sandwich, iced cupcake and an apple, he kept a sideways eye out for her arrival.

And there she was, tit-tupping along in that dreadful long

black skirt — *lord*, that was a hideous outfit! — looking so regal, so self-possessed, so *Melissande*, it brought a lump to his throat. Six months and more since he'd seen her? It felt like six years ... and at the same time, six minutes. She was Monk Markham's young lady and, after the events of New Ottosland, the next-best thing he had to a sister.

Disdainfully she wandered by him, ever-so-artfully letting the book she was carrying with her lunchbox slip to the grass. He dived for it and held it up.

'Excuse me, Miss! Oh, Miss? I think you dropped this.'

Turning, she looked over her glasses-rims and down her nose at him. *Just* the way she'd looked when he stepped out of the portal in her brother's palace. It was all he could do not to smile like a loon.

'I beg your pardon?' she said, deliciously snooty. 'Did you address me, sir?'

He stood. 'Yes. Yes. Gerald Dunwoody at your service, Miss. You dropped this,' he said, thrusting the book towards her.

As she reached out to take it from him he heard a soft, muffled thud close by. And then one of Permelia Wycliffe's other gels shrieked and pointed.

'Oh! Oh! How *awful*! A bird just dropped *dead*, right out of that *tree*!'

Melissande whipped round, book in hand, and stiffened. 'Oh, blimey,' she muttered. 'Don't look now, but Reg just fainted.'

Reg? *Reg* was here? He turned and yes, there she was, his very own Reg, toes turned up on the mulched garden bed beneath an ornamental fig-tree.

Reg.

'Don't worry, Miss!' he said to the horrified gel, now being supported by two of her equally horrified friends. 'I'll take care of it. Don't you distress yourself, or come any closer. For all we know it could be diseased.'

'*Gerald —*'

He pulled a hush-up face at Melissande and rushed over to the garden bed where Reg lay unmoving. Heart thudding so hard he felt sick, he dropped to his knees beside her and stroked a fingertip down her limp wing.

A cold cave. A dead bird. A cruel hoax that he'd believed.

'Reg,' he whispered, trying not to move his lips. 'Reg, can you hear me? Reg, it's me. Gerald. Come on, Reg, *please*, open your eyes.'

Two of her toes twitched. Then she coughed, faintly, and half-raised her closed eyelids. 'Gerald? Gerald, is that really you?'

He choked down a laugh, relieved almost to tears. 'Yes, it's really me.'

Both of her eyes popped wide open. '*Gerald Dunwoody*!' she said, out of the side of her beak. 'How long have you been back in town? And what do you mean, not coming to see me? I've been worried sick about you, sunshine. I'm going to have your guts for garters, I'm going to hang your silver eyeball as a New Year's decoration, I'm going to —'

He snatched her up and kissed the top of her head. 'I'm fine,' he whispered. 'I miss you. Fly home. We'll talk properly when this job's done, I promise.' Standing, he tossed her high into the air. Watched her scramble her wings into action and flap away squawking her outrage like a fishwife.

'Oh!' cried Permelia Wycliffe's gel. 'I thought it was dead.'

'No, Miss,' he said politely, offering her a bow. 'Merely a slight case of sunstroke. No harm done.'

The gel and her companions returned to their seat, and Gerald rejoined Melissande. 'How very gallant of you, Mister Dunwoody,' she said, still haughty. Behind the prim glasses her eyes were sparkling.

'Not at all, Miss — ah —'

'Carstairs. Molly Carstairs.'

Really? 'A pleasure to make your acquaintance, Miss Carstairs. Perhaps you'd care to join me for lunch?'

'That would be very pleasant,' said Melissande, dropping to the bench. 'Reg is all right?' she added softly.

'She's fine. Cross as two sticks, but fine,' he replied, equally softly. 'Melissande . . . what are you doing here?'

'*Molly*. And I was about to ask you the same question.'

'I'm on an assignment for the Department.'

She smiled, a very chilly curve of her lips, just in case they were being watched. 'Fancy that. *I'm* on an assignment for the agency.'

He stared. 'Who hired you?'

'Permelia Wycliffe. Who hired you?'

'Nobody.' In case anyone was watching, he pulled his fish-paste sandwich out of his lunch sack and took a bite. 'I can't talk about it.'

'You can't talk about it *here*,' she said, opening her lunch box and taking out her own sandwich. It was ham and tomato, and looked singularly unappetising. The tomato had turned the bread all pink and soggy. 'But you are going to talk about it, Gerald. There's a very good chance you and I could help each other.'

'I doubt it,' he replied, and laughed as though she'd just said something amusing. 'In fact, I think you should forget all about your job for the agency. Things around here might get a little . . . tricky . . . soon.'

'You mean you might try and blow something up?' she replied, and put her soggy sandwich back in the lunch box with a refined shudder. 'That would have all the charm of novelty.'

He turned his shoulder to the rest of the garden and squinted his blind eye meaningfully. 'I'm not joking, Melissande. You've no idea what's brewing around this place.'

'Not right now, no,' she agreed. 'But I will as soon as you tell me. And Reg, and Bibbie. Tonight. At Monk's new establishment. Nine o'clock sharp. Don't be late.'

What? 'Monk's *what*? What are you talking about?'

She reached into his lunch sack and took out the cupcake. The icing was luridly green: it had been the only one left in the baker's that morning. 'You haven't heard? Great-uncle Throgmorton died and left him two houses,' she said around a mouthful. 'He's living behind the Old Barracks in Central Ott. Twenty-four Chatterly Crescent.' She finished the cupcake, pulled a napkin from her lunchbox and daintily dabbed her lips clean. 'You know where that is?'

'I'll find it,' he said, then shook his head. 'That is, when I can find time to visit him. Which won't be tonight, or any night soon. Mel —'

'Say you'll come or I'll make a scene,' she said, dropping the napkin back in her lunchbox. Her lips were smiling, but her eyes were deadly serious. 'Do you have any idea how worried Reg has been about you? She's in such a state she's practically moulting.'

A pang of guilt spiked through him. 'Yes, well, I'm sorry about that, but —'

'Not as sorry as you're going to be if you're not at Monk's place by nine,' she said, and stood. 'Say you'll be there. Go on. Say it.'

Oh, lord. Sir Alec was going to roast him alive. *Or he will if he finds out. So I'd best make sure he never does.* 'All right,' he snapped. *Bloody woman. I must have been mad thinking I was pleased to see her.* 'Nine o'clock. But don't get your hopes up, thinking I'm going to give you chapter and verse about my assignment, because —'

'Well, Mister Dunwoody, thank you so much for the pleasant chat,' she said loudly in her best royal highness voice. Holding her lunchbox like a shield ... or a weapon. 'We must do it again sometime. Good day.'

Dumbfounded, he watched her mince out of the garden, collecting other black-clad gels along the way. Honestly, she was *impossible*. Hah. Miss Carstairs his — his *arse*. Melissande was born a princess, she'd die a princess, and live every damn day in between a princess.

Just like Reg.

Moulting? Reg had been so worried she was *moulting*? Oh no. She was so vain about her feathers ...

Flayed with remorse, appetite ruined, he put his lunch back together and returned to the R&D complex. Three steps through the side door a hand clamped mercilessly around his upper arm.

'A moment, Dunwoody. I want a word with you.'

Gerald felt his heart plummet. *Errol, Errol. Do we have to do this now?* Making certain to keep his expression suitably chastened and subservient, to keep the surge of anger from showing in his eyes, he didn't fight but let Errol drag him sideways into a convenient corner.

'Ah — Mister Haythwaite — I really am sorry about your staff,' he muttered, keeping his gaze lowered. 'I'll purchase you a new one, you have my word. It might take some time — my salary, you know — but —'

Errol, whose blistered hand had been bandaged, let go of him and leaned close. As always when he was displeased his immaculate accent had sharpened to a lethal edge. 'What are you playing at, Dunwoody? What exactly are you doing here?'

Abruptly, he decided to drop a little of his Third Grade act. He'd never bowed and scraped to Errol at the Wizards' Club and, assignment or no assignment, he saw no reason to completely humiliate himself.

'I'm earning a living,' he said, meeting Errol's savage stare calmly. 'Just like you.'

Errol ignored that. 'What really happened in New Ottosland, Dunwoody? The *truth*. Because I don't for a moment believe King Lional broke his neck hunting. Not if *you* were anywhere around.'

Damn. Trust Errol to let his petty vindictiveness spoil everything. They'd been doing such a good job of avoiding each other, too. And now the time had come for him to lie through his teeth.

Please, please, let me be a good liar.

'I'm sorry you feel that way, Errol,' he said carefully. 'But there's nothing more I can tell you. King Lional's death was a horrible accident. One in which I was *not* involved. And I'm back in Ottosland because the new king didn't want a royal wizard. That's the truth, but whether you choose to believe it or not is entirely up to you.'

Errol was staring at him, his contempt mixed with — with *confusion*? 'There's something ... different about you, Dunnywood. I don't know what — I can't put my finger on it — but it's there. I can feel it. And I'll work out what it is, I promise you that.'

Oh, *really* damn. Errol wasn't supposed to be able to sense anything through the anti-thaumic shield. *He really is a bloody good wizard.* 'I'm sorry, Errol. I don't know what you're talking about. Please, I need to get back to work.'

'*Work*.' Errol fairly spat the word. 'You're a waste of space, Dunwoody. Truscott's must have a screw loose, sending you somewhere like this.' He leaned close again. 'Ambrose is too stupid to see that you're a menace. A bloody great disaster waiting to happen. He won't sack you. At least not yet. But until he does you stay away from me and my projects. I don't want you so much as sharpening one of my pencils, is that clear? And if I catch you even *looking* at the next Mark VI prototype I will tear you limb from limb. Is *that* clear? Do you believe me? *Gerald*?'

Without waiting for an answer, Errol stalked away.

Gerald looked after him, shocked to realise he was actually shaken. Errol was positively overflowing with venomous hatred. He didn't understand it.

At least he could wait till I've proven he's the traitor Sir Alec's looking for.

'Mister Dunwoody!' called Robert Methven, standing beside a crowded lab bench. 'If you've quite finished wasting Mister Wycliffe's time, there are several pieces of apparatus here that need to be cleaned.'

Gerald closed his eyes, took a deep breath and rearranged his expression into the epitome of suitably Third Grade submission.

'Yes, Mister Methven,' he said. 'Coming, Mister Methven.' And he hurried forward to do Robert Methven's bidding.

This bloody assignment can't end fast enough.

CHAPTER TWELVE

'Blimey,' said Monk, standing at his open front door. 'Gerald?'

'Oy,' said Gerald, glancing over his shoulder at the late night emptiness of Chatterly Crescent. 'Not so loud. Voices carry. Can I come in?'

'Come in?' said Monk, still staring. 'Oh! Of course, mate. Sorry.'

As Monk retreated he stepped over the dilapidated but still stately house's threshold into the old-fashioned vestibule, which was — to put it very kindly — sadly shabby.

'What are you doing, Markham, answering your own door?' he demanded. 'Isn't a place like this meant to come with a butler?'

'It did, but — well. Long story,' said Monk, pushing the front door closed again. 'And anyway, I don't really need ancient retainers hobbling about the place. They just get in the way. Gerald, I can't *believe* you're standing in my vestibule.'

Grinning, he accepted Monk's back-slapping embrace. 'Neither can I. Mind you, I can't believe you've *got* a vestibule. *Two* vestibules. Greedy sod.'

'How did you hear about that?' said Monk, stepping back. His eyes widened in alarm. 'Gerald, are you telling me Sir Alec's got —'

'Don't be stupid. Melissande told me.'

Monk frowned. 'Melissande? When did you run into Melissande?'

'She hasn't said?'

'I haven't seen her. Or heard from her,' said Monk. 'She, Bibs and Reg are up to their eyeballs in a job.'

He pulled a face. 'I know. At the Wycliffe Airship Company. That's where we bumped into each other.'

'*You're* at Wycliffe's?' said Monk, eyebrows shooting up. 'Since when?'

'Look, I'll tell you what I can,' he said, shrugging out of his overcoat, 'but isn't there somewhere we can talk in comfort?'

'Sure, sure,' said Monk, then took the coat and slung it onto the vestibule's coat stand. 'Sorry. Come into the parlour.'

Gerald followed Monk down the creaky-floorboarded hallway into another shabby room made cheerfully warm by a leaping fire in the fireplace. A laden drinks trolley stood beside the curtained window and a lopsided table took up half of one wall. Two overstuffed armchairs were angled to take comfortable advantage of the warmth. The armchairs were both so elderly their leather had crazed and cracked, leaving tufts of horsehair stuffing poking out like bristles on a caterpillar. A faded, cosy two-seater sofa completed the room's furnishings.

'What?' he said, looking around. 'No experiments all over the floor? Don't tell me you've reformed.'

Grinning, Monk collapsed into the nearest armchair. 'Who, me? Perish the thought. No, they're all over the attic.'

He grinned back at his friend and sat himself in the matching chair. 'Of course they are.' Typical Markham. 'It's good to see you, Monk.'

'And you. I notice that colour-incant's worn off. How's it working out?'

He rubbed his silver eye. 'Good. It's good. I had to tweak it a bit — I'm putting in a ten-hour at Wycliffe's. Can't afford it fading at an embarrassing moment.'

Monk sat up. 'You what? You tweaked one of my incants? Oooh, Gerald, you shouldn't have done that. You might explode your eyeball.'

'Ah ... no,' he said, gently smiling. 'I don't think so.'

'Oh,' said Monk, slumping again. 'You know, for a moment there I forgot.' He shook his head, bemused. 'Huh. You tweaked one of my incants. There's a turn-up for the books.'

Was he jealous? No. Not Monk. There wasn't a jealous bone in his friend's lanky body. He was just ... adjusting.

And he isn't the only one. I'm still not used to it and I've spent the last six months finding out what I can do.

'It'd be good if you could tweak it a bit more, though,' he added. 'Whatever I did to it makes my eye itch.'

'Sure,' said Monk. 'Remind me to take care of it before you leave. So. If you're at Wycliffe's, that means ...'

'Yeah. I'm in the field. My first assignment.'

A slow smile spread over Monk's thin, anarchic face. 'You passed the final test.'

'Well, I didn't *fail*.'

'Eh? What's that supposed to mean?'

'You tell me and we'll both know,' he said wryly. 'Hey, I don't suppose the bar's open, is it?'

'Been one of those days?' said Monk, sympathetic.

'You have no idea.'

Monk uncoiled from his armchair. 'Brandy all right?'

'Bless you, my son,' he said, letting his head fall back. 'Brandy is perfect.'

Monk frowned as he sloshed a generous amount of liquor into the first of two balloon glasses. 'Wycliffe's,' he murmured. 'Hang on ... hang on ...' His eyebrows shot up, and he stared.

'Errol Haythwaite's working for Wycliffe's. Very smartly turned down the Aframbigi post and … oh. Oh, Gerald. Tell me you're not.'

Trust Monk to leap to the right conclusion. 'Not what?'

'Tell me you're not investigating Errol Haythwaite!'

Careful now, careful. 'I'm not investigating him specifically.'

Monk poured the second brandy, brought both glasses back to the armchairs and held one out. 'But …'

He took the brandy and swallowed a generous mouthful. The smooth bite of fermented apple flamed across his tongue and down his throat, and he smiled.

'That's good stuff.'

'Yeah, well, Great-uncle Throgmorton was a cranky old sod but he kept a good cellar,' said Monk, sitting again. '*Gerald*. What's going on?'

'Look, I'm not trying to be coy, honestly,' he said, 'but can we wait till the girls get here before I spill the beans?'

Monk frowned. 'The girls?'

Terrific. 'They didn't warn you?'

'Warn me about what?'

'That we'd all be meeting here tonight. At nine.'

'No,' Monk sighed. 'They didn't.'

'Probably they wanted it to be a surprise.'

'Or Mel was just being regal again.' Monk grinned. 'She does that, you know.'

'I had noticed,' he said. 'So … you and Melissande … you're still …'

'Yes, Gerald,' Monk said primly. 'We are still — what's the word? Courting?'

'I think so. Though when it comes to Melissande it must be like courting disaster.'

'It has its moments,' Monk admitted. 'I'm busy. She's busy. And she's the next in line to a throne, at least until Rupert marries and has a sprog. She's genuine working royalty, mate. That kind of complicates things.'

'Only if you let it, Monk. Unless, of course, you're looking for an excuse.'

'An excuse?' said Monk, startled. 'To do what — exit stage left? No. No. I just — I don't know — I'm not good at this, Gerald.'

'Not good at what?'

'You know. *Romance*,' said Monk, harassed. 'I don't think I know what women *want*. What do they *want*?'

He swallowed laughter, along with more brandy. 'How would I know? Ask Reg. She'll tell you — at length.'

'Yeah …' Monk half-drained his glass. 'So. How are you? What's it like being a janitor? Answering to Sir Alec? Is he as tricky as everyone says?'

Instead of replying, Gerald stared into his brandy balloon. He shouldn't answer. In fact, he should leave. He'd been told, point blank, not to make contact with his friends.

And I didn't. I tripped over them, which is hardly my fault. The damage — if there is damage — is done, so there's no point in me leaving. Besides, I wouldn't be doing my job if I didn't find out what Melissande and Reg are up to at Wycliffe's.

As for Monk, well, he wasn't just anybody. He was the best friend who'd risked everything for him in New Ottosland and had come damn close to losing his career on the strength of it. Monk Markham knew the same secrets as he did. Which meant, in his book, they were practically the same person.

Which means the rules don't apply.

Besides, he really needed someone to talk to about … stuff. And he had questions that only Monk could answer.

He looked up. 'Remember in New Ottosland when you said to me, "*Don't do it*". Not unless I really wanted to? You meant the janitoring, right?'

Monk considered him warily. 'Yeah. Right.'

'So what did you know that you weren't telling me?'

'Gerald ...' Monk shoved out of his armchair and returned to the drinks trolley, sloshed more apple brandy into his glass and brought the bottle back with him.

He held out his own glass. In the fireplace the flames crackled merrily, devouring wood. 'Don't mess me about, Monk. I really need to know.'

His expression derisive, Monk topped up the brandy balloon. 'That was fast. I thought it'd take longer.'

'Thought what would take longer?'

'For Sir Alec to mess with your head. Seven months? That must be some kind of record. From what I hear, most agents are good for a couple of years at least.' He sat down again and plonked the bottle of brandy by his feet. 'So. What happened?'

Gerald put down his drink. 'In a minute. First tell me why you tried to warn me off.'

'Why d'you think?' Monk muttered, brooding into his glass. 'Because I'm your friend.'

'That's not an answer.'

Monk took a much bigger mouthful of brandy, swallowed, spluttered and made a big production out of coughing and wheezing and banging his chest. Playing for time. Trying to avoid the truth.

'*Monk* ...'

Monk sighed and gave up. 'I had a cousin. On my mum's side of the family. Mordecai Thackeray. He was a fair bit older than me, and he was an agent too. Not for your lot. He worked for a different Department. Same business, though. Dirty tricks. Investigations. Swimming in the political sewers. Domestic, not international. Though sometimes the two spheres ... well, they crossed paths. They still do from time to time.'

Gerald nodded. He'd been fully briefed on the government's other thaumaturgical investigative branch. Been made blisteringly aware of their not-always-cordial relationship and warned he was never to tread on their toes. Not unless it couldn't be helped. The last thing Sir Alec wanted was junior janitors muddying already murky waters.

'And this Mordecai,' he said. 'What happened to him?'

Shifting in his armchair, Monk glowered at the fire's leaping flames. 'Short answer? He died.'

Oh. 'And the long answer?' Not that he was sure he wanted to hear it. Not with a look like that on Monk's face. Monk was the most resilient, the most stubbornly uncrushable man he knew. For him to look stricken ...

But if I'm going to be this — this person, this agent, then I have to know. I never want to be taken unawares again.

'I don't have a long answer,' said Monk eventually. 'At least, not one I can swear to. I was only a nipper when we lost Mordy. Bibbie was still in nappies. And the folks never talk about it.' He brooded into his glass of brandy. 'I think Aylesbury knows something. I think he overheard something he wasn't meant to hear — but you know Aylesbury. If I asked he'd know it mattered, so he'd let himself be torn apart by wild dogs before telling.'

'Yeah,' he said. 'Tell me again how sad it is I'm an only child.'

Monk smiled, but his amusement was brief. 'The *official* story,' he continued, looking up after another long pause, 'is that Mordy contracted Assowary Fever and didn't run to the nearest hospital because he thought it was only a bad cold. By the time he realised he was wrong it was too late.'

'And *un*officially?'

'Unofficially — from what I've been able to glean and ferret and snoop and fossick — he was involved in a case that went spectacularly wrong. Good people died, another agent included. He blamed himself. And ... he didn't want to live any more.' Monk shrugged. 'But none of that's official. It's just me leaping to conclusions.'

Gerald rubbed a finger over the shiny spot on the knee of his trousers. 'Yeah. But you're good at that. So, what? You think that could be me one day?' A charming thought. But Monk was wrong. He'd never do it. Not to his parents. Not to Reg.

Monk swallowed more brandy, avoiding his gaze. 'Didn't say that.'

'*Monk.*'

'It's just, you remind me of him a bit, right?' said Monk, goaded. 'Like I said, I was only a nipper but I never forgot him. Mordy was a good man. He cared about things. About right and wrong and helping people who needed to be helped, no matter what it cost him. Looking back, I can see there was something sad about him. Something driven.'

Gerald felt his jaw drop. 'And you think that's *me*? You think *I'm* sad and driven? Bloody hell, Monk. Don't beat around the bush — you think I'm pathetic!'

'Not pathetic,' Monk protested. 'You just ... take things to heart. Like Mordy did.' He got up again and crossed to the fire. Stared down into the mesmerising flames. 'And if you are feeling a bit ... down ... no-one could blame you. Not after what you've been through.'

Gerald reached for his glass and knocked back the remains of his brandy in one swallow. 'Well, I'm not down. Right? I'm fine. I mean, I'm sorry about your uncle, but I'm not him.'

'No?' Monk swung round. 'Then what's the problem? And don't tell me there isn't one, mate, because I've still got two good eyes.'

Brought to it, suddenly he wasn't sure what to say.

'Hey,' said Monk. 'If you're worried I'm going to let something slip ...'

'No. Lord, no.' He shrugged. 'It's just hard to explain.'

'Explain what?'

'The final test.'

'What about it?'

'It was bloody peculiar, that's what!' he replied, flooded once more with baffled unease. 'Even now, Monk, I'm not sure how much of it actually happened. I mean, I *know* I got on a train in Central Ott. I know I got *off* the train in Finkley Meadows and a cart took me into the countryside and left me at the front gates of an obscure Department property. And I *know* I ended up drinking tea with Sir Alec and driving back to Nettleworth with him in a car. But everything that happened in between?' Another shrug. 'I can't explain it. It felt real. *Too* real. But I don't think it *was* real.'

Monk frowned at the hearth. 'How do you mean, not real?'

'It felt like a dream,' he said. 'Things happening that make sense at the time, even while a part of you knows they're impossible. You know?'

'Mmm,' said Monk, and gulped some brandy. 'Maybe. Did you, ah, ask Sir Alec?'

'Of course I asked Sir Alec! Sir Alec said it wasn't Department policy to discuss testing with agents.'

'Ah,' said Monk. Suddenly he was looking . . . uncomfortable. No, more than uncomfortable. He was looking *guilty*.

Gerald put down his empty glass. 'Monk? What's going on? Do you know something? If you do you'd better tell me.'

'Mmm,' said Monk. 'Well. This is bloody awkward.'

He stood. 'Awkward? What do you mean *awkward*?'

Now Monk's face was a picture of woe. 'I'm sorry, Gerald. I had no idea they'd use it. At least, not on you. They said they were exploring some new ideas. They said they were *considering* its application, maybe, sometime in the future. Once the kinks were ironed out.'

'*They* said?'

Monk winced. 'He said. Sir Alec.'

Sir Alec. Again, and at every turn. 'And what is it?'

'The *delerioso* incant,' Monk mumbled.

'Never heard of it.'

'No. Well, you wouldn't have,' said Monk, still mumbling. 'It's on the proscribed list.'

'The *proscribed* list?' He stared. 'Then how the hell did you —' Monk rubbed his nose. 'I invented it.'

'Of course you did,' he said, dazed, and sat down again. 'Enlighten me, Monk, before I punch you. Or worse.'

On a deep sigh Monk dropped cross-legged onto the fireplace's cindery hearth. 'What can I say? It was a stupid university prank. Something I dreamed up in second year. Back when I was smart enough to do that kind of thing but too stupid to realise it might backfire.'

'Oh, well, it's good to know things have changed,' he said, giving sarcasm full rein.

'Bloody hell, Gerald,' Monk muttered. 'I said I was sorry, didn't I? I'm telling you I *didn't know*.'

'Never mind the grovelling,' he retorted. 'You can save that for later. What the hell is a *delerioso* incant?'

'It was *meant* to be a bit of harmless fun,' said Monk. 'Good for a giggle, and embarrassing people you don't like.' His sharkish grin flashed, irrepressible. 'Worked a treat on Errol. He didn't show his face for a week after, stupid git.'

'*Monk.*'

'Oh. Yeah. Right.' Monk cleared his throat. 'The *delerioso* tickles the subconscious. Gets you reliving a dream, or a memory, as vividly as if it's happening right in that moment. You know, you *think* you're dancing with some bird on the last night of school but in reality you're making a fool of yourself in the quad waltzing with a broom. Stuff like that.' Monk couldn't help himself: he grinned again. 'So anyway, I tried it on Errol and *he* re-lived the time his mother dressed him in a sailor suit and it all got very ugly. The upshot was I got sent down for three weeks ...

and noticed by the Department of Thaumaturgy. They recruited me on the spot. Well, I *say* recruited but it was more like being strong-armed.'

'Like me,' said Gerald, slowly. 'How come you never mentioned this before?'

'Water under the bridge, mate,' said Monk simply. 'Turns out it was the right choice. I'm happy where I am. I do good work.'

'I don't know about *good*,' he said, feeling bitter. 'It's bloody *effective*, I'll give you that. Although …' He frowned. 'I was doing more than re-living memories. I was experiencing new things as though they were real.'

'Yeah. Sorry about that,' said Monk, wincing. 'They — he — Sir Alec — got me to kind of — you know — soup up the original incant. He said they were thinking of using the *delerioso* as an interrogation tool. A way of tricking villains into giving up vital information without having to — to —'

'Make them uncomfortable?' he suggested, with a savage delicacy.

'Well … yeah,' Monk admitted, thoroughly miserable now. 'Something like that. I thought it was a good idea. We find out what we need to know and nobody gets hurt in the process.'

'Yes, it's all very noble, really. So … what? I was your guinea pig?'

Monk rubbed his nose again. 'I suppose. Sir Alec's guinea pig, anyway.'

Bloody Sir Alec. Gerald reached for the brandy bottle beside Monk's chair. *Someone remind me to have words with him the next time we meet.* Not bothering with his glass, he swallowed deeply.

'I really am sorry, Gerald,' Monk said quietly. 'You know that, right?'

He shook his head. 'It's funny. I should've twigged you had something to do with it. There was this hex I had to break. Your fingerprints were all over it. Yours, and a bunch of other wizards.'

'They put that in?' said Monk, surprised. 'Huh.'

'Something else you were playing at?'

'Ah …' Monk's face coloured. 'Yeah. The hex Lional used to lock Mel in her palace apartments. Remember? I kind of … borrowed it, and gave it the old Markham touch.'

He swallowed from the bottle a second time then wiped his mouth on his sleeve. 'Speaking of Lional, he and I had an interesting conversation — courtesy of your *delerioso* incant. Congratulations. Your souping up efforts are a spectacular success.'

'Hell's bells,' said Monk, and dropped his head into his hands. 'Gerald, I'm sorry. I *swear* I didn't know what Sir Alec had planned.'

With exacting precision Gerald put down the brandy bottle, temper bubbling beneath the warm apple glow. 'And when I finished chatting with Lional I tortured someone to make them talk,' he added, feeling ruthless. The horror of those moments still hadn't receded. 'At least I thought I did.'

'*What*?' said Monk, his head snapping up. 'Gerald, I *never* —'

'His name was William. Sir Alec told me people were going to die if he didn't tell us what we needed to know. And because I thought it was real, I started to dismantle the shadbolt that was keeping him quiet. But he screamed and I couldn't finish. I walked out. And instead of failing me, Sir Alec offered me tea and sent me to Wycliffe's.'

The fire crackled merrily into the silence.

'It must've been the only test they could think of,' Monk murmured. 'Using your own strength, your own memories, against you. I mean, if you could break those gate-hexes … you did break them, didn't you?'

Gerald nodded, remembering the delight he'd felt at outwitting the great Monk Markham. 'Oh, yes. I broke them.'

'No-one at the Department could crack them, you know. The best First Graders in the country couldn't make a dent.

Bloody hell, Gerald. You're *good*.' And then Monk shook his head. 'I can't believe they used my *delerioso* against you. That's — that's bloody *wrong*, that is. They *know* we're friends. We're on the same side. You don't use team mates *against* each other.'

He felt his lips tug in a small, sardonic smile. 'Don't look now but the game's changed, Monk — and we'd better keep up. And don't forget ... it's all for the greater good.'

'Yeah, well, to hell with the greater good!' said Monk, bouncing to his feet. 'First thing in the morning, *first bloody thing*, I'm going to —'

'No, you're not,' he said tiredly, his bubble of temper abruptly burst by Monk's genuine distress. 'You're not saying a word about this to anyone. I'm not even supposed to be here. I wasn't supposed to breathe a syllable of what happened in Finkley Meadows. It's janitor business.' Picking up the brandy bottle again, this time he splashed a little into his glass. 'I just ... I didn't know .... I wasn't sure ...' He sighed. 'Well. At least I know it wasn't real. I didn't *actually* —'

'Gerald, you're not the villain here,' Monk insisted. 'Like you said, that wasn't real. It was a hypothetical situation. And *nobody* got hurt.'

'This time,' he whispered, and drained his glass. 'But what about next time, Monk? What happens when there really *is* a William, and a shadbolt, and innocent lives on the line? What do I do then?'

Before Monk could answer they heard a loud banging on the front door — just as the clock on the mantel struck nine.

Gerald pulled a face. 'That'll be the girls. We'd better let them in before they kick down the door.'

Monk, his expression still deeply troubled, didn't move. 'Hey, Gerald. You believe me, don't you? That I didn't know what Sir Alec wanted that incant for? That I had no idea he was going to —'

'Don't be stupid, Monk,' he said, and put aside his empty glass. 'Come on. They really are going to kick their way in.'

But Monk just stood there, hands shoved in his pockets, his frowning gaze fixed on the past.

'Well, it's about time, Gerald!' grumbled Melissande, marching into the vestibule with Reg perched piratically on her right shoulder. She'd changed out of the hideous black blouse and skirt into her familiar tweed trousers and a pale yellow blouse with a sensible coat on top. Not hideous, but not terribly flattering either. Just quintessentially Melissande. Her rust-red hair hung down her back in a plait. 'Bibbie was about to blast the door into matchsticks.'

Bibbie. *Emmerabiblia*. Closing her brother's front door behind her, Gerald felt his heart stutter. Lord, she was so incredibly, blindingly beautiful. Every time he saw her it was like being struck with a hammer.

She gave him a cheeky, dimpled smile. 'Hello, Gerald.'

'Yes, hello again,' said Melissande, looking him up and down. 'I have to say I'm a bit surprised you came. You didn't look at all a sure thing when I left you in the employee garden.'

He couldn't help smiling. She was so *tart*, like the best lemons. 'It'd take a braver man than me to refuse your gracious royal command,' he said, then shifted his gaze. 'Hello, Reg.'

Reg looked at the ceiling. 'I'm not speaking to you.'

'*Reg . . .*'

Monk stuck his head through the open parlour door. 'In here, everyone. If you two are going to fight you might as well do it in comfort.'

They trooped into the parlour, and Monk closed the door to keep the heat in. Melissande twitched her shoulder so Reg could flap to the back of the sofa, then graciously allowed Monk to slip off her coat and hang it on the door hook. Bibbie tossed her own coat on the floor then collapsed in one armchair, swivelling till she could dangle both legs over its arm. *Very* unladylike, and totally Bibbie. Melissande joined Reg on the sofa and Monk sat beside her, gently taking her hand in his. They hadn't spoken a word to each other but the look they exchanged was eloquent.

Gerald, hiding a smile, stood with his back to the fire. *So. Monk's really smitten, eh? I think this time he might be in trouble ...*

'I hope you appreciate all the effort we're going to, Gerald,' said Melissande. 'Meeting late so no-one will see you. I start at Wycliffe's at the crack of dawn, practically. I'm giving up precious sleep to be here.'

'You didn't have to,' he pointed out. 'You could've told me at lunch what you're doing at Wycliffe's.'

'With all those people around?' she retorted. 'Nonsense. We have to thrash this out properly, Gerald. For all I know we're working on the same case and I'm not going to have Witches Inc. shoved aside by the Ottish government.'

'The same case, Mel?' said Bibbie, sounding amused. 'Oh, I don't think —'

Melissande tilted her chin. 'It's possible! Stranger things have happened — and frequently to me.'

'I wouldn't worry,' he said dryly. 'I very much doubt Witches Inc. would be retained to investigate my case.'

'Oy!' said Reg. 'That's enough patriarchal superiority from you, sunshine. Witches are perfectly capable of solving mysteries of international significance, just like any common-or-garden, backstabbing, inconsiderate, selfish wizard you care to think of.'

Ouch. 'I thought you weren't speaking to me?'

'I'm not,' she snapped. 'I'm making a general observation to the room at large.'

Oh, *Reg*. 'You knew I'd be gone for a while,' he said quietly. 'You knew I wouldn't be able to contact you.'

'While you were off training, yes,' she retorted. 'But you're not training *now*, are you? You're *janitoring*. You're back in town and you never *told* us.'

'Because I wasn't allowed to, Reg.' He looked at all of them, his three dearest friends and Bibbie. Whom he knew a bit, through Monk … and would very much like to know better. 'Strict instructions from Sir Alec. If he finds out I've spoken to you he won't be happy.' *Which is putting it mildly.* 'And he *really* won't be happy when he finds out you three are investigating at Wycliffe's. What in the name of Saint Snodgrass are you *doing* there?'

'We could ask you the same question,' said Melissande. 'In fact, I think I will.'

'I asked first.'

She looked at him over the top of her glasses. '*That* is a particularly childish answer, Gerald.'

'Melissande, please. This is important. Just — tell me what's going on, all right?'

He was immediately treated to a tangled three-way tale of sprites and cheating pastry cooks and public unmaskings and exploding gooseberry sponges and a mystery thief with a penchant for nicking biscuits and sundry office equipment. When the riotous tale was told, and the girls finally stopped shouting over the top of each other, contradicting and complaining, he looked at Monk and shook his head.

'An interdimensional portal opener?' he said. 'Bloody hell, Markham. Only you.'

Monk tried to look penitent and failed, abjectly. 'What can I say? It was an accident.'

It was an accident. *They're going to be his last words, I just know it.* 'I take it you haven't told anyone … official?'

'Not yet,' said Monk, shaking his head. 'To be honest I don't know if I will. Once I calmed down and thought about it, I wondered if an interdimensional portal opener might not be a bit dangerous to have around.'

Melissande rolled her eyes. '*Now* it occurs to him. *After* he's let the interdimensional sprite loose on the world.'

'Hey,' said Monk. 'It got your agency out of financial hot water, didn't it?'

'But Monk,' said Bibbie, 'if you keep the IPO under wraps that means you won't get another article in *The Golden Staff*.'

'He'll survive,' said Gerald. 'And *I'll* forget I even heard about it . . . if *you* promise to forget it exists, Monk.'

'Yeah, yeah,' Monk sighed. 'I know the drill. Stop being such an old mother hen, mate.'

Reg nipped him on the ear. 'Oy. That's enough disparaging of mature female birds, thank you. And anyway, what you did was daft and you know it.'

'Ow,' said Monk. 'Fine. Sorry. The point is, Gerald, there's no need to fuss. I learned my lesson. No more interdimensional portal opening for me.'

'Okay,' he said, relieved. Monk might be a raving nutter, but once he gave his word that was that. 'Good.'

'And now,' said Melissande, 'it's your turn, Gerald. Why are *you* skulking at Wycliffe's?'

Damn. 'If I tell you on my honour, cross my heart and hope to get haemorrhoids that I'm *not* on the trail of a rascally biscuit thief, will you believe me and let it go? *Please*?'

Melissande looked at Reg, then Bibbie. 'Sorry,' she said, stubborn to the last. 'For all you know our biscuit thief could be — could be —'

'Diversifying,' said Bibbie brightly. 'They've gone so long without being caught they've been emboldened, and now they're — they're —'

'Upping the ante,' said Reg.

He sighed. 'No, girls. Trust me. They're really not.'

'You don't know that,' said Melissande, with another belligerent lift of her chin. 'How can you know that?'

'Because it's my job,' he said, striving for patience. 'Secret government agent now, remember?'

'That just makes you badly paid,' said Bibbie. 'Not infallible.'

'So, Gerald, what *are* you doing at Wycliffe's?' said Melissande. 'It's the dullest place imaginable. *And* it's well on the road to insolvency, if I'm any judge. And as a former prime minister of a practically bankrupt kingdom you'd best believe I am. These scooters and velocipedes and what-have-yous they're trying to flog are rubbish.'

He shook his head. 'Sorry. I can't tell you.'

Reg rattled her tail feathers ominously. 'Sauce for the goose, sunshine. If you don't give us chapter and verse about what you're up to, well, this Markham boy's still got his interdimensional portal opener around here somewhere. Fancy a little jaunt to the twelfth dimension, do you? With an extra helping of sprites?'

Gerald stared at them, feeling his frustration churn. 'Look, girls, I know you think I'm being a spoilsport but I'm only trying to protect you. In fact ...' He took a deep breath. 'For your own safety, I think you should tell Permelia Wycliffe you can't solve the case and get out of there while you still can. Because if you keep on poking around in that place you might accidentally poke the person I'm after ... and that could be dangerous.'

'Turn tail and run, you mean?' said Bibbie. 'Absolutely *not*! We're *witches*, not *shrinking violets*.'

Gerald shoved his hands in his pockets. 'That's not quite accurate. You're a witch, Bibbie, but as for your colleagues ... well, Melissande's a born organiser and Reg is a bird. Trust me, that's not enough this time. We're not talking hexed cakes. We're talking big trouble. And I don't want you three anywhere near it.'

Now they were all glaring at him. 'You — you — insufferable prig!' spluttered Melissande. 'Is that what they taught you on your Department training course? How to be an insufferable prig?'

'Steady on, Mel,' Monk murmured. 'He's only —'

She snatched her hand free of his. 'Don't you *dare* defend him to me, Monk Markham! Patting me on the head and telling me to sit in the corner like a good little girl? After *Lional*?'

Monk pulled a face, hands raised. 'Sorry, mate. You're on your own.'

Wonderful. He couldn't be handling this worse if he'd planned it. 'Look, that's not what I meant. I know you're brave, Melissande. You're *ridiculously* brave. You and Reg are the bravest women I've ever met. And Bibbie, you'd be just as brave if you had to be, I'm sure.'

Reg's eyes were glinting dangerously. 'That's right, sunshine. Keep on digging. Graves are generally six feet deep.'

He stared at them, despairing. 'Why won't you trust me when I say you shouldn't be there? *I'm* the one with the inside information. *I'm* the one working for the secret government Department that knows things. If anybody's being priggish here it's you, dismissing my expertise out of hand.'

The girls looked at each other. Then Bibbie shrugged. 'I hate to admit it but he's got a point.'

'Fine,' said Melissande, and folded her arms. 'All right, Gerald. You tell us *why* it's too dangerous for Witches Inc. to continue investigating at Wycliffe's . . . and we'll consider leaving.'

CHAPTER THIRTEEN

Gerald stared at her, silenced. *Why me?* 'Melissande, aren't you *listening*? I'm not *allowed* to tell you why.'

She sniffed. 'Then we'll just have to make sure we're on different lunchbreaks, won't we?'

'Don't look at me, mate,' said Monk, reprehensibly grinning. 'I want to know what's going on as badly as they do.'

'Oh, thank you very much,' he said bitterly. 'You're a big help, you are.'

'Hey,' said Monk. 'Whatever you tell us won't go beyond these four walls.'

'I *know* that,' he said, close to shouting. 'This isn't about me not trusting you, it's about the fact I'm working on something huge. If somehow I manage to mess things up by telling you about it, the consequences could be catastrophic.' He felt like tearing his hair out. 'Damn, this is a bloody disaster. With the girls involved suddenly everything's getting *complicated* — and you know what *that* means.'

'The girls are sitting right here, Gerald, in case you've suddenly gone blind in your other eye,' said Melissande. 'And they don't appreciate being treated like three pieces of furniture.'

'I don't care! I wish you *were* three pieces of furniture!' he retorted. 'Because then I could put you under lock and key and not have to worry about you getting in the way!'

She leapt to her feet. '*Gerald Dunwoody* — I am not a *foot stool*! Who the hell do you think you *are*, to stand there telling *me* what I can and can't —'

'Oh, put a sock in it, ducky,' said Reg, with a sigh. 'You won't get anywhere browbeating him. And all your shouting is giving me a headache.'

Surprised, Gerald blinked at her. 'Thanks, Reg. It's nice to know I'm forgiven.'

Reg looked down her beak at him. 'Did I say you were forgiven? Trust me, you're not.'

Of course he wasn't. It couldn't possibly be that easy. He frowned at the threadbare carpet, marshalling his thoughts. Trying to work out how much he could tell them ... what was safe ... what wasn't ... and came to a depressing conclusion. He either told them everything or nothing at all. And if he decided to tell them nothing, if he turned around and walked out of Monk's house right now, Melissande and Bibbie and Reg might end up paying the ultimate price. Because they wouldn't give up investigating at Wycliffe's. They wouldn't back down. They didn't know how.

Of course I could always just tip this into Sir Alec's lap. Leave him to deal with it. Sure, I could do that ... and lose their friendship forever.

Because Sir Alec really would put Witches Inc. under lock and key — most likely metaphorically but possibly in a literal sense. Either way they'd be shoved to one side. Treated like *gels*. Even though Reg hadn't been a *gel* for centuries, and Melissande ... well, Melissande had *never* been a *gel*. But Sir Alec would make no allowances for that, despite knowing the kind of women they were. Knowing they'd already proven beyond doubt they could be trusted.

And then there was Bibbie. She wasn't like Melissande and Reg. Hell, she might well be a genius, like Monk, but she was practically a slip of a girl. Not part of the New Ottosland mess, she'd never had to face the things that slithered beneath the world's stones, and feasted.

And I don't want her to face them. At least not while she's still so young. So innocent. Bibbie's why I'm doing this. Aren't I supposed to keep her — and everyone like her — safe?

But Reg would say that wasn't his decision. Reg would say it was Bibbie's choice, her right to risk herself if she wanted to. Hell, Monk would say the same thing and he was her brother. And what did that mean? That he was indifferent? Or that he cared so much for Bibbie that he was prepared to treat her exactly as he treated himself, and let her take the risks *he* took without a second thought?

Gerald sighed and looked at his friends. He could protect them or he could lose them . . . but he couldn't do both. Rightly or wrongly they weren't going to let him. And rightly or wrongly he wasn't prepared to give them up.

Oh lord. Sir Alec is going to kill me . . .

'Well,' he said slowly, 'it all started with the portal accidents.'

As Melissande sank back onto the sofa, Monk pulled a face. 'They weren't accidents.'

Sometimes I don't know why I bother. 'How do you know that? Have you been listening at the wrong keyholes again?'

'No,' said Monk, suspiciously self-righteous. 'I worked it out, that's all. Well, me and Macklewhite and Barkett worked it out. We were just tossing ideas around. Speculating, after the second incident, that maybe someone was messing with the portal matrixes. We even set up a couple of experiments to see if we could do it. You know. In our spare time.'

Fascinated, Gerald stared at him. 'In your spare time,' he murmured. *I wonder if Sir Alec has any idea . . .* 'And?'

'Oh, we managed it,' Monk said cheerfully. 'Wasn't easy, mind you. They've built about forty levels of security and redundancy and failsafes into the portal system, Gerald. Not only would you have to be bloody good, you'd have to bloody lucky to actually splotz one.'

'Well, someone was both,' he said. 'More's the pity.'

'But — but that's just *wicked*,' said Bibbie, eyes wide. 'I mean, people have been hurt. *Badly* hurt. Why would someone do an awful thing like that?'

'Ha,' said Reg, still perched on the back of the sofa. 'That's easy. First question any good investigator asks is *Who benefits*?'

'Or,' said Gerald, his brain newly stuffed with all that training, '*Who loses?*'

'You mean who's been hurt by the growing popularity of portal travel?' said Melissande.

'Smart girl I've got here,' said Monk, and kissed her hand. Melissande blushed: seemingly Monk wasn't the only one smitten.

Gerald nodded. 'Yes. In the three years since it was introduced, portal travel's become commonplace and very popular. It's had a major impact on the way people get around.'

'Fewer cars and carriages,' said Bibbie. 'Reduced rail services. And —'

'Hardly any airships,' said Reg. 'There was a time I couldn't fly a mile without bumping into one. Mind you, they did come in useful when I felt like resting my wings. Except of course then I could never find one going my way. Typical. I remember once —'

'Reg,' said Gerald, and pulled an apologetic face. 'If we could just stick to the topic ...?'

She sniffed. 'Yes. Well. What I was *about* to say is I'm guessing that once the public realised they wouldn't go up in a puff of smoke if they used a portal, the bottom fell out of the airship business. Am I right? Of course I'm right. And while fashions change, people don't. I remember when steerable hot-air balloons first came in — all the carriage and wagon-makers went into a decline. There were riots, you know.' Another sniff. 'Bit before your time, of course.'

'Just a bit, yes,' he said, grinning. 'But the point's sound. Three years ago Wycliffe's was Ottosland's premier airship company, having put the other two out of business. People who know about these things fully expected them to make it to world number one within a couple of years. And then came the major breakthrough in portal thaumaturgics, our government patented the incants and sold them internationally ... and overnight, everything changed.'

'Permelia Wycliffe said they'd endured some crushing disappointments,' said Melissande, frowning. 'I suppose this is what she was talking about. The collapse of their domestic *and* foreign markets.'

'So what you're saying is, Gerald, someone at Wycliffe's is trying to scare people away from using the portal system?' Monk chewed his lip. 'By unravelling the matrixes? That's a bit bloody drastic, don't you think?'

Very drastic. But — 'Desperate people do desperate things, Monk.'

'Well, yeah, obviously, but why now? Like you said, public portals have been around for three years.'

'Maybe whoever's doing this thought portals would be a passing fad,' said Bibbie. 'Maybe they thought there *would* be accidents and then people would go back to using airships. Maybe they kept hoping they wouldn't have to do something so awful as wrecking portals and hurting people. And they kept putting it off, and putting it off, and hoping things would go back to the way they were. And they didn't.'

She really was a very sweet girl. Mad as a hatter, just like her brother, but sweet. Gerald smiled at her. 'I suppose that's as good an explanation as any.'

'Wait a minute,' said Melissande, sitting up. 'Orville Wycliffe, the company's founder, died a year ago.'

Gerald nodded. 'And his son Ambrose took over the firm. We know.'

'*Huh*,' said Melissande, scowling. '*Ambrose*. I tell you, Gerald, he's bloody lucky I'm not Bibbie or I'd have fried him where he stood today. "*Gels interfere with the thaumaturgical ether.*" I'll give him ether, the insulting old frog.'

He had to smile. 'Yes, well, Ambrose is a bit old-fashioned.'

'Old-fashioned *and* incompetent,' she said. 'Ever since he got control of the company he's tried to diversify it, with spectacularly unimpressive results. From what I can tell its scooters and velocipedes and jalopies are *hopeless*. They practically fall apart if you sneeze on them. If Ambrose thought he was going to save the business that way he was sadly mistaken.'

'Then it's obvious, isn't it?' said Monk. 'Ambrose Wycliffe's your villain. He's trying to get his company back in the air by sabotaging the portal network.'

Gerald shook his head. 'I wish it was that straightforward, but it's not. We looked at Wycliffe's financials and, yes, they are shaky, but business incompetence isn't proof of a crime. We also looked at Ambrose himself, very hard, but he's squeaky clean. There's not a shred of evidence connecting him to the portal accidents. If there was then trust me, we'd have found it.'

Melissande cleared her throat. 'What about Permelia?'

'*Permelia*?' Gerald stared. 'No. It's not her, either. And yes, we *did* look into the possibility,' he added as she opened her mouth to argue. 'The Department is perfectly aware that women can be criminals too. But she's as squeaky clean as her fiscally inept brother.'

'So really,' said Monk, 'all you've got against Wycliffe's is a suspicious-looking coincidence. As far as you and Sir Alec know the portals are being sabotaged by some anti-thaumaturgic nutter out to save the world from the dangers of meddling with etheretic particles. And that's even if it *is* sabotage. I mean, me and Macklewhite and Barkett could've been wrong.'

'No, you're not wrong,' Gerald sighed. 'There were some trace thaumic signatures left after the last incident that can't be explained away by the existing portal matrixes or as a by-product of the random thaumic fluctuations caused by normal portal operations. It looks like some very powerful hexes were used to pull the portals apart.'

'In that case,' said Bibbie, 'can't Monk also be right about who's responsible? Everyone knows what those anti-thaumaturgical people are like. Quite dotty, the lot of them. Or jealous because they can't hex themselves out of a wet paper bag.'

'I wish he was right,' he said. 'Because then this would be over. But we know for a fact that nobody in the anti-thaumic movement is behind the portal sabotage.'

'Ah,' said Monk. 'You've got agents on the inside?'

He pulled a face. 'All I can tell you is there's only a handful of wizards worldwide capable of using the kind of thaumaturgy we're dealing with ... and shady enough to try.'

'And none of them belongs to an anti-thaumic group?'

'No,' said Gerald. 'That's another dead end, I'm afraid.'

Monk drummed his fingers on the arm of the sofa. 'This shady wizard. You've got a name, haven't you?'

'There's someone we're looking at, yes,' he admitted.

Monk's eyes widened. '*Errol*?'

Bibbie sat up. 'Really? *Really* Errol?' She clapped her hands. 'Oh, that would be too perfect!'

'Who's Errol?' said Melissande.

Bibbie made a rude noise. 'Errol Haythwaite. Tall, dark and handsome, yes, but *such* a plonker.'

'Did you say Haythwaite?' said Melissande. 'I know that name. Gerald, does she mean that horrible wizard today who —'

He nodded. 'Yes. Him.'

'You've met Errol?' said Bibbie, surprised.

'No. At least, we've not been introduced,' said Melissande, with fastidious distaste. 'But I caught him in action at Wycliffe's this afternoon. As you say, Bibbie, the man's an utter plonker.'

'Worse,' said Bibbie. 'He's the kind of First Grade wizard who thinks Third Graders should be rounded up and set adrift on barges in the middle of the nearest ocean. Rich, of course. His sort always are.' She wrinkled her nose. 'Whenever we meet at swanky parties he always tries to look down my dress. I think he thinks I should be swooning all over him. I *know* he'd like to marry me because of the important people Father knows.'

Monk was staring at her, his mouth open. 'What? He tries to look down your *dress*? How come you never —'

'Because I'm perfectly capable of squashing a bug like Errol Haythwaite without assistance,' said Bibbie airily. 'Besides, he and Aylesbury are chummy and you know what Aylesbury's like. Honestly, Monk,' she added, seeing he was still upset. 'Errol knows better than to push his luck with me.'

'All right, Bibs. If you say so.' He turned. 'But Gerald — look, fine, so Errol's a plonker. You'll get no argument from me about that. But it doesn't mean he's behind the sabotaged portals.'

Gerald shrugged. 'We think he's connected. Through another wizard, whose thaumic signature has a few things in common with the one we found at the last accident site. He's already raised a few eyebrows in the past. Nothing's been proven, it's just ... suspicions, but smoke and fire. You know how it goes. Given what's at stake we can't afford to ignore the possibility. So Sir Alec put me into Wycliffe's on a watching brief.'

'And have you seen anything?'

He shook his head. 'Not yet.'

'What about this eyebrow-raising wizard? Has he got a name?'

'Haf Rottlezinder.'

Monk's jaw dropped again. '*Rottlezinder*? Are you sure?'

'Yes.'

'Blimey,' Monk muttered. 'I knew a Haf Rottlezinder. Third year at university. He came over from West Uphantica as an exchange student. He was generally touted as a thaumaturgical prodigy. Stayed with —'

'Yes. We know, Monk,' said Gerald, meeting his friend's gaze steadily. 'With Errol. And from what we've been able to learn, he and Haf got to be very good friends.'

'And that's your connection?' said Monk, incredulous. 'I got to be friendly with Rottlezinder too. Does that mean you're looking sideways at *me*?'

He tried to smile. 'Come on, Monk. Sir Alec's been looking sideways at you for *years*.'

But Monk ignored that. Beside him, Melissande tightened her hold on his hand. 'Sorry, Gerald, it's got to be a stupid coincidence. Errol's a tick, but he's not — not —'

'Not what, Monk? A saboteur? An attempted murderer? Or at the very least mixed up with one?' He felt his temper stir. 'Why not? Because his family's rich and influential and he's a wizard Grand Master? Because even though you loathe him you went through university together and that means you belong to some kind of wizardly brotherhood? Because he's *one of us*?'

'Don't be a bloody idiot,' Monk retorted. 'That's got nothing to do with it. It's just I know Errol and I'm telling you, Gerald, this isn't his style. He's got no *reason* to —'

'Actually, he does,' he replied. 'Errol's got a lot invested in Wycliffe's. He's head of Research and Development and this new project he's working on, the Ambrose Mark VI, could put his name up in lights on the international stage. But *only* if the public loses confidence in portal travel, bringing back the age of the airship.'

'You have to admit, Monk,' Melissande said softly. 'It does make sense.'

Monk tugged his fingers through his hair. 'I don't know, Gerald. It sounds pretty far-fetched to me, Errol and Haf Rottlezinder in cahoots to bring down Ottosland's portal system and return Wycliffe's to its glory days. I mean, what's in it for Haf?'

'Money,' he said. 'Errol's rich enough to make it more than worth Rottlezinder's while.'

'True,' Monk admitted reluctantly. 'All right then — where's your evidence? Besides the fact they knew each other at university?'

Trust Monk to find the weak spots in the Department's argument. 'We haven't found any yet. But that doesn't mean we won't.'

'I don't understand,' said Melissande. 'If you're so sure this Haf Rottlezinder is behind the portal incidents, why don't you bring him in for questioning?'

What a shame Melissande was no less astute than Monk. 'We can't.'

'Because he's in West Uphantica? But I thought your Department had all kinds of international extradition arrangements?'

Abruptly tired of standing, Gerald dropped into the other armchair. 'We do.'

'Hang on,' said Monk. '*Is* Rottlezinder in West Uphantica?'

'He was.'

'But he's not now? You mean you lost him?'

'Well done,' said Reg. 'That's the kind of competence we're looking for in a secret government Department.'

'No, he's *not* lost,' he said, giving Reg a look. 'We just don't have a definite location for him at the moment.'

'Gerald, that means you lost him,' said Bibbie. 'How terribly careless of you.'

'So what happened?' said Monk. 'I'm guessing nothing good.'

Gerald frowned at his interlaced fingers, remembering the look in Sir Alec's eyes when he'd come to this part of the mission briefing. 'One of our best men was sent in to extract Rottlezinder, quickly and quietly. It ... didn't work out. Rottlezinder had already gone — and he left a nasty little surprise behind him.'

'The fatal kind?' said Monk.

Looking up, he nodded. 'I'm afraid so.'

Now Monk gave Bibbie a vaguely disquieted glance. As though he were having sudden second thoughts about his little sister getting mixed up with this kind of ugliness.

'Forget it, Monk,' Bibbie snapped, glaring. 'I'm staying. Try and push me aside and I'll tell Uncle Ralph about the Mushtarkan diplomat's cousin and the —'

'*Hey!*' said Monk, sitting bolt upright. 'You can't do that! We had an agreement, remember?'

Gerald looked at Melissande. *The Mushtarkan diplomat's cousin and the what?* She shrugged; either she didn't know or she was protecting Monk.

'I remember everything,' said Bibbie, smiling dangerously now. 'I *especially* remember how you promised you wouldn't interfere in any of my cases.'

'But this isn't your case,' he retorted. 'It's Gerald's.'

'And Gerald is perfectly happy for me to stay.' She turned. 'Aren't you, Gerald?'

Oh, thank you so very much, Emmerabiblia. He looked at Monk, apologetic. 'I think it's a bit late to get cold feet now.'

Monk knew when he was beaten. 'Fine,' he muttered. 'But if you stub your toe, Bibbie, don't come crying to me afterwards.'

'Look, I'm sure it's very sad this agent died,' said Melissande, as the Markhams exchanged incendiary glares. 'And I hope he didn't have a family that's grieving for him. But, Gerald, his death doesn't actually prove what you're saying, does it?'

He shook his head. 'Unfortunately not. And the incant Rottlezinder used to cover his tracks was comprehensive. All it left behind was a great big smoking hole in the ground. If there was evidence connecting him and Errol, it went up in flames along with everything else. And no. Crawford didn't have a family. Just . . . us.'

It felt odd saying that. Those two words suddenly seemed to put him on the other side of a line. Them and us. *You* and us. He didn't like it. It made him feel horribly . . . *alone*.

'Hey,' said Monk, noticing. 'There's more than one kind of *us* in the world, mate. Don't you go forgetting that.'

Sometimes it was quite alarming, how well Monk could tell what he was thinking.

'I know,' he said, dredging up a smile. 'Would I be telling you lot any of this if I didn't?'

'Why's your Department involved anyway?' said Monk, fingers drumming again. 'It's a domestic matter, isn't it? Shouldn't Mordy's old outfit be handling the investigation?'

'Ah,' said Gerald, wincing. 'That's a bit of a sore spot actually. They looked at the first incident and ruled out any hanky-panky. Turned the case over to the Transport Department's safety committee. But Sir Alec had a feeling so he reached out to an old chum who kept him apprised, and when Rottlezinder's name came up he grabbed the case with both hands. Of course *now* the other mob's screaming blue murder, accusing us of breaching jurisdiction.'

'Well, they would, wouldn't they?' said Monk, derisive. 'All that egg on their faces. Stupid bastards. As if jurisdiction matters when lives are at stake.'

'Yeah, well, try telling them that.'

'So,' said Monk. 'Rottlezinder's the saboteur, Errol's the

brains behind the scheme, and you're at Wycliffe's to find the evidence to prove it. Is that it?'

'That's the theory,' he agreed.

Monk nodded slowly. 'Well, it's a reasonable working hypothesis, I suppose. *If* you accept Errol's that far gone. But Gerald — why did Sir Alec pick you for the Wycliffe job? No offence, mate, but you're so wet behind the ears you're practically dripping. And given one agent's been murdered already, wouldn't they want an experienced man behind the wheel?'

He shrugged. 'Sir Alec couldn't get anyone else into Wycliffe's at such short notice. There weren't any vacancies for a First or Second Grader in the R&D lab. But Ambrose goes through Third Graders like shaving cream because the work's so bloody stultifying . . . and Errol makes our lives hell.'

'Poor Gerald,' said Bibbie, scowling, and reached over to pat him on the arm. 'Having to take orders from the likes of Errol Haythwaite when you can run rings around him as a wizard.'

'Oh, it's not so bad,' he said. 'And it's not as if being treated like something you'd scrape off your shoe is a novel experience. *Actually*, being a Third Grader is coming in quite handy. I mean, it's true I don't get to work on any important projects but I do get to poke my nose in pretty well everywhere, even if it's only to play canary in the coal mine and clean up after the important work gets done. And *that* gives me plenty of scope for snooping. It's like being a housemaid. Nobody notices the poor bugger stuck cleaning out the test tubes.'

Despite all his concerns, Monk unleashed another of his anarchic grins. 'Errol can't be too happy about it. Having you peering over his shoulder must be getting right up his sinuses.'

He remembered the look on Errol's face after the failure of the Mark VI's experimental engine. Remembered the way Errol had gripped his arm, so furious. 'You could say that.'

'Hmm,' said Monk, thoughtful. 'Maybe that's another reason why Sir Alec sent you in there. To rattle Errol.'

'Why would Sir Alec think that strategy could work?' said Melissande.

'Because what he doesn't know about people isn't worth knowing,' said Monk. 'And he'll use anything or anyone to get what he wants. I'll bet he knows Errol used to like using Gerald as a verbal dartboard. *And* that Errol was furious about losing his precious custom-designed First Grade staff when Stuttley's went up. I'll bet he's betting that if Gerald can throw Errol far enough off-stride he might make a mistake.'

'*If* he's in cahoots with this Haf Rottlezinder,' said Reg. 'That's not been proven. Your precious Sir Alec doesn't even know where that bounder's stashed himself.'

'No, but we'll find him,' said Gerald. 'We have to. The Department of Transport's keeping things low-key, not blabbing to the press, but it seems the sabotage is working. People are going back to airships for domestic and international travel. Who knows? A few more "accidents" and the public might lose all confidence in the portal network. It could easily collapse.'

'Which means Wycliffe's would be saved,' said Melissande. 'Which brings us back to *who benefits?*'

'And there's no denying that's Errol,' said Bibbie. 'It all fits.'

They looked at each other as the clock on the mantel ticked slowly towards midnight and the logs in the fireplace collapsed into glowing coals.

'It's a bit awful, really, isn't it?' said Melissande eventually. 'Because *really*, what would help you to catch this Errol Haythwaite — or whoever's responsible — is another portal accident.'

Gerald nodded glumly. 'I hate to say it, but ... yes.'

'Except Monk's right,' she added. 'Catching your quarry's not important. Not compared to the public's safety. The Department of Transport should shut down the portal network until you find whoever's behind this. What if there is another attack? What if people just aren't hurt next time? What if they *die*?'

As if he hadn't already thought of that. But what was it Sir Alec had said to him, back in New Ottosland?

In war there are always innocent casualties. It's regrettable but unavoidable. The sooner you come to terms with that the better.

'The other agents Sir Alec's got working on this are very good,' he said. 'We'll find Rottlezinder before anyone else gets hurt.'

Melissande snorted. 'You mean you *hope* you will. But hope isn't good enough, Gerald. Hope doesn't save lives. Actions save lives. And lack of action costs them.'

She stared at him, so accusing, and he stared back. Crowding Monk's parlour, the ghosts of those ninety-seven New Ottoslanders who'd perished because of Lional. Because of him.

Stabbed with guilt, he shoved out of his armchair. 'Look. I'm as worried as you are that more innocent people might get caught up in this. But we need Rottlezinder and Errol — or whoever he'd working with — to think they're safe. And we can't afford to start a panic.'

'Who said anything about starting a panic?' she retorted. 'You say it's for an equipment review. That won't worry people, it'll reassure them.'

'Perhaps, but it would also be disruptive, causing a great deal of distress and delay ... and almost certainly would send our villains back into the shadows to wait until the fuss died down so they could strike again.'

'Which means what, exactly? You're going to do nothing?' she demanded, leaping up to face him. 'Gerald, that's — that's *wrong*.'

'We're not doing *nothing*.'

'Then what *are* you doing?'

'Things I can't talk about,' he said, harassed. 'You'll just have to trust me, Melissande. We're doing our very best to keep the public safe *and* catch whoever's responsible.'

Melissande's chin lifted again. Behind the prim glasses her eyes were glittering. 'And what if your best's not good enough, Gerald?'

Oh, lord. I know that look. 'Melissande, you can't repeat a word of what I've said tonight. I've risked *everything* telling you this. I know it's hard but you *have* to sit on it.'

'She will,' said Reg. 'She's got her knickers twisted right now but they'll untwist when she's had a moment to think this through.'

'Don't you dare put words in my mouth!' snapped Melissande.

Tipping her head to one side, Reg chattered her beak. 'What, so you *are* going to talk out of turn? See Gerald sent to prison? Help these villains get away with their dastardly plan?'

'Mel,' said Monk, very quietly, and reached for her hand. 'You're right. It's a risk. But it has to be taken.'

'And you're happy about taking it?' she asked, her voice unsteady.

'No,' said Monk, his gaze intent on her. As though they were the only two people in the world. 'But we don't have a choice. And let's be fair … we're the ones who pressured Gerald into telling us this stuff. He didn't want to. We used our friendship as a lever. Are you going to beat him over the head with it too?'

'Monk's right, Mel,' Bibbie said in a small voice. 'We can't get Gerald into trouble. It wouldn't be fair.'

Melissande's lips trembled, just for a moment. Then she sat down again hard. 'I liked it better when we were chasing stupid interdimensional sprites and blowing up sponge cakes,' she said, her voice unsteady again. 'I think after this is over we should stick with *frippery*.'

Gerald perched on the edge of the armchair. 'Can you see now why I don't want you three anywhere near Wycliffe's? If Sir Alec's right and Errol is somehow involved with this portal business, things could get very ugly very fast. And I'd never forgive myself if any of you got hurt. You need to tell Permelia Wycliffe that you can't find her biscuit thief and get the hell out of that place while the getting's still good.'

'No,' said Melissande, and folded her arms, her momentary vulnerability squashed flat as a pancake. 'We are Witches Incorporated. Once we take on a job we see it through to the bitter end. If we walk out on Permelia Wycliffe now all the good we achieved by unmasking that *ridiculous* Millicent Grimwade will be wasted. We might as well shut up shop and — and get married. We won't be in your way, I promise. And who knows? There's a chance we could help you and your precious Sir Alec save the day.'

Damn. He turned to Monk. 'Come on. You have to help me here. This is your young lady we're talking about.'

Monk grimaced. 'Trust me, mate. If I try and stick a spoke in her wheel she won't be my young lady any more.'

'Well — well — what about Bibbie? She's your sister, your own flesh and blood! Are you going to let her put her life at risk? Or is it more important for you to cover your tracks over — what was it? Your whoopsie with the Mushtarkan diplomat's cousin?'

'Hey!' Monk protested. 'That's not fair!'

'And Bibbie's not at Wycliffe's,' Melissande added. 'She's holding the fort back at the agency.'

'But even if I *was* undercover at Wycliffe's,' said Bibbie, pink with crossness, 'I wouldn't leave either. What do you take me for, Gerald? Some lisping, chicken-hearted, lily-livered *gel*?'

'And what about your *future*?' he retorted. 'I'm assuming you want one!'

Melissande rolled her eyes. 'Oh, do stop trying to frighten us, Gerald. It won't work. If you want to be useful, concentrate on rattling Errol Haythwaite and finding this dreadful Rottlezinder person.'

Sighing, he looked at conspicuously silent Reg. 'What? You don't have anything to add?'

'No,' she said, staring down her beak at him. 'You're still digging your own grave perfectly well without my assistance, Gerald.'

He felt his jaw clench. 'Right. Fine. That's very helpful. Thank you.'

Melissande stood again. 'Excellent. And now *that's* settled we'll be on our way. It's despicably late and we've got an early start.'

She headed for the closed parlour door, Bibbie on her heels, coat dangling from one hand. Monk jumped up. 'I'll see you out,' he said, and snatched Melissande's coat from its hook.

'Fine,' Gerald called after them. 'Good. This is wonderful, girls. I'm glad we got this all straightened out.'

Instead of following her colleagues, Reg flapped from the sofa to the arm of the chair. 'Well,' she said, considering him with a bright eye. 'I did say it was going to be interesting, didn't I?'

Groaning, he slid into the chair properly and dropped his head into his hands. 'Oh, Reg. I don't mind interesting. It's impossible I'm having a problem with.' He lifted his head again. 'You look well. Are you well?'

She sniffed. 'Much you care if I'm well or not, Gerald Dunwoody.'

'Oh, *Reg* . . .'

'I'm fine,' she said gruffly. 'But you're looking peaked. Don't let that plonker Errol Haythwaite boss you about. *Or* that government stooge, Sir Alec. And don't worry about madam. I'll make sure she keeps her mouth shut.'

'Thanks, Reg,' he said, subdued. 'I'd really appreciate it.' He hesitated then added, 'I meant what I said in the garden, you know. I miss you. A lot.'

Monk stuck his head back in through the open parlour doorway. 'Reg, they're going.'

'I miss you too, sunshine,' said Reg, and flapped out of the room.

After she was gone, Gerald sat back in the chair and closed his eyes, his head pounding.

Oh, lord. Oh, Saint Snodgrass. Sir Alec is going to kill me.

CHAPTER FOURTEEN

'I think it's time you stopped sulking, madam,' said Reg, with a rattle of tail feathers. 'You can't tell me you don't understand about difficult choices. Every princess knows all about those. Well. Every princess worth her tiara, anyway.'

Melissande looked up from her horribly early breakfast of hard-boiled egg and glowered. 'I am *not* sulking.'

'All right, then. *Moping* ... with a snooty look on your face,' said Reg. 'Same thing.'

She sprinkled more salt on her egg. 'I don't want to talk about it.'

'Look,' said Reg, hopping down from the bedpost onto the bed, and strutting back and forth like a teacher in front of her class. 'What did you think was going to happen when Gerald agreed to work for that Sir Alec? Did you think he was going to be romping through alpen fields picking daisies? He's in a dirty business now, ducky. He's going to get *grimy*.'

'Fine,' she snapped. 'If he wants to get grimy that's his choice. But now there's a chance his grime is going to rub off on *me*!'

Reg stopped strutting and fixed her with an angrily gleaming eye. 'Like your grime rubbed off on him, do you mean? Back in New Ottosland?'

'That was different,' she muttered. 'I didn't know Lional was a raving lunatic.'

'Yes, well, I think we'll leave what you did and didn't know about Lional for another argument,' said Reg. 'Let's stick to this one for now, shall we?'

Shocked, Melissande stared at her. 'I don't — what are you — I *resent* that insinuation, Reg!'

'Yes, I'm sure you do,' said Reg, looking down her beak. 'Now as I was saying, it's time you pulled yourself together, madam. Gerald risked everything by telling us why he's at Wycliffe's. And since it has nothing whatsoever to do with why *we're* at Wycliffe's we are going to leave him alone to get on with things. We're still owed half our retainer, remember?'

'I don't understand why you're defending him,' she complained, ignoring that. 'I thought you weren't even *talking* to Gerald.'

'Ha!' said Reg. 'Didn't you know? I'm ambidextrous. I can be itching to kick his arse *and* yours at the same time.'

Abandoning her other egg, Melissande got off the bed and stalked over to the window. Gazing across the rooftops, she caught sight of something floating through the sky, flashing silver in the light of the rising sun. A Wycliffe airship.

Floating not on the air but on a river of innocent blood.

She turned. 'I'm not just worried about me, you know. About how *I'll* feel if there's another portal incident and more people get hurt or — or even die. What about Gerald?'

'Gerald's a big boy,' Reg said quietly. 'He knew what he was getting into when he jumped in the boat and started rowing with that Sir Alec. There's no such thing as a perfect solution, ducky. There's the best you can do at any given moment on any given day and that's *all*. Besides, we don't know what else that Sir Alec knows. If we go wading into the middle of this now, throwing our weight about just because we're royalty and we think we were born knowing better than everyone else, we could make things worse, not improve them. Is that what you want?'

'No, of course it's not,' she said. 'And I do *not* think I was born knowing better than everyone else!'

'No?' said Reg. 'Oh well. If you say so.'

Melissande choked down the impulse to scream. Reg was the most impossible, infuriating, *outrageous* —

'Hey!' Bibbie called from beyond the closed door. 'Is anybody here?'

She marched to the bedsit door and flung it open. 'Of course,' she said, stamping into the office. 'Where else would we be?'

'All right, calm down. There's no need to bite my head off,' said Bibbie, perching on the edge of her desk.

'Well?' she said, ignoring that. 'Did you bring the hexes?'

Bibbie rolled her eyes. 'No. I just slaved through the night finishing the last of them, and making sure they worked, and then left them behind at the boarding house for Mistress Mossop to find. She snoops, you know. I'm starting to think I might have to take Monk up on his house-sharing offer after all.'

'Good idea,' said Reg, gliding in from the bedsit to land on her ram skull. 'Then you can play chaperone and we can move in with you. I'd very much appreciate a bedroom of my own. Madam here snores like a combine harvester.'

Melissande gasped. 'I do *not*!'

'No?' said Reg. 'Then get Mad Miss Markham to leave a recording incant on in the bedroom and prove me a liar.'

'I don't care if Mel snores so loudly all the roof tiles fall off,' snapped Bibbie. 'Why would I want to share a house with two people who can't be bothered to say thank you after someone's slaved through the night on their behalf!'

Oh dear. Melissande exchanged a guilty glance with Reg and cleared her throat. 'Sorry, Bibbie. Did you really slave through the night?'

Bibbie stifled a yawn. 'I slaved through *two* nights,' she said, waspish. 'Because as you very well know my days have been spent slaving in here!'

'Yes, I do know,' she said in a small voice. 'And I appreciate it. We both appreciate it, don't we, Reg?'

'I'd appreciate a good night's sleep more,' said Reg.

'Oh well,' said Bibbie, with another of her lightning-swift mood shifts. 'I suppose it could be worse. I could be impersonating a Wycliffe gel.' She tipped her head, consideringly. 'Because honestly, Mel, that awful blouse-and-skirt ensemble doesn't get *any* more attractive with the passage of time.'

Melissande looked down at her black-clad self and sighed. 'It doesn't, does it?'

'And you being such a fashion plate I'm sure it's breaking your heart,' said Reg. 'But you need to glue the pieces back together again, ducky, because if you don't leave in the next five minutes you're not going to get into Wycliffe's early enough to set our trap. So haul out those hexes, Emmerabiblia, and let's get cracking.'

The single most irritating thing about Reg was that too often she was right. 'Yes, Bibbie,' she said. 'Quickly, explain what I'm supposed to do with them.'

Bibbie reached into the carpetbag she'd dumped on her desk and pulled out a smoked-glass jar with its lid screwed on. 'All right. So what you *do* is put a hex on any item you think is at risk of being stolen. Things that generally speaking stay put in the office, that don't have any business being taken *out* of it? Yes?'

Melissande pulled a face. 'That's easier said than done. You're talking about practically everything in the place.'

'Then choose the thief's favourite targets,' said Bibbie. 'Like Permelia's special biscuits. One hex for each item, and whatever you do *be careful*. Anyone who touches a hexed item with bare skin is sort of painted with a detectable thaumic signature, so whatever you do *don't* handle the hexes or the items you're marking without wearing gloves. Otherwise we'll be wasting a lot of time chasing you instead of our mystery pilferer.' She held out the jar. 'I made a hundred. Please don't tell me you'll need more than that.'

'A *hundred*?' she said, cautiously taking the jar. 'Bibbie, that must have cost a *fortune*. We may be getting more clients now but we can't afford —'

'Yes, well,' said Bibbie, beautifully blushing. 'You forget I'm a Markham, which means I'm not exactly poor.'

Ambushed by sudden emotion, Melissande blinked hard then cleared her throat. 'Oh, Bibbie. You used your own money? You shouldn't have done that.'

'What are you talking about?' said Reg. 'Of course she should. We each do what we can, ducky. You wave your tiara about, Little Miss Markham here empties her piggy bank and I — I —'

'Remind us of things we keep forgetting,' said Melissande. 'Especially when we don't want to remember them.'

As her eyes met Reg's she managed a very small smile. Reg sniffed, pretending not to understand, but her feathers ruffled ever so slightly.

'Anyway,' said Bibbie, and pulled a stoppered test tube out of the carpetbag. 'Once you've marked all the at-risk items, put one of *these* hexes on all the doors and windows. Gloves again or there'll be hell to pay. The two hexes react antithetically, you see. They're a lot like dogs and cats, they start snarling and spitting when they get too close to each other.' She grinned. 'Just like Monk and Aylesbury, actually. Probably that's what gave me the idea. Well. When *that* happens —' She handed over the stoppered test tube and pulled out a small blue crystal. '— this hex detector will light up. It's different from the first one we tried. Much more powerful, and operating on a different etheretic vibration.'

Melissande shook her head. 'That's marvellous, Bibbie.' And it was. Her inventiveness was amazing. 'Except — what happens if the thief triggers the hex detector when I'm not around to see it?'

'Well, if you're not on the premises then we're out of luck,' said Bibbie. 'But if you are — even if you're at lunch in the garden — the hex detector will still react. Its range is good enough, I made sure of that.'

'And if it does go off while I'm at lunch?'

'Then you'll have to find a way to sort of — wave it past everybody,' said Bibbie, shrugging. 'It'll go off again when it detects the presence of the triggered hex-marker on the guilty party.'

'Excellent,' said Melissande. She retrieved her own carpetbag from the bedsit, stowed the smoked-glass jar, the stoppered test tube and the blue crystal hex detector inside, and straightened. 'Is that it?'

'Not quite,' said Bibbie, and fished again in her own carpetbag. 'This is a confounder,' she added, handing over a small perfume spritzer. 'For the picking of locks both large and small. One tiny squirt in the keyhole will get you into Permelia's office, and anywhere else you need.'

'A confounder,' she repeated. 'I see. Ah — something tells me this is a gift horse I shouldn't look in the mouth.'

Bibbie grinned. 'And something tells *me* you're right. Illegal doesn't *begin* to cover it.'

'So is it one of Monk's little —'

'Monk?' said Bibbie. She sounded annoyed. 'Why do you assume Monk had something to do with it? Honestly, Mel, if you let being sweet on my brother turn your brains to slush I'm going to be very disappointed in you.'

'Sorry, sorry,' she said hastily. 'I wasn't thinking. So — *you* made it?'

Mollified, Bibbie tapped a finger to her nose. 'Gift horse, remember? No peeking allowed. And whatever you do, don't let anyone catch you with it. Since it's a liquid hex, at a pinch you really can pretend it's perfume but I don't recommend more than a single short spritz. Now shoo. So many hexes to distribute, not very much time.'

Melissande looked at Bibbie's inventive and illegal gift then closed her fingers around it. *Saint Snodgrass give me strength.* 'Fine. I'm shooing. But are you sure you'll be all right here on your own again? Maybe Reg should stay in the office today.'

'No, maybe Reg shouldn't,' said Bibbie, sharply. 'Do you mind? It's bad enough when Gerald and Monk get all patriarchal on me. Don't *you* start or I'll have an apoplexy. Besides, that chap in Births, Deaths and Marriages I sweet-talked is letting me have a peek at some personal information about Permelia Wycliffe's gels today, remember?'

Oh. 'Well, yes, but —'

'So probably, Mel, you should just wobble on your way, yes?' said Bibbie, with a dangerous smile.

'Yes,' said Reg. 'She should. And so should I. There's a tree in that employee garden with my name on it, unfortunately. But I'm telling both of you, duckies, I'm giving you fair warning: if that constipated male pigeon living in the roof of the R&D building tries *one more time* to look up my feathers those gels really *will* have a dead bird to scream about.'

Uncomfortably aware that time wasn't on their side, Melissande took a cab almost the whole way to the old Wycliffe estate on the outskirts of West Ott, where the family company did its business. After paying the driver, hiding her wince behind a polite smile, she half-walked, half-jogged along the quiet road, through the open gates with their enormous 'W's and decorative ironwork airships, under the not-quite-life-sized tethered model airship and up the long tree-lined driveway towards the administration office.

According to her watch it was a few minutes after half-past six. The early autumn air had a nip to it, and the birds were yet to finish their rousing dawn chorus. Somewhere over to the left, behind a carefully cultivated swathe of greenery, Permelia was hopefully still abed in the family mansion. Ambrose, too. Unlike Monk, he'd been able to persuade his unwed sister to run his household for him.

Holding her breath, praying this wasn't the one morning that Permelia or Ambrose decided to greet the dawn in person, or that one of Ambrose's wizards hadn't succumbed to a fit of dedication — or worse, that officious Miss Petterly wasn't doing some investigating of her own — she crept to the administration office's front door, fished Bibbie's highly suspect confounder out of the carpetbag and squirted some hex over the front door's lock. There was a subdued hum, a discreet flash of green light, and the handle turned without resistance.

'Oh, Bibbie,' she whispered. 'Promise you'll only ever use your powers for good!'

Biting her lip with nerves, she let herself in to the ground-floor reception area. It was hushed and empty, thank Saint Snodgrass. Miss Fisher, the receptionist, never arrived before eight. Climbing the stairs up to the office as quickly and quietly as she could, uncomfortably aware of her heart thudding against her ribs, she clutched the carpetbag in one hand, the confounder in the other and begged the muse of good luck not to desert her.

The door into the administration office was also locked. Melissande pressed her ear against it but couldn't hear a sound. Bibbie's confounder took care of that minor impediment and she found herself alone in the grey, cubicle-crammed dimness.

Oh, lord. Where to start, where to start . . .

Permelia's office seemed the logical place. Closing the door behind her, she put down the carpetbag then made her way through the gloom to the curtained window behind Permelia's desk. After letting in the morning light, she unlocked Permelia's private supply cupboard, put on the gloves she'd stuffed into the carpetbag and quickly hexed everything she could think of that the office thief might decide to pinch.

That done, she took a moment to inspect the crowded wall of framed photographs. Permelia starred in each one, the collection seeming to span at least three decades. There was Permelia at around Bibbie's age, standing beside a younger and slightly less flinty Orville Wycliffe than the one in the portrait. Behind them hovered an enormous tethered airship — the *Ambrose*. There didn't seem to be a corresponding photo of an airship called the *Permelia*. Sad, but perhaps not entirely unexpected. After all, Permelia was only a *gel*.

Other Permelias, gradually aging, proudly posed with various cakes and pies, each one adorned with either a ribbon or a cup or, in sixteen repetitive cases, a Golden Whisk. The award's design hadn't changed a whit over the years. Many of the photographs showed Permelia with an assortment of apparently important and exotically-attired women from around the world: given the cake-themed badges pinned to their breasts it seemed reasonable to assume they were international sister-Guild members.

And lastly there was a very recent photo indeed: Permelia clutching her most controversial and hard-won seventeenth Golden Whisk.

'Blimey,' she muttered. 'That didn't take you long, Permelia.'

Although really, could she blame the woman for surrounding herself with the trappings of her success? At least in the Baking and Pastry Guild Permelia was someone of influence and importance. In the Guild she wasn't treated like a housekeeper. In the Guild she wasn't a *gel*. Or if she was, at least she was the head gel.

I suppose it makes up for not having an airship named after you. Or being banned from setting foot in your own research laboratory.

Again, she was aware of that inconvenient tug of sympathy — but she thrust it aside, quickly, because time was marching on and she still had an entire office to hex.

First she took care of the contents of Miss Petterly's jealously guarded office supply cupboard. Then she hexed everything locked in the staff tea room's cupboard: packets of plain biscuits and sugar and all the teacups, just in case. After that she hexed the portable items on each cubicle's grim, impersonal desk: typewriter, abacus, pens and pencils, rulers.

Bibbie was right about going to Monk for help, drat her. Without his friend in the Births, Deaths and Marriages Bureau we'd never learn a thing about these girls. Honestly, would one little picture bring productivity screaming to a halt?

Last of all she hexed the windows and the door. Then, task finally accomplished, she bolted back downstairs and out to the employee garden.

'Well?' said Reg from her camouflaged position in the bushiest fig tree. 'Any trouble?'

'Of course not,' she said, shoving the carpetbag and her plain, work purse under a handy low-growing shrub. 'Why would there be?'

Reg snorted. 'Why does flypaper attract flies, ducky?'

Charming. 'Everything's fine,' she said. 'Now all we have to do is wait.'

'You can wait if you like,' said Reg. 'Me, I'm going back to sleep.'

Yes, well, it was all right for Reg. 'Fine,' she said, feeling grumpy. 'And I'm going for a walk.'

As she left the garden she saw a posh silver car glide down the driveway towards the hallowed Research and Development complex, which was strategically distant from the administration building in case of unfortunate thaumaturgical accidents. As it passed she caught a glimpse of the driver: none other than that handsome plonker Errol Haythwaite.

She looked at her watch, pinned tidily to her ghastly black blouse. Just gone half-past seven. Goodness, Errol started work early, didn't he? All the better to hide his treachery, perhaps? Curiosity piqued, she started down the long, hedge-trimmed driveway towards the sprawling R&D building.

Errol's flash car was the only vehicle in the staff car park adjacent to the main R&D laboratory. Squished against the hedge, peering through a straggly patch, Melissande watched him unfold himself from its sleek interior, retrieve an expensive-looking briefcase and even more expensive-looking staff from the passenger seat, secure the car and make his way to the laboratory. A touch of the staff to a brass plate beside the doors unlocked them, and he went in.

'Rats,' she said, under her breath. 'If only I could follow him inside. Saint Snodgrass knows what he's getting up to in there.'

On impulse she scuttled across the almost empty car park and over to the imposing laboratory complex. There were no windows along the front, but perhaps along the back? Hardly daring to breathe, she crept around the corner of the building and peered along its rear length. She was in luck. There was indeed a scattering of windows. None of them was open but not all were screened by curtains. And one of them, it turned out, belonged to Errol Haythwaite's office.

Nose pressed against the narrow width of uncurtained glass, quaking in fear that he'd look up and see her, Melissande held her breath again and spied on Gerald's nemesis and number one suspect.

Tall, lean and indisputably dazzling, Errol stood in front of a large drawing-desk, a series of blueprints spread out before him. Even though he was facing the window, he didn't notice he was being stared at, so intently was he focused upon his work. He'd taken off his expensive suit-coat and hung it on the back of his closed office door. His white shirt shone with a definite silkish shimmer, and his tiepin looked like solid gold. *Definitely* he wasn't short of dosh.

Melissande glared. *Come on, you rich plonker, do something incriminating. You're owed such a smacking for the way you spoke to Gerald.*

Errol, unobliging, picked up a wax pen and began to scribble all over his blueprints. Every so often he paused and stood back to consider his handiwork. Sometimes he smiled, which made him even more handsome.

On the desk behind him, his crystal ball pulsed red. Irritated, Errol turned and glared at it. Almost ignored it … and then changed his mind. Tossing down the wax pen he answered his incoming call.

'Rats,' said Melissande. She could see his lips move, but she couldn't hear a thing. 'I wonder if Bibbie's invented an eavesdropping-hex too …'

Whatever was being said to Errol by his mystery caller, one thing was clear: he didn't like it. Not at all. Now he was pacing his small, tidy office, hands fisted on his hips, and as he strode in and out of view Melissande saw his face was contracted in a scowl. But even angry and upset he was still shockingly handsome.

Just like Lional. Don't let his looks fool you …

With Errol moving around so much it was far more likely he'd catch sight of her at his window. Time to go … especially since according to her watch it was nearly a quarter to eight and she still had to make her way back to the office.

She met up with Gerald on the way.

'Melissande!' he said, looking suitably Third Grade in a worn brown suit, a limp white shirt and slightly threadbare blue tie. His gaze narrowed suspiciously. 'What have you been doing?'

Trust him to notice. 'Doing, Gerald? I don't know what you mean.'

With a quick look around to make sure no-one was coming, he took her elbow and tugged her against the hedge. 'You know perfectly well what I mean. The only thing at the end of this driveway is the R&D lab. Melissande, please, *stay out of my case.* I know you're only trying to help, but you can't.'

'No?' she said, tugging her elbow free.

'No.'

'Does that mean you're not interested in what I just saw?'

A riot of emotions chased over his face. '*Melissande . . .*'

She patted his cheek. 'I'll tell you if you'd like to know. I'll even waive my regular fee as a professional courtesy.'

He closed his eyes. 'Yes. I'd like to know.'

'Say please.'

'*Please.*'

Two more wizards were walking down the driveway. As much as she enjoyed teasing Gerald, she'd have to make this fast. 'Someone contacted Errol,' she said quickly. 'Through his crystal ball. Whoever it was made him very angry.'

Gerald took her arm again, his eyes intent, his grip veering towards painful. 'Who was it? What did they talk about?'

'I don't know,' she said. 'I couldn't hear, I could only see. Gerald —'

Abruptly aware of himself, he let go of her arm. 'Sorry. I'm sorry. Of course you couldn't hear him, Errol's got his office thaumaturgically sound-proofed. But did you see anything else?'

'No,' she said, resisting the urge to rub where his fingers had gripped her. 'Well ... except I don't think he was just angry. I think he was afraid, too.'

Gerald laughed, unamused. 'Errol? Afraid? That doesn't seem likely.'

She shrugged. 'Maybe not, but he was.'

The other wizards were much closer now, their shoes scrunching the driveway's loose gravel. Gerald glanced over his shoulder. 'We shouldn't be seen together. Melissande —' He shook his head. 'Thank you. That might be important. But please, I'm *begging* you — stay out of my way. If anything happened to you, or Reg, or Bibbie ...'

This was only the third time she'd seen him since New Ottosland, and Lional. Even so — she could tell that he'd changed. That tentative, sweet man she'd met his first day in the palace was gone. Vanished, as though he'd never lived. And in his place stood this quietly haunted man, with one good eye that showed her dreadful things.

I wonder what he can see that's different in me.

'You mustn't worry,' she said gently. 'Nothing's going to happen. Have a good day, Gerald. I expect we'll talk again quite soon.'

With a nod and a smile she walked away, heading back to the employee garden so she could retrieve her reticule. She could feel Gerald stare after her, his gaze heavy between her shoulder-blades.

When she was clear of the two approaching wizards she broke into an unladylike jog. If she wasn't careful she was going to be late ... and getting fired was the last thing she needed.

'Here you go, Gerald,' said Japhet Morgan, fellow Third Grade menial, wheeling yet another trolley-load of thaumaturgically-stained beakers and test tubes and etheretic containers into R&D's industrial-sized scullery. 'Compliments of Mister Haythwaite.'

Gerald looked round, and managed — just — to keep his face blank. That made five trolley-loads washed and six waiting for his attention. He'd been at this for nearly four hours now with no sign of a reprieve. So much for spying on Errol. And with what Melissande had told him this morning, he really, *really* needed to spy.

'Fine, Japh,' he sighed. 'Just leave them with the others.'

Japhet parked the trolley, then lingered. 'So. It was really you who blew up Stuttley's?'

Was there any point in yet again protesting his innocence? No. People believed what they wanted to believe. Especially when someone like Errol was telling the tale.

'Yes, Japh,' he said wearily. 'It was really me.'

Japhet, young and pimpled and easily awed, whistled soundlessly. 'Gosh. No wonder Mister Haythwaite hates your guts. He says that staff of his you ruined cost *thousands*.'

'Does he?' He reached for another manky beaker. 'Then I guess it did.'

'He says everywhere you go, disaster follows. He says you probably got a *king* killed. You didn't, did you?'

What? He put down the scrubbing brush and turned to face Japhet. 'No. I didn't. And you should know better than to listen to gossip, Mister Morgan.'

Japhet flushed. 'It's not gossip. It's what Mister Haythwaite says.'

Gerald turned back to the sink. 'Yes, well, Mister Haythwaite's going to say a lot more than that if he catches you in here idling. So you'd best leave me to my scrubbing and get back to work.'

'Right. Yes,' said Japhet, suitably cowed. 'Sorry, Gerald. It's only what Mister Haythwaite says.'

Alone again, Gerald rinsed the beaker and stacked it with the other twelve on the draining board. Outrage at Errol tangled with his ongoing remorse for blabbing to Monk and the girls about his true purpose here at Wycliffe's. Reaching for yet another beaker, plunging it into the sink's scalding, soapy water, he throttled the urgent desire to run out to the lab and beat Errol about the head with his brand new First Grade staff.

Stupid, stupid, mingy pillock. He's trying to turn everyone here against me. He's trying to get me fired. Does he know I've got my eye on him? Has he guessed? Did I give myself away somehow? He said he could sense there was something different about me. What if he really can? What if that wasn't just bluster? Oh lord. If he gets me fired Sir Alec will be furious.

He scrubbed and scrubbed at the dirty beaker, feeling his shoulders ache. Feeling the heat of the scalding water. Even wearing rubber gloves he was developing dishpan hands. He could feel his fingers shrivelling; a few more hours of this and he'd have no fingers left.

But I'd better get used to it. If I let Errol get me fired this'll be my first and last field assignment. Of course it'll be my first and last field assignment anyway if Sir Alec finds out I spilled the beans on the investigation . . .

He wouldn't feel so bad about it if he'd managed to convince the girls to give up working for Permelia Wycliffe. But he'd been mad to think he could talk them out of it by telling them the truth.

If anything, he'd actually made things worse. Melissande spying on Errol? The stupid girl had lost her mind. Maybe if he put a call through to Rupert . . .

I can't. Melissande would never forgive me. Besides, Rupert would tell Sir Alec and that'd be that.

He'd just have to trust that, between them, Melissande and Reg would be able to find their biscuit thief. Maybe he could help them. Solving their stupid case would get them out of the way and he could breathe easily again. Focus on finding the link between Errol and Haf Rottlezinder.

Assuming there is one. I really want there to be one. I suppose that makes me a bad person. But he's telling people I killed a king! All right, I did. But that's not the point! And anyway, he was a bad king. The point is —

His disjointed train of thought was derailed by a commotion beyond the scullery's open door. As he turned, half-cleaned beaker in hand, Japhet Morgan rushed back in.

'You'll never guess!' he panted. 'There's been another portal accident! It's all over the wireless. Quick, come and listen!'

Japhet rushed out again. Gerald, staring, didn't even feel the beaker slip from his grasp. Hardly flinched as it smashed to splinters on the scullery's brick floor.

Oh, damn. This is my fault. I should've found a way to stop it.

He stepped over the shards of glass, dreamlike, and drifted out to the complex of laboratories.

The wizards of R&D were huddled around the lab wireless. Even Errol was listening. But was that to learn first-hand of his success or because — like everyone else — he was horrified and wanted to know what had happened?

Was this what that crystal ball communication was about? Did Rottlezinder call Errol for permission to proceed?

He didn't know. He had to find out.

'— *and details are scarce at this time,*' the news announcer was saying. '*There is no word yet of casualties. We shall update as new information comes to hand. I repeat, there has been an accident at the Central Ott General Post Office Portal. No official statement has been released by the Department of Transport, as yet, and details are scarce at this time. There is no word —*'

Turning blindly away from the huddle of wizards, from the ruthlessly unemotional voice emanating from the wireless, Gerald nearly smacked face-first into Ambrose Wycliffe. The company's hapless owner stood in the wide aisle that separated the two long rows of laboratories, his jowly, whiskered face unhealthily flushed.

'What's that? What's going on? Why aren't you men going about your work? You know the rule about the wireless, gentlemen, it's only for —'

'There's been another portal accident,' said Gerald. Sweat was tormenting its way down his spine. 'In Central Ott. Mister Wycliffe — I'm sorry — I have to go down there. My — my mother — was coming in to town today. She always uses the Central Post Office Portal. Please, sir, I really, *really* need to —'

'What?' said Ambrose Wycliffe, and shook himself. Paid attention. 'Your mother, Dunwoody? I'm sorry to hear it. Naturally you must go. But don't forget to punch out. You'll need to make up the lost time.'

Of course he would.

As he made his surreptitious way out of the R&D block Gerald looked back at Errol, still standing closest to the wireless, still listening to the repetitive droning of the plummy-voiced announcer. If his dismay was an act, he belonged on the stage. But then traitors had to be good actors, didn't they?

Feeling himself watched, Errol glanced up. Seeing who stared at him, his face hardened and his eyes chilled as his expression shifted from shock to sneering contempt. Then it shifted again, to a dawning suspicion . . .

Bugger. Before Errol could challenge him Gerald ducked out of the side door. Ranged down the length of the R&D block was a collection of prototype scooters and velocipedes. Rubbish, Melissande had called them. And she was right: the first three scooters he tried to start just spluttered at him, protesting. The fourth one kicked over, but chugged so pathetically he feared it would expire altogether before he could cover the distance between Wycliffe's and the Central General Post Office.

Put-put-puttering down the driveway that led to Wycliffe's front gates, he heard a wild flapping of wings and looked up.

'*Reg*? What are you doing?' he whispered, as she landed on the back of the scooter. He was chugging past the main office building, past window after window that could at any moment contain an inconvenient witness. 'Go away. Someone might see you!'

'Not likely,' said Reg, flapping herself into a more comfortable and secure position, pillion on the scooter. 'Any gel caught looking out of the window is summarily dismissed, sunshine. And it's only gels working in there.'

'Yes, all right, fine, if you say so, but —'

'I was stretching my wings and I saw you making a desperate getaway,' she said. 'What's going on, Gerald? Don't tell me that pillock Errol Haythwaite's put the wind up you?'

He risked a glance over his shoulder at her. Felt the most enormous wave of relief wash over him. *I'm not alone. I'm not alone.* 'If only,' he said, and heard his voice shake. 'There's been another portal incident, Reg.'

'Bugger,' she said. 'Anybody dead this time?'

'I don't know. I'm going down there. I have to see — maybe I can help, maybe I can —' His throat closed. 'Melissande was right.'

'No, she wasn't,' said Reg, as they bumped over the gratings set between the front gates of the Wycliffe Airship Company. Above their heads the tethered, antiquated airship bobbed in the light breeze. 'You know she wasn't. *She* knows she wasn't. And even if she was this wouldn't be your fault. You're not a miracle worker. Incidentally, why are you wearing bright pink rubber gloves?'

He looked at his hands as though he'd never seen them before. 'Oh. Yes.' With a bit of precarious manoeuvring, he managed to get the gloves off and shove them in his pocket. 'I was —' The scooter's engine gurgled, threatening imminent expiration. 'Oh, this useless, hopeless, *rubbish* piece of —'

'Then fix it,' said Reg. 'Soup it up. What's the matter with you, Gerald? You're not a Third Grade wizard any more, sunshine. You're just playing one!'

Oh. Yes. So he was. He'd forgotten ...

The road outside Wycliffe's wasn't the busiest of thoroughfares, but there were a few cars, and some carriages, and even a handful of scooters. Not Wycliffe models, that he could tell. Even so, he should be all right. The slowest carriage was still moving too quickly to tell what he was doing on his pathetic little piece of Wycliffe machinery.

He switched off his shield-incant. Took a deep breath, feeling his rogue powers stir. Thought for a moment, sorting through his repertoire of incants, chose the good old reliable Speed-em-up hex, gave it a twist, then zapped the gasping engine to within a thaumicle of its life.

The scooter roared like a ravenous tiger.

'Blimey!' said Reg, startled. 'Do you know what you're doing?'

'Hold on,' he said grimly. 'We're about to go really, *really* fast.'

'Gerald — now Gerald —' said Reg, warbling with unease. 'You're not that Markham boy, remember, just you think about this — just you — Gerald — *Geraaaaaald!*'

CHAPTER FIFTEEN

'And you're perfectly certain, are you, Miss Cadwallader, that these — these *hexes* of yours will do the trick?' said Permelia Wycliffe, coldly displeased behind her desk. 'Because up to this point I cannot see that you've made any progress. Worse than that, I have just discovered that three more boxes of Buttle's Best Assorted Cream Biscuits are missing from my executive cupboard.'

Melissande managed not to squirm. 'Oh dear. I am so very sorry, Miss Wycliffe. Still. Biscuits. It could be worse, couldn't it? I mean, all your Golden Whisks are still here.'

'It's not the biscuits, it's the principle!' snapped Permelia Wycliffe. 'We continue to succour a thief in our midst! And you seem to have taken steps to apprehend this — this criminal only this morning!'

'Yes, well, as I explained, Miss Wycliffe, the hexes we've employed to identify your miscreant are extremely complicated and delicate. Moreover they are unique. My colleague Miss Markham has invented them specifically for your use. Hours and hours of work have gone into them. I assure you they will do the trick.'

Mention of Bibbie softened the severe pinching of Permelia Wycliffe's lips. 'Yes. Well,' she said, fractionally mollified. 'No less could be expected of Antigone Markham's great-niece. Nevertheless, Miss Cadwallader, I must insist that you —'

The telephone on Permelia Wycliffe's desk buzzed, one long blurt of noise indicating an internal communication.

As Permelia Wycliffe answered the summons — it was her horrible brother, Ambrose — Melissande rested her gaze on that crowded wall of boastful photographs. Honestly, the more she thought about it the crazier it seemed. How was it possible that so many women around the world, important women — or at least women who were married to important men — could get so excited about baking cakes? Surely there was a better way of solving world hunger ...

She realised then that Permelia Wycliffe had stopped talking. Had hung up the telephone. Was sitting behind her desk like a woman carved from meringue, sugar-white of face with a hectic dot of strawberry jam on each sunken cheek.

'Miss Wycliffe?' she said, alarmed. 'Miss Wycliffe, are you all right?'

Permelia Wycliffe was breathing with such harsh restraint she seemed in danger of bursting a blood vessel. 'There has been,' she said, though her jaw was clenched to breaking point, 'another portal incident, Miss Cadwallader. It is *very* distressing.'

Melissande felt herself go cold. 'Oh. Oh, no. Oh, that's awful. Has anyone been —'

'You must excuse me, Miss Cadwallader,' said Permelia Wycliffe stiffly. 'My brother will be joining me shortly. A confidential business meeting.'

'Of course, Miss Wycliffe,' said Melissande, standing. 'I'll just — I'll leave you to — I'll go now. Thank you.'

As she reached the office door, Permelia Wycliffe said, 'Miss Cadwallader?'

She turned, desperately hoping her face wasn't betraying how close she was to tears. 'Yes, Miss Wycliffe?'

'You must appreciate, given the current business climate, that the Wycliffe Airship Company cannot be expected to pay for your services indefinitely. Particularly when you seem unable to reach a satisfactory conclusion to your investigation. I believe the amount of your retainer covers one more day? Then you have one more day, Miss Cadwallader, to unmask the thief. After that your services shall no longer be required.'

'Oh,' she said faintly. 'I see. Yes. Well. I'm sure Witches Inc. will do its utmost to provide satisfaction, Miss Wycliffe.'

'I certainly hope so,' said Permelia Wycliffe. 'Because people do talk, Miss Cadwallader. It would be unfortunate if they were talking about you for all the wrong reasons.'

'Yes, Miss Wycliffe,' she said, and made her escape past horrible Miss Petterly, who looked at her with deep disfavour as she returned to her horrible little grey cubicle. Safely hidden she sat for a moment, willing the tears and nausea to subside, then mechanically reached for the next purchase order requiring her attention.

Another portal accident? So was last night a premonition? And was I wrong to let Gerald and Reg talk me into staying silent? Oh, Saint Snodgrass, if anyone has perished . . .

The spectre of leaving Wycliffe's a failure paled before this latest dreadful news. Heart pounding, stomach churning, she tried to focus on the paperwork . . .

But all she could see were her dead and dying people sprawled on the palace forecourt, struck down by Lional, innocent in death . . .

Like fingernails down a classroom blackboard, Miss Petterly's horrible handbell rang out. Melissande held her breath, knowing every gel in the office was doing the same.

'Miss Carstairs. *Miss Carstairs.* To me, if you please!'

Well . . . *bugger.* Biting her lip, she went to face Miss Petterly.

'What is the meaning of this, Miss Carstairs?' demanded Miss Petterly, brandishing a sheaf of paperwork. 'You have been *altering* the customers' *purchase orders*!'

What? Oh, yes. Tantivy Tourist Extravaganza's order, from first thing that morning. 'I'm sorry, Miss Petterly. I was just trying to help. They seem to have confused themselves and ordered the Gyrating Pandoscopic Side-mirror when what they really needed was the —'

Miss Petterly leapt to her feet. '*Miss Carstairs*. No gel under *my* supervision presumes to tell a *customer* he is *confused*! Are you *trying* to cost this company *business*?'

'Well, no, Miss Petterly, I was trying to —'

'Don't you talk back to me, young lady! No gel under *my* supervision shall —'

At the other end of the office, somebody's silver handbell tinkled.

'Wait here,' said Miss Petterly coldly. 'This conversation is *not* concluded.'

Miss Petterly stalked off to make someone else's life miserable. Melissande pulled a face at her retreating back, then took the blue hex-detector from her black skirt pocket and surreptitiously waved it over the horrible woman's desk. Sadly there was no reaction.

Bugger. How wonderful it would be if Miss Petterly was the thief.

In Permelia Wycliffe's office, behind Miss Petterly's guard-dog desk, Permelia Wycliffe and her useless brother Ambrose were deep in private consultation. Although the door was closed and the curtains before the internal window were almost completely drawn, she caught a snatch of raised voices.

'— *I* would take care of it, Ambrose! You must be *mad* to ... such a foolish decision ... quite *despair*! If Father were alive, he'd ... clearly up to *me* to save the company. So this is what you're ...'

She didn't catch the end of the sentence.

Trying to be nonchalant, trying not to attract unwelcome attention, Melissande inched her way around Miss Petterly's desk, to see if she could overhear anything else.

'... not the success we'd hoped for, but ... *my* fault I had to buy inferior equipment. There *is* a market for ... need better quality wizards, Permelia ... purse strings ... had to do *something*! ... You haven't saved us ... shall prevail!'

And that was brother Ambrose, sounding petulant and henpecked. Probably Permelia was complaining about the awfulness of the latest Wycliffe City Scooter. If the number of purchase orders coming in were any indication, it was a lemon to outshine any previous citrus product Wycliffe's had managed to produce so far.

'*Miss Carstairs*! Do you *mind*?' demanded Miss Petterly, marching towards her. 'No gel under *my* supervision stands on *my* side of the desk!'

Rats. She really wanted to know what Permelia and Ambrose were arguing about. 'Sorry, Miss Petterly,' she murmured, leaping back to her proper place.

'Indeed,' said Miss Petterly, taking her seat. 'I should think so. *Never* let me have to tell you again. *Now*, Miss Carstairs. Regarding these altered purchase orders ...'

There was so much traffic snarled on the approach to the Central Ott General Post Office that Gerald had to abandon the souped-up scooter with a don't-steal-me hex on it, and walk the last half a mile. Reg rode on his shoulder, scolding without bothering, it seemed, to take any breaths at all.

'— practically turned my feathers inside out, you raving *nutter*! If this is what being a rogue wizard has done for you, Gerald, all I can say is it's a great pity you ever learned the truth of your condition! You are officially worse than that Markham boy and I never thought the day would come when I'd say *that* with a straight face! Well? Well? Aren't you even going to apologise?'

'Not right now,' he said, scarcely paying her attention. The

Central Ott streets were clogged with gawkers and police, so much shouting and whistle-blowing and shoving and pushing and clanging alarm bells. He was being poked by elbows, prodded by parasols: if one more person trod on his feet he was going to break down and *cry*. 'Reg ... we're there. Can you please fly around a bit? See what you can see? Chances are they won't let me get much closer than this.'

'*Well*!' she spluttered. 'If you aren't the most *impossible*, the most *outrageous*, the most —'

'Thanks, Reg,' he said, and heaved her off his shoulder with one enormous shrug.

Swearing a blue streak she took to the air. Good thing there was so much noise and mayhem or somebody would have heard her, and that might have been awkward.

He put his head down and tried to forge his way through the wall of gathered onlookers, to get to the front of the crowd so he would at least have some hope of seeing what was going on.

No luck. The human wall refused to budge. Thwarted, Gerald let out a hard breath.

This is important. This is government business. I'm a government agent. If people won't get out of my way I'll just have to ... nudge them. A bit. Not hard. Just enough.

He hadn't switched his etheretic shield back on. Another breach of protocol, but by now who was counting? With a pang of guilt he whispered a hex beneath his breath, and heated a thin layer of air around him. Agitated the ether, making its thaumicles dance.

Without even knowing why, the crowd parted for him then closed up behind. Like a fish in water he swam to the edge of the street ... and got his first look at the Central Ott Portal.

It was intact. At least, from the outside it looked intact. For a moment he was so giddy with relief he thought he might fall over. If there weren't so many people in the crowd around him, practically propping him up, he probably would have.

Blotting sweat from his forehead with his sleeve, he stared past the imposing line of policemen who'd been posted to keep the milling spectators at a safe distance. A row of ambulances was lined up at the portal entrance, but the drivers were just lounging about, chatting. No frantic scramble to haul out the injured or — or the dead. He caught sight of a couple of Government-looking types, with bright purple badges fixed to their coat lapels. Officials from the Department of Transport, they were. Deep in solemn conversation but not looking panicked. Looking *cheerful*, if anything. So did that mean there really *weren't* any casualties this time?

Oh please, oh please . . .

Off to one side of the portal entrance a huddle of regular townsfolk were in animated discussion with more men from the Department of Transport. Portal passengers, then? Witnesses to whatever had happened? He caught sight of Reg, bless her, perched on top of a street sign announcing the portal's entrance, almost on top of them, flagrantly eavesdropping for all she was worth.

All around him the crowd was muttering and agitating and speculating. '*Heard it was just a breakdown, not like the other times . . . I don't know, they tell us all these thaumaturgics are safe, Harry, but I don't think I'm going to trust them any more . . . new airships, did you see that advertisement? Yes, they might be slower but they're safer, you can't deny they're safer . . . are we quite certain no-one got hurt this time? . . .*'

He nearly turned to see who'd said *that*. It was disgusting, the speaker had sounded positively *disappointed*. But his attention was caught by more movement at the portal entrance. Someone was coming out.

Lord, it was *Dalby*, the senior janitor with the inexplicable fondness for stewed tea. Gerald held his breath and stared at the cobbled street in front of him, willing the rumpled, bruised-looking agent not to see him, not to feel so much of a skerrick of his presence. He didn't dare switch his shield back on in case Dalby felt the etheretic disturbance and came to investigate what had caused it.

He risked a glance up, just in time to see Dalby nod to one of the Department of Transport officials, get into a small, nondescript car parked a little way past the ambulances and drive off.

Gerald, lungs aching, let out an enormously relieved rush of air.

The Department of Transport officials said something to the idling ambulance drivers. They nodded and touched their caps, then returned to their emergency vehicles. One by one they drove away too. A few moments later an empty bus pulled up in the space left by the ambulances, and the people who'd been eagerly talking to the Department of Transport officials loaded onto it.

Reg bounced up and down on top of the street sign, flipping her wing towards the grand Central Ott Post Office building with its imposing colonnaded entrance and carved sandstone cherubim and gargoyles, half a block down from the portal station.

Gerald stared. *What*? How was he supposed to get to the Post Office with all these policemen and Department of Transport officials clogging the street?

Reg bounced harder then flew from the street sign down to the Post Office, where she perched on a gargoyle making more impatient *come on, hurry up* gestures with her wing. Which was all well and good for *her*, but she was a *bird*, wasn't she? Who paid any attention to *her*?

He looked up and down the crowded street. No sign of any other agents. Well, not agents he could recognise, anyway. No regular wizards he could recognise either. Just lots of ordinary people, starting to drift away now that it seemed the excitement was over.

He took a deep breath and drifted with them.

When he was finally opposite the Post Office he stopped drifting — quite a few people swore and cursed — and looked across the street to where Reg on her gargoyle was bouncing up and down so violently she was in danger, surely, of giving herself a concussion.

One of the crowd-control policemen stepped forward, his expression stern. 'Thank you, sir, move it along if you please. We need to clear this area now so folk can get back to minding their own business.'

Gerald looked up into the policeman's uncompromising face. The brass buttons on his dark green uniform shone brightly in the sunshine. 'Yes, Constable. Of course, Constable. Sorry to be a nuisance, Constable.'

The policeman nodded, then turned to chivvy someone else. Gerald shuffled along as slowly as he could, thinking furiously. He wasn't going to get across the street unnoticed, not with so many policemen still about. What he needed was a diversion ...

I am not supposed to do this. If Sir Alec finds out he'll have my guts for garters. The problem is I don't have much choice.

He agitated the ether again, a little harder this time. Hard enough to tingle. Sent the ripple running back the way he'd come so the crowd leapt and exclaimed and fussed. And then, as the startled policemen rushed to investigate, he nipped across the closed-off street to the Post Office and dived for shelter in its inky-deep shadows.

Reg flapped down to join him. 'Nicely done,' she said, landing on his shoulder. 'Gerald Dunwoody, you've got a real talent for sneakiness.'

'Let's just hope Sir Alec doesn't find out,' he muttered. 'I've lost count of the rules I've broken so far and it doesn't seem like this case is anywhere near over.'

'I thought sneaky would be an advantage in your game,' said Reg. 'As for rules, well, if they're getting in the way they're not much use to you, are they?'

He wasn't too sure about that, but this wasn't the time or place for a philosophical debate. 'What did you overhear, Reg?'

'Well, the good news is nobody got hurt,' she said. 'Mainly because someone called in a warning, apparently. There was enough time to get folks to safety and put some kind of dampening field in place so the portal just fizzled out instead of unravelling like the others.'

A wave of giddy relief crashed over him. 'Who called in the warning?'

'Don't know,' said Reg. 'But bless his mother's apron, whoever he is. Or she, of course.'

Of course. 'And the bad news?'

Reg ruffled her feathers. 'The bad news is that every single witness was bleating how they'd never travel by portal again,' she said. 'And you can bet your warmest flannel long johns they won't be the only ones. So if this *is* a big conspiracy to put the portal network out of business and usher in the Second Great Age of the Airship, whoever's behind it is on a winning formula, sunshine.'

Damn. 'I need to speak to Sir Alec,' he said, chewing the side of his thumb. 'I've got more information for him which may or may not mean something.' He glanced through the small window in the Post Office's grandiloquent front doors, to the bank of recently installed public telephones in the lobby. Glanced back at the street, where his small etheretic sleight-of-hand still kept the crowd and the policemen usefully preoccupied. Then he twitched his shoulder. 'Stay out here, would you? And keep both eyes open in case someone looks like coming in.'

With a rattle of tail feathers Reg flapped up to perch precariously on a little bit of jutting stonework. 'All right, but make it snappy,' she said. 'I'm not being paid to help you out, sunshine. *I've* still got a job to do back at Wycliffe's. Melissande's all alone, getting into who-knows-what kind of mischief without me.'

He smiled, briefly. 'You're really enjoying this whole Witches Inc. adventure, aren't you?'

'It's something to pass the time,' she said, pretending indifference. In the gloom beneath the Post Office's porticoed entrance her eyes gleamed.

'Yeah. You love it,' he said. 'Okay. Sit tight. I won't be long.'

The Post Office's front doors surrendered to a particularly sneaky unlocking hex he'd learned during his training. Feeling a no-doubt reprehensible flicker of satisfaction, he slipped into the lobby and hurried to the nearest public telephone. He could have hexed that too but somehow the notion seemed wrong so he fished out a few coins from his pocket and called Sir Alec's *very* private number.

'*What are you playing at, Mister Dunwoody?*' Sir Alec demanded. His voice was so cold it was a wonder the telephone receiver didn't freeze solid. '*Mister Dalby has already told me where you are. You are not supposed to be there, Mister Dunwoody. Your brief is simple: keep a close eye on Errol Haythwaite.*'

Dalby had noticed him? *Damn.* 'I'm sorry, Sir Alec,' he said. 'I just — I had to — when I heard on the wireless about the new accident, I —'

'*Mister Dunwoody,*' said Sir Alec, his icy voice warming the smallest fraction. '*You will not last five minutes in this business if you don't learn how to find a proper distance — and follow explicit instructions imparted to you by your superiors. Do I make myself clear?*'

He leaned his forehead against the public telephone booth. 'Yes, Sir Alec. Sorry. Ah — there was one thing I thought you might like to know.'

'*Yes?*'

'Errol was contacted early this morning. I don't know who by, but the conversation upset him.' *Oh Mel, please be right about this.* 'He was angry and afraid, and that's very out of character.'

'*I see. Anything else?*'

'No, sir.'

'*Then return to Wycliffe's at once, Mister Dunwoody, and make sure to keep both eyes on our quarry. Thanks to Mister Dalby the destructive hex was contained, and we've been able to ascertain without a doubt that it was authored by Haf Rottlezinder. It is now imperative that we either establish a link between him and Haythwaite or discount that avenue of investigation once and for all, thus freeing our resources.*'

Thanks to Mister Dalby? Him? That stringy, bruised-looking chap had managed to foil a Rottlezinder hex? Gosh. Nothing about him had suggested *that* kind of power.

In other words, Gerald, books and covers. You shouldn't need to be reminded of that.

'That's good news, sir.'

'*Indeed,*' said Sir Alec. '*Now follow my instructions, Mister Dunwoody, and in future curb the temptation to meddle. I am not new to this tea party, which is why you should be less concerned with doing my job and more concerned with doing your own.*'

'Yes, Sir Alec,' he whispered, wincing. 'I'll — ah — I'll get back to Wycliffe's, then.'

'*Please do. And bear in mind that I did not supply you with this telephone number for the purpose of engaging in cosy chats.*'

Gerald stared at the buzzing telephone receiver for a moment, then replaced it.

Gosh, that went well. I can just imagine how my first mission debrief is going to play out.

Especially when he told Sir Alec about his crowd dispersal techniques ...

'So?' said Reg, flapping back down to his shoulder. 'What now?'

'Now it's back to Wycliffe's,' he said, hiding in the shadows again. 'Are you coming with me, or don't you want to risk it?'

'I'll risk it,' she said grudgingly. 'I'm supposed to be on duty in the employee garden, and madam'll go spare if I've missed any important gossip. But when this romp is over, sunshine, you and I are going to have a serious talk about finding you a few less mad-as-hatter friends!'

Thanks to the appallingly tyrannical Miss Petterly, Melissande was forced to work through nearly all of her lunchbreak, painstakingly uncorrecting all of Tantivy Tourist Extravaganza's corrected orders. When the last mistake was re-made, certainly guaranteeing Wycliffe's yet another massively dissatisfied customer, she dumped the pile of purchase orders on Miss Petterly's empty desk.

Miss Petterly, of course, was indulging her own *long* lunchbreak, as she did every day.

As she rushed downstairs, lunch box in hand, determined to have at least five minutes in the fresh air to clear her head and stave off imminent starvation, she heard a familiar voice at the front reception desk. Instead of turning left, to leave the office block via the staff entrance at the back of the building, she turned right and hovered around the corner, straining to hear the conversation.

'Yes, that's right, Eudora Telford,' said the familiar voice. 'Here to see Miss Permelia Wycliffe on a personal matter of the utmost urgency. She sent for me, you know. Personally. I am Miss Permelia Wycliffe's Baking and Pastry Guild secretary, you know. Highly trusted. Highly valuable. I am the person she calls upon when something important must be done.'

'Yes, Miss Telford,' said bored-sounding Miss Fisher, the

receptionist. 'Miss Wycliffe has just stepped out for a moment. If you'd care to wait ...'

Melissande eased back from the corner before somebody saw her. What was so urgent that Permelia Wycliffe would send for a wet hen like Eudora Telford to take care of?

It's probably nothing really important. That's just Eudora puffing herself up. It's definitely none of my business. But it's certainly curious ...

It was so late now the employee garden was empty of everyone save two of the R&D wizards, and they never deigned to speak to any of the *gels*. Just as she sat on a sun-soaked bench, desperate to devour her lunch, she heard a rattling of tail feathers in the garden's bushiest ornamental fig-tree. Ignoring the wretched bird, she opened her lunch box. One mouthful, just one, and then she'd find out what Reg wanted.

'*Pssst. Pssst! Oy! Are you deaf?*'

No, but very soon now she was going to starve to death. Abandoning her lunch, she stamped over to the nearby garden bed and bent over, pretending to admire the pansies. '*What*? Can't this *wait*? I am *famished* beyond your wildest imagination!'

'Never mind about that, ducky,' said Reg, almost hidden amongst the foliage. 'Last time I looked you weren't anywhere near skin-and-bone. Have you heard about the Central Ott portal?'

She felt her rumbling stomach lurch. 'Yes.'

'Well, I've just come back from there and thought you might like to know there's nobody been hurt. It's all under control.'

She looked up, startled. 'Oh, that's *wonderful*, Reg. But what were you —'

'I went for a little look-see with Gerald. He was all het up about it, convinced you were right and he was responsible for more death and destruction.' She sniffed. 'You know, you really want to be a bit more careful, madam. My Gerald takes things very much to heart.'

'Sorry,' she mumbled. 'I will. Listen —' She bent again to the pansies, just in case anyone was wondering why she was talking to an ornamental fig tree.

'What?'

'It's probably nothing, probably I'm just being nosy, but how about you go perch on the sill of Permelia Wycliffe's office window and see if you can hear what she and Eudora Telford are talking about? Eudora's claiming Permelia's sent for her, some desperately urgent and important errand that needs doing. I think I'd like to know what it is.'

'Hmm,' said Reg. 'I thought we weren't investigating our own clients?'

'Well, yes, but — that was before we found out about Gerald and why he's here. I think it's our duty to investigate anything that smells fishy. And I've already overheard a row between Permelia and Ambrose.' She stood up straight. 'And d'you know, it was just after she found out about the latest portal accident.'

'Gerald said that Sir Alec said Ambrose Wycliffe wasn't involved.'

'Sir Alec could be wrong,' she said. 'Men have been known to be wrong from time to time, haven't they?'

Reg snorted. 'Not to hear them talk. All right. I'll go and have a stickybeak into Permelia Wycliffe's business.'

'Yes, do that. Only be *careful*, Reg! They both know who you are, remember?'

Another snort. 'Good. Yes. Thanks for that, ducky. Are you finished? Or would you like to teach your grandmother how to suck eggs while you're at it?'

Shaking her head, Melissande watched the wretched bird flap away. Then she returned to her lunch. Finally, finally, something to eat.

'Miss Carstairs! *Miss Carstairs!* What do you think you're *doing*, Miss Carstairs? Lunchtime is *over* for *gels*, Miss Carstairs!'

Incredulous, she turned. And there was Miss Petterly standing at the employee garden's entrance, a skinny black-clad scarecrow with her fists on her hips and a face like peevish thunder.

Her gurgling stomach rumbled a fresh protest.

If I throw my lunch at her she'll make sure I'm fired ... and that'll be it for Witches Inc. Curtains. Coda. Dead in the water before we've barely begun swimming.

She let her chin drop to her chest. Swallowed her pride, which wasn't anywhere near as satisfying as a ham and cheese sandwich.

'Yes, Miss Petterly,' she said, trudging towards the horrible woman. 'I'm coming, Miss Petterly.'

And somehow, sometime, I'll pay you back for this.

After returning to the R&D block, Gerald was hustled back into the scullery by a sneering Errol and only set foot out of it again to collect more trolley-loads of equipment to clean. It seemed he no longer even rated the likes of Japhet Morgan to give him a hand.

On his third trundle round the laboratory complex, feeling like a tea lady with his trolley and pink gloves, he caught sight of an arrival he wasn't expecting: James Kirkby-Hackett. He stared, immediately curious. What was one of Errol's revolting First Grade chums doing here? In person? Looking ... perturbed.

Of course the worry in Kirkby-Hackett's face was wiped away by incredulous delight upon seeing who it was trundling the dirty equipment trolley round the lab.

It doesn't matter, Dunwoody. It really doesn't matter. Who cares what Kirkby-Hackett thinks? You know what you are. You know what you're doing here. Other people's opinions mean nothing at all.

And still ... and still ... his belly burned with dull pain.

Philpott, Methven's off-sider, went to fetch Errol, who came out of the Mark VI lab a moment later. Was it a trick of the light or did he — just for a heartbeat — seem monumentally displeased to see his friend?

Gerald hastily got busy restacking his trolley, just in case it became obvious he was sneakily eavesdropping.

'James! What a surprise,' said Errol, all cordial good-nature. 'Fancy seeing you here. You should have called ahead, I'd have arranged a tour for you.' He laughed, the faintest of edges under his voice. 'Well, of anything that's not classified top secret of course.'

Kirkby-Hackett hesitated then shook Errol's outstretched hand. 'No. No. That's quite all right, Errol. No need to go to any trouble for me. Fact is, just passing, thought I'd swing by and give you a nod.'

'A nod,' said Errol, his eyes narrowing. 'Right. I see. Well, let's go into my office, we can —'

'Office?' said Kirkby-Hackett. He was definitely jumpy. Ill at ease. *Concerned*. 'Right. Yes. Only I thought we might have a quick word in the fresh air, Errol. You cooped up in here. Me cooped up at Masterly's. Yes. Fresh air. Just the thing.'

'All right,' said Errol, after a moment. He didn't sound at all pleased. 'We'll stroll around the staff garden a time or two.' He turned. 'Dunwoody! What the hell are you doing? Can't you even put beakers in a trolley without creating a catastrophe? Get on with it, man. I swear, if so much as one stage of one project is held up because we've run out of clean equipment —'

Hastily, Gerald backed up his trolley. 'Sorry, Mister Haythwaite. Getting right on that, Mister Haythwaite.'

Kirkby-Hackett said something, his voice too low to carry. Errol laughed and Kirkby-Hackett laughed with him, despite his obvious worry.

'Oh, yes,' said Errol, clapping a hand to Kirkby-Hackett's

expensively suited shoulder. 'That's right. Found his true level at last, has our old chum Dunnywood.'

Gerald watched them saunter out of the building, furious that he couldn't follow them. Desperate to know what had brought Kirkby-Hackett here, so patently uneasy.

Oh Reg, Reg, don't fail me now. Be in the garden . . .

'You'd better do as Mister Haythwaite says, Mister Dunwoody,' said Robert Methven, in passing. 'There's plenty of desperate Third Grade wizards in the world. Do you want to keep this job or don't you?'

'Yes, Mister Methven,' he said, suitably chastened. 'Right away, Mister Methven.'

He was just finishing up the latest load of stained lab equipment when Reg appeared without warning at the closed scullery window. He nearly dropped another beaker, which would have been a disaster. He'd already been lambasted by Errol for the one he'd smashed after hearing about the latest portal incident.

Reg banged her beak on the glass. 'Don't just stand there gawping, sunshine!' she shouted, her voice muffled. 'Open it up! I've got something to tell you!'

Bloody hell. He looked over his shoulder through the open scullery door but nobody had heard her. Praise Saint Snodgrass for small mercies. Grabbing a trolley, he eased the door closed and barricaded it then rushed to open the window before Reg broke it.

'What? What? Reg, are you crazy? Are you trying to get me fired?'

'Put a sock in it and listen, Gerald,' she retorted. 'Because I've just been doing your dirty work again. Do you know —'

Irritation disappeared in a flood of hope. 'You overheard them? Errol and Kirkby-Hackett? Oh, Reg. That's terrific. What did they —'

'*Do you know*,' said Reg, glaring, 'I've a good mind to send that Sir Alec a bill when this is over. All this wear and tear on my nerves! First I'm scouting for *you*, then I'm eavesdropping for *madam*, then I'm back eavesdropping for *you* again! And I'm only getting paid to help madam! You're taking me for granted, Gerald Dunwoody, and I don't like it. I'll have you know my feelings are *hurt*.'

He snatched her off the windowsill, dropped a kiss on her head then put her back. 'Sorry. I'll make it up to you, I promise. What did Errol and Kirkby-Hackett talk about?'

Reg fluffed out all her feathers. 'Have you got a stool in here? You should be sitting down for this. *Haf Rottlezinder*. Someone official was asking Kirkby-Hackett about him. Had they been in contact recently, old university chums catching up sort of thing. And did he know if Rottlezinder had been in touch with any *other* old university chums, like, say, for instance, one *Errol Haythwaite*?' She cackled. 'That pillock Errol turned fourteen different shades of puce when he heard *that*.'

Gerald frowned at the barricaded scullery door. He wouldn't have much longer, surely, before someone tried to barge in. 'And what did Errol say, once he was finished turning fourteen different shades of puce?'

Reg shrugged. 'Said he hadn't spoken to Rottlezinder in years. Said he didn't want anything to do with him, something about rumours of unsavoury thaumaturgical practices. Said if Kirkby-Hackett had the brains of a gnat *he'd* not have anything to do with their old chum Haf, either. And then he sent Kirkby-Hackett on his way with a flea in his ear. Properly put out, he was, the poncy prat.'

'Do you think Errol was lying? Or was he telling the truth?'

'Hmm,' said Reg, and thoughtfully scratched her head. 'That's a good question. Wish I could answer it, sunshine, but the truth is — I couldn't tell.'

Damn. 'I'll bet Sir Alec's behind Kirkby-Hackett's quizzing,' he murmured. 'He's stirring the pot a bit to give me a better chance of seeing what floats to the surface.' Snatching Reg up again he rested his cheek on her head, briefly. 'You're wonderful. You're marvellous. I couldn't do this without you.'

'Ha,' she said, trying hard not to show she was pleased. 'Tell me something I don't already know.'

'I've got to get back to work,' he said, still holding her. 'Thanks. I'll be in touch.' And he settled her gently back on the windowsill.

'Yes, all right,' she said, sleeking her feathers ready for flight. 'But — look here, Gerald, just you be careful. I don't care how much thaumaturgic power you've got at your fingertips these days, my boy — if I've told you once, I haven't told you often enough. *You're not indestructible.* And I can't be in two places at the same time.'

And on that final trenchant note, she flapped away.

CHAPTER SIXTEEN

Gerald watched her out of sight, missing her so much, then hurriedly unbarricaded the scullery door and shoved his trolley back out into the lab for yet another round of hunt-the-dirty-beaker.

He didn't see Errol again, but he heard him inside the Mark VI lab, shouting at some unfortunate inferior or other. Even for Errol, the vitriol was vicious. Look after wary look was exchanged around the complex. Heads ducked lower, shoulders hunched. Even the other First Graders tried to make themselves inconspicuous, just in case Errol stormed out of his lab in search of fresh prey.

At length, Robert Methven came out of the Mark VI lab, looking alarmingly close to tears.

Gerald put his head down and got on with his beaker-hunting. Sir Alec had stirred the pot all right: Errol was as rattled as he'd ever seen him. In fact, he'd *never* seen Errol rattled like this. It certainly was ... suggestive.

The work-day dragged to its eventual conclusion. One by one Wycliffe's wizards began to go home. First Japhet Morgan and his two fellow Third Graders. Then Robert Methven, set-faced and silent, followed soon after by Wycliffe's other three First Graders. The seven Second Graders weren't long behind them. That just left Errol. And of course Ambrose Wycliffe, shut uncharacteristically late in his office.

Gerald was ready with an explanation if anyone asked why he was still working when the other Third Grade wizards had bolted. Making up for the time he took earlier, he intended to say. But nobody asked. Nobody gave a toss about Dunnywood or what he was up to. Not a single wizard was stupid enough to risk Errol's wrath by showing any interest in a man their superior so openly despised.

When Ambrose Wycliffe finally emerged from his office into the complex, florid and preoccupied, Gerald ducked into one of the small labs so he wouldn't be seen. He heard Ambrose exhort Errol not to kill himself on the Mark VI prototype. Things were looking up. The market would wait a little longer for the greatest airship in history. Errol's reply wasn't loud enough to be heard. Shortly after that, Ambrose bid Errol goodnight, dimmed the main lights to a mere glow and departed. Silence descended, full of unsolved mysteries.

Risking discovery, Gerald looked through the small lab's almost-closed door. Where was Errol? What was he doing?

Please, please, let me catch him in a treacherous act. I want this bloody assignment to be over.

A moment later Errol stamped out of his own lab, swearing and muttering under his breath. In the subdued lighting his face was a portrait of furious indecision as he half-paced, half-dithered in the complex's wide aisle. He looked like a man attached to invisible strings tugging him first this way, then that. The fingers of one elegant hand dragged through and through his disordered dark hair. His jaw was set hard, and shadowed with stubble. He was a far cry from the urbane, polished and sophisticated Errol Haythwaite who'd paraded himself for obsequious admiration at the Wizards' Club and through the pages of newspapers and thaumaturgical publications alike.

'*Dammit,*' Errol said at last, furious. 'I'll have to chance it. I'll *have* to. *Dammit.*'

Spinning on his heel he headed back to his office, which was tucked between the Ambrose Mark VI lab and the complex's outer wall. Breath hard-held, Gerald watched him go in — and couldn't believe his luck. Errol left his office door open, which meant the thaumaturgic soundproofing wouldn't work. It was a gift . . . and a hint. *Time to spy.* But with the lab complex so quiet and empty of all other wizards, there was a chance he'd be heard. And even if he wasn't, Errol would undoubtedly sense his presence. Unless . . . unless . . .

What if he threw out an obfuscation hex to cover any inadvertent sound he might make and mask his thaumic signature completely? It was a neat solution, except —

I'd need to drop my shield. Will Errol feel it disengage? Will he feel me cast the hex? I may hate his guts but I can't deny the truth: he is a phenomenal wizard. Dare I risk it? Is he upset enough to be sufficiently distracted?

Sadly, there was only one way to find out.

As softly and gently as he knew how, he switched off his shield-incant then held his breath again. Waited for Errol to storm out of his office, searching for the source of the strange surge in the ether.

No Errol. No storming. The lab remained as quiet as a tomb.

Not my tomb, please. I don't feel like dying today.

Under his breath, Gerald whispered an obfuscation hex Reg had taught him years ago. Despite all of the new incants and hexes Sir Alec's people had given him he hadn't found one of theirs to beat it for flexibility. And he hadn't shared it with them, either. It was important to keep safe some things from his old life.

Besides, as Reg liked to say, it never hurt to keep a trick or two stuffed down your knickers.

He crept out of the darkened lab, into the almost dark complex and along the aisle towards Errol's office. Flattened himself against the wall beside the door and closed his eyes ... hoping that would help him hear more clearly what was happening.

'— were right and I was wrong. See? I can admit it.'

Errol, sounding oddly subdued. Conciliatory. Almost ... entreating. Speaking not on the telephone, but through a crystal ball. He could feel the connection vibrating the ether: yet another legacy of his roguish, barely-charted powers. If there was time, he could very likely trace that connection all the way back to its source, but there wasn't.

Who the hell is he talking to? Please, let it be Rottlezinder. Come on, Errol, give yourself away.

The person on the other end of the conversation said something in reply. The crystal ball's volume was turned down so low there was no hope of hearing it.

'Yes. And I'm sorry, Haf,' Errol replied. He actually sounded *humble*. Was he sickening for something? 'I want to make it up to you, old friend. Please, can we meet? Tonight? We need to sort this out.'

Though he'd been hoping for it ... expecting it ... Gerald felt his muscles slacken with shock. Confirmation at last. Errol *was* in cahoots with Haf Rottlezinder. Even as a small, vindictive part of himself that he hated to admit even existed let out a glorious, gloating yell — he thought: *damn*.

Because Errol was one of Ottosland's leading thaumaturgical lights. But to serve his own base ambitions he'd turned against his own people. Their blood was on his elegant hands. There was going to be *such* a scandal ... and the people who tended to look sideways at wizards, who supported the nutty anti-thaumaturgical brigade, who eschewed lives that took advantage of thaumic advances ... their blind prejudices would be reinforced and they'd end up with more converts to their short-sighted cause.

Dammit, Errol. How could you?

He realised Errol was talking again. '— know where that is, yes. It's too early to risk coming now, so wait for me. If you don't — please, Haf. Just make sure you're there.'

There? Where was *there*? Damn, if only he'd been able to hear Rottlezinder's half of the conversation, or had time to trace the etheretic connection between the crystal balls back to Errol's partner in crime. Now he'd have to remain hidden here until Errol left the lab then follow him … a venture fraught with the very real chance of discovery and failure.

But never mind. At least we know Rottlezinder's here in Ottosland. At least he's within our reach, at last.

So, should he contact Sir Alec? Call for some more agents? No. That would only further complicate an already complicated situation. Besides, he'd had it drummed into him repeatedly during the last six months: nine times out of ten, janitors worked solo. They relied on themselves and nobody else. A janitor was a lone resourceful wolf.

Gerald slunk back to the shadows, prepared to wait for as long it took.

Lord. I wish Reg was here.

'You know, Bibbie,' said Monk, tucking his hands into his armpits. 'I'm starting to have second thoughts about this.'

'Really?' said Bibbie brightly, wrapping a striped scarf around her neck. 'I'm not.'

He stamped his feet. 'Bibs, you've only had your driving certificate for five minutes.'

'Excuse me? It's been almost three months, thank you.'

'Where you're concerned that's pretty much the same thing,' he retorted. 'And it's dark, Bibs. Worse, you don't even know where you're going! For all you know you could end up in a not-very-salubrious part of town. Truly, I think you need to reconsider.'

Bibbie pulled on a battered old pair of gauntlet-style driving gloves. 'I don't.'

'Then at least you should let me come with you.'

'*No*.'

'I think it's quite interesting,' said Melissande, 'that you're not showing the *least* bit of concern for *my* welfare.'

'Yes, well,' said Monk, harassed, 'you're not my sister.'

'And a good thing too,' said Reg. 'Or things might be a bit awkward.'

They were standing in the rear court of Monk's Chatterly Crescent establishment. Once upon a time, before the invention of the thaumic engine, the rear court had been the stable yard. But the stables had been converted to woodwormed storage sheds and a single falling-down garage, which housed the battered jalopy that Great-uncle Throgmorton had left behind when he died. All the house's back lights were on, casting everything into varying shades of black and white. Reg sat on the jalopy's bug-eyed left headlight, feathers plumped against the night's chill.

Monk looked at Melissande, his gaze owlish with distraction. 'Please, Mel, don't take me the wrong way. It's just that if anything happens to *you* my parents aren't going to come after *me* with a shotgun.'

She smiled her very thinnest smile. 'True. But my brother might well come after you with an army borrowed from his friendly next-door neighbour Sultan Zazoor. You remember him, don't you? He's the one with the very nice war camel and quite a lot of swords.'

'I remember,' Monk said darkly. 'But Zazoor's half a world away. My parents are only two suburbs over.'

He had a point. 'Monk, we'll be fine.'

'The famous last words of disaster victims through the ages,' he said and tugged at his untidy hair. 'Honestly, girls, I *really* think this is a bad idea.'

'So you said, Monk,' Bibbie replied. 'But we didn't ask you what you thought, we asked you to lend us the jalopy and you said yes. And *then* you asked what for, but you know the rules. Once you say yes, you can't take it back.'

'*Nursery* rules?' he said, incredulous. 'Made up when we were five years old? Honestly, Bibs. You need to take this *seriously*. You're talented but you're not witching's answer to Gerald Dunwoody.'

She shrugged. 'I could be, one day. Or I could be a famous explorer and paddle a canoe single-handed down the great and mysterious Lanruvian River. Or I could try to solve the riddle of the singing forests of Fandawandi. I am Emmerabiblia Markham and I can do anything I want. Which tonight means I'm taking your rackety old jalopy and investigating a peculiar occurrence with my colleagues from Witches Inc. Because *you* said yes and now you can't take it back.'

Melissande exchanged an eye-rolling look with Reg then patted Monk on the arm. 'Truly, you mustn't worry. I'll make sure she doesn't get into any trouble.'

'Will you?' he said, his expression so woebegone. 'Really? Because I wasn't joking about the shotgun, you know. Ma and Pa dote on her, Saint Snodgrass knows why. I know *I* don't when she's in *this* mood.'

'Oh, *pooh*,' said Bibbie. 'And likewise *fiddlesticks* and furthermore *pishwash*.' She marched to the jalopy and flung open the driver's side door. 'Are we going or are we standing around here watching Monk be a wet hen?'

'Oy,' said Reg crossly. 'How many times do I have to —'

'And you can stop being a wet hen too,' said Bibbie. 'Are you going to come with us or fly? Make up your mind.'

Reg sniffed. 'I'll go with you. But you'd best leave a window down in case I need to make a fast getaway.'

And she flapped herself into the jalopy's back seat as Bibbie slid behind the wheel and patted it, like a pet.

Now Monk was chewing the side of his thumb. 'Oh blimey,' he muttered. 'This is what comes of giving girls an education. And the vote. And familial emancipation.'

'I *beg* your pardon?' said Melissande, and instead of kissing his cheek punched him hard on the shoulder. 'Would you like to withdraw those gormless, brainless, mannerless remarks?'

'No,' he said sulkily. 'And what's more I'm starting to regret ever introducing you to Bibbie.'

'What? You're saying she's *my* fault?'

'I'm saying that ever since you three started up Witches Inc. she's — she's — Mel, she could get *hurt*.'

Outrage surrendered to his genuine concern. Melissande, offended and touched at the same time, patted the shoulder she'd just punched. 'Monk, honestly, stop *fussing*. We're *not* trying to be Gerald. We're just keeping an eye on a silly old biddy who agreed to go traipsing about the streets of Ott late at night for her very dear friend Permelia Wycliffe, when Permelia Wycliffe appears to be perfectly capable of doing her own traipsing . . . yet doesn't want to.'

'Yes, but why?' wailed Monk. 'I thought you were *working* for Permelia Wycliffe, not *investigating* her!'

It was another excellent point.

'Yes, we are.'

'You are what? Doing both?'

She sighed. 'I know it looks like that at the moment. But Monk, something's not right. There's too much of the peculiar going on at Wycliffe's. Raised voices. Mysterious meetings. Even more mysterious crystal ball conversations. And now Permelia's got that dotty Eudora Telford running secret errands for her. It's just very *odd*, Monk, and I don't *like* odd. I like things neat and tidy and properly explained — and if possible filed alphabetically and correctly taxed. Besides. Eudora Telford's such a scatty old thing she really does need a few guardian angels making sure she's safe.'

'Well, yes, I suppose so,' said Monk, still unhappy. 'But why do you three have to take on the job?'

'Because nobody else was available at such short notice.'

'You know,' he said, sounding desperate, 'I could stop you. I could whammy the engine. Swallow the ignition key.'

Bibbie tugged down the driver's window. 'You could certainly try. Tell me, Monk, would you prefer one black eye or a matched pair?'

'*Bibbie* —'

She shrugged. 'It's only polite to offer you a choice.'

'Then please, *please*, at least let me come with you!'

Melissande sighed, and this time did reach up to kiss Monk's cheek. 'No. Now stop *worrying*, Monk. I'm a princess, remember, *and* an ex-prime minister. I'm perfectly capable of driving around the city for an evening. Reg is in no danger at all, and as for Bibbie ... you mustn't let her youth and extravagant beauty fool you. Your sister is as tough as nails. A match for anyone and anything.'

His shoulders slumped. 'I'm really not talking you out of this, am I?'

'No, Monk, you're not,' said Bibbie. 'You're just making us cross.'

'Reg and I will take good care of her,' Melissande promised. 'Our royal word of honour.'

Monk kissed her cheek, a little closer to her lips than was entirely proper. 'I'll hold you to that.'

She felt herself blush. 'Yes. Well,' she said, flustered. How embarrassing. 'We should get going or we'll be late. Don't wait up. We'll bring the jalopy back to you first thing in the morning.'

Leaving him adrift in the middle of the old stable yard, she squashed herself into the elderly car beside Bibbie and banged shut the passenger door.

'Right,' she said, as Bibbie closed her window. 'You two do realise that we're mad as hatters, attempting this?'

'Certainly,' said Bibbie.

'Stark staring bonkers,' said Reg.

'If Permelia Wycliffe finds out we were spying on her friend instead of trying to find her biscuit thief, she'll sack us and make it her life's work to see us ruined.'

'Of course she will,' said Bibbie.

'And she'd do a good job of it, too,' said Reg.

'So perhaps we should follow Monk's suggestion, and stay home toasting crumpets?'

'I don't think so,' said Bibbie, and started the engine.

'Wash your mouth out,' said Reg. 'That's a shameful suggestion.'

She sat back, feeling enormously pleased. 'My sentiments exactly, gels. All right, then. Let's get this done. Witches Inc. ho!'

An hour later they were still sitting in the jalopy, which they'd parked in the street outside Eudora Telford's fussily neat little bungalow. It was located on the outskirts of North Ott, which wasn't the richest part of the city, really it was rather shabby-genteel, but at least it wasn't insalubrious. The low, steady thaumic lighting threw odd shadows over the world.

Melissande wriggled in her saggy-springed passenger seat, trying to find a comfortable way of squishing too much of herself into not enough space. 'I don't know, Reg. I do wish you'd managed to overhear a bit more of Permelia's conversation with Eudora. I'd rather like to know if she's a victim or a villain.'

'No, would you really?' said Reg. 'I wouldn't have cottoned onto that if you hadn't already mentioned it forty-seven times.'

'Oh, come on, girls,' said Bibbie, sighing. 'Enough squabbling. Let's look on the bright side for once. At least we know for certain now that I can charm pertinent information out of government officials if I have to. That's *two* young men at the Births, Deaths and Marriages Bureau who couldn't have been more helpful.'

'Well, yes,' said Melissande. 'Only I'm starting to have second thoughts about that.'

Bibbie stared at her. 'About what?'

'You using your feminine wiles on unsuspecting file clerks.'

'I didn't do anything unseemly!' Bibbie protested. 'I just batted my eyelashes a bit and acted helpless, that's all.'

'*All?*' she echoed, letting her scepticism show.

'Well …' Bibbie's lips twitched in a small smile. 'Maybe I shed a few heartbreaking tears as well, and told an affecting tale of my ailing auntie whose address I'd misplaced. But honestly, Mel, how is it my fault if these clerks are so stupid they fall for that kind of nonsense?'

'Mmm,' said Melissande, and decided to let the subject drop. Mainly because she had a nasty sneaking suspicion that she wouldn't feel so critical if she possessed the kind of wiles that would work on unsuspecting file clerks. 'It's just a shame you couldn't learn anything useful about the office staff. Especially since nobody's triggered those hexes. I wonder if our thief realises we're onto her?'

'I suppose it's possible,' said Bibbie. 'But let's worry about that later.' She rubbed her gauntleted hands together. 'Reg, are you sure Permelia told Eudora not to run this errand until after eight o'clock?'

Reg sighed. 'Yes.'

'And you're absolutely certain that's the only piece of useful information you discovered? I mean, you were hanging upside down on the other side of a window with a curtain in front of it. And you're not as young as you used to be. Maybe your memory's playing tricks or —'

'And maybe *you'd* like to put a sock in it!' Reg retorted. 'I heard what I heard and I know what I heard and I've *told* you everything I heard. It's not *my* fault if three-quarters of the conversation was done with by the time I got there!'

'No, no, of course it's not,' Melissande soothed, and shot Bibbie an annoyed look. 'You did wonderfully well to hear what you did and make sense of it. But I do have to agree with Bibbie. I'd much rather be waiting for Eudora Telford at her destination than here outside her home. I mean, we're not exactly what you'd call experienced at following people, are we?'

Reg sniffed. 'Speak for yourself, ducky. I'm very good at it.'

'Yes, well, you've got what they call a natural advantage, haven't you? But we're stuck in this jalopy and — ow! What?'

Bibbie let go of her arm and pointed down the street. 'Look. There's a cab coming.'

'And here comes that wet hen Eudora Telford,' said Reg, staring at the bungalow. 'We're in business, girls.'

Melissande and Bibbie stared at her.

'What? I'm allowed to say wet hen,' said Reg. 'I'm a bird.'

'Ha,' Bibbie muttered. 'Only when it suits you.'

'Oh hush up, the pair of you,' said Melissande. 'And get down, quick. We don't want her to see us.'

As one they hunched down in their seats to watch Eudora Telford lock her front door behind her and hurry out to the waiting cab. She was wearing a dark coat over a plain dark dress and carrying a small reticule.

'Right,' said Reg, bobbing up as the cab pulled away with Eudora Telford inside it. 'Follow that wet hen!'

There was a slight delay as an excited Bibbie momentarily forgot everything she'd ever been taught about driving a car. But after a fraught few moments filled with unladylike exclamations, the jalopy fired up and Bibbie steered it in Eudora Telford's wake.

'Not too close!' said Reg. 'You don't want to put the wind up that cab driver. He might come over all chivalrous and try to do us a mischief. And not too far back either. There's not a lot of traffic but we don't want to lose them.'

Bibbie flung an exasperated look over her shoulder. 'Would you like to drive, Reg?'

'Love to,' Reg said promptly. 'I'd be very good at it, you mark my words. If you could've seen me with my coach-and-four ...'

Melissande saw the words *Four what?* flit across Bibbie's face, ready to be disastrously uttered. 'Don't say it, Bibbie!' she snapped. 'Just pay attention to what you're doing.'

They followed Eudora Telford out of the shabby-gentility of North Ott, around the edge of West Ott then over the Ott Bridge and onto the main Ott road. That led them eventually into the outskirts of South Ott, where a great many people of limited means were anonymously crowded into a definitely insalubrious stretch of township squashed between a looping bend in the Ott River and the huddled conglomeration of thaumic distilleries on the edge of the noisome Ott marshes.

'Hmm,' said Melissande, starting to feel ever so slightly uncomfortable. 'This isn't what you'd call a desirable locale, is it? What was Permelia thinking, sending Eudora all the way out here?'

'Nothing good, I'll bet you,' said Reg. 'And as for Eudora Telford, she's the kind of silly, clinging woman who'd do anything for a friend. The trouble with her sort is they think they're being needed but they're only being used.'

In this part of town the cobbled streets were narrow and poorly lit. From the looks of things the people of this sad, grimy district still relied on gas lighting, and many of the lamps had gone out. The night was moonless dark and empty of people. Eerily quiet.

'Hang back a bit more, Bibbie,' said Melissande. 'We really do stick out like a sore thumb.'

Bibbie slowed until the jalopy threatened to stop altogether. Up ahead, Eudora Telford's cab turned into a side street.

'Quick! Quick!' said Melissande. 'Don't lose her!'

Bibbie ground her teeth. 'Melissande Cadwallader, make up your *mind*!'

They crawled a bit faster towards the side street, then had to slam on the brakes as the cab appeared again. It pulled out of the side street and drove away.

'What? What? Did they make a wrong turn?' said Bibbie. 'Was Eudora Telford still in the back? I couldn't see! What —'

'Someone open a window,' said Reg. 'I'll go and look.'

Melissande pulled her passenger window down and Reg took off like a rocket.

'Well,' said Bibbie, after a moment. 'This is exciting.'

'I suppose,' said Melissande, sticking her head as far out of the jalopy as she could manage without decapitating herself. 'Drat these broken streetlamps, I can't see Reg at all! And if Eudora Telford's not in that cab then she's getting away in another direction altogether. If we lose sight of her then this was all for nothing.' She pulled her head back inside and gave Bibbie her sternest, most prime ministerly look. 'Right. New plan. You stay here and wait for Reg. Whatever you do, *don't* get out of this jalopy. The last thing we need is for it to get nicked.'

Bibbie gave her a look. 'It won't get nicked, Mel, not with the kind of don't-steal-me hexes I —'

'Then don't get out because I *said* don't get out!' she snapped. 'If anything happens to you it'll be *me* your parents come after with a shotgun — and Monk'll be right behind them carrying the spare ammunition! *Please*, Bibbie. *Stay put.*'

Without giving Monk's appalling sister a chance to draw breath for her next objection, she shoved out of the jalopy, eked the door closed and hurried towards the side street where she hoped she'd be able to see Eudora Telford.

Because if we've lost her ... and something awful happens to the silly old biddy ...

She made her way as quickly and quietly as she could over the uneven cobblestones. What a piece of luck she hadn't bothered to change out of her hideous Wycliffe uniform — she was practically a shadow herself, slipping through the darkness like a real secret agent.

Reaching the corner of the side street she took a quick look behind her. Miracle of miracles, Bibbie was still inside the jalopy. She lifted her hand in a half wave, half *you bloody well stay there* gesture in the hope that Bibbie could see her clearly, then ducked clandestinely into the side street.

Tall, decrepit tenement houses squashed shoulder to shoulder, marching down both sides of the street as far as she could see. Smoke drifted above them, thick and stinking. A few doorways here and there were illuminated by gas lamps, shedding just enough light to be useful. More light from a street brazier, cheerfully burning. But where was Eudora Telford? The street was silent — deserted. She was nowhere in sight.

Melissande hugged herself, as close to dithering as she'd ever been in her life. What to do? What to *do*? How had Eudora managed to get so far ahead? Or had she been in that cab after all?

Oh, where was Reg? Surely the wretched bird had caught up with it by now? So should she push on to see if Eudora was in fact ahead of her or should she go back to Bibbie, who was probably fine all alone in the jalopy. She was a witch with incants to spare, after all, she was perfectly safe, of course she was, but —

'*Melissande*?' said an astonished whispering voice behind her. 'Melissande, what the hell are *you* doing here?'

Swallowing an undignified yelp, she swung around. '*Gerald*?'

Bundled in a long dark coat, an impressive-looking First Grade staff in one hand, Gerald stared at her in dismay. 'I don't believe this. How can you *possibly* be here?'

'I could say the same thing of you,' she retorted. 'Don't tell me, let me guess. You're following a clue?'

'Not a clue. A person,' said Gerald.

'What a coincidence,' she replied. 'So are we.'

His jaw dropped. 'We? We? What do you mean *we*?' He looked around wildly. 'Is Reg here?'

'Not at the moment, but she's around. And Bibbie's back that way —' She jerked a thumb. 'Minding Monk's jalopy.'

Gerald grabbed her arm. 'Mind it somewhere else, Melissande. Go back. Now. All three of you. Get out of here, quickly!'

Honestly. Some people never learned, did they? 'Save your breath, Gerald,' she said, pulling her arm free. 'Witches Inc. is on a case and —'

'Hey ho,' said Reg, joining them in a rustle of feathers. 'What are you doing here, Gerald? Don't tell me Eudora Telford's an international master criminal!'

'Who? Eudora who?' said Gerald, distracted. 'What are you talking about? Who the hell is Eudora Telford?'

Melissande winced, just a little bit, as Reg settled onto her shoulder, claws pricking through her black blouse. 'If you have to ask, Gerald,' the bird said, 'then probably she isn't an international master criminal. At least not the one you're looking for.'

'Well, Reg?' said Melissande. 'Was Eudora in the cab?'

Reg shook her head. 'No.'

Rats. 'That means she must've been dropped off somewhere along this street. Right then, we'd better push on. See where this thoroughfare leads, and if we can still find her.'

'What?' said Gerald. 'No! You can't do that. You have to get *out* of here, you two, and take Bibbie with you. Any second now the person I'm following is going to come out of the laneway over there and —'

'How do you know?' said Reg.

He looked at her. 'I know.'

'Yes, but *how* do you know?' Reg persisted.

'I know because I've had a few tricks shoved down my kni — up my sleeve over the last six months,' he said, exasperated. 'Which I don't have time to explain right now. *Please*, will you just *trust* me? You have to — oh, *damn*.'

Further down the street, a tall figure wearing a long black coat emerged from a deeply shadowed laneway and turned right.

'Oy,' said Reg, flapping upwards to get a better line of sight. '*That's* Errol Haythwaite.'

Melissande peered around Gerald. 'Are you sure? How can you tell?'

'These eyes don't lie,' said Reg, still hovering. 'So. He *is* up to something nefarious. And he's about to get done for it.' Sniffing, she dropped back to her human perch. 'Couldn't happen to a nicer pillock.'

Gerald rounded on them. 'He's only going to get done for it if you two skedaddle.'

She sighed, irritated. 'Gerald, are you sure turning into a rogue wizard hasn't done something to your hearing as well as your eye? *We are on a case. We are not skedaddling anywhere.*'

'Melissande —' He sounded like he wanted to shout. 'Why are you following this Eudora Telford?'

'Because she's a wet hen running some kind of errand for Permelia Wycliffe,' said Reg. 'Why are you following Errol Haythwaite?'

'Good question,' said Melissande. 'If he's as upper crusty as you and Monk say, what's he doing in crustless, mouldy South Ott?'

Gerald muttered something impolite under his breath. 'He's meeting with Haf Rottlezinder — which is why I don't want you two anywhere in the vicinity.'

'Haf Rottlezinder?' Melissande looked at Reg. 'You don't suppose that's who *Eudora* — no. That makes no sense. Why would *Permelia* need to — unless she's the one — and we've accidentally crossed paths with — Reg, are you *sure* you didn't hear anything else Permelia told Eudora?'

'*Yes*,' said Reg, and chattered her beak crossly.

'Melissande, what are you talking about?' said Gerald.

She turned to him. 'Earlier this morning I overhead bits and pieces of an argument between Permelia and Ambrose. They were fighting over something to do with the company. And not long after that Eudora turned up, and Reg overheard Permelia begging her for a favour. But surely she wouldn't send Eudora to see —'

'She might,' said Reg, slowly. 'If she wanted to keep a prudent distance between herself and a questionable character like Haf Rottlezinder.'

'But that would mean Permelia *is* behind the portal sabotage.'

'Who says she isn't?' said Reg. 'Or maybe she and Ambrose are in on it together.'

'But — but Gerald said Permelia and Ambrose were in the clear.'

Gerald pulled a face. 'I might've been wrong about that. Obviously there's more going on here than Sir Alec's team managed to uncover.'

Reg chortled. '*We* uncovered it all right, sunshine.'

'Yes, well, there'll be plenty of time to gloat later,' he muttered. 'And we both know you will.'

'But — *Permelia*?' said Melissande. 'She's so — so law-abiding. Such a stickler for the rules. Why hire us to find a biscuit thief if she's merrily romping around Ottosland blowing up portals? It doesn't make any sense. And where does Errol Haythwaite fit in? He and Permelia don't have anything to do with each other.'

'Apart from the fact she's his employer, once removed?' said Reg.

'*That's* what I'm trying to find out!' said Gerald. 'But you two are making it *very difficult*!'

She opened her mouth to say something blighting, but was interrupted by a door opening further down the street. She and Gerald stepped back, flattening themselves against the wall behind them, as a well-wrapped figure emerged from the house.

It was Eudora Telford. 'Thank you so much,' she said to someone standing in the open doorway. 'Yes, I do feel much better now. And I understand perfectly where it is I need to go. I do appreciate you giving me such clear directions.'

A murmuring, as the person she was speaking to said something indistinct.

'Oh, no, no, I mustn't put you to any more trouble,' said Eudora Telford. 'I shall be quite all right. Thank you again.'

The door closed and Eudora Telford stepped back. In the dim gas lamp lighting she looked quite limp with fear.

'Oh, Permelia,' they heard her say. 'Oh, this is dreadful. If you weren't such a dear friend — if you didn't *need* me ...'

She turned and started walking away, following in Errol Haythwaite's footsteps.

'Oh lord,' groaned Gerald. 'Go after her, Melissande. *Stop* her. It might be nothing more than a bizarre coincidence that she's here ... but even if that's so, this situation — this area — they're far too dangerous for a woman like her. Please. Get her to safety.'

'And what are you going to do, sunshine?' said Reg.

'My job,' said Gerald. 'Now go on. Get out of here. *Hurry*.'

'All right, ducky,' said Reg, with a rattle of tail feathers. 'You heard the boy. Let's go.'

Melissande looked at Gerald. In the flickering brazier-light his face was older and grimmer than she'd ever seen it. Very nearly the face of a stranger. 'Um — did you know you've — ah — turned silver again?'

He touched his blind eye. 'Oh.' On a deep breath he covered it with the palm of his hand and muttered something. The air shivered. And when he lowered his hand she saw that his silver eye had turned brown. How eerie. 'Thanks.'

She nodded. 'All right then.' She wanted to say, *You be careful, Gerald*. She wanted to say, *Don't get killed*. But nothing she said could make any difference. He had a job to do, and so did she. 'So, I suppose we'll hear from you later?'

'Hopefully,' said Gerald, staring after Eudora Telford. '*Melissande* —'

'Yes, yes, we're going!'

Reg leapt off her shoulder, flapping ahead. Melissande hitched up her horrible long black skirt and ran after her.

Oooh, Saint Snodgrass, don't you let me go arse over teakettle on these stupid cobbles!

There was no sign of Errol Haythwaite when she and Reg caught up with Eudora, some ten doors down from where they'd last seen her. The silly woman shrieked and turned when she heard her name called.

'Gracious! Your Highness!' she squeaked, eyes popped wide with shock. 'What are *you* doing here?'

CHAPTER SEVENTEEN

Reg had settled on top of a defunct lamp post, sufficiently shadowed for Eudora Telford not to see her. Melissande flicked her a glance, hoping she'd get the message to stay put. From the corner of her eye she saw a running shadow — Gerald — sprinting down the other side of the street as he chased after Errol Haythwaite.

'What am I doing here, Miss Telford?' she said, wrenching her attention back to Eudora, and then realised she had no idea what to say next.

Obviously she couldn't tell the silly woman the truth. *Spying on you and Permelia* wouldn't help matters at all. She could say Permelia had changed her mind, but then Eudora Telford would go back to Permelia Wycliffe and, lo, see the cat making a meal of the pigeons.

'Um —' she said, knowing she now looked exceedingly silly herself ... not to mention suspicious. *Eudora Telford. Eudora Telford. What do I know about Eudora Telford . . .* 'Ah — well — His Majesty sent me.'

Eudora Telford stared. 'His Majesty? You mean —'

'Yes, Miss Telford. My brother. King Rupert the First of New Ottosland.'

'But — but *why*?'

Oh, what a very good question. On top of the lamp post, Reg was shaking with suppressed laughter.

'Well, Miss Telford, the thing is, Rupert — I mean, His Majesty — has — has a sweet tooth,' she said, frantically wracking her imagination. 'Yes. He's very fond of his cakes and pastries. And I — um — well, I mentioned to him that I knew you, a luminary of the internationally renowned Ottosland Baking and Pastry Guild — and he's very anxious to meet you himself.'

'*Me?*' said Eudora Telford faintly. 'Not Permelia? Your Highness, are you sure?'

Ignoring the pangs of guilt — *I'm only lying to save her* — she nodded. 'Quite sure, Miss Telford. His Majesty is hoping you might — ah — make a visit to New Ottosland so you can teach the royal kitchen staff how to — to — create a better jam roll.'

Now Reg was hanging upside down off the lamp post, wings waving as she whooped with silent hilarity. Melissande risked glaring at her, but the wretched bird took no notice.

Eudora Telford was trembling. 'Oh, Your Highness, I don't know what to say! Except — however did you find me all the way out here in South Ott?'

Melissande looked around the grim, poorly-lit street. 'Yes, it is rather an odd place for you to visit, Miss Telford. Do you mind if I ask what's brought you so far from home?'

Eudora Telford clutched her reticule more tightly. 'Nothing important, Your Highness. A favour for a friend. Nothing for you to worry about. You — you were going to tell me how you found me.'

I was? Oh. 'Yes, well, His Majesty is a wonderful man, Miss Telford, but when he gets a bee in his bonnet he does rather want things to get *done*. No delay. And he's so very excited about the thought of you visiting New Ottosland that he instructed me to — to —' *Oh, Rupert, I'm sorry about this . . .* '— to extend his invitation to you immediately. Nothing would satisfy him but that I rush out this very evening and see you on his behalf. But when I reached your charming little bungalow I saw you leaving in a cab, so I followed you. I'm sorry. It's just — I didn't want to disappoint the king.'

'Oh,' said Eudora Telford, and looked down at her tightly clutched purse. 'Well. That's perfectly understandable, Your Highness. Disappointing people is awful, isn't it? One — one is prepared to brave anything, no matter how frightening it might be, if that means not letting down the person who's relying on you.'

Despite the good news about Rupert, the poor silly woman was still trembling. Still pale. Melissande lightly touched her cold hands. 'Yes, Miss Telford,' she said gently. 'One is.'

She risked another glance at Reg. The horrible bird had recovered her composure and was sitting on top of the lamp post again, rolling her eyes.

'And now,' she added, 'I think we should return to North Ott so we can discuss the particulars of your visit to His Majesty's court. I have a car standing by, which should be here any moment.'

Looking at Reg again, she waggled her eyebrows in what she hoped was a clear hint to go and fetch Bibbie. But instead of flying off, Reg turned to look along the street in the direction Gerald had run.

Drat. 'Yes, *any moment* now my car should arrive.'

'That's very kind of you, Your Highness,' Eudora Telford murmured. 'Only, you see, there is the small matter of this errand, this favour . . .'

'I'm sure your friend would understand that you had to delay,' said Melissande, and looked again at Reg. 'Friends know that sometimes you have to *make a choice*. And being friends they don't hold it against you.'

'Yes, yes,' said Eudora Telford. She didn't look convinced. Reg didn't look convinced either but she flew off, away from Gerald, back towards the mouth of the side street and Bibbie.

'Honestly, Miss Telford,' said Melissande earnestly, tucking a hand in the crook of Eudora's arm. 'What true friend would deny you such a splendid opportunity?' With a little tug and a smile, she started the woman walking back along the street. 'Did I mention His Majesty has heard of your light touch with sweet pastry?'

Eudora Telford gasped. 'King Rupert's heard of my pastry? Your *Highness*!'

Melissande felt another stab of guilt. It was awful, playing on Eudora's pathetic sensibilities like this, but what other choice did she have?

I'll make it up to her somehow. Even if I have to arm-wrestle Rupert into extending her a real invitation. She is the Guild's secretary, after all. How bad could her jam rolls be?

Loud in the night-time silence, the wheezing chug-chug of Monk's approaching jalopy. 'And here's the car,' she said, waving at Bibby as two bug-eyed headlights cut through the gloom.

'Your Highness, Miss Telford,' said Bibbie through the open driver's window. 'All set to go?'

'Oh,' said Eudora Telford, taken aback. 'Miss Markham. You — you *drive*?'

Bibbie's perfect teeth gleamed. 'Certainly, Miss Telford. Would you expect anything less from the great-niece of Antigone Markham?' Leaving the jalopy to idle, she got out and held the rear passenger door wide. 'Please. Do have a seat.'

But Eudora Telford hesitated. 'Oh. Yes. D'you know, I'm just wondering, since you have this — this interesting vehicle, Your Highness, whether it would be possible for us to — to just drive a little further along so I can do this important favour for — for my friend. You know, before we discuss my visit to New

Ottosland. The thing is — you see — that if I don't do what I promised, my — my friend will be dreadfully ... disappointed.'

Melissande looked at Eudora's white and frightened face. Drat that Permelia Wycliffe. She really had this rabbit browbeaten.

'Oh, we can't,' said Bibbie quickly. 'I'm so sorry, Miss Telford. There's been a gas leak in the area, and we really should leave. You can come back in the morning. I'll bring you myself.'

'Gas leak?' said Eudora Telford, bewildered. 'I didn't hear anything about a —'

'The car has a wireless in it,' said Bibbie, with another dazzling smile. 'I just heard the announcement.' She began to usher Eudora Telford into the jalopy. 'Come along. No time to waste. That's it, upsadaisy —'

'Go on, ducky,' said Reg, from the shadows. 'Get that silly woman out of here. I'm going back to help Gerald.'

Of course she was.

'You're quite sure we can come back in the morning?' said Eudora Telford, settled in the back seat.

'Yes,' said Melissande, stepping forward. 'Of course. Because helping friends is always important. Come along, Miss Telford. I can't wait to tell you all about New Ottosland.'

Reaching the far end of the street at last, Gerald ducked into the final darkened doorway and pulled the tracer crystal from his pocket. Good. The activation was still holding. He'd attached the other half of the tracer to Errol's black cashmere overcoat, while Errol was in his lab killing time by working on the new Ambrose Mark VI prototype.

Please, Errol, whatever you do, don't take it off.

The crystal pulsed a medium bright green, which meant Errol was about three hundred yards ahead, still moving. He'd have to be careful not to get too close. He'd had to keep his etheretic shield deactivated, and Errol would almost certainly notice something amiss in the ether now.

He slipped out of the doorway and started walking again, throwing a glance down the street behind him. Thankfully there was neither sight nor sound of Melissande or that dratted Eudora Telford, best friend of Ambrose's sister Permelia. Who was, apparently, upset about something going on in the company. Something a bit more disturbing than petty biscuit pilfering.

There's definitely a connection here. I don't know what, but there is one. Another problem I need to sort out ...

A familiar rustling sound ... a stirring in the air ...

'Right,' said Reg, landing hard on his shoulder. 'Care to tell me what's really going on?'

He'd been expecting her, of course. 'I already did,' he said, resigned ... but not displeased. 'Errol's leading me to Haf Rottlezinder.'

'And you're convinced, are you, that Errol's a villain?'

'Yes,' he said shortly. 'What I heard was ... incriminating.'

He'd left the poor residential neighbourhood behind. Now the surrounding buildings looked like warehouses. Abandoned. Dilapidated. Old businesses gone to rack and ruin. The industrial smoke was thicker here, gritty and tainted with a thaumic tang. Under that was the stench of sour water, spoiled with the effluvium from some factory or other. The darkness was oppressive, the silence a shroud. It even felt like he was breathing too loudly.

Reg cleared her throat. 'So how did you get here from Wycliffe's?'

'The scooter.'

'Then why are we walking? It can't be too safe walking around here.'

'I'm just following Errol's lead,' he said. 'He drove from Wycliffe's to the other end of that laneway back there and parked. If he's walking now it's because Haf Rottlezinder told him to.'

'And where is our pretty plonker?'

'Up ahead somewhere.' He checked the tracer crystal. As he watched, the green pulse slowed … slowed … stopped. 'All right. Either he's lost or he's reached his destination.'

'The Errol Haythwaites of this world don't get lost, sunshine,' said Reg. 'Right. Stay here. I'll see what's what and come right back.'

'No — Reg —'

But she was gone, her wings whispering through the menacing night.

Shivering, he hunched a little deeper into his own cheap coat and shoved the tracer in one pocket. Shrugged his left shoulder up and down against the slowly building ache. He was starting to regret bringing his First Grade staff with him. It had seemed like a good idea when he left Wycliffe's, but now it was getting heavier with every step. At times like this he missed his lowly Third Grade cherrywood staff, which had fitted so neatly inside his coat.

Maybe I can get Monk to — to fiddle a First Grader down to Third Grade size somehow. A sort of stealth staff. That might come in handy.

He was standing opposite a narrow, vacant lot that sat between two run-down buildings. It looked a bit like a missing tooth in a rotten smile. In the faint illumination from the gas lamps on the buildings behind it he saw that the lot was overrun with weeds. A rustle. A snarling hiss. A panicked squeak, silenced. Two large yellow eyes gleamed briefly then disappeared.

He shivered again. *That's me. Slinking through the weeds in the dark, hunting. My father was a tailor. How did I get to be this?*

The world around him looked slightly … flattened. With only one good eye he'd lost his depth perception. He hardly ever noticed the difference any more. Only at times like this, with so little light around, and so much danger. That was when he remembered that while he'd gained a lot, he'd lost something too.

He frowned into the distance, trying to see Reg. Oh, lord, Reg. How was he going to explain her to Sir Alec? Her *and* the girls. Because he couldn't not include them in his final report. Lying to Sir Alec was out of the question. If his intimidating superior didn't understand about their serendipitous involvement — about how hard it was to stop Reg sticking her beak in to save him at every opportunity ...

Exactly how influential was Sir Alec? *Could* he take reprisals against Witches Inc.? Have Melissande recalled to New Ottosland? See Bibbie stripped of her thaumaturgical licence? Make Monk pay for his irrepressible sister? And what about Reg? All right, probably he couldn't do anything to her. If nothing else, she could outfly him. But what if he made things so difficult she had to leave Ottosland? Where would she go? Back to New Ottosland, probably, with Melissande ...

But I don't want her to! Why does everything have to be so bloody difficult?

'Right,' said Reg, gliding out of the gloom. 'I've got him spotted.' She landed on his shoulder again. 'He's outside an old boot factory, five hundred yards down on the left. Looks like that Rottlezinder's up on the top floor. You can just see a crack of light shining between the closed shutters. We'd better get hopping, sunshine, we don't want to miss what's going on.'

Letting his staff drop, Gerald plucked her off his shoulder and kissed her beak. 'There's no *we*, Reg. Not this time. You've been marvellous but now you have to go.'

'Gerald —'

'*No.* You can't be here, Reg. *Please.*'

She rattled her tail feathers. 'If there was time I'd argue with you, but there's not. Gerald, that place is hexed into the middle of next week. It was like flying into a brick wall, just about knocked me eyeballs over toenails. I'd say that's why Errol's waiting on the footpath — so his nasty little friend can let him in. You'd better not try taking that fancy staff of yours anywhere near it — you'll probably start fireworks.'

He kissed her again. 'I won't. Goodbye!'

As she flapped away he slid his gold-filigreed staff into the undergrowth on the vacant lot and obscured it with a hex. Then, because Errol was so close, he reactivated his shield-incant and broke into a soft-footed jog down the empty street towards Errol, and Haf Rottlezinder.

The warding hexes Rottlezinder had put on the boot factory struck him while he was still some fifty feet from its partially boarded-up entrance. The criminal wizard's thaumic signature stank of power, and malice. Dropping back to a stealthy walk he slunk from shadow to shadow, inching his way closer ... and closer ...

Yes, there was Errol, still standing on the footpath, impatiently waiting. A single working lamppost a little further down the street washed him with a faint light. He looked ill. Angry. Uncertain.

Then Gerald felt the ether shiver. Saw a ripple in the air, gentle at first and then more forceful. Errol's hair ruffled, as though blown by a breeze, and detritus in the shallow gutter — some old leaves, a few sheets of torn, tattered newspaper — picked itself up and danced, coquettish. Hazing smoke from the looming factories eddied, sharpening the ambient stink.

Rottlezinder was opening the front door.

Gerald bit his lip. He needed access to his full range of *potentia* now. Trying to spy on Errol and Rottlezinder muffled by his shield would be a waste of time ... and dangerous. So he held his breath, and at the height of the warding hexes' deactivation switched his shield off. Trusting, hoping, that any disturbance it caused would be lost in the already agitated ether, he stood still and mute in the deepest shadow he could find, and waited.

It worked.

With the oddest sensation — like the soundless snapping of a taut elastic — the warding hexes around Rottlezinder's hideout collapsed. Gasping, Errol rocked a little on his heels. A moment later the partially-boarded factory entrance shifted sideways, and an indistinct figure stepped onto the broken-bricked path to the door.

'Haythwaite,' it said, the accent heavily West Uphantican, guttural and grating.

'Haf,' said Errol curtly. 'It's safe to approach?'

'The hexes, they are down,' said Rottlezinder. He sounded bleakly amused. 'If it is safe, that is up to you. You're alone?'

Errol nodded. 'Of course. I don't want trouble.'

'Mmm-hmm,' said Rottlezinder. 'Such a funny fellow. You think I have not heard that before?'

Mist clouded as Errol breathed out, hard. 'Not from me, you haven't. Can we go inside? I don't care to discuss this in the street, like some beggar.'

'But you are a beggar, Errol,' said Rottlezinder, amused. 'You asked to see me, remember?'

Gerald saw Errol's lips pinch bloodless. Saw his hands clench into fists. *No, no, no, Errol, don't you bloody dare! How am I supposed to get to the bottom of this if you kill each other before I've got you dead to rights!*

'Yes, I asked to see you,' said Errol, mastering himself. 'But you approached me first. You got me involved. *Please*, Haf. We need to talk.'

Frowning, Rottlezinder looked past Errol to the street beyond. 'No, you want to talk. There is a difference.'

'What are you looking for?' said Errol, turning. 'I told you, Haf, I came alone.'

'You saw no-one else in the street?'

'Not a soul,' said Errol. 'Why? Are you expecting more visitors?'

Rottlezinder's face stilled, then he shook his head. 'No. I'm not one for company, Errol. You know that.'

Gerald, watching, thought that was a lie. *I'll bet he's waiting for Eudora Telford. But why? This is getting more complicated by the minute. Lord, how much do I hate complications?*

'Yes,' said Errol. 'And this won't take long. Please, can we go inside?'

The suggestion of a careless shrug. 'Sure,' said Rottlezinder. 'In you come.'

Errol walked up the uneven brick path, treading carefully, his head tipped back a little as though braced for a blow. Rottlezinder didn't shift aside when Errol reached him. Instead he made Errol squeeze past him. Errol stepped off the broken brick path and into a slimy puddle of something. The gluggy splash, and his exclamation of disgust, made Rottlezinder laugh again.

'Haf,' said Errol, his voice low. 'There's no need for this to be unpleasant.'

'No?' said Rottlezinder, then pulled aside the entrance's boarding. 'You first, *old friend.*'

As Errol shoved his way into the abandoned factory, Rottlezinder wandered a little way down the path and frowned out into the night. With the very edge of the street lamp's murky light touching him, Gerald saw that he was of middling height, very broad and blocky. Built more like a brawler than a wizard, one might think. His face was bony, his pale hair clipped very close to his skull, and he was dressed in black from head to toe. Around his right wrist a gold bracelet set with rubies winked and leered.

Gerald felt a tremble on the edges of the ether. Felt

Rottlezinder's *potentia* gather itself, like a fist. The criminal wizard was going to reactivate his warding hexes, and once they were brought back to life there'd be no hope of getting into that factory, no hope of learning the truth about him and Errol, no chance of thwarting whatever wickedness they had planned next.

No, no, no . . . I can't be locked out, I can't. Come on, Dunnywood, you tosser. Think . . .

Time spiralled around him. Years ago . . . he was a small boy playing in the kitchen while his mother baked fresh scones. A knock on the door. Someone unexpected. Mother went to answer it — some kind of travelling salesman. He remembered standing behind her, his four-year-old head not quite level with her hips, clutching her green skirt, listening to her tell him, 'No thank you, not today.' Remembered her closing the door, and the toe of the salesman's shoe jamming it open. Remembered his voice, persistent and argumentative. She'd threatened him with her rolling pin and he'd run away, the nasty man.

Jamming his toe in the closing door . . .

Was it even possible? Was there an equivalent incant? If there was he'd never come across it. He'd have to improvise one, and quick.

Oh lord. Where's Monk when I need him?

As Haf Rottlezinder rewove the strands of his guarding hexes, Gerald took a deep, desperate breath and insinuated the barest sliver of his *potentia* into the turbulence of the thaumic mix. Not even so much as a toe in the door . . . more like a toenail . . . or a tiny toenail clipping . . . If Rottlezinder felt it, if he noticed any shift in the etheretic balance, this would get very ugly, very fast. And his best weapon, his First Grade staff, was yards and yards behind him in a patch of weeds.

'Hey!' said Errol from the abandoned factory's entrance. 'What the hell are you playing at, Haf? Do you think I came all this way to stand around watching you show off?'

Distracted, displeased, Rottlezinder swung round. And as he swung round he snapped the fingers of his right hand. Dull ruby fire flashed, the bracelet round his wrist shivering, and the warding hexes slammed back into place.

'You should watch your mouth, Errol,' said Rottlezinder, not amused now but threatening. 'A fight with me is not something you should be looking for.'

'All right,' said Errol. He sounded ... cautious. And beneath the caution was something else. *Fear.* 'I don't want to fight, Haf. I came to talk. So let's talk.'

The factory's partially boarded-up door clattered shut behind them. Gerald let out his held breath, light-headed, and bent over, gasping, hands braced on his knees. Too close. That was too close. Rivulets of sweat trickled down his spine and face.

I read all those case files. I studied the last ten years of the Department's doings. Even with the censored bits blacked out, and nobody wanting Sir Alec to think they thought they were writing adventure fiction, I could see what this life is. So why am I surprised I'm so scared I could vomit?

Looked like Reg was right after all. *Living is believing, sunshine,* she was fond of saying. *Until you've lived it you don't know what's possible.*

Carefully he straightened, willing the dry-mouthed heaves to subside. Then he reached out and tugged, so *very* gently, on the thin thread of his *potentia* that was caught up in Haf Rottlezinder's warding hexes. Had he been right? Had his desperate gamble paid off? Or was he about to trigger the hexes and bring this entire investigation crashing down around his inexperienced ears?

He nearly fell over.

Oh, lord. Oh, Reg. It worked. How could it work? I don't know what I'm doing. I'm making this up as I go along.

Incredibly, what he'd managed to achieve, it seemed, was the insertion of his *potentia* into the actual matrix of Rottlezinder's warding hexes. It was still his, but somehow it was *mimicking* Rottlezinder's thaumic signature. The most fortuitous fluke, surely: this could only have worked because he stuck his toe in the door at a precisely perfect split-second of the hexing process.

If I'd tried to do it on purpose I'd never have managed it. Gosh. When Monk hears about this he's going to go spare.

But while it was exciting, he wasn't sure what it meant. Could he now *break* Rottlezinder's wardings? Or could he — maybe — possibly —

He walked through them as though the hexes weren't there. As though he were Haf Rottlezinder himself.

Dazed, he spun about to look behind him. To the ordinary eye the wizard's hexes were invisible, but he could sense them in the ether, thaumic barbed wire, slashing claws and tearing teeth.

That shouldn't be possible. I shouldn't have done that. Could anybody do that ... or is it just me?

In the pit of his belly, a faint, sickening tremble. If that wasn't something any First Grader could do ... if what he'd just done was a trick reserved for rogue wizards ...

What else can I do that we don't know about yet? And how long will it take for my own side to start thinking I'm more wizard than they can handle?

Horrible thoughts ... but he'd have to think them through later. Right now he had to get inside the factory and find out what Errol and Haf Rottlezinder were planning next.

With enormous care he cloaked himself in another obfuscation hex; not Reg's, this time, but one he'd learned from Sir Alec. The good news was that it muffled his thaumic signature until he was practically invisible. The *bad* news was that it interfered with his *potentia*, but he'd have to live with that. Secrecy was the most important thing right now.

He looked up. There, just as Reg had said, was the faint trace of light leaking between the top floor windows' shutters. That was where he needed to be, and quickly. Before Errol and Haf concluded their treacherous business.

Scarcely daring to breathe, he eased himself into the abandoned boot factory. It was pitch dark inside, like being smothered with black velvet. His half-blindness wasn't much help, either ... but he didn't dare try an *illuminato* incant.

The tracer crystal.

He dug it out of his pocket and held it in front of his good eye, squinting. The tracer glowed steadily, indicating Errol's nearby presence, but it wasn't bright enough to make a difference to the dark.

Damn.

Shoving the useless thing back in his pocket, he reached out with his muffled senses and began to pick his way across the floor to where he thought, he hoped, the stairs were located — heart-thuddingly aware that time was ticking past, that Errol and Haf could be planning another devastating portal attack and he wasn't anywhere near enough to overhear and stop them.

Come on, come on, Dunnywood. Get a move on. Don't let them win.

He found the stairs and, tread by uncertain, unseen tread, climbed them. Up one floor. Then another. Another. He was breathing in dust and who-knew-what kinds of filth; he wanted to sneeze and cough, but couldn't. His sinuses were burning. His legs were burning too — climbing stairs was hard work and he'd never been an athlete. Maybe Reg should have nagged him a little harder about getting outdoors for some healthy fresh air and callisthenics.

As he reached the top floor at last, the blood thundering through his veins and arteries, he heard raised voices. Errol and Haf Rottlezinder were arguing. Under the cover of their anger he crept along a little faster, guided by the spill of light from a room at the end of the corridor that lead off from the staircase.

'— always were one of the best, Haf,' Errol was saying. 'But is this any way to prove it? I thought you'd learned your lesson five years ago.'

'I'm not trying to prove anything,' Rottlezinder sneered. 'That was your game, as I recall. Appearances always mattered to you. They always will. Me? I don't care how a thing looks. I never did. The world is a lie. Everyone is a liar. Even you, Errol. *Especially* you, I think.'

The ether shivered again, teeth and claws returning.

'I don't know what you mean, Haf,' said Errol, sounding cautious again.

'Of course you do,' said Rottlezinder, softly dangerous. 'Don't treat me like one of your pathetic subordinates, Errol. We both know you didn't ask to see me because you changed your mind.'

A gentle sigh. 'You're right,' said Errol. 'I didn't. I've no intention of joining you, Haf.'

Gerald froze, shocked to a standstill. *What*? Errol *wasn't* involved? But —

'You're a fool,' said Rottlezinder, contemptuous. 'We are talking about a great deal of money.'

'I don't care about the money!' Errol spat. 'I've got plenty of money. I *care* that the wrong people are asking questions about me!'

'So let them ask. What is that to you? You don't have anything to hide, do you, old friend?'

Rottlezinder's voice was taunting now. What the hell was going on? Gerald stared at the open doorway. It was six feet away but he didn't dare creep any closer. Obfuscated or not, the risk was too great.

'Why should you worry?' Rottlezinder continued. 'The records were sealed. What we did — what *you* did — was winked at. Youthful indiscretions, isn't that what they call them?'

'It's what they were, Haf!' Errol was close to shouting. 'I was young and ignorant and I *never* would've dabbled in that — that *business* if it hadn't been for you. Why do you think I turned you down this time? Do you think I'm stupid? You used me at university and you wanted to use me again.'

'Ah ... you hurt my feelings,' said Rottlezinder, mocking.

'Believe me, Haf, I'll hurt a lot more than that if you don't stop this insanity,' said Errol. 'I *told* you not to get involved with this mess. But you couldn't resist, could you? Not the money, and not the chance to make the little people squirm. You always were greedy. Well, *friend*, now your greed is threatening *me* and I won't put up with it. I have a reputation, Haf. I am one of Ottosland's elite. And I'll not stand idly by while your hatred and greed threaten what I've worked so hard to achieve!'

'Oh, such a typical Haythwaite response,' said Rottlezinder, contemptuous again. 'Errol, you have not changed a bit. Always you are so — so *predictable*. All your outrage reserved for yourself. None left for the little people caught up in the madness.'

'I'm not interested in your personal opinion of me,' said Errol. 'I'm interested in watching you leave the country.'

Rottlezinder laughed. 'I'm not leaving. I still have work to do.'

'No, you haven't. Get it through your thick skull, Haf. This ends here tonight. I'm ending it, is that clear?'

As Rottlezinder laughed again, Gerald felt the hair prickle on the back of his neck. *Careful, Errol. Can't you tell he's dangerous? He's not some Third Grade minion you can order around.* But that was Errol's problem, wasn't it? His arrogance was blinding.

'Oh, Errol,' said Rottlezinder, spuriously sad. 'You think you're so much better than everyone else, don't you? You think because you have old blood, because the roots of your family tree go down so deep in Ottosland's rotten soil, you can snap your fingers and everyone will fall in line. You think *I* will fall in line. This is not true.'

'Yes, it is,' said Errol, his voice strained to breaking point. 'Did you not hear today's news? Your sabotage of the Post Office portal failed. Now the net's closing around you, and if you don't leave you'll be caught. For old times' sake I'm giving you this once chance to escape. But if you don't take it — well ...'

So close to the open door, to Errol and Rottlezinder, Gerald felt another ominous shiver in the ether. Even muffled he felt it, blowing through him like a wind full of knives.

Oh, lord. That's not good.

'Errol ... Errol ... what did you do?' Rottlezinder whispered. 'Did you call the authorities? Did you *tattle* on me?'

'Of course I bloody called them, Haf! What choice did you leave me?' Errol demanded. 'It was only a matter of time before somebody *died*!'

'How could you?' said Rottlezinder. He sounded ... bemused. 'After I turned to you for help. After everything I shared with you. Everything we did. *This* is how you thank me? With *betrayal*?'

'I haven't betrayed you, Haf,' said Errol. 'Nobody knows you're here. Nobody *will* know. Not from me. Do you think I want anyone knowing I'm involved with this madness? Just ... *leave*. I'm begging you. Let it all end tonight.'

'I am a fool,' said Rottlezinder, his voice thickened with rage. 'I let sentiment defeat pragmatism. Get out, Haythwaite, and do not come back. Next time my wards will tear you apart.'

'I'll go when you do,' said Errol, defiant. 'Come on, Haf. It's *over*.'

'No, it is *not* over!' shouted Rottlezinder. 'Not until *I* say so!'

'Then you *are* a fool!' Errol retorted. 'You're forcing me to stop you. And you know I can, Haf. You know —'

And then Errol let out a shout of pain.

Flattened against the cracked corridor wall, Gerald felt Rottlezinder's *potentia* flare, felt the saboteur lash out at Errol with an incant full of flame and fury. He heard Errol shout again, felt his instinctive defence. Felt the ether writhe and shudder as Errol fought back.

'Haf! Are you mad? Stand down, man, before you trigger that bloody hex!'

His head snapped up. What? What bloody hex? What did Rottlezinder have in that room? Surely not another incant destined to destroy a portal?

Oh, no. This madman could blow up the whole building. Lord, he could blow up half of South Ott.

Heart pounding, Gerald tried to control his panicked breathing. Booming in his ears, Sir Alec's inviolate first rule: *Never ever compromise your identity.*

But if he didn't do something . . . people were going to die.

Sorry, Sir Alec. I don't have a choice.

CHAPTER EIGHTEEN

But as he took a deep breath and stepped into the open doorway Errol and Rottlezinder hurled grotesque hexes in a desperate attempt to vanquish each other. Colliding, the hexes ignited in an eye-searing thaumic explosion.

The etheretic wave trembled the factory on its foundations. Tossed him into the corridor's far wall. His head thwacked the rotting plaster so hard he saw stars. Teeth rattling in their sockets, he dropped to his hands and knees. Dazed, giddy, he looked up — and choked on a shout.

Errol and Rottlezinder lay crumpled on the room's filthy floor. On a rough workbench near its shuttered window sat a clear crystal container, and inside the container — pulsing malevolently — was Rottlezinder's next portal hex: activated and close to discharge.

'Oh, no.'

He could feel the hex's matrixes coalescing ... constricting ... drawing in a deep thaumic breath before exhaling annihilation.

This wasn't like Stuttley's. He wouldn't survive this explosion. He had to get out. He had to get Errol and Rottlezinder out. But there wasn't time — there wasn't time — he could save one man, but not both. So who? Rottlezinder, the saboteur, who could unmask his employer? Or Errol, who wasn't guilty. Not of this crime, anyway.

Inside its crystal prison the wicked hex began to shudder. The ill-lit room washed with red light, and all around him the ether started to scream.

Gerald threw himself into the room, grabbed hold of Errol's ankles and dragged him into the corridor. Haythwaite was insensible, blood trickling from his nostrils, his face sweaty and chalk-white. Bending over him, Gerald grabbed Errol's wrists, hauled him upright then let him topple over his shoulder. Staggering like an inebriate he made for the staircase at the end of the corridor.

Not having to hide any more, he panted out the *illuminato* incant, his spine buckling under the strain of running with Errol on his back. He could feel the ether torquing, feel Rottlezinder's hex warping and distorting its delicate fabric.

Down the stairs, three treads at a time, sobbing for air, sobbing for speed, punishing his bones and muscles, knowing he had scant moments . . . knowing he might die. That Rottlezinder would die. Another death at his door. How many more before he'd not be able to open it?

A scream was building in his chest and throat, terror and pain and despair throttling him. Blinding him. He skidded down the final staircase, almost fell as he hit the floor, blundered across the refuse-scattered factory entrance towards its partially-boarded front door. He had enough wit and strength left to smash the door with a demolishing incant, then staggered through the rain of splinters into the chill night air. The *illuminato* floated with him like a tethered balloon.

Five steps closer to the deserted street, Haf Rottlezinder's portal hex exploded. Gerald felt the unravelling in the ether as the malevolence of the hex reached its destructive peak. He let his knees fold. Let himself and Errol crash to the stony, brick-strewn ground, bright lights of pain bursting behind his closed eyes. Trapped air escaped his lungs in an agonised grunt. He managed to reach for a warding incant, managed to raise it partway ...

... and then the shock wave from Rottlezinder's detonated hex rolled over them. Gerald folded himself across Errol, wrapped his arms round his head and held his breath.

Going to die now. We're going to die.

Great booming echoes of sound, loud enough to hurt his eardrums. A silent shrieking of thaumic energies, released. The thud and clatter and deadly rainfall of debris, plaster and brickwork and tiles and tin. The retching stink of overheated thaumicles, of scorched ether, of burning wood. The grinding, groaning collapse of the ruined boot factory.

After a little while, Gerald sat up. Everything hurt, but he wasn't dead. Errol wasn't dead either, he was twitching and moaning. He had cuts on his face and a swelling bruise on his forehead. His shamelessly expensive black cashmere overcoat was ruined.

Faintly, in the distance, the sound of sirens, wailing.

'Right,' he said, and was surprised to hear that his voice still worked. 'Probably it'd be a good idea to make ourselves scarce.'

Groaning, Errol opened his eyes. Blinked into the *illuminato*'s faint light. 'What the hell? Dunwoody, is that you?'

Bugger. 'No, Errol, it's your fairy godfather. Can you stand? We've got to leave before the authorities arrive.'

'Dunwoody, what are you *doing* here?' said Errol, sounding querulous. 'I was — I was —' His confused expression cleared, and he wrenched himself upright on a sharp gasp of pain. 'Haf. I came to see Haf — where the hell is he, we were fighting, he —'

Gerald grabbed Errol's shoulder. 'Haf Rottlezinder's dead, Errol. He went up with the factory. Now come on. We have to *go*.'

Shrugging free, Errol got his feet under him and managed to stand. Swaying, he looked at the charred and smoking remains of the abandoned boot factory, then turned. 'What the *hell*? Did you do this, Dunwoody? Did you kill Haf?'

Oh lord. Painfully Gerald pushed to his feet. 'No. He killed himself. Errol —'

Errol took a step back. 'How did you get here? Did you *follow* me? What's going on? What are you —'

'I can't tell you,' he said. The sirens were inconveniently close now. 'Errol, listen, there's no time, we have to —'

Stepping back again, Errol nearly tripped on a twisted section of guttering. 'You get the hell away from me, Dunwoody. I don't know what you're up to but I've had more than enough of you. I'll see you're decertified for this. I'll see you back in your family tailor shop by the end of the week. That's if I don't see you in prison first — and if I can, I will. You're a bloody menace. You always were. You must've bribed someone to get your Third Grade credentials, and I promise you this, too — I'll find out who it was. I'll see them in a prison cell beside you, I'll —'

Gerald let Errol's ravings wash over him. Took a deep breath, feeling his battered flesh and bones protest.

He'll never be reasonable. He won't let me explain. And anyway, I can't. Not without telling him the truth.

'Errol,' he said quietly.

Errol ignored him, still ranting.

'*Errol!*' he said, and snapped his fingers in Errol's face. Recited a new incant under his breath. One word to trigger it. Just one word. The incant itself was a little more ... complicated. A lot more treacherous. In anyone else's hands, internationally illegal. Gleaned, he'd been told, from an obscure proscribed text. Turned out it was closely related to the hex Lional had used on *him* to ensure his obedience. But that was all right, apparently. He was a janitor so he could be trusted with it. They only had to worry about *bad* people using *that* kind of thaumaturgy.

He hadn't wanted to learn the incant. Hated knowing it

existed. Couldn't stand the idea of one day having to use it. Not after his first-hand experience with its effects.

'*For emergencies only,*' said Sir Alec. '*Most agents never have to resort to the* docilianti. *I understand your concerns, Mister Dunwoody, but you are going to learn it. After all, isn't it better to be safe than sorry?*'

'Yeah? Well now I'm both,' Gerald muttered to the still-agitated ether. 'And for the record, Sir Alec? *I think this is wrong.*'

His free will thaumaturgically suspended, hexed from man to compliant puppet, Errol Haythwaite smiled a vacant smile.

Gerald took him by the elbow and tugged. 'I'm sorry, Errol. I really am.' Then he sighed. 'Come on. Let's go.'

'More tea, Your Highness?' said Eudora Telford, hopefully brandishing the pot. It was covered in a badly-knitted puce and mustard yellow cosy, with a bobble on top.

Melissande shook her head. One more mouthful of tea and her bladder was going to explode. 'No, thank you, Miss Telford.'

Eudora Telford's face fell. 'Oh.' Then she brightened. 'Then perhaps another macaroon?'

Saint Snodgrass save her. Another crumb of Eudora Telford's macaroons and the chair she was sitting on was going to collapse. They were so lumpen they could easily be used to weight sacks full of unwanted kittens, for the drowning thereof. Or scuttle an entire fleet of the Ottosland Navy's battleships.

If I end up having to send her to visit Rupert he will never, ever, in a million years forgive me. No wonder she's never been in contention for the Golden Whisk. She wouldn't be considered for an old tin teaspoon. Not even if it was the consolation prize and she was the only contestant!

Realising that silence was another rejection, Eudora Telford took a step back.

'I'd love another macaroon, Miss Telford,' said Bibbie, as the end of the wretched woman's nose turned an emotional pink. 'I can eat anything.'

'And never gain an ounce,' Melissande added quickly. 'Alas, if I could only say the same.'

'Oh,' said Miss Telford, marginally cheered. 'Yes. Well.' She put down the teapot and offered the plate of macaroons to Bibbie. 'Have as many as you like, Miss Markham. It's a great honour for my little cakes to win the acclaim of Antigone Markham's great-niece.'

As Bibbie got in some practice on her skills at deception, praising Eudora Telford's dreadful macaroons, Melissande stared out of the horribly knick-knacked parlour window. Still no sign of Reg. Where was the dratted bird? More than an hour they'd been stuck here with Eudora, listening to her prattle on and on and on, and all she had to show for it was indigestion, a full bladder, and the sinking feeling there was no way she could extricate Rupert from a life-threatening encounter with the silly woman's horrendous cooking.

Oh dear. Nature could not be ignored a moment longer. She leapt up. 'I'm so sorry, Miss Telford. Might you excuse me to the — the powder room?'

Eudora Telford's plump cheeks coloured. 'Why certainly, Your Highness. Let me show you —'

'No, no, just point me in the right direction,' she said. 'I don't want to put you to trouble. Besides, now that we've heard all about your exciting life in the Guild, I'm sure there are some stirring tales of Antigone Markham my colleague's just dying to share with you.'

'Oh!' said Eudora Telford, hands clasped to her bosom. 'Oh, Miss Markham, *would* you? I didn't like to ask ... I didn't want to — to thrust myself forward — but I *must* confess to you, Antigone Markham has been a lifelong *heroine* of mine. *Any* story you could share — *any* snippet of information to shed light on her illustrious career ...'

Melissande winced as Bibbie shot her a look that would've

scalded a burned cake tin clean. But the smile she gave Eudora was as sweet as plum pie. 'Well, I think I can oblige you, Miss Telford. Only you must promise never to breathe a word to another soul. Antigone *never* liked to boast, you know.'

Eudora Telford dropped to the edge of the sofa, which was antimacassared to within an inch of its upholstery. 'Not a word … not a *syllable* … I *swear* it, Miss Markham.' Then, remembering, she looked up. 'Through the parlour door, Your Highness, turn right, up the little staircase, second door on your left.'

Melissande smiled. 'Thank you, Miss Telford.'

Coming back downstairs again afterwards, half-an-ear tuned to Bibbie's enthusiastic retelling of some notorious Pastry Guild scandal of the past, she caught sight of Eudora Telford's reticule on the hall stand … and stopped. The *most* appalling thought had occurred.

Upon their return to Miss Telford's bungalow, the sad little woman had begged them to come indoors to partake of tea and cakes and perhaps a little conversation. Of course she and Bibbie agreed. Not only did they need to find out what Eudora had been up to in South Ott, there was also the danger she might think better of abandoning her errand for Permelia Wycliffe and call another cab to go back there … where all she could do was get herself in terrible trouble.

So they'd accompanied Eudora Telford into her little home, and paid for their dedication with ghastly tea and worse cakes. Upon entering her residence, Eudora placed her reticule on the hall stand … and clearly hadn't gone back to it since.

Like Boris at a mouse hole, Melissande stared at the fussily beaded purse.

I shouldn't. I really shouldn't. It would be dreadfully uncivil. A brute violation of the laws of decent society, common courtesy and the debt one owes one's hostess.

On the other hand, she was one third of Witches Inc. An investigator of the unusual and the odd. And after Lional she had sworn a solemn, private oath *never* to shirk a difficult duty again.

Bugger it.

She snatched up Eudora Telford's reticule, loosened its drawstrings and stuck her hand inside. Her fingers closed around a soft pouch, which felt heavy and full of suspiciously small, hard items.

She glanced over her shoulder at the almost-closed parlour door. Bibbie was still regaling Eudora with saucy Guild stories. Keeping her spellbound. *Good girl, Bibs. Don't run out of inspiration now, whatever you do.* Holding her breath she pulled the pouch out of Eudora's reticule, loosened its drawstrings and looked inside.

Gemstones flashed in the hall's mellow lamplight: diamonds, rubies, sapphires and emeralds. Enough jewels for a king's ransom, surely.

Good grief. Where did Permelia Wycliffe get her hands on these?

She fished in the reticule again, and this time came up with a folded scrap of paper. Heart racing, she unfolded it.

Haf Rottlezinder. The old boot factory, Laceup Lane, South Ott. After dark. Enter from Button Street. Approach only on foot.

The last instruction was heavily underlined. The entire note was written in Permelia Wycliffe's unembellished hand.

Melissande stared at it, horrified. So Permelia *was* mixed up with the portal saboteur. But how? *Why?* She couldn't be the one behind the attacks, could she? It had to be her horrible brother Ambrose, didn't it?

Or am I letting Lional get in the way? Am I making the fatal mistake of assuming that because Ambrose is horrible it also follows that he's evil?

Surely, as an intelligent woman, an investigator, a staunch advocate of women's suffrage, she had to accept the possibility that Permelia Wycliffe was the mastermind behind the portal sabotage? That somehow she'd suborned Errol Haythwaite to her cause and used him as a conduit between herself and Haf Rottlezinder? After all, she did love — excessively — the company her father had built. And no-one could deny that Permelia was ambitious, and ruthless.

Or it could be both of them, Permelia and Ambrose. They might not care for each other the way she and Rupert cared, but that didn't mean they'd not join forces to save the family business from bankruptcy and ruin. If politics made strange bedfellows, money had the power to join enemies at the hip.

Rats. I really don't want Permelia to be guilty. I want it to be Ambrose, because he's such an old frog. But I have to face facts: the note. The gemstones. Eudora Telford. One way or another, Permelia's involved.

With another glance at the not-quite-closed parlour door, heart pounding harder than ever, Melissande stuffed the note and the gemstones back inside Eudora Telford's reticule and replaced it on the hall stand exactly as she'd found it.

Then she took a deep breath, poked a stray hairpin into her bun and sailed back into the parlour as though nothing whatsoever out of the ordinary had just occurred.

'— and *that*,' Bibbie was saying, 'is the true story of what happened at the Coconut Cookoff of 1884. But I warn you, Miss Telford, you did *not* hear it from *me*.'

Eudora Telford clapped her hands together, delighted. 'Oh, Miss Markham, I shall *never* breathe a *word*, I promise. Not even to Permelia, and *she* is my dearest bosom friend, you know.'

Melissande cleared her throat. 'Miss Telford, it's been truly delightful having this wonderful opportunity to get to know you better. His Majesty is going to be so excited when I tell him about this charming interlude. I'm sure he won't know what to do with himself until you and he meet in person.' She flicked a glance at Bibbie. 'But I'm afraid we'll have to leave you now. It's getting rather late, and there's something we have to tidy up back at the agency.'

'Oh,' said Eudora Telford, woeful again. 'Yes, of course, Your Highness. You've been too gracious. Too kind.'

'And speaking of Miss Wycliffe,' she added, 'we've not forgotten the errand you were to perform on her behalf this evening.'

Eudora Telford blushed. 'You know?'

'We guessed, Eudora,' she said gently. 'I can't imagine there's anyone else for whom you'd have braved the streets of South Ott.'

'Please, Your Highness,' Eudora whispered. 'You mustn't tell a soul. I promised Permelia I'd take her secret to my grave.' She sobbed. 'Just as I promised I'd help her, but I haven't. I've let her down.'

'No, you haven't,' said Melissande. 'Miss Markham and I shall return tomorrow morning, promptly at ten, and escort you back to South Ott, so you can keep your word to Permelia.'

'Oh, no, I couldn't impose, Your Highness,' gasped Eudora. 'I couldn't *possibly* —'

'Oh, but we *insist*, Miss Telford,' said Bibbie, smoothly taking her cue. 'It's the least we can do. Besides, I have so many more stories about Antigone to tell you.'

Flustered and flattered, Eudora Telford surrendered. 'Well, as long as you don't consider it a dreadful inconvenience. Only, the thing is — if you'd not mind —' Her blush deepened. 'You must promise not to mention it,' she said beseechingly. 'Permelia would be so displeased with me if she were to discover —'

'Miss Telford,' said Melissande, 'we shan't breathe a *word*. The *last* thing we want is for Permelia Wycliffe to know that we know anything about your errand to South Ott.'

'Oh *thank* you,' said Eudora Telford, and showed them out with a fervent promise to be ready for them again in the morning.

'*Gemstones*?' said Bibbie in shocked disbelief, once she'd heard what was hidden in Eudora Telford's reticule. She fired up the jalopy's engine. 'Are you *sure*?'

'Trust me,' said Melissande. 'If there's one thing I know about it's jewels. I had to sell off most of ours to pay the palace gardeners towards the end.'

Bibbie whistled. 'Gemstones *and* Haf Rottlezinder. Gosh. Things aren't looking too good for Permelia, are they?'

'No,' she said shortly. 'But let's not jump to conclusions, Bibbie. We need to meet with Gerald and see what he found out. Let's get back to the office, shall we? Fingers crossed Reg is waiting there for us, and she can fill in at least some of the blanks.'

It nearly killed him, but Gerald finally got Errol safely back to Wycliffe's.

He came up with his plan of action during the mildly precarious journey to Errol's parked car. Precarious not because the *docilianti* compulsion was in danger of wearing off, but because scant minutes after they left the ruined boot factory various civilian and government folk began descending on the area. Having paused to retrieve his staff from the vacant lot, he'd been forced to drag Errol further into the smelly shadows to avoid them being noticed. He'd stared anxiously at each passing vehicle but hadn't — praise Saint Snodgrass — caught sight of Sir Alec. He did see Dalby, though, and thought his heart would stop altogether. But Dalby couldn't see him this time ... which meant he could start breathing again.

Once it was safe to get moving, he hauled Errol into an awkward dog-trot and hustled him as fast as he dared back to the wizard's silver Orion. The old boot factory's destruction had enticed quite a few people out of their homes, which was helpful. He and Errol lost themselves in the general excitement and reached the car without incident. It was still there, of course, its don't-steal-me hex glowing a bold red warning on the windscreen.

'Unhex it, Errol. We have to get out of here.'

Dreamily, Errol did as he was told then let himself be bundled into the driver's seat.

'Right,' he said, stowing his staff in the back and clambering into the passenger seat. 'To Wycliffe's, Errol. Slowly. Don't draw any attention to us, whatever you do.'

Still trammelled in the *docilianti*, all the mean, superior sharpness in his face smoothed away, leaving it peculiarly pleasant, Errol obeyed. And as they glided through the advancing night in a car that cost more money than Gerald knew he could hope to earn in ten years, he ran through his plan again, looking for any holes that Sir Alec might poke in it. And then, when he couldn't find any, hunched in the passenger seat and worked very hard at not thinking about *anything* ... most *especially* what had just happened back there at the factory.

Wycliffe's front gates were locked, but he took care of that with a touch of his staff. Still beautifully obedient, Errol drove them round to the R&D block. Gerald had to admit it: while he didn't at all care for the *docilianti*, or having to use it, he couldn't deny it was coming in handy.

As he and Errol got out of the car a winged shadow swooped down from one of the nearby tall and spindly balibob trees.

'Reg?' he said, then shook his head. *Surprise, surprise. Nothing changes.* 'What are you doing here?'

'What does it look like, sunshine?' she said, landing on his outstretched arm. 'I'm waiting for you.'

'But — but how did you know —'

'I didn't,' she said, shrugging. 'Not for sure. But it seemed like a safe bet. When I saw you and Mister Puppet, here, weren't blown to smithereens along with that boot factory, I —'

'*Reg*! You were *there*? But I *told* you to —'

'Yes, well,' she said, insufferably complacent, her eyes gleaming sardonically in the meagre light from his newly-kindled *illuminato*. 'I don't take orders from you, Gerald. I might, every now and then, adopt a politely worded *suggestion*, but —'

'So you saw what happened?'

She sniffed. 'I saw you save Errol, here. I saw the factory blow itself to matchsticks — you're making a bit of a habit of that, aren't you? — and then when I saw all the bigwigs rolling in, I scarpered. So what happened?'

Briefly, he told her.

'Well, well,' she said when he was done. 'You're turning lucky escapes into an art form, aren't you?' Considering him closely, she tipped her head to one side. 'Gerald . . .'

He roused himself from unpleasant memory. 'What?'

'It's not your fault if that Rottlezinder's dead.'

'*If* he's dead? Come on, Reg. That explosion spread him across half of South Ott.'

'Half?' She snorted. 'You do exaggerate, Gerald. I'd say a quarter, if you're lucky.'

'*Reg*!'

'Oh, don't start,' she snapped. 'If you could've saved Rottlezinder too, you would have. But you had to choose, and you chose pillocking Errol Haythwaite. Though why —'

'Because he's innocent.'

'*Innocent*?' Incredulous, Reg stared at him. '*Errol Haythwaite*?'

'Yes. He went to see Rottlezinder to make him stop the portal sabotage. *And* he tipped off the authorities about today's attack.'

'Blimey!' she said. 'I don't mind admitting I never saw *that* coming.' Feathers ruffled with surprise, she hopped from his arm onto Errol's head. Obligingly docile, Errol said nothing. He barely flinched. Seemed hardly aware he was wearing a bird for a hat. Reg's gaze sharpened. 'All right, Gerald. What have you done to him?'

He turned back to the car and fished out his staff. 'Nothing permanent,' he muttered. 'Just encouraged his co-operation.'

'Oh, yes? Using one of Sir Alec's dirty tricks, I take it?'

'Please, Reg,' he sighed. 'Not now.'

Relenting, she chattered her beak thoughtfully. 'I'll say this much. Dirty trick or not, the incant works a treat.' Suddenly her eyes gleamed with wicked mischief. 'What d'you think? I mean, this chance won't come again, Gerald. I could pretend I'm a pigeon and Errol's a statue.'

Despite everything, he grinned. 'I think I don't have time for this,' he said, trying to sound severe. 'I have to get him inside and make it look like there's been a laboratory accident.'

'Hmm,' she said. 'Well, as cover stories go I suppose I've heard worse. Are you sure it'll hold?'

'It'll have to. At least long enough for me to do what needs to be done.' He pulled a face. 'After that he can be Sir Alec's problem. I've had enough of Errol Haythwaite to last me a lifetime.'

'And you're quite sure he's innocent?' said Reg, wistful.

He frowned, remembering the cryptic comments he'd overheard about sealed records and youthful indiscretions. 'Of the portal sabotage? Yes.'

'Bugger.' She rattled her tail feathers. 'And there was me looking forward to him being publicly disgraced.'

He pushed Errol's car door closed again. 'Reg, that's not very nice.'

'Yes, well, neither is Errol,' she retorted. 'All right then, so if he's in the clear then who hired that bounder Rottlezinder?'

He shrugged. 'I don't know. Not yet. Now please, Reg, you need to leave. Again. And I mean *really* leave this time. The girls must be going spare, wondering what's happened to you.'

'No they're not, Gerald. They know I'd never leave you in the lurch.' She sleeked her feathers, getting ready to fly off. 'You know, sunshine,' she added, abruptly serious. 'That was some pretty fancy thaumaturgy you managed tonight. I'm talking about getting past Rottlezinder's warding hexes. If I were you, I might be a bit … careful … about what I said in my report to that Sir Alec. After all, he's a very busy man. Probably he doesn't need to know every little pettifogging detail. Broad brushstrokes. Big picture. That's what you should be focusing on.'

In silence they looked at each other. Then he nodded. 'Thanks for everything, Reg. Tell the girls I'll be in touch. I still need to know what part Eudora Telford played in this — if any.'

As she flapped away, he took hold of Errol's sleeve. 'All right, you. Come along. Let's make this look good, shall we?'

The laboratory complex was dark and deserted, just the way they'd left it. Still passively compliant, Errol deactivated the warding hexes on the side door and they slipped inside. It didn't take long to set up the latest Ambrose Mark VI prototype for destruction. A fiddle here … a tweak there … a clumsy adjustment or three to the thaumic regulation chamber …

When he was done, Gerald looked at Errol. In the bright laboratory lights all his scrapes, bumps and bruises from the factory explosion were starkly revealed. The damage to his expensive coat was equally impressive.

'Haythwaite,' he said, and put one hand on Errol's shoulder. Snapped the fingers of his other hand in front of Errol's face, reinvigorating the *docilianti*. Priming Errol for what was to come. Thrusting aside any nasty, niggling qualms.

I'm one of the good guys. That means I'm doing good.

'You need to listen to me now, Errol. Are you listening? Can you hear me?'

'Oh, yes,' said Errol. His altered face was quite blank. Waiting for someone to write his thoughts upon it.

Slowly, carefully, Gerald reconstructed the evening's events. 'We've been working here all night, Errol. Just you and me. Working on the Mark VI prototype. We haven't set so much as a toe outside of the lab complex. You made me stay behind and work with you to make up for the time I took to go into town. You were very angry about that, Errol. You thought I had no business leaving the laboratory. Do you understand me?'

Errol nodded. 'Yes.'

'How did you feel about me leaving the laboratory, Errol?'

Slowly, Errol's face contorted. 'Bloody Dunnywood,' he said, contemptuous. 'Have to twist his arm practically out of its socket to get a decent day's work from him. Well, I won't have it, you mingy little turd. I'm in charge of this facility and you'll bloody well work all the hours I say. You'll work till you drop, do I make myself clear?'

'Yes, Mister Haythwaite,' he said, letting his voice cringe. 'I'm sorry, Mister Haythwaite. Of course I'll work back with you, as long as it takes, Mister Haythwaite.'

'Yes indeed, you will,' said Errol. 'Or I'll see that Ambrose sacks you first thing in the morning.'

'Good, Errol,' said Gerald, and patted his shoulder. 'That's what you remember. That's all you remember. And Haf Rottlezinder is nothing to you but a vague memory from your youth. You didn't know he was in the country. You had no idea what he was up to. Do you understand me, Errol?'

Errol nodded. 'Yes, I understand.'

Gerald let out a long, unsteady breath. *Lord, this is despicable.*

Even in a good cause. 'Excellent. Oh! Yes!' He'd nearly forgotten. 'One last thing, Errol. If anyone asks, what happened tonight wasn't my fault. In fact, I did everything I could to help you prevent this horrible accident. Ah ... yes ... which wasn't much, because I am a thoroughly useless lump of a Third Grade wizard ... but still. I tried. Right? You got that?'

'Right,' said Errol. 'Got it.'

He nodded. 'Good. So I think that's everything. Now, Errol, you mustn't worry. You're perfectly safe.'

Using his staff this time, he washed a filtering protective wall around them, leaving it just porous enough for authenticity. Then, on a deep breath, he destabilised the hovering Ambrose Mark VI airship prototype ... and watched it explode. Felt the rolling wave of thaumic discharge tumble through the carefully calibrated protective shield and leave the appropriate amount of thaumic residue all over himself and Errol. Not enough to hurt them — though he did feel his eyebrows frizzle — but a sufficient quantity to completely obscure what still remained of the residue from the old boot factory's destruction.

Ears ringing, exposed skin smarting ever so slightly, he satisfied himself that Errol was unharmed then looked at the totally ruined prototype airship. Another one. How many did that make now? Four? No. Five. Fresh scorch marks seared the laboratory walls. Smoke swirled beneath its buckled ceiling.

After deactivating the protective barrier he turned back to Errol. Snapped his fingers again, severing the *docilianti*'s hold. Errol's eyes rolled back in his head and he dropped where he stood, his head rapping too hard on the laboratory's unforgiving concrete floor. He'd have a nasty goose-egg for sure. Ah well, Just another touch of authenticity.

Feeling bleak, Gerald stared down at him.

Reg is right. I'm far too good at this. Nobody can know just how good at this I am.

And then he went to make his panicked phone call to the authorities. On the whole, it wasn't going to take much acting.

CHAPTER NINETEEN

A great deal of fuss and chaos ensued.

Some time later ... he wasn't sure exactly how much time had passed, he wasn't keeping an eye on the clock and besides, he had a thumping headache ... Ambrose Wycliffe and his sister Permelia arrived to force their loudly blustering way through the milling Department inspectors and ambulance orderlies.

'Mister Dunnywood, is it?' Ambrose Wycliffe demanded. 'What is the meaning of this? What's going on? Who are all these people and why are they here before me?'

'Before *us*,' said his sister sharply. 'Well, young man? Answer my brother!'

Gerald, sitting at one of the central aisle benches, flicked an apologetic glance at the junior ambulance attendant who was pressing a strip of sticking plaster to his forehead. 'It's — ah — it's Dunwoody, actually, Mister Wycliffe,' he said, at his most humble. 'And I'm sorry, but I thought proper procedure was to inform the authorities in the case of a thaumaturgical accident. So I did.'

'An accident?' said Permelia Wycliffe. 'What are you talking about? What kind of accident?'

Gerald arranged his face into an expression of servile distress. 'We lost another Mark VI prototype, I'm sorry to say. We —'

'What do you mean *we*?' Ambrose Wycliffe interrupted. 'Who is *we*, pray tell?'

'Mister Haythwaite and myself, sir,' said Gerald, earnestly. 'We —'

'Mister Haythwaite?' echoed Ambrose Wycliffe, his florid face paling. 'D'you mean to tell me Errol's been *blown up*?'

He bit his lip. *Yes indeed, Ambrose, that's exactly what happened. In fact, our Errol's been blown up twice. In one night. I wonder if that's some kind of record?* Throttling the urge to laugh — *am I in shock?* — he cleared his throat.

'It's all right, Mister Wycliffe. Mister Haythwaite's not dead. Some other ambulance officers are taking excellent care of him.'

Dazed, Ambrose Wycliffe fished a large blue handkerchief from his coat pocket and mopped his forehead. 'Oh. I see. Good. What a relief.'

'The accident, young man!' snapped Permelia Wycliffe. '*What happened*?'

'Well, we stayed back, you see, to do some more work on the prototype's engine,' he explained, glancing uncertainly at Ambrose's intimidating sister. If her brother was florid, she was pale as snow. In her eyes, the most unnerving glitter. 'Ah — Mister Haythwaite was very keen to see that little — er — little hiccup in the thaumic regulation chamber sorted before —'

'What?' said Ambrose Wycliffe, startled out of his bewilderment, and glared at the junior ambulance orderly who was packing up his little tin of plasters and salves. 'Be quiet, Dunwoody! You're discussing private company matters in front of witnesses, you *dolt*!'

'Oh,' said Gerald. 'Sorry, sir. I'm not thinking straight, got rather a nasty bump on the head.'

But if he was hoping for some sympathy from the Wycliffes he was wasting his breath.

'Let me see if I understand you, young man,' said Permelia Wycliffe. 'You and another wizard were working here alone in the laboratory tonight?'

He nodded. 'Yes, Miss Wycliffe. That's correct.'

'*All* night?'

'All night, Miss Wycliffe,' he said virtuously. 'We never left. Everyone else left, but we stayed behind to work. As Mister Wycliffe knows, Mister Haythwaite is devoted heart and soul to the Ambrose Mark VI and he particularly ordered me to assist him. And of course I was only too happy to obey.'

Now Permelia Wycliffe was staring at him with the *most* peculiar look on her face. As though she'd swallowed a whole swarm of flies and couldn't quite believe it.

'You *never* left?' she said. 'Not even for a late supper?'

'No, Miss Wycliffe,' he replied. 'Mister Haythwaite wouldn't hear of it.'

'I'm sorry,' said Permelia Wycliffe. 'But I —'

'Oh, do *hush*, Permelia,' snapped her brother Ambrose. 'You're a gel. You can't possibly understand my wizards' dedication and loyalty. Good lord, woman, you shouldn't even *be* here. You know perfect well that gels interfere with —'

'*Yes*, Ambrose,' said Permelia Wycliffe sharply. 'But I think tonight, of all nights, we can make an exception. Don't you?'

Surprisingly, Ambrose backed down. 'Ah — yes, well, perhaps this once,' he mumbled. 'But only this once.'

'Actually, sir,' said Gerald, remembering Melissande's outrage, 'I'm pretty sure the notion of gels upsetting the thaumic balance has been thoroughly disproved by —'

'Who asked for your opinion, Dunwoody?' Ambrose shouted, spittle flying. 'Keep your mouth shut, you Third Grade ignoramus. You've already said quite enough for one evening.' He rounded on the waiting ambulance orderly. 'You there. What is Mister Haythwaite's condition? He's my best First Grade wizard. The man without whom Wycliffe's resurgence is doomed! I *demand* to know —'

The orderly leaned away from Ambrose's rabid intensity. 'Ah, sorry sir, I'm not permitted to discuss the —'

'*Don't you stand there telling me what you're not permitted! I want to know how he is!*'

Everyone within earshot of Ambrose Wycliffe jumped, even Permelia. Well. Everyone except for Dalby, who was hovering around the edges of the lab, bruised-looking and completely unremarkable. Gerald let his gaze glide right over the man, then turned again to the quaking orderly.

'Look, I'm fine. Just a few bruises,' he said. 'And I'm not important, I'm just Mister Haythwaite's lowly assistant. I think —'

'Ha!' said Ambrose Wycliffe. 'His *former* lowly assistant, you mean! Dunwoody, you're *sacked*. I *never* want to see your incompetent face again. Getting the government involved in private Wycliffe company business — not having the courtesy to call *me*, your employer, before these interfering government busybodies — it's *outrageous*! And I have *no* doubt this accident is *your* fault, just like —'

'Now, now, Ambrose,' said Permelia Wycliffe. The peculiar expression still hadn't quite left her face. 'I think you're being a bit hasty. The young man is right, he is required by law to inform the authorities first. Doubtless they instructed him not to tell anyone else, even us.' She turned. 'Isn't that so, young man?'

Gerald blinked. Permelia was protecting him? How *odd*. But since the popular theory was not to go kicking gift horses in the teeth … 'Yes, Miss Wycliffe. That's exactly right, Miss Wycliffe. It'd be my licence if I disobeyed the authorities, Miss Wycliffe.'

She gave her brother a sharp, satisfied nod. 'You see, Ambrose? And besides, you don't know what caused this unfortunate explosion. You won't know until you've spoken with Mister Haythwaite. You can't sack a man who might be innocent of wrongdoing. That flies in the face of everything Wycliffe's represents. Father would never have stood for it, you know.'

Ambrose Wycliffe's face burned an even brighter red. 'Really? Well, Permelia, in case you've not noticed, Father's not here any more. But *I* am and *I* say —'

'That you've had a horrible shock,' said Permelia Wycliffe, and took her brother's arm. 'You're quite overset, Ambrose, and who can blame you? But what kind of a devoted sister would I be, to stand by and let you make a poor decision without trying to stop you? Can you imagine I'd ever do such a thing?'

Ambrose Wycliffe stared at his sister, and she stared back. Some of the hectic colour died out of his jowly, whiskered face, and he cleared his throat. 'No. Of course not,' he said hoarsely, tugging his arm free. 'Very well. Mister Dunwoody here is not sacked outright.' Recapturing his authority, he puffed out his chest. 'But you are suspended, Mister Dunwoody. Pending a thorough investigation into this disgraceful affair.'

'Suspended with full salary and benefits,' Permelia Wycliffe added smoothly. 'In fact, don't think of it as a suspension at all, young man. Think of it as a nice little holiday, to help you recover from your nasty experience. After all, it's a wonder you weren't blown to pieces.'

'Ah — yes — thank you, Mister Wycliffe. Miss Wycliffe,' Gerald said, very carefully not letting his gaze touch on the still-hovering Dalby. 'I — ah — well, it has all been a bit upsetting. In fact, is it all right if I go home now? I've spoken with the men from the Department of Thaumaturgy. They know where to reach me if they need anything else.'

'All right,' said Ambrose Wycliffe, grudgingly. 'You can go. But I don't mind telling you, Dunwoody, you've handled this whole thing poorly. Very poorly indeed.' His disgruntled gaze swept around the now brightly-lit lab complex, crowded with busily investigating outsiders. 'You might well have done irreparable harm to this establishment's reputation. And if *that* proves to be the case —' Ambrose Wycliffe leaned close. 'Not even my tender-hearted sister will save you.'

With an effort, Gerald kept his face under control. 'I understand, Mister Wycliffe.'

'You'd better,' snapped Ambrose Wycliffe, then glared at the ambulance orderly. 'And you. Take me to Errol Haythwaite at once.'

As the orderly hesitated, Gerald nodded. 'Truly. I'm fine. I'll be right as rain come the morning.'

'Very well, sir,' said the orderly, reluctant. 'But you should see your own doctor, soon as you can.'

The Wycliffes followed the junior orderly to the other side of the laboratory complex, where two senior ambulance orderlies were still fussing over Errol. Permelia Wycliffe cast one last, puzzled look behind her. Gerald nodded and smiled gratefully, pretending not to notice anything was wrong.

Then he slid off his stool and made his circumspect way through the ongoing bustle to the lab's main door ... making sure to catch Dalby's eye as he passed.

Outside it was cool and much more quiet, the aftermath of the accident mercifully muffled. Aching all over, his various scrapes and bruises vigorously complaining, Gerald folded his arms tight to his chest and waited.

A brief increase in noise, as the doors opened then closed again. The scrape of boots on the pathway. A roughly cleared throat.

'Dear me,' said Dalby sourly, very quiet. 'What a hurly-burly to be sure. Never a dull moment when you're around, is there, Dunwoody?'

Gerald didn't turn. 'Does Sir Alec know?'

'You could say that,' said Dalby, with a soft, derisive snort. 'He wants to see you. Soon as. Proper put out, he is.'

Proper put out? *I bet that's an understatement.* 'Fine. I don't suppose you could —'

'Don't make me laugh,' said Dalby, and spat. 'I've got to keep an eye on what's happening here. Take Haythwaite in when the leeches have cleared him. You'll have to make your own way to Nettleworth, boyo.'

Oh. In which case, he'd have to soup-up another scooter. But that still left the one he'd ridden to South Ott. Somehow he'd have to get it back here before someone noticed its absence.

Damn. Why can't anything ever be simple?

'Fine,' he sighed. 'Only there's one small problem, Dalby.'

Another derisive snort. 'No, there's not. The scooter you left across town's shoved in the garden, over there.'

'You found it?'

'Course I bloody found it,' said Dalby, scornful. 'The amount of hexing you did on that thing, it's a wonder every bloody wizard in town didn't find it. Bloody show-off, Dunwoody, that's what you are.'

Gerald felt his face heat. 'Thanks.'

'Yeah,' said Dalby. 'That makes my night, that does.'

And he went back inside.

Still aching, and now dry-mouthed with nerves on top of it, Gerald retrieved the scooter . . . and went to face the formidable Sir Alec.

'So you see, sir,' he finished, at the end of his long and convoluted explanation of the night's events — keeping the girls out of it had been interesting, to say the least — 'Errol Haythwaite is in the clear. But it looks like we'll have to take another look at the Wycliffes.'

Leaning back in his chair, elbows propped on its arms, Sir Alec steepled his fingers and gazed at the ceiling. 'Hmm. Yes. That certainly appears to be the case, doesn't it?'

The night was so late now it was very nearly morning. Beyond Sir Alec's office window the sky above Nettleworth was shifting towards dawn, blushing pale pearly grey with the merest suggestion of pink. Gerald was so tired he felt light-headed and not quite real. Strangely insubstantial, as though his bones were made of paper and his flesh of cotton stuffing. Thanks to some noxious brew Sir Alec had made him drink, his aches and pains were mostly subsided. But oddly, he was hungry ... and he desperately wanted to sleep.

'I'm sorry I couldn't get Rottlezinder out in time,' he added. 'I know you were anxious to speak with him, sir.'

Gaze lowered again, Sir Alec raised an eyebrow. '*Anxious*, Mister Dunwoody? I'm not in the habit of feeling *anxious*. Certainly it would've been useful if we'd been able to chat with Mestre Rottlezinder, but alas. In this business we quite often encounter disappointment. However experience has taught me that things often do work themselves out, though perhaps not as swiftly as one might prefer.'

Gerald frowned. 'I suppose,' he said slowly, 'the fact that Rottlezinder's dead will give us a bit of breathing space. Finding his replacement won't be easy. Perhaps we'll get lucky, and the search itself will help us identify who's behind the portal sabotage. Ambrose Wycliffe, or whoever.'

The faintest hint of weariness touched Sir Alec's cool eyes. 'Indeed. In our business, success too frequently hinges upon fortuitous serendipity.'

While failure turned on the lack of it. 'I'm sorry about the boot factory, too. Even though I didn't see anything in Rottlezinder's room except for him, Errol and the portal hex, there might've been information hidden elsewhere in the building. I wish I'd been able to investigate more thoroughly. Still ... maybe Mister Dalby can find something in the debris.'

'It's unlikely,' said Sir Alec. 'Which is also unfortunate. But under the circumstances — all things considered — I appreciate that your choices at the time were limited.'

Gerald waited for the inevitable, sardonic reference to Stuttley's. When it didn't come he felt himself relax, just a little bit.

'So, all in all, an eventful evening,' Sir Alec said, his steepled fingers tapping each other.

'Yes, sir,' he sighed. 'Eventful is one word that springs to mind.'

Sir Alec's gaze narrowed. 'The thing is, Mister Dunwoody, that when one is assigned a watching brief, the emphasis is generally placed upon *watching*. But it seems there has been rather a lot of running about in this instance. Also some very ... creative ... uses of thaumaturgy.'

He swallowed. 'As you say, sir. Things got a bit eventful.'

'And then, of course, there's the matter of the *docilianti* compulsion,' Sir Alec continued, ignoring that. 'If I recall correctly, I believe I made quite a point of telling you how rarely such a dangerous incant is to be employed. And yet here we have you, a junior janitor, whipping it out at the first opportunity. Tell me, Mister Dunwoody, do I misremember the facts or were you *not* quite ... opinionated ... regarding the uses of such thaumaturgics?'

Sir Alec's voice was mild enough, his expression perfectly bland, but behind his grey eyes something dangerous waited. Gerald felt his jaw tighten.

'I know what I said about that kind of thaumaturgy, Sir Alec. And my opinion hasn't changed. But under the circumstances I didn't think I had a choice. We had to get out of there, and Errol — well, I knew Errol wasn't going to co-operate. And there wasn't a lie I could tell him that he'd believe.'

'No, no I don't suppose there was,' Sir Alec said at last, musingly. 'Given your colourful history. Tell me, Mister Dunwoody, how did you manage to breach Rottlezinder's perimeter warding hexes? I don't recall you mentioning that.'

He kept his gaze steady, his expression unchanged. *Watch yourself, Gerald. This man is no-one's fool.* 'I don't recall mentioning that there were any warding hexes, Sir Alec.'

Sir Alec smiled. 'Perhaps you didn't. But there must have been some, surely. A man like Haf Rottlezinder would never leave himself exposed and unprotected, even in such an obscure location. Everything we know about the man suggests he'd have himself warded to the stars. So. How did you successfully breach his defences?'

Seated on the other side of Sir Alec's imposing desk, in the remarkably uncomfortable wooden visitor's chair, Gerald dropped his gaze to his knees. Well. Hadn't he been an idiot, to hope Sir Alec wouldn't put his finger precisely on his story's omission? The question before him now was how did he handle the situation. Reg's uncharacteristically solemn warning echoed in his memory.

If I were you, I might be a bit . . . careful . . . about what I said in my reports to that Sir Alec.

The warning only echoed his own misgivings. He might've spent the last six months here in Nettleworth, being poked and prodded, but that didn't mean he knew Sir Alec any better now than five minutes after they first met.

All right, yes, Monk says I can trust him to fight the good fight, but how does Monk know that? He'd never lie to me . . . but that doesn't mean someone wouldn't lie to him. And I have no idea what Sir Alec really thinks of my abilities. For all I know he already sees me as a threat . . .

Sir Alec cleared his throat, very mildly. Too mildly. 'Mister Dunwoody,' he said, suspiciously pleasant. 'I feel it would be a great pity for you to thrust a spoke in the wheel of your brand-new career by choosing, at this point, to tell me anything less than the whole, unvarnished truth.'

He looked up, straight into Sir Alec's unnerving grey eyes. Eyes that had looked upon death, and worse than death, for more years than he cared to think about. And he realised he'd reached a kind of crossroads, without ever noticing the journey or its destination. He'd thought he'd made his final choice in New Ottosland. That Sir Alec's offer of joining the Department was the defining moment of his life.

But he'd been wrong. *This* was the defining moment of his life. Because after the factory, and Rottlezinder, he knew from the inside just what he was getting himself into. It was the difference between looking at a rapid-filled river … and swimming in it.

So. Did he want to keep swimming? Or did he want to get out? Was Sir Alec a man with a life preserver or was he someone with a long pole waiting to push him under the surface to watch him drown? There was no way of knowing. Not for certain. It all came down to a question of faith.

Either you trust him or you don't, Dunwoody. The time has come to make your choice: piss or get off the Department pot.

'I don't know how I did it,' he said, shrugging. 'I was thinking about sticking my toe in the door, and the next thing I knew a tiny thread of my *potentia* had woven itself into Rottlezinder's warding hex. I didn't plan it. It just happened. And somehow I was able to pass through the barrier undetected.'

'I see,' said Sir Alec, after a moment. 'How very … creative … of you, Mister Dunwoody.'

He shrugged again. 'I don't know about creative, Sir Alec. All I know is that it turned out lucky for Errol. If I hadn't — improvised — he would've been blown to bits, just like Haf Rottlezinder.'

'Yes indeed, he certainly would have,' murmured Sir Alec.

He leaned forward. 'Look, sir. I've no idea what you know about me that I don't. I don't know what all those tests have told you. And to be honest, right now I'm too tired to care. But let me tell you what *I* know about me. I agreed to join your Department so I could make up for what happened in New Ottosland. All I'm interested in is stopping people who hurt other people with thaumaturgy.'

Sir Alec unsteepled his fingers, and instead laced them across his lean belly. 'Yes, Mister Dunwoody. I am perfectly aware of your motives for joining this Department.'

'Maybe, but I don't want there to be any misunderstandings,' he retorted. 'I never asked to be a rogue wizard, Sir Alec. If I could undo it right now, believe me: I would.'

Sir Alec's eyebrows lifted. 'Really?'

'You asked for the truth. That's it. I'll always be truthful with you, provided honesty doesn't get someone hurt.'

'Mister Dunwoody ...' Sir Alec sighed. 'Surely you've learned by now that life is rarely so cut-and-dried. Telling the truth frequently results in casualties. That is the nature of our business. It is sadly too often how this wicked world of ours works.'

'I know,' he said, uncomfortable. 'I suppose what I'm trying to say, Sir Alec, is that while I might work for you, that doesn't mean you own me. And it doesn't mean I'm going to let you spend six more months poking and prodding and *investigating* me to satisfy your curiosity about just what makes me tick. You take me or leave me the way I am, flaws and all, right here and now. And if there's more about me and my rogue powers to discover, then I say let's discover them while I do what I joined this Department to do. Because otherwise, I don't see any point in me staying.'

Sir Alec's wintry smile appeared then disappeared, like a

sparkle of sunlight on dancing water. 'What a forthright young man you are, Mister Dunwoody.'

'I try to be,' he said, making himself meet Sir Alec's unforgiving gaze. 'And I try to learn from my mistakes.'

'Yes, well, I'd advise you to learn from this one,' said Sir Alec. 'Do not edit your reports to me, Mister Dunwoody. I'm not sure if it's occurred to you, but trust is in fact a two-way street.'

The girls. He winced. *But I can't drop them in it. Nor Monk. I'll just have to do a better job of keeping them out of things after this.* 'Yes, sir.'

'Hmm,' said Sir Alec, eyes narrowed. Then his expression relaxed. 'And now, to celebrate the establishment of our new and deeper, more trusting relationship, I will share with you some rather alarming news about your erstwhile superior Errol Haythwaite.'

Gerald sat up. 'He's not dead, is he? I mean, I took every precaution with that lab explosion, Sir Alec. I know I timed it right, and jiggled the prototype's engine matrix not a single thaumicle past what I needed to, and I absolutely protected him with —'

'*Relax*, Mister Dunwoody!' Sir Alec said sharply. 'I realise you've had a morbid night but there's no need to assume *everything* is about death.'

He swallowed. 'Sorry. So — Errol's all right?'

'He's not dead,' said Sir Alec. 'But I'm afraid to say that he's far from all right.'

Oh, lord. 'What's happened now?'

Sir Alec got out of his chair and moved to stand at the window, gazing into the slowly lightening sky. 'What can you tell me of Jandria, Mister Dunwoody?'

'Ah … not an awful lot,' he said, staring. 'Um. They were the instigators of the last big war. Must be coming up to forty years ago. They lost. They were required to pay some pretty steep reparations and made to agree not to rebuild their — *oh*.'

'Yes,' said Sir Alec, at his blandest. '*Oh* indeed. They were made to agree not to rebuild their military capabilities.'

He felt his heart thud, sickeningly. 'Are you saying the Jandrians have broken the terms of the armistice?'

'I'm saying we've received reliable intelligence that they are working on a secret fleet of military airships,' said Sir Alec. 'Incorporating some of Errol Haythwaite's most innovative thaumaturgical designs.'

Gerald felt his jaw drop. '*What*? No. That can't be right. I mean, Errol's a lot of things, Sir Alec —' *pillock ... plonker ... tosser ...* 'but he's not a *traitor*.'

Sir Alec turned from the window. 'No? And what makes you so sure of that? It wouldn't be the first time a Haythwaite has let down his country.'

I'm so tired, and this is all going too fast. 'Sorry, Sir Alec. I don't know what you mean.'

'Never mind,' said Sir Alec, and resumed his chair. 'The Haythwaite family history is not germane to this conversation. Let us instead look at the unpalatable facts of this new development, shall we?'

Yes, please. 'You said we've received reliable intelligence?'

'We have a janitor in play,' said Sir Alec, nodding. 'A long term undercover agent inserted into Jandria more than ten years ago, against the possibility of just this event.'

More than ten years? One of Sir Alec's men had been living in a deceptive, hostile foreign country for more than *ten years*? But — but —

'Yes, Mister Dunwoody,' said Sir Alec, very dry. 'A confronting notion, is it not? What one might describe as the very antithesis of treachery. More than ten years of looking over your shoulder, hoping and praying you don't make a slip, not one single, infinitesimal mistake, that would reveal to those around you that you're not at all what you seem. And all the while on alert, living on your nerves, looking for the clue that might save countless lives. Prevent another devastating war. Save the entire world from a thaumaturgical conflagration.'

Gerald swallowed, his mouth suddenly like sand. 'It sounds —' He shook his head. 'Very lonely.'

'It is,' said Sir Alec, his sharp gaze losing its focus. 'Lonely and dangerous.'

Something in the way he said it, some odd little note in his voice, had Gerald looking at him even more closely. *He's speaking from personal experience.* But he knew better than to comment on it. *Think about Errol, instead. That's a lot safer. And more comfortable.*

'And this agent in Jandria has seen some of Errol's airship designs?'

Sir Alec nodded. 'He's seen copies, yes.'

Leaning forward, he willed Sir Alec to believe him. 'Sir, I don't mean to contradict you or the janitor who passed you this information, but I really can't believe Errol would do this. He's got too much *pride.* Appearances matter to Errol Haythwaite. Hell, appearances are *everything.* If you'd heard him tonight, talking to Rottlezinder. He was *furious* he'd been dragged into this portal investigation.'

'Perhaps because this investigation threatened to uncover what he's really been up to,' Sir Alec suggested. 'I accept your assertion that Haythwaite is not involved in the portal sabotage. But that in no way means he is innocent of industrial espionage and treason.'

'But — but — it doesn't make *sense.*'

Again, a swift flash of that chilly smile. 'You'll find, Mister Dunwoody, once you've been in this line of work for slightly longer than a few weeks, that many things on their surface do not appear to make sense. Nevertheless they are true. And in due course they often *do* make sense. At least to the criminals we apprehend. Usually we come to understand their twisted logic, in time. But understanding them is not a prerequisite for catching them. I think that principle was discussed in some depth during your training.'

'It was,' Gerald admitted. 'Except —'

'Exceptions exist to prove the rule, Mister Dunwoody,' Sir Alec said briskly.

'So is there any more evidence against Errol? Aside from the fact that his airship design-work has turned up in Jandria? Rottlezinder mentioned some ... youthful indiscretions.' He sat back, staring. 'Is *that* why you're so quick to believe Errol's trucking treason with Jandria? Because he and Haf Rottlezinder made some mischief when they were students?'

'*Made some mischief* ...' Sir Alec murmured. 'Are you by any chance comparing Rottlezinder to Monk Markham? I wouldn't. Your friend is flamboyant and frequently thoughtless, but he lacks the cruel streak that marked Rottlezinder's chequered career.'

Cruel streak? 'Are you saying he and Errol —'

Sir Alec shook his head. 'I'm not saying anything, Mister Dunwoody. As you pointed out, that record is sealed.'

'Maybe, but whatever's in it has you believing Errol's a traitor.'

'No, Mister Dunwoody,' said Sir Alec, his cool gaze direct and impatient. 'The fact that Errol Haythwaite signs his design-work has convinced me of that.'

Gerald slumped. 'Oh.'

'Yes. *Oh.*'

So, things were looking pretty grim for Errol. *And why do I care? He's never done me any favours. He'd see me on the scrap heap, given half a chance.* Except ... he expected more of himself than that.

'But that doesn't mean he's the one passing his work to the Jandrians, does it?' he said, thoughts racing despite his crushing weariness. 'Couldn't someone be stealing it from him?'

'If you're thinking of another Wycliffe wizard, it's most unlikely,' said Sir Alec. 'They've all been exhaustively investigated. None of them has access to Jandria.'

'But Errol does?'

Sir Alec nodded. 'There are some family connections, which are being investigated as we speak. And you mustn't forget, Mister Dunwoody — the only wizard at Wycliffe's capable of breaching Errol Haythwaite's privacy hexes is you, and I'm assuming you've not been passing Mister Haythwaite's designs to the Jandrian government?'

Oh, ha ha, Sir Alec. Very funny. 'Still,' he muttered. 'Despite all the evidence, I can't bring myself to believe Errol's guilty.'

'Mister Dunwoody, you have me perplexed,' said Sir Alec, and drummed his fingers on the arm of his chair. 'There is no love lost between you and Errol Haythwaite. Why are you so determined to defend him in this matter?'

'Because — well, *because* I don't like him,' Gerald said at last, goaded. 'It's too easy to believe the worst of someone you loathe and despise. If it was *Monk* you were accusing I'd never stand for it, because he's my friend. So what kind of man would I be if I didn't apply the same kind of rigour to someone I *don't* like, for the sole simple reason that I don't like him?'

'What kind of man indeed?' Sir Alec murmured, leaning back in his chair and staring across his desk with a contemplative, narrowed gaze. 'That, Mister Dunwoody, is an interesting question.'

'Where's Errol now? Is he under arrest? Is he *here*?'

Sir Alec glanced at the quietly ticking clock on the wall. 'Not yet. But he will be, soon. We wanted to make sure he was cleared by a medical specialist before bringing him into the Department for questioning.'

'Dalby's bringing him?'

Another disapproving pinch of lip. '*Senior Janitor* Dalby, yes.'

He pushed to his feet and shoved his hands in his pockets. 'You need to let me talk to Errol. Alone.'

'That's out of the question,' said Sir Alec. 'For one thing it's been determined at the highest levels that you are never to be publicly identified with this Department. And for another, Mister Dunwoody, you are hardly a qualified interrogator. You are barely a janitor at all. I think you're allowing tonight's little achievements to overrule your —'

You sanctimonious bastard. 'If I'm not an interrogator,' he said, his heart thudding, 'then what the hell was that business with Monk's souped-up *delerioso* incant?'

Sir Alec's face hardened. 'I don't recall mentioning a *delerioso* incant.'

Oh . . . bugger. *Sorry, Monk.* 'Sir Alec, don't dismiss me. I can —'

But Sir Alec wasn't so easily sidetracked. 'Mister Dunwoody, am I to understand you have violated protocol and contacted —'

'You made me think I had to *torture* someone!' he shouted. 'And I did. At least, I started to. And then you refused to discuss it afterwards! What did you *think* I was going to do, Sir Alec? After what Lional did to me, what did you *think*? Did you think I was going to smile and shrug and laugh it off?'

'What I thought or did not think is irrelevant,' Sir Alec snapped. 'Mister Dunwoody, this is a serious breach. You have discussed confidential Department business with a non-Department individual.'

'Oh, don't give me that!' he snapped. 'You're the one who went to Monk and got him to soup up his incant in the first place! And don't you go blaming him for this either. He didn't come to me, I went to him — because what I did in that final test *disturbed* me and *you* refused to talk about it.'

For quite some time, Sir Alec said nothing. Then he nodded at the hard wooden chair. 'Sit down, Mister Dunwoody. And do make an effort to moderate your tone. I'm not in the habit of permitting subordinates to shout at me in my own office. Or anywhere else, for that matter.'

Gerald thudded back into the chair. 'I'm sorry. But —'

'I think, Mister Dunwoody,' Sir Alec said, lowering his hand, 'that your best course of action is to leave it at "I'm sorry".' He steepled his fingers again, his pale grey eyes coldly intent. 'Now. What makes you think you're qualified to successfully interrogate Errol Haythwaite?'

'I don't want to interrogate him,' he said tiredly. 'I just want to talk to him. I mean, you put me into Wycliffe's in the first place because you know he doesn't like me any more than I like him. I get under his skin. I throw him off-stride. So *let* me throw him off-stride. Let me use what I overheard tonight —' He looked at the early morning sky and shrugged. 'Last night. If he thinks I believe him about not being in cahoots with Rottlezinder, maybe I can get him talking about this other thing with Jandria, and one of your real interrogators can maybe catch him in a lie. *If* he's lying.'

And I really don't think he is.

'I'm sure that sounds terribly exciting in theory, Mister Dunwoody, but there remains the matter of your anonymity,' said Sir Alec.

Gerald shrugged. 'We both know you can fix that, Sir Alec. This Department's got access to any number of useful, despicable incants.' He snorted. 'Probably we invent most of them ourselves.'

Sir Alec was silent again, one forefinger tapping his lips. 'You'd sanction that?' he said at last. No emotion in his voice, no hint of what he was thinking or feeling. 'The use of despicable incants against Errol Haythwaite?'

'Given that I've already rearranged his memories once tonight, I'd be a bit bloody hypocritical to complain now, wouldn't I?' he retorted. 'Besides ... if it means we stop Jandria from starting another war?' Staring at his knees, he thought about New Ottosland. Remembered all those charred, twisted bodies in the streets. Imagined the same kind of bloodshed here … and in other cities … but with a death toll in the thousands. Imagined death raining down from the sky from military airships. Just another kind of dragon. Looking up, he nodded. 'Yes. I can live with hexing Errol. Besides, nothing could hurt him worse than being falsely accused of treason and maybe found guilty of something he didn't do.'

Sighing, Sir Alec passed a hand across his face. 'Mister Dunwoody,' he murmured. 'What a trial you are proving to be.'

'Um …' said Gerald. 'So, would that be a yes?'

CHAPTER TWENTY

Pale and dishevelled, his face motley with bruises, its cuts and scrapes covered with sticking plaster, Errol looked up as Gerald entered the small interrogation room. His mouth dropped open and his tired, bloodshot eyes stretched wide.

'What the *hell*? What is this rubbish? *Dunnywood*?'

Sighing, Gerald dropped into the other chair at the interrogation room's table. 'Hello, Errol.'

This interrogation room was identical to the one from Monk's *delerioso* incant. Four walls. Two doors. No windows. No sign of the scrying crystal that would be feeding images back to Sir Alec and whoever else was observing this ... conversation.

Errol was still staring at him in shock. 'Is this some kind of unamusing joke? Or are you under arrest too? Now *that* I have *no* trouble believing. I don't care what I said, you're responsible for what happened to the new Mark VI prototype. To *both* prototypes. You're a walking bloody disaster, Dunwoody. I knew you were trouble the first day I laid eyes on you. And at Wycliffe's I was convinced. I could *smell* trouble on you, I could *sense* it. I could *feel* there was something very *wrong* about you.'

Gerald looked at him. *Here we go.* 'Actually, Errol, what you felt was *this*.'

And he let his full rogue wizard *potentia* flare all around him like the raging nimbus of a newborn sun.

Every last bit of colour drained from Errol's face. He scrambled out of his chair and retreated until he hit the nearest wall.

'That's not possible,' he whispered, his voice hitching with shock. 'That's a trick. What the hell is going on here? You get out, Dunwoody. I won't share a room with you. I want nothing to do with you!'

'Sorry, Errol,' he said, and pulled his *potentia* back inside himself. 'We're stuck with each other for a little while yet.' He nodded at the chair. 'Sit down. There are some things we need to discuss.'

'Are you bloody deaf, you cretin?' Errol spat. 'I'm not talking to you. I don't know how but you're responsible for all of this!'

'No,' he said. 'Not all of it. Maybe some of it, in a roundabout kind of way. Look ... maybe this will be easier on both of us if I put things back the way they were.' And with a snap of his fingers, and the whisper of a few cruel words, he undid what he'd done to Errol's memory at Wycliffe's.

It took a moment for reality to reassert itself. And then, as Gerald watched, Errol ... remembered.

'I'm sorry about Rottlezinder,' he said, as Errol blindly groped for the chair. 'I know you were friends. Used to be friends. And I'm sorry about what I did to you. But you didn't really give me a choice, Errol.'

Errol thudded into the chair and pressed his hands flat to his face. It was quite astonishing, to see the polished, sophisticated, exquisitely urbane Errol Haythwaite so completely dismayed. Once, he'd have been delighted to see his nemesis brought so low. But witnessing it now, all he could feel was a tired pity.

Errol let his hands drop to the table, revealing a bone-white, ravaged face. 'Who the hell *are* you, Dunwoody? *What* are you?'

He grimaced. 'Yes, well, it seems nobody's managed to figure that out yet. But I can tell you what I'm not. I'm not your enemy, Errol. I'm trying to help you.'

'*Help* me?' said Errol, and wrestled for self-control. 'Fine. Then you can answer some questions.'

'Sure. If I can.'

'What is this place?' Errol demanded, looking around the cold, unfriendly room. 'What am I doing here? What are *you* doing here? That man — *Dalby*, is it? — he said there were one or two things about the lab accident that needed clearing up — and then he took me to see some *doctor*. Said it was a new DoT policy. Except —' He shook his head, dazed. 'There wasn't any lab accident. You — you faked that. So is this about Haf? About him sabotaging Ottosland's portal network?' Errol leaned across the table, the closest to desperate that Gerald had ever seen him. 'Because I had *nothing* to do with that! You were there at the boot factory, Dunwoody, God knows how or why. Didn't you hear what I told Haf, didn't you hear me —'

'Yes, Errol, I heard,' he said quietly. 'We know you weren't working with Haf Rottlezinder.'

Errol sat back. 'Good. That's good,' he said unsteadily. 'Then I can go.'

'Not quite yet,' he said. 'There's something else we need to discuss. But before we do … I have to tell you, Errol, I am curious about something.'

'As if I had the slightest interest in you or your curiosity,' said Errol, sneering. His confidence was seeping back. In his eyes a familiar, icy glitter of dislike. 'Get out of here, Dunwoody. I've nothing to say to you.'

Oh, Errol. How can you be such a brilliant wizard and such a fool?

'Come on, Errol,' he said, and rested his clasped hands on the table. 'Indulge me, just this once. After all, I did save your life. Go on. What can it hurt?'

Errol blew out a hard breath and waved his hand. 'Fine. Ask what you like. But that doesn't mean I'll answer.'

As invitations went, it was hardly gracious — but given that this was Errol Haythwaite, he'd take what he could get. 'Okay. So here's the thing that has me puzzled, Errol. After Rottlezinder first approached you, why didn't you tell the Department of Thaumaturgy?'

'Tell them what?' said Errol, scathing. 'That an old friend contacted me out of the blue and asked if I'd like to work with him on a lucrative project?'

He frowned. 'That's all he said? He didn't tell you what the project was? Where the money was coming from?'

'No.'

'And you didn't ask?'

'I wasn't interested.'

'And why was that, Errol?' he asked quietly. 'Because you knew there was a good chance that if Haf was involved the project would be ... questionable?'

Errol glared at the table. 'This is ridiculous.'

'All right,' he said. 'I accept that Haf played his cards close to his chest. I accept that on the face of it there was no reason for you to alert the authorities. Not in the beginning. But Errol ... after that first portal accident, and knowing the kind of man Rottlezinder was, you must've realised there was a connection. Or at least *suspected* — but still you kept quiet. And because you kept quiet, scores more people were hurt. For what? So you could protect your precious career? Are you really that shallow, Errol?'

Errol's pale, bruised face flushed a dull red. 'Watch your mouth, Dunwoody. I don't take that kind of cheek from tailor's brats.'

'Don't say things like that, Errol,' he said, shaking his head. 'I'm the only friend you've got in this place.'

'Ha!' said Errol. 'Then I really am in trouble, aren't I?'

Oh, lord. 'Errol, don't you get it? You're in so much hot water right now it's a wonder you can't feel the steam.'

Errol breathed hard, torn between contempt and uncertainty. Then he dropped his gaze and folded his arms. 'Of course I knew something was wrong,' he muttered. 'But he threatened me. When I turned him down. He threatened my family. He threatened my friends. He said if I knew what was good for me I'd pay no attention to the newspapers. He said if I didn't want to spend the next six months attending funerals I'd mind my own business.'

'And you believed him?'

'*Yes*, I believed him!' said Errol, violently. 'God, you'd have believed him too if —'

'If I'd shared a few youthful indiscretions with him?'

Stark silence, as Errol stared. 'You know about that?' he said at last, dully, emptied abruptly of fire and fight. He shrugged. 'Well, then.'

Sympathy flickered. Resenting it, Gerald frowned. 'Errol, while it's true you've been cleared of involvement in the portal sabotage, we have learned something else. Something very … disquieting. I wanted to know what you thought about it.'

'*You* wanted to —' Errol glared, his anger rekindling. '*You*?' Unfolding his arms, he shoved to his feet. '*You* aren't fit to polish my shoes, Dunwoody. As far as I'm concerned this conversation is over. I'm leaving. And you can rest assured, you and —' His gaze swept the small room. '— whoever else is party to this charade, that Lord Attaby shall shortly be receiving a visit from my legal counsel. This has been nothing but a farrago of harassment, assault and intimidation. And if you think you can get away with it you are sorely mistaken. I shall take immense pleasure, Dunwoody, in seeing you broken in a very public Court of —'

'Sit down, Errol,' Gerald said softly. 'We're not finished here.'

'We most certainly are!' snapped Errol. '*You're* finished, Dunnywood, you're —'

'*I said sit down*!'

Errol gaped at him, stunned.

'Please, Errol,' he said. 'Sit. Don't make me make you.'

Errol sat jerkily, like a puppet with faulty strings.

'The Jandrians are building a fleet of military airships using your designs,' he said flatly. 'Would you care to explain how that's come about?'

'I'm sorry?' said Errol, after another long silence. His voice was faint. Uncertain. 'I don't — I don't understand.'

He leaned forward across the table. 'I think you do, Errol. You're not deaf, or stupid. The Jandrian government has broken the armistice. The Jandrians are dreaming of war again. And you're helping them. I don't understand. Why would you do that? Betray your country, most likely to its death?'

'But I didn't,' said Errol. 'I would *never* —' He shook his head, stunned. 'The Jandrians? You think I'd crawl into bed with *those* filthy scum? My God, they're barely one rung up the ladder from *animals*.'

'Perhaps,' said Gerald, shrugging, and sat back. 'But they're wealthy, Errol. And you have expensive tastes. Perhaps you lied to Rottlezinder about not needing money. Perhaps your trust fund has run dry.'

He wasn't sure what he'd been expecting from Errol, once the accusation of treason was made. Fury. Wild denials. Possibly even a physical or thaumaturgical attack. He was braced for all of that.

What he wasn't prepared for was ... *anguish*.

Errol leaned forward, his hands splayed flat and hard on the table. 'No. No. You must believe me. On my wizard's oath, I *did not do this*. I haven't betrayed Ottosland to Jandria.' He swallowed convulsively, a terrible desperation in his eyes. 'I swear it.'

'Then how do you explain copies of your airship designs being found there?'

A bead of sweat trickled down Errol's blanched cheek. 'I

can't. All my work is triple-warded and kept in my office at Wycliffe's. I don't let anybody touch it, not even Ambrose.'

He shrugged, feigning indifference. 'Then like I said, Errol. You're in very hot water.'

'Oh, God,' said Errol. It was almost a sob. 'This can't be happening.' On a gasp he pressed his hands flat to his face, then let them drop. 'You have to help me, Gerald. Whatever you are, whatever freakish powers you possess, *use* them. Winnow my memories. Break my mind, if you have to. I don't care. *I am not a traitor.* And I'm asking you … I'm *begging* you … help me to prove it.'

Sighing, Gerald stood up. Looked to the ceiling, where he suspected the scrying crystals were concealed. 'Sir Alec? If you know anything about Errol, you know what asking that cost him. He's telling the truth. You need to look for your traitor somewhere else. And now, if you don't mind, it's been a long night. I'm going home.'

And he walked out, closing the interrogation room door very gently behind him.

But the idea of returning to his rented bedsit, which was hardly better than that horrible attic room in the Wizards' Club, depressed him beyond bearing. Besides. After everything that had happened … he didn't want to be alone.

Monk answered his front door wearing the harassed, distracted expression that meant he'd just been talking to his sister.

'*Gerald*? Blimey, you look like death dragged backwards,' he said. 'Come on in. Amuse yourself for a moment, I'm on the telephone with Bibbie.'

As Monk muttered his way down the corridor, Gerald pushed the front door closed behind him and heaved a deep sigh. Lord, he was so *tired*. He was also, technically, in possession of stolen property, having ridden his pilfered, souped-up Wycliffe scooter straight here from Nettleworth. He'd have to take it back to the airship company sooner or later, but now all he could think about was sitting down before he fell down.

Monk's voice drifted into the corridor from the parlour. '— was Gerald. — Yes, he just got here. — No, I don't know what's going on. Didn't I say he just got here? *Blimey.* — Well yes, I think you *should* come round right away. I want my jalopy back. — No, I *didn't* say you could keep it indefinitely, I said you could borrow it for one night and — Bibbie. *Bibbie.* Bibbie, I *swear*, if you don't bring my jalopy back I will tell the folks about the time you and Tiffany McSweeney — yes, I do know what you did. — It doesn't matter *how* I know. I *know.* — Yes. Good. I'll see you soon.'

Gerald leaned against the parlour's open doorway, frowning muzzily. 'Everything all right?'

Monk stopped glaring at the telephone. 'Sisters! You can't say no to 'em and you can't kill 'em. Doesn't leave much else, does it?'

'I'll take your word on that.'

'She's bringing my car back,' said Monk. 'And it goes without saying she'll have Mel and Reg with her. Are you feeling strong enough to face them? Or would you rather escape while there's still time?'

He managed a smile. 'I'd love to, but after what happened last night I need to talk to them.'

Monk paled. 'Why? What happened last night?'

'I ran into them while they were gallivanting about South Ott.'

Monk stared. '*What*? They were gallivanting *where*?'

'In South Ott. In the old factory district. I can't *believe* you let them go there, Monk. It's a dreadful part of town!'

'Hey, it's not *my* fault!' Monk protested. 'I had no idea where they were headed!'

Unbelievable. 'You mean you lent those three maniacs your

jalopy and you didn't know what they had in mind? What the hell is *wrong* with you, Monk?'

'Well — well — I tried to stop them,' Monk said feebly. 'But you know what women are like. You know what *those* three are like, especially.'

'Yes! They're maniacs!' he retorted. 'And they nearly ended up getting themselves blown to bits. All because you lent them your jalopy, you *idiot*.'

'Blown to bits?' Monk said, his voice faint with horror. 'What are you talking about, blown to bits?'

'You haven't listened to the wireless this morning?'

'Come on, Gerald. You know I never listen to the wireless.'

There seemed little point now in slavishly following Department protocols. That boat had not only sailed, it had sunk. 'I suppose Reg will have already told the girls,' he sighed. 'So. An abandoned boot factory blew up in South Ott last night.'

Monk stared at him, lips twitching. 'Don't tell me. Let me guess. Son of Stuttley's?'

He raised a warning finger. 'Don't. Just *don't*, all right? Not this morning, Markham. I'm not in the mood.'

'Yeah,' said Monk, sobering, and looked him up and down. 'Yeah, I can see that. Maybe you'd better sit down, mate, before you fall down.'

'Funny. I was just thinking the same thing.' He weaved his way across the parlour's dingy, threadbare carpet and collapsed onto the two-seater sofa. 'Monk, I could murder a cup of tea. And some toast. And some scrambled eggs.'

'And after that sleep for a week, it looks like,' Monk added. He held out his hand. 'Here. Give me that staff and I'll put it somewhere safe.'

Vaguely surprised, Gerald looked down at the gold-filigreed First Grade staff still clutched in his right hand. 'Oh. Yes. I forgot about this.'

'Right,' said Monk carefully. 'Okay. So maybe you shouldn't be making any sudden moves.' He grabbed the staff and lifted it out of the way. 'Just ... sit there. Don't think about the girls, or my jalopy, or South Ott, or exploding factories. Think — think *happy* thoughts, Gerald. You can do it if you try, I know you can.'

He stared at his friend, bemused. 'Monk, what are you going on about? I'm fine. I'm tired and starving, but aside from that I'm fine.'

'Really?' said Monk. 'Then you and I have very different definitions of "fine", mate. Look — you relax. I'll be right back. Don't go anywhere.'

'I wasn't planning to,' he said, around a jaw-cracking yawn. 'Bloody hell, Monk. You won't believe what's been going on. Exploding factories is just the beginning.'

'I'll believe anything if you're mixed up in it,' said Monk. 'I should've known what I'd be in for after you turned that mad king's bloody cat into a lion.'

Monk was only joking, he was trying to play the fool, like he always did ... but suddenly nothing felt funny any more. 'Give it a rest, Monk,' he said, appalled to hear the little quaver in his voice. 'Can you?'

'Oh, God,' said Monk, equally appalled. 'Who died?'

'Haf Rottlezinder.'

Monk's eyes nearly started out of his head. '*Really*? Someone *died*? You're not joking?'

He gave Monk his most jaundiced look. 'Is this my joking face, Markham? Is it?'

'You don't have a joking face, Gerald.'

'Then take the hint.'

'Bloody hell,' Monk muttered. 'Rottlezinder's really dead?'

'Yes. He's really dead.' Very dead. Comprehensively dead. Unmistakably, unreservedly dead. Every time he closed his eyes he heard the annihilating boom of the factory exploding.

Smelled the tinny thaumic discharge. Imagined himself enveloped in a fine red mist ...

Don't think about it. Don't think about it. What's done is done.

Monk cleared his throat. 'Did you — you didn't — bloody hell, Gerald —'

With a grating effort, he dragged his eyelids open. 'If you mean did I actually, personally kill him, then no. Not exactly. He was killed by his own unstable hex. But I had to choose between saving him and saving Errol.'

'Blimey,' said Monk. 'Rather you than me, mate.' Then he winced. 'Sorry.'

He shrugged. 'Yeah. That makes two of us.'

'Look, I want to hear all about it, but — let me get you some breakfast first.'

'I don't want to make you late for work. I can —'

'I'll call in sick,' said Monk. 'Or late. Or something. Don't worry about that. You just — take some deep breaths. Cultivate your appetite. I'll be right back.'

The remains of Monk's breakfast were sitting on the parlour table. He'd buttered his bread roll but hadn't eaten it. Perhaps the telephone call from Bibbie had distracted him. With a heartfelt groan, Gerald staggered off the sofa, snatched the bread roll off its plate and devoured it. Then he fell onto the sofa again and enjoyed the sensation of being still and quiet. Could eyelashes ache? He rather thought that they could.

Time meandered by. He didn't quite fall asleep, but he did drift into a kind of aimless doze. The room was pleasantly warm, with a cheerful little fire crackling in the fireplace. It was like being in a shabby cocoon ...

'Here you go,' said Monk, returning to the parlour with a mug of tea and a plate of scrambled eggs, only slightly charred bacon and four thick slices of butter-dripping toast. Bless him and the camel he rode in on. 'Wrap your laughing gear around this, mate. You'll feel like a new man, afterwards. And while you're eating you can fill me in on the rest.'

So he did. When both breakfast and tale were finished he sat back, replete, the worst of his dizziness subsiding. Looked at Monk, who was staring at him with dazed fascination.

'Bloody hell, Gerald.'

'Yeah,' he sighed. 'I know.'

'So what's going to happen to Errol?'

He shrugged. 'Don't know. Don't much care. He's Sir Alec's problem now.'

'But you're convinced he didn't sell his work to the Jandrians?'

'You're the one who didn't believe he'd sabotage the portal network. Does Errol selling secrets to an enemy government sound likely to you?'

Monk shook his head. 'No. I said from the start he's a pillock, not a traitor.'

Which reminded him . . . 'So which Haythwaite was it then, who did the dirty on Ottosland?'

'What are you talking about?'

'It was something Sir Alec said. About Errol maybe not being the first treacherous Haythwaite.'

'Dunno,' said Monk, his interest piqued. 'I'll ask Uncle Ralph. He'll know for sure. He's got closets full of other people's skeletons and he hates the Haythwaites as much as we do.' Monk shook his head again, this time with a tinge of admiration. 'I can't believe you read the riot act to Sir Alec. And I *really* can't believe he didn't skin you for it!'

Oh. Yes. Damn. He cleared his throat. 'Ah, Monk? There is one more thing. In the course of the mission debrief I, well, I sort of lost my temper a bit and — well, frankly, I got a trifle carried away and, um, I let it slip that I knew where he got the *delerioso* incant.'

'Oh,' said Monk, after a moment's horrified silence.

'I'm sorry. I didn't mean to. But I swear you won't hear a word about it,' he said quickly. 'Sir Alec and I came to a definite understanding.'

'Yeah,' Monk said slowly. 'And by a definite understanding, did you actually hear him say, *I will not string Monk Markham up by his short and curlies for blabbing about his super-secret hex?*'

'Well, no,' he said. 'I mean, not in so many words. You could say the understanding was definite, but not … articulated.'

'Right,' said Monk, his expression glum. 'In other words it's back to Probationville for me — if I'm lucky.'

He shook his head. 'No. Not this time. Not on my account. Not again.'

Monk sighed. 'You say that, Gerald, and I know you mean it, but —'

They both turned their heads at a loud banging on the front door.

'This has an eerily familiar feel to it,' said Monk. 'All right. I'll let them in, but after that you're on your own.' He took a deep breath and blew it out, hard. 'Brace yourself, mate.'

Reg flapped into the parlour first to circle under the ceiling, closely followed by Melissande and Bibbie, their long skirts swishing. All three of them were talking a mile a minute. On his feet to greet them, Gerald waited till Monk came in and closed the door behind them, then raised both hands.

'*Put a sock in it, all of you!*' he said loudly. '*I mean it!*' And to show them he was serious, he stirred the ether with a short, sharp breeze. The flames in the fireplace leapt up, roaring. The heavy curtains swayed, creaking the old timber curtain rods. The girls' skirts whipped around their legs and Reg's feathers fluttered wildly.

'Oy!' said Reg, gliding down to the arm of the sofa. 'Do you mind?'

'Sorry,' he said, and settled the ether. 'But I know what you three are like when you're in full spate.'

'Monk Markham, you wipe that grin off your face *right this instant*,' said Melissande, without turning her head. 'Or there *will* be blood on the carpet and I promise it won't be mine.'

'Sorry,' said Monk, hastily sobering.

'Gerald,' said Bibbie, 'you look dreadful.'

'I'm fine,' he said, trying hard not to be distracted by her. Really, she was so beautiful it was ridiculous. She was so beautiful she made Ambrose's ban on gels in the laboratory almost seem *reasonable*.

'He looks like he's been blown up,' said Reg. 'I told you, didn't I?'

'Yes, but you've been known to exaggerate,' said Bibbie, and shook her head. 'Really, Gerald? Really, you blew up another factory? I mean, I heard about the explosion on the boarding house wireless, but —'

'Yes, Bibbie,' he sighed. 'Another one. Son of Stuttley's and so forth and et cetera and so on.'

She wrinkled her nose. 'Son of Stuttley's? That's a silly thing to say —' Her gaze shifted sideways. '*Monk.*'

'Oh, find a sock and swallow it, ducky,' said Reg. 'Then put your bum in the nearest chair. Gerald needs to know what we know and vice versa.'

Grumbling under their breaths, Melissande and Bibbie sat, taking an armchair each. Monk stood in front of the dwindling fire, one elbow propped on the mantel. When everyone was settled, Gerald sat on the sofa again and looked at the girls.

'All right,' he said. 'Tell me everything.'

'In a minute,' said Melissande. 'First, is what Reg told us true? Have you stopped suspecting Errol Haythwaite?'

'For the portal sabotage? Yes,' he said, with a warning glance at Monk. 'It's true. Your turn.'

'We found out what Eudora Telford was doing in South Ott last night. She was taking a fortune in gemstones to Haf Rottlezinder.'

He stared at her. 'I'm sorry — she was what?'

'On Permelia Wycliffe's behalf,' Reg added. 'Which you never would've found out if it hadn't been for us.' She sniffed. 'A nice bit of grovelling wouldn't go astray right about now, sunshine.'

Sometimes the only way to survive Reg was to ignore her. 'Permelia Wycliffe was paying Haf Rottlezinder?' he echoed. *If that's the case, Sir Alec's going to go spare.* 'Are you quite certain?'

'Of course we are, Gerald,' said Bibbie. 'When Mel and I took that silly Eudora Telford back to her bungalow we ended up staying for cakes and tea. Mel snooped in Eudora's purse and found a fortune in sparkly stones. *And* a note in Permelia Wycliffe's handwriting, directing Eudora to Haf Rottlezinder in the old boot factory that you blew up.'

'Actually,' he said, 'for the record? I didn't blow it up. Rottlezinder did. I was just ... there.'

'Oh, who cares?' said Reg, fluffing out her feathers. 'It was abandoned. No-one was using it.'

'No-one except Haf Rottlezinder,' he said quietly.

'Yes, well, he was a rotter and he blew himself to smithereens so good riddance to *him*,' said Reg. 'What matters, Gerald, is we've solved your case.'

He considered her blankly. 'No, you haven't.'

'Yes, we have,' said Melissande. '*Gerald*, we caught Permelia red-handed, paying off the wizard who blew up the portals!'

Monk cleared his throat. 'Except that you didn't, Mel. Permelia Wycliffe was nowhere near South Ott last night.'

'But —'

'Melissande,' said Gerald, as kindly as he could. 'Look. I know you're trying to help, but Monk's right. Have you got the gemstones? Have you got this note you think was written by Permelia? Have you got *anything* connecting her to Haf Rottlezinder?'

'I *told* you,' said Melissande, rolling her eyes. 'I overheard Permelia and Ambrose arguing about saving the company, and Reg overhead Permelia asking Eudora for a favour and —'

'In other words, no. You've got no proof at all.'

Reg, Melissande and Bibbie looked at each other. Then Bibbie shrugged. 'Well ... we've got Eudora Telford.'

'What?' said Monk, alarmed. 'What do you mean you've got Eudora Telford? Do you mean you've actually *got* her? Are you telling me there's some old bat trussed up and — and stuffed in the boot of my jalopy?'

'No, Monk, you *idiot*,' said Melissande, throwing a cushion at him. '*Honestly.* She's at her place, waiting for me and Bibbie to pick her up and take her out to South Ott so she can honour her promise to Permelia Wycliffe and deliver the gemstones to Haf Rottlezinder.'

'Which of course she can't do now, because he's blown himself to smithereens,' said Bibbie. She pulled a thoughtful face. 'It's a funny word that, isn't it? *Smithereens.* How big is a smithereen, do you suppose? Do you think it's smaller than a —'

'One more word out of you, ducky,' said Reg, 'and I'll blow you to smithereens myself and you can investigate the mystery *personally*.'

Bibbie stared at her. 'What did I say?'

'I'll explain later,' said Monk, and threw the cushion at his offended sister.

'What Bibbie means,' said Melissande, with teeth-gritted restraint, 'is that we've established quite a cosy little rapport with Eudora Telford. She — ah — she thinks she's got an invitation to visit Rupert and cook pastries for him.'

Gerald raised an eyebrow. 'Really? And whatever gave her that idea?'

'Ah,' said Melissande, her freckles disappearing in a tide of pink. 'Well. I might have ... you know ... um ...'

'Told her a big fat lie? Got her to trust you under false pretences?' He had to grin, even though he was so tired. 'Oh, Melissande. Can this Telford woman even cook?'

'Only very, *very* badly,' she said. 'But I'm trying hard not to think about that.'

'Good idea,' said Reg. 'So — forgetting New Ottosland's Butterfly King and his future digestive dilemmas for a moment — let's agree, shall we, that Mad Miss Markham's right for once and Eudora Telford's our gold-plated key. Because with that pillock Errol Haythwaite ruled out of the guilty picture it's obvious that Permelia and her brother are — are —' She chattered her beak. '*Gerald* ...?'

'What?' said Melissande. 'Reg, what's wrong?'

Feeling Reg's narrowed gaze on him, Gerald closed his eyes. How had he forgotten that she, like Monk, could read him like a book written in crayon with very big letters?

Damn. I'm even more tired than I thought.

'What's *wrong*,' Reg said snippily, 'is that we've not been told the whole story, ducky. Come on, Gerald. I know that look. What have you ever-so-slightly neglected to mention?'

He sighed. 'Nothing that has anything to do with Permelia.'

'How would you know?' Reg retorted. 'You lot wrote Permelia off as pure as the driven snow. You're just lucky we're around, sunshine, or there'd be egg all over your face about now.'

Regrettably, he couldn't argue with that.

'Tell them, Gerald,' said Monk, reprehensibly amused. 'You'll get no peace until you do.'

And he couldn't argue with *that*, either. 'Something else has come up,' he muttered. 'A question of treason. Errol's in Department custody, helping Sir Alec with his enquiries. And it looks like I'm the only person who still thinks he's innocent.'

'Blimey,' said Reg. 'You're *defending* that plonker now? Cor.' She let loose a cackle of laughter. 'That has to be giving you piles.'

'Right now the only thing I've got is a headache,' he said, 'and that's because people keep on *interrupting*.'

'Someone's been passing Errol's airship designs to the Jandrians,' said Monk. 'The Department thinks that someone is Errol.'

'Don't tell me, let me guess,' said Reg. 'The Jandrians are building military airships under the bed.' She shook her head. 'Those buggers. Twisty as a corkscrew, the bloody lot of 'em. Always have been, for as long as I can remember.'

'But — but — they can't *do* that,' said Bibbie. 'The treaty of 1846 expressly forbids them from rebuilding their military capabilities. Their airship fleet is limited to five civilian carriers, and the routes are·restricted *and* monitored.'

Melissande blinked at her. 'How do you *know* these things?'

'Uncle Ralph was a junior clerk during the post-war tribunals,' said Bibbie, shrugging. 'Every time he's had one whiskey too many he bangs on about how he was present at the making of history. Silly old turtle. It was boring the first time he told the story.'

Melissande looked at Monk. 'What *isn't* your family connected to in this country?'

Monk and Bibbie exchanged resigned looks. 'Not much,' he said. 'Sorry.'

'So if Errol's not selling us out, who is?' said Reg. 'And how are you going to find this villain?'

Gerald sighed. *Good question.* 'I'm not. Sir Alec's looking into that. Officially I'm still assigned to the portal sabotage case. Which I have to crack, fast, because there's the risk that once our mystery villain realises Rottlezinder's dead, he'll find himself another bent wizard and keep on attacking the portal network.'

'In that case, Gerald,' said Melissande, standing, 'you'll have to come with us to see Eudora Telford and help us to convince her it's her patriotic duty to sell Permelia down the river. Once we've got the gemstones and Permelia's handwritten note, the rest of this crazy jigsaw should fall into place.'

It wasn't a bad idea, actually. There was only one small problem. 'Melissande, nobody's supposed to know that I work for the government.'

Melissande smiled, and behind her glasses her eyes sparkled wickedly. 'Don't worry. Eudora won't have the first idea.'

Before he could explore that alarming answer further, completely not trusting the gleam in her eyes, Bibbie scrambled out of her own chair. 'I think that's an excellent plan, Mel.' She turned to her brother. 'Monk, Mel, Reg and I need to —'

'No,' said Monk, and folded his arms. 'Absolutely not. I am never lending you my jalopy again. If you want to go somewhere I'll drive you, but I'm not letting you loose on the streets of Ott unsupervised. Not after last night. Not until you've turned fifty. Or possibly sixty. Ott's not a perfect city, not by a long shot, but it hasn't done anything bad enough to deserve *you*.'

Bibbie flushed pink with temper. 'Monk Debinger Aloysius Markham, don't you *dare* try to boss me around like you're Father!'

'I'm not bossing you, I'm saving you!' Monk retorted, scrambling to his feet. 'You came within a whisker of getting yourself blown to bits last night, you — you — gawking great gossoon of a girl!'

Under cover of yet another Markham sibling squabble, Gerald looked at Melissande. 'This might take a while. Care to conference?'

CHAPTER TWENTY-ONE

Melissande grinned. 'Good idea, Gerald. We can discuss what your Sir Alec's going to pay us for practically solving the Department's portal case single-handed.'

Oh, lord. *When he finds out how deeply Witches Inc. is involved in this ... and he is going to find out. I'll have no choice but to tell him.* 'Ah, well, I wouldn't presume to speak for Sir Alec. Tell me, how's your own case coming along?'

Monk and Bibbie were still squabbling hammer and tongs. Melissande pulled a face at them, then smoothed the front of her primrose-yellow blouse. 'Oh. That. I'm afraid it's hit a dead end. The office is hexed to the eyeballs but nothing's been set off, and Bibbie's investigations into the gels' backgrounds haven't helped us a bit. Whoever's been pinching Permelia's assorted creams is a lot sneakier and more accomplished than I anticipated, I'm afraid.'

Now Bibbie was jabbing Monk in the chest with a particularly pointed finger, and Monk was waving his arms around ... a solid gold sign he'd reached the end of his tether.

Wonderful. As if I haven't had enough explosions for one lifetime.

With an effort he turned his attention back to Melissande. 'I'm sorry. That must be very aggravating.'

A look of surprise crossed her face. 'D'you know, it is. Our case might not be as important as portal sabotage but even so, my professional pride is at stake. The thought of being outsmarted by a *biscuit thief*...'

'Don't give up hope,' he said. 'I know things look bad for Permelia, but she's not been proven guilty yet. There's still a chance you'll get to unmask Wycliffe's dastardly petty pilferer.'

'Huh,' said Melissande gloomily. 'Don't bet on it. Our retainer runs out today, and without a culprit to wave under Permelia's nose we're fired.'

'Tell you what, Gerald,' said Reg, hopping from the arm of the sofa to Melissande's shoulder. 'Since it looks like we're solving your case for you, once your portal saboteur's nabbed you can show your gratitude by returning the favour.'

He looked at her. 'And how am I supposed to do that, Reg?'

'How? How?' She rattled her tail feathers. 'How should I know, Gerald? You're the rogue wizard, *you* think of a way. Blimey. I don't see why *I* should be expected to do *everything*.'

He was exhausted, all his bangs and bruises hurting. Haf Rottlezinder was dead and innocent Errol Haythwaite faced an uncertain future. Somewhere in Ottosland a venal man or woman plotted more indiscriminate destruction.

And for reasons I don't begin to understand, I'm the one who's expected to make everything all right.

Consumed by their own nonsensical fight, Monk and Bibbie hurled more insults at each other.

Honestly, you two. Enough is enough.

Taking a deep breath he snapped his fingers twice. The ether leapt to his command, cracking like thunder above Monk and Bibbie's heads. 'Oy, you raving tossers! Put a bloody sock in it!'

Mouths open, they gaped at him.

'Monk,' he said as the ether trembled, 'if you are going to call in sick do it now.' He turned. 'What about you, Melissande? Aren't you supposed to be at Wycliffe's?'

'Yes, but they can do without me for the morning,' she said. 'Let Miss Petterly take my place. It's about time she did an honest day's work.'

'Fine. Then let's go. Monk, you can drive us to Eudora Telford's place. And after we've heard what she has to say we'll make a decision as to what to do next.'

'Right,' said Monk faintly. 'So, Gerald — this is you being a janitor, is it?'

He bared his teeth in a savage smile. 'No, Monk. This is me being tired and cranky. When I'm being a janitor, buildings tend to explode. I take it you're getting quite fond of this house?'

Things happened with satisfying speed after that.

With Monk behind the wheel, himself and his First Grade staff in the passenger seat and Reg, Melissande and Bibbie squashed in the back, the jalopy chugged its way to shabby-genteel North Ott.

'There,' said Melissande, pointing to a low-roofed bungalow painted the most confronting shade of cupcake-icing pink. Its trim was a blinding shade of blue. 'That's the place, Monk. Pull up out the front.'

'Blimey,' said Reg. 'If she cooks like she decorates, old Rupes better have the royal physician on standby.'

'Unfortunately she does,' said Melissande glumly. 'Rupert is never going to forgive me.'

As Monk coasted the jalopy to a halt and switched off the engine, Melissande leaned forward. 'Right, you two. Listen carefully. For the purposes of this exercise I'm *not* Miss Cadwallader, is that clear? I'm Her Royal Highness Princess Melissande. So don't speak unless you're spoken to, the more obsequious grovelling the better, and whatever you do, *don't you dare laugh.*'

Gerald stared at Monk, who was staring at him. 'Don't look at me,' he said. 'She's not my young lady.'

'Yeah,' said Monk. 'Ah — Gerald? Your eye's turned silver again.'

He sighed. 'Of course it has. Hang on —'

'Allow me,' said Monk, and with a sizzle of thaumic energy he rejuiced the eye-colour incant. 'There you go, mate. Good as new.'

'Excuse me?' said Melissande. 'If you two have *quite* finished with the male bonding rituals, can we go?'

Head held high, as snooty as she'd ever been in New Ottosland, she led the way to Eudora Telford's front door and rapped on it with a consummate authority. Gerald, bringing up the rear with Reg ensconced comfortably, familiarly, on his right shoulder, tried to imagine what Sir Alec would say if he could see this ... and nearly turned tail and ran.

Reg nipped his ear affectionately. 'Just like old times, sunshine,' she whispered. 'Only they've got a bit more crowded.'

Smiling, he stroked her wing with one finger. 'I do miss you, you know.'

She sniffed. 'Miss my brilliant deductive reasoning, my rapier wit and wing speed more like it.'

'Well yes,' he said. 'Them too.'

Before she could nip him again, less than affectionately, the bungalow's front door opened, revealing a plump, middle-aged lady dressed in unbecoming puce, with mildly myopic eyes and a permanently apologetic expression.

'Oh!' she said, flustered. 'Your Highness! It's not — it can't be — is it ten o'clock already? I thought the clock said — but perhaps it's wrong — although —'

'No, no, Miss Telford, I expect your clock is quite correct,' said Melissande, her vowels so plummy she sounded like an orchard. 'I'm afraid we're early. Something rather important has arisen and it was urgent that we speak with you at once.'

Miss Telford looked past Melissande, her brow furrowing in a frown. 'All of you?'

'Yes, I'm afraid so,' said Melissande grandly. 'May we come in? This isn't the sort of conversation one conducts on a doorstep.'

'Oh — oh yes, of course,' said Miss Telford, and backed away from the door. 'Do come in, Your Highness. Miss Markham. Go directly to the parlour. And — oh dear — these gentlemen are …?'

'This is my factotum, Miss Telford,' said Melissande, flicking her fingers at Monk. 'And the other one is my factotum's factotum. They aren't important enough to have names. They barely have faces. Pay them no attention. I never do. It only gives them ideas.'

'Oh,' said Miss Telford, as they tramped into her small home. 'I see. A factotum with a factotum. How very unusual.'

'Not in New Ottosland, Miss Telford,' said Melissande, leading the way into the parlour. 'In New Ottosland, royalty is accustomed to an extensive entourage.'

Having shut the front door, Miss Telford joined them in the now uncomfortably crowded parlour. 'I see, Your Highness,' she said. 'Except — I thought you wanted to remain incog —'

'Oh, I did,' said Melissande. 'I mean, I do. But of course you *know* my secret, Miss Telford. So it's all right. I can surround myself with all the factotums I want.'

'Yes, yes,' said Miss Telford. She was eyeing Reg with a nervous air. 'And I see you brought your bird.'

'But not just any bird, remember?' said Bibbie, anarchically dimpling. 'She's the National Bird of New Ottosland and figures prominently on the kingdom's coat of arms. I'm sure King Rupert will be thrilled when you tell him you've entertained his national symbol in your very own home.'

Miss Telford brightened. 'Really? He will?'

'Certainly,' said Melissande, with a repressive look at Bibbie. 'But let's not tease ourselves with the prospect of delights to come. I'm afraid, Miss Telford, that we must discuss a considerably more serious matter.'

'Oh,' said Miss Telford, wilting slightly. 'Then please, Your Highness, do have a seat.'

'Thank you,' said Melissande. 'Miss Markham and I shall gladly sit. And you, of course, Miss Telford. Factotums don't sit. Factotums stand and wait for royal commands.'

'Blimey,' Reg muttered in Gerald's ear. 'Princess Pushy's off and running now. Let's hope for all our sakes she doesn't sprain a bloody ankle.'

Moving to stand before the fireplace, whose mantel was crowded with spinsterly knick-knacks, he nodded. *Let's hope indeed*. He'd just have to trust that Melissande knew what she was doing. Or at least had sense enough to know when it was time to let him step in. He flicked a glance at Monk, who rolled his eyes and took an unobtrusive position by the parlour's curtained window.

'Miss Telford,' said Melissande, perched on the edge of the ugliest looking armchair he'd ever seen. 'I'm afraid that what I'm about to say might well shock you. It will doubtless distress you, and quite possibly alarm you. Of course I'm sorry about that, but — well — as a royal princess I have always done my duty.'

'Your duty?' said Eudora Telford, who'd chosen an equally ugly armchair to sit in. She plucked a lace-edged hanky from her sleeve and pressed it to her lips. 'Are you saying it's your duty to shock, distress and alarm me?'

'Miss Telford,' said Bibbie, who was seated on a hideous sofa, 'she is. And speaking as the great-niece of Antigone Markham, the greatest president in the history of Otttosland's Baking and Pastry Guild, I'd like you to accept my apologies also. You are a credit to the sisterhood, Eudora. More than that, you're a credit to your country. And your poor country needs you now. Will you be brave? Will you be bold and resolute? Will you bear up under the burden Her Royal Highness is about to place upon your frail, womanly shoulders?'

Miss Telford was pressed so far back in her armchair it was in danger of tipping over. 'Oh dear,' she whispered. 'How terribly unexpected. I   I really don't know.'

Melissande leaned forward and reached for Eudora Telford's hand. 'If you were anyone else, Eudora, I would quail at the thought of what I'm about to reveal. But I know the stuff you're made of and I believe I can trust you'll do the right thing, though it may be hard. Though it may break your kind and generous heart. Have I misjudged you, Eudora? Or can I now trust you with this dread secret?'

Eudora Telford nodded, mute as a swan.

Reg was gurgling into his ear. 'Mad as mice, her *and* that Bibbie! And that gormless guppy Eudora's twice as bad. Falling for that load of melodramatic poppycock? She's a *disgrace* to the sisterhood, that's what *she* is!'

'Eudora,' said Melissande gravely, 'something very wrong is going on at Wycliffe's Airship Company. Something that's endangering a great many lives.'

'What?' said Eudora Telford, stiffening. 'Oh, no, Your Highness, you must be —'

'*Eudora.*' Melissande gave the woman's plump hand a little shake. 'Trust, remember?'

'I'm sorry,' whispered Eudora Telford. 'Please, do go on.'

'Miss Markham and I have been investigating a case of theft in the office,' Melissande continued. 'By any chance did Permelia mention that to you?'

Eudora Telford shook her head, looking hurt. 'No. No, she didn't. And Permelia tells me *everything*.'

'Ha,' Reg muttered. 'That's what *she* thinks.'

'Never mind,' said Melissande. 'I expect she was trying to

protect the company. But you see, Eudora, the thing is, while we were looking into that trifling matter we stumbled across something far more serious. Something with dire implications for Ottosland. Something I think *you've* become tangled in. Because you're such a very good friend, Eudora, and Permelia Wycliffe trusts you.'

'Oh,' said Eudora Telford faintly.

'And now I must make a confession, Eudora,' said Melissande. 'Once you've heard it I only hope you can forgive me.'

Gerald exchanged an alarmed look with Monk. What? She wasn't going to tell the silly woman about snooping through her purse, was she? About finding the gemstones? Because that would be a big mistake. Silly old biddies like Eudora Telford tended to have rigid views about certain things, like privacy and propriety and —

'Settle down, settle down,' Reg muttered. 'Give madam some credit. She's not going to scuttle this, I've taught her far too well.'

Eudora Telford's eyes were enormous. '*Me* forgive *you*, Your Highness?'

Melissande nodded. 'Yes. Because you see, Eudora, last night . . . I lied to you.'

'Lied, Your Highness?' said Eudora Telford, in a very small voice. Tears brimmed in her faded eyes. 'D'you mean — d'you mean His Majesty *doesn't* want me to come to Court and cook for him?' The tears spilled down her cheeks. 'Oh. Oh, my.'

Transfixed, Melissande stared at the woman. Gerald could almost see the thoughts whirligigging behind her eyes. 'Ah —'

'Of course he does, Eudora!' said Bibbie. 'That's not what Her Highness meant. Tell Eudora what you meant, Melissande.'

Melissande stirred. 'Yes. Of course. Ah — what I meant, Eudora, is that the invitation could've waited. The reason we followed you to South Ott is because we feared you were in danger.'

'In danger?' said Eudora Telford, dabbing her cheeks dry with her hanky. 'Me?'

'Oh yes,' said Bibbie fervently. 'Terrible danger. Awful danger. *Dreadful* danger. The kind of danger that —'

'*Thank you*, Emmerabiblia,' said Melissande, glaring. 'I think the lily is sufficiently gilded.' She looked again at Eudora Telford. 'I'm sorry, Eudora. Please be brave, because there's more. We believe Permelia is in peril too.'

'*Permelia*?' gasped Eudora, her hanky dropping unheeded to the carpet. 'Oh no! Are you sure?'

'Yes,' said Melissande. 'Which is why it's imperative that you tell me what you were doing in South Ott, Eudora. Because there's a good chance you hold the key not only to saving Ottosland from a terrible tragedy ... but more importantly, saving Permelia as well.'

'Blimey,' Reg muttered. 'Madam's getting really good at this.'

Watching Melissande's excruciatingly manipulative performance, Gerald could only agree. Heartfelt sincerity was practically oozing from her pores. She was wasted being plain Miss Cadwallader: Rupert should get her onto New Ottosland's diplomatic merry-go-round without delay. He glanced at Monk, who was staring at Melissande with *such* a fatuous look on his face ...

Blimey. Smitten doesn't even begin to cover it.

'Eudora,' said Melissande, her green eyes terrifyingly intent behind her glasses. 'I know it feels like you'd be betraying a confidence. I know what it's like to care so much for someone that you'd do practically *anything* to keep them safe ... even when that little voice in your head is trying to tell you that might not be what's best for them. *Listen* to that little voice, Eudora. You and I both know it *always* speaks the truth.'

Silly Eudora Telford blinked, her plump face softly undecided. And then it settled into firmer lines. Something approaching determination pressed her plump lips together. Melissande, seeing the change, released the woman's hand and sat back.

'Do excuse me for a moment, Your Highness,' said Eudora Telford with a kind of crumpled dignity. 'I think I have something in my room that might assist you.'

'Good work, Melissande,' said Gerald softly, as soon as Eudora Telford had left the parlour. 'You've got her, I think.'

'And *I* think I need a bath,' said Melissande, just as softly, with a shiver of distaste. '*Honestly*. That poor, silly, gullible woman! I'm as bad as Permelia Wycliffe, taking advantage of her like that.'

'Oh, give it a rest, ducky,' said Reg. 'You're only doing what needs to be done.'

'She's right, Mel,' said Monk. 'You don't have a choice. And you're being as kind as you can. So don't —'

'Shut up everyone,' hissed Bibbie, who'd leapt up to keep watch at the half-closed parlour door. 'She's coming back.'

A moment later Eudora Telford returned, a small black pouch in one hand and a piece of folded paper in the other. Resuming her seat, she clutched them in her lap.

'Permelia called me,' she said, her voice unsteady. 'She begged me to help her. She said I was the only person in the world whom she could trust.'

'And of course you said yes,' said Melissande, her voice gently encouraging. 'You said you'd love to help.'

Eudora Telford nodded. 'I always help Permelia. We've been friends since childhood. That's what friendship is, isn't it? Relying on each other. Knowing there'll always be someone there to help you.'

'Ha,' Reg muttered. '*She* calls it friendship. *I* call it being a dogsbody at the beck and call of a domestic tyrant.'

Gerald agreed, but twitched his shoulder again. The last thing they needed was for Eudora Telford to hear Reg's sarcastic running commentary.

'That's certainly how I always think of friendship, yes,' said Melissande. 'So, Eudora, when Permelia called you ... what exactly did she say?'

Eudora cleared her throat. 'She — she told me Ambrose had done something very foolish, and that if anyone found out about it he'd get into terrible trouble. She wouldn't tell me what it was that he'd done, and naturally I didn't ask. I just promised to do whatever I could to help him.' She blushed. 'There was a time once, many years ago now, when Ambrose and I — but alas. It was not to be. Ambrose had a higher calling.'

'The family company,' said Melissande, nodding. 'Of course. How noble of you, Eudora, to give Ambrose his freedom like that. Few women would be so self-sacrificing.'

Fresh tears glimmered in Eudora Telford's eyes. 'I loved him,' she whispered. 'What else could I do?'

Melissande cleared her throat. 'Nothing, of course,' she said, her voice husky. 'All right. So Permelia called you. What happened next?'

'I went to see her,' said Eudora. 'She gave me this pouch and these instructions and swore me to secrecy. Oh dear ...'

'And then you went all the way to South Ott,' Melissande said quickly, before Eudora Telford changed her mind. 'To meet with someone on Permelia's behalf. Is that right?'

Eudora Telford nodded. 'Yes, Your Highness.'

'South Ott's not a very nice part of town, Eudora,' said Bibbie. 'Even I was a bit nervous going there, and I'm a witch.'

Eudora Telford nodded. 'Yes, it was rather frightening,' she said unhappily. 'But Permelia was so worried she'd be recognised, which would cause more trouble for Ambrose, and — and — she *asked* me. Friends do things for friends. How could I say no?'

Gerald found himself glancing at Reg, and then Monk, who raised an eyebrow in wry resignation. Eudora Telford was right. Friends *did* do things for friends. How could they criticise the silly woman after the risks *they'd* taken?

'Yes, well,' sighed Melissande. 'It mightn't have been terribly sensible of you to go off like that alone, Eudora, but I'm not going to fault you for your loyalty.' Reaching out, she touched her fingertips to the woman's knee. 'Have you any idea what's in that pouch?'

Eudora Telford shook her head vehemently. 'Oh, no. No. Permelia told me I mustn't open it.'

'I understand. But I think *I* should open it, Eudora. I think I need to see what's inside. And I need to know what she wrote in that note, too.' Melissande held out her hand. 'May I?'

Gerald held his breath, and heard a little gasp as Reg held hers too. If Eudora Telford got cold feet ... if she decided not to betray Permelia Wycliffe's confidence ...

Now they were all holding their breath, staring at poor Miss Eudora Telford — who should never have been put in this awful position.

'Oh dear,' she said, and handed over both note and small black pouch.

Melissande briefly closed her eyes. 'Thank you, Eudora.' In silence she unfolded the note and pretended to be reading it for the very first time. When she was finished she looked at Eudora Telford, her face grave. 'I don't suppose you've listened to your wireless this morning?'

'No,' said Eudora Telford. 'The knob's broken and I can't aff— that's to say, I haven't had time to get it fixed.'

'Then you wouldn't have heard. Soon after we left South Ott last night there was an explosion, Eudora. In an old, abandoned boot factory. One man was killed. His name was Haf Rottlezinder.'

Eudora Telford turned parchment pale. 'But — but —'

'Yes, Eudora,' said Bibbie. 'That might've been you if we hadn't convinced you to leave with us.'

For a moment it looked as though Eudora Telford might faint. 'Oh — oh, I do feel unwell.'

Bibbie snapped her fingers at Monk. 'You there. Factotum. Run to Miss Telford's kitchen and bring her a glass of water. Well? What are you gaping at, you silly man? Go!'

Glaring at his impossible sister, Monk went.

Melissande was holding Eudora Telford's hand again. 'Deep breaths, Eudora. I know it's an awful shock.'

'Give me the pouch, Your Highness,' said Bibbie. 'Let's see what Permelia — I mean, Miss Wycliffe — wanted you to give the late Haf Rottlezinder.'

Melissande handed over the pouch. Bibbie opened it ... upended it ... and a stream of gemstones poured into her cupped hand.

'*Mercy*!' gasped Eudora Telford. 'Do you mean to say I was carrying a fortune in precious stones on my person?'

Bibbie was frowning at the sparkling diamonds, rubies and sapphires. 'Actually ...' She tipped the gemstones into her lap, stripped off one glove and plunged her bare fingers into the bounty. 'Hmmm,' she murmured, wearing an expression like a chef tasting soup. 'Let me see ...'

Gerald half-closed his eyes and extended his thaumic senses. Damn. Bibbie was definitely onto something.

Monk returned with the glass of water for Eudora Telford. Catching his eye, Gerald nodded to the puddle of gemstones in Bibbie's lap. Monk dropped one eyelid in a wink, gave Eudora the glass then clumsily turned and knocked into his sister, scattering the gemstones on the carpet.

'Oh! Oh, I'm sorry, Miss, I'm sorry!' he cried in a dreadful parody of a working-class accent, dropping to his knees. 'Let me get 'em for you, I'll pick 'em up, let me!'

'Honestly,' said Bibbie. 'Good factotums are *so* hard to find.'

Melissande was staring, eyebrows raised high. Gerald pulled a warning face at her then looked at Monk, who was tipping the last of the diamonds back into the pouch Bibbie held out for him. As he got off his knees he gave his head the smallest shake, then flicked his sister a meaningful look. Bibbie dropped one eyelid in an acknowledging wink.

'Actually, Eudora, these gemstones are fake,' she said. 'Good enough to — ah — fool a lay-person,' she added, with an apologetic glance at Melissande. 'But I'm afraid any wizard worth his salt would've immediately detected them as forgeries.'

'*Forgeries?*' said Eudora Telford and leapt to her feet. The glass of water slid through her fingers, splashing her skirt then rolling under the chair. 'Oh, Your Highness,' she whispered, hands pressed to her breast. 'Oh, Miss Markham! I hope you don't think that — I would *never* — I wouldn't know *how* to —' Overcome, she burst into tears.

Melissande stood and put an arm around the damp, distraught woman. 'Now Eudora, don't be silly. We know you wouldn't exchange the real gemstones for fakes. You'd *never* cheat Permelia like that. After all, *you're* not a Millicent Grimwade.'

'Or a Permelia Wycliffe,' Reg muttered. 'The hide of that woman, Gerald. Next time I see her I'll bloody well pluck her bald, sending this — this *wet hen* into the wilds of South Ott to do her dirty work for her! She must've known what would happen if Rottlezinder got wind of the fake jewels!'

He nodded. It really was diabolical . . . or desperate.

As Melissande comforted her, Eudora Telford continued to tearfully deny any wrongdoing. 'I know, I know, Eudora,' said Melissande, 'but everything's going to be all right, I promise. Eudora — *Eudora, put a sock in it! Carrying on like a watering can isn't going to help!*'

Shocked tearless, Eudora Telford stared at her.

Melissande stepped back. 'Sorry,' she said, very pink around her freckles. 'But it was either shout at you or slap you. I thought you'd prefer the shouting.'

'I don't understand,' said Eudora Telford, her voice quavering. 'None of this makes any sense.'

'I know,' said Melissande. 'And I'm so sorry you're caught up in it. You're a very sweet person, and none of this is fair.'

'Please, Your Highness,' said Eudora, her eyes red-rimmed, her lips trembling. 'Am I in trouble?'

Melissande took her by the shoulders. '*No*, Eudora. You've done nothing wrong. In fact you're halfway to being a heroine.'

'A heroine?' gasped Eudora. 'Me? Oh, surely not.'

'Absolutely, Eudora,' said Bibbie. 'In fact you're crucial to an ongoing government investigation that —'

'That we can't talk about,' said Melissande quickly, glaring at Bibbie. 'Nevertheless, Eudora, it's the truth. And we need you to help us help the government. The future of Ottosland could be at stake.'

Eudora Telford's knees gave way, and she dropped back into her chair. 'Gracious. I don't — this is so *sudden* — are you *sure* I —'

'I'm certain,' said Melissande firmly. 'Eudora, please, you need to trust me. It appears you've stumbled across a dangerous business, but you mustn't worry — as a princess and the former prime minister of New Ottosland, I have — ah — access to government sources not available to most people.'

'Ha,' Reg snickered. 'That's one way of putting it.'

'I'll make sure you're perfectly safe,' Melissande added. 'But I shan't lie to you, Eudora — doing your duty won't be easy. You'll have to talk about Permelia, and Ambrose, and everything you know about the Wycliffe Airship Company.'

'Oh, *no* — oh, I *couldn't*,' said Eudora Telford, horrified.

Melissande held up a cautioning finger. 'Eudora, you must.

I know you want to protect Permelia — and Ambrose. But don't you see? Telling the truth is the only way you can do that.'

'But I don't know anything, not really,' Eudora whispered. 'Oh, Your Highness, please, can't you explain for me?'

'I wish I could,' said Melissande. 'I know you're frightened, Eudora. But you mustn't be. Everything will work out for the best, you'll see. Now, what I need you to do for me is change out of your wet skirt so that one of my factotums can escort you to see — to see —'

'Sir Ralph Markham,' said Bibbie. 'My uncle. Antigone's nephew, as it happens. Only don't mention pastry to him. It's a bit of a sore point. But he will want to hear everything else you've got to say.'

'Oh gracious,' said Eudora. 'Are you *quite* sure this is the right thing to do?'

'*Positive*,' said Melissande and Bibbie together.

'Blimey!' said Reg, after Eudora Telford had tottered from the parlour. 'If that woman was any wetter she'd be a registered weather system!'

'Don't be horrible, Reg,' Melissande snapped. 'Gerald, sorry, I didn't mean to take over but —'

'*Ha!*' said Reg. 'Pull the other one, ducky, it plays nursery rhymes!'

'Reg,' said Gerald, and twitched his shoulder again. Then he looked at Melissande. 'It's fine. You're right, she does have to speak to the authorities. And Sir Ralph's as good a place to start as any. If Sir Alec needs to get involved, Sir Ralph will bring him in.'

'Just make sure you remind her about the pastry thing,' said Bibbie. 'I wasn't kidding about that — was I, Monk?'

Monk was inspecting the occasional table under the parlour window, looking at the forest of framed photographs Eudora had planted there.

'Hmm? What?' he said absently. 'No. It's no joke. Antigone single-handedly gave Uncle Ralph a pastry phobia. Insisted on him helping her bake fairy-cakes. In an apron. With frills. When he was twenty.'

Reg shook her head, then looked at Melissande. 'Do you remember our conversation about the children, ducky?'

'What?' said Melissande, frowning. 'No.'

'Offspring,' said Reg. 'Sprogs. Yours and his.'

Melissande blushed. 'Oh. That. Reg —'

'Only the more I learn about this Markham boy's family,' Reg continued, undaunted, 'the more I start to wonder if paddling in his gene pool is really —'

'Reg, *shut up!*'

'Mind you,' said Reg, oblivious, staring around Eudora Telford's fussy, frilly, knick-knack crowded parlour. 'Things could be worse. You could end up living like this. All I can say is it's a wonder the place isn't crawling with cats.' She sniffed. 'Unmarried women tend to break out in cats, I've noticed.' She gave Melissande a pointed look. 'You'd best be careful, ducky. You've already got one toe in *that* manky pond.'

'And to think I *ever* wondered why your husband hexed you!' said Bibbie, very pink. 'If you don't mind, you deranged feather duster, that's my brother and my family you're —'

'Don't, Bibbie,' said Melissande. 'Really. You'll only encourage her.' As Reg chortled and Bibbie spluttered she looked at Monk. 'Can you see that Eudora gets to your uncle safely? Obviously Bibbie and I can't be officially involved in any of this. Besides, with the portal sabotage case practically solved we really have to focus on *our* case now or Permelia Wycliffe is going to fire us *and* sue us for breach of contract.'

'Not necessarily,' said Reg. 'It's a bit hard to sue someone when you're behind bars yourself. Don't forget she's up to her eyeballs in this portal business.'

'Good point,' said Melissande. 'But I hope you're wrong, because I'd like us to get paid the rest of our retainer and keep our growing reputation intact.'

'So what's our next move?' said Bibbie.

'Well,' said Reg, 'while that Markham boy's taking the tropical depression in to see your Uncle Ralph, you and I and Princess Pushy and Gerald are going to —'

'Oh, Your Highness,' said Eudora Telford, returning to the parlour, dressed now in cheerful primrose-yellow silk. 'So sorry to have kept you waiting, I —' She saw Monk at the occasional table and blushed. 'Oh, I see you've noticed my — my — oh dear —' She cleared her throat. 'My little bragging table.'

'I'm sorry. Your bragging table?' said Melissande, advancing on the collection of photos.

'Yes,' said Eudora, fluttering after her. 'Mementos of my years in the Baking and Pastry Guild. Photographs of Permelia and myself with some of the illustrious women it's been our pleasure to meet. Quite a few of them are terribly important, you know.'

Monk, playing his role of servile factotum to the hilt, tugged his forelock and backed off as Melissande and Eudora reached the table.

'Oh,' said Melissande. 'Yes. I've seen these photos before, I think. On Permelia's wall.' She frowned. 'Did you say you're in them, Eudora?'

'Oh yes,' said Eudora Telford, and snatched up the nearest framed photograph. 'See?' She thrust it under Melissande's nose. 'This is me — and Permelia — with the wife of the Kalif of Ninifar. That was at the year-before-last's Golden Whisk.'

Melissande considered the photo. 'Well, I see Permelia and the Kalifa but — I'm sorry, I don't quite —'

'There! That's me!' said Eudora Telford, pointing. 'That's my elbow, and the edge of my purple silk dress.'

'Blimey,' Reg muttered. 'Her elbow? I take it back, Gerald. She's not a tropical depression, she's a candidate for the asylum.'

'Hush,' he hissed at her under his breath.

'And this one — this one, you see?' said Eudora Telford. 'Here I am with the Mogul of Fandawandi's forty-third wife, and Permelia, at the opening of the Ott Homeland District's annual fair. Four years ago.'

Melissande peered. 'Ah. Yes. I take it this is your foot, Eudora?'

'That's right,' said Eudora Telford. 'I'm afraid I'm rather hopeless in photographs,' she confided. 'Always moving at the wrong moment, or sneezing.'

'Yes, having your photograph taken is terribly tedious I know,' said Melissande, staring fixedly at one framed photo in particular.

'Hello,' said Reg. 'What's madam seen now?'

Gerald couldn't tell. But from the look on her face . . .

'This lady here,' said Melissande, picking up the photograph. 'She looks familiar for some reason. Do you know who she is?'

Eudora looked. 'Yes. Of course. That's me — well, the back of my head — and Permelia with the Prime Minister of Jandria's wife. Madam Manawa Tambotan. *That* one was taken not quite two months ago, at the Annual Baking and Pastry Guild Charity Ball. Madam Tambotan was this year's charity patron. She and Permelia were great chums at school, you know. And of course *she's* the president of Jandria's Baking and Pastry Guild.'

'Bloody hell,' Reg muttered. 'Gerald . . .'

But he didn't need Reg's alarm tickling in his ear. He didn't need Melissande's startled expression, or Bibbie's wide-eyed stare, or the swiftly-extinguished flare in Monk's etheretic aura.

Jandria.

CHAPTER TWENTY-TWO

Gerald felt his heart hammering at his ribs. *Permelia* was the connection between Errol and Jandria? But how could that be? She never set foot in Ambrose's jealously guarded lab.

He realised then that something was nudging him ... a thought ... a memory ... something important ...

'Um,' said Melissande. 'So Permelia and the prime minister's wife — you're saying they're still good friends?'

'Oh yes, indeed,' said Eudora. 'They're always exchanging letters. They even talk on the telephone, though the calls are so expensive.' Her expression dimmed a little. 'Doubtless there are things only two presidents can discuss.'

Gerald felt the nudging, niggling thought sharpen into a jabbing realisation. *Permelia.*

'Oy!' Reg muttered. 'What's wrong?'

Ignoring Reg, he cleared his throat. 'I'm sorry, Your Highness, excuse me, Your Highness.'

Melissande gave him her snootiest look. 'What?'

'We should — ah — the jalopy, Your Highness. We should warm it up before you and the ladies get into it. Me and — um — him.' He jerked his thumb at Monk, who was staring at him as though he'd gone mad. 'Um. Can we? Please?'

Melissande heaved a sigh. 'I suppose so. If you must. But don't take all day. We'll be joining you shortly.'

'What the hell are you going on about, Gerald?' said Monk, once they'd escaped Eudora Telford's bungalow. 'The jalopy doesn't need warming up.'

'I know,' he said. 'But I had to talk to you about Permelia Wycliffe.'

'Ah,' said Monk. 'Yeah. She and Errol must be in cahoots. Him passing his work to her so she can pass it on to Jandria through her good chum the prime minister's wife. Could be he's the one behind the faked gemstones, too, which means sorry, mate, he also lied to you about not being involved with the portal sabotage.'

'You think so?' he demanded. 'So you detected Errol's thaumic signature on those fake jewels, did you?'

Monk frowned. 'Well, no, but —'

'But nothing. I'm telling you, Monk, Errol didn't make them. And he's not passing his work to Jandria through Permelia Wycliffe either.'

Still anchored to his shoulder, Reg rattled her tail feathers. 'Gerald, what's going on? What is this obsession with Errol Haythwaite's innocence?'

'This isn't about Errol,' he snapped. 'It's about the principle of protecting the unjustly accused.' He plucked Reg off his shoulder, set her down on the roof of the jalopy and stared into her worried eyes. 'The Janitorial Department — Sir Alec — *me* — we've got an awful lot of power, Reg. You don't know how much. You don't know the kind of incants they've given me or what I've learned to do in the last six months.'

'Then tell me,' she said. 'Secrets aren't healthy, Gerald.'

He shook his head. 'I can't. There's no time.'

'Not at the moment, no,' she agreed. 'But when this is done you can make time. That is, if you want to.'

'Reg,' Monk said quietly. 'Don't nag him, all right?'

Her feathers flattened. 'I see.' She sniffed. 'I suppose *you* know all about it, do you?'

And now her feelings were hurt. Gerald laid his hands flat on either side of her and touched his chin lightly to the top of her head. 'Don't be angry,' he whispered. 'I'm *dangerous* now. I have to be careful. I can't ever let myself be too convinced that I'm right.' Stepping back, he looked at Monk. 'Eudora Telford's not the only one with a voice in her head ... and right now mine's *screaming*.'

'All right, mate, all right,' said Monk, glancing at the bungalow. 'Calm down. What is it screaming?'

Calm down. It was good advice. His heart was still racing, his thoughts tumbled and jumbled. Just as Melissande predicted, the pieces of the jigsaw were falling into place.

'Last night,' he said slowly, 'after I'd faked the laboratory explosion and Wycliffe's was crawling with inspectors, Ambrose and Permelia turned up ... and something odd happened. I didn't pay much attention at the time, but now I realise how important it was. When I was explaining to Ambrose what had happened —'

'Ha,' said Reg, eyes bright with sardonic amusement. 'When you were lying through your teeth, you mean.'

'Yes, all right, when I was lying through my teeth,' he said, impatient, 'I told them Errol and I had been working in the lab all night without a break.'

Monk frowned at him. 'So?'

'So when Permelia Wycliffe heard that she nearly swallowed her tongue. I'm telling you, Monk, she couldn't believe her ears. Ambrose assumed it was because she didn't think we were dedicated enough to work back late, but *I* think it was more than that.'

'You mean she knew it was a lie?' said Monk. 'But how would she know? Unless —'

He nodded. 'Exactly. Unless she'd already been to the lab that night, sometime between when Errol and I left and when we got back. Permelia has no business setting foot in the place. R&D's out of bounds for her *and* her gels.'

Monk's face screwed up in a sceptical frown. 'You're thinking she snuck in there and stole some of Errol's blueprints while you were both in South Ott? But how could she? Errol used to ward his school pencil box so we couldn't nick his eraser. There's no way that woman could get past one of his anti-theft hexes.' He shook his head. 'Sorry, Gerald, but I think you're stretching the facts a bit thin.'

Maybe, but what choice did he have? 'The blueprints that ended up in Jandria were copies,' he said. 'So maybe whatever black market thaumaturgist Permelia found to make her the fake jewels put together a recording incant and a hex-breaker, too.'

Reg rattled her tail feathers. 'That's not a bad theory.'

'It's not a bad theory if you believe Errol's innocent,' Monk said slowly.

'And I *do*,' said Gerald. 'In fact I *know* he is. Please Monk, you have to trust me. I was *there*. I saw his face. He *begged* me to — to —' He blew out a hard breath. 'Take my word for it, Errol's not involved.'

'All right,' said Monk. 'I'll take your word for it.'

'Great,' said Gerald, giddy with relief. 'In that case, how do you feel about selling my theory to Sir Alec?'

'What?' said Monk. '*Me*? After you told him what I said about the *delerioso*? Bloody hell, Gerald. Are you trying to get me sacked?'

He pulled an apologetic face. 'Yeah. I know. Sorry. But he was going to bollocks you over that anyway. At least if you've got some good news on the investigation you might distract him. And someone's got to take Eudora Telford in so they can interview her.'

'What, skip Uncle Ralph altogether, you mean?' Monk brightened. 'Take her straight to your people? I could do that.'

'Yeah. Look, I'm sorry to dump this on you, Monk. It's just that I don't want the girls going back to Wycliffe's alone. And anyway, I need to get into Errol's office. If Permelia did pinch more of his work last night there might still be some thaumic signature traces I can read.'

'Good idea,' said Monk, and fished in his pocket. 'Here — take these. I palmed them when I was ever-so-helpfully picking up Eudora's spilled booty.'

Gerald grinned at the fake diamonds Monk gave him. 'Thanks,' he said, slipping the imposters into his own pocket. 'If the thaumic signatures match that'll be one more nail in somebody's coffin. Y'know, anyone'd think you were a genius or something.'

Reg cleared her throat ominously. 'Just so you don't think I'm not paying attention, *the girls* are perfectly capable of handling themselves in Wycliffe's, or anywhere else you care to name.'

'Sorry,' he sighed. 'Of course you are. I just —'

'I mean,' she said, 'we pretty well solved this case for you, sunshine. Without Witches Inc. you'd still be staggering around the lab, wouldn't you, blowing up prototype airships?'

'I *didn't* blow up the Ambrose Mark VI!' he protested. 'Errol got the etheretic intermix balance wrong.'

'Yes, well, you can throw all the syllables around that you like, sunshine,' said Reg, sniffing, 'it doesn't alter the fact that without our connection to that wet hen Eudora Telford —'

'Who's coming out of her bungalow right now,' said Monk. 'So put a sock in it. Gerald —'

'You take her to Sir Alec in the jalopy,' he said quickly. 'We'll get a taxi to Wycliffe's. Tell Sir Alec I'll call him as soon as I've got the proof of Permelia's tampering so he can send in Dalby and his team.'

'Will do.'

He turned to Reg. 'Quick, flap on over to Melissande. Make a big fuss of her.'

'What do you mean, make a big fuss of her?' said Reg. 'I don't go around making big fusses. That girl's problem is she's already too big for her britches — and I'm not just talking about her buttocks, either.'

He stared nose to beak at the wretched bird. '*What*?'

'Don't ask,' said Monk, resigned. 'Really. Just don't.'

'Reg, I need you to tell her what the plan is,' he hissed, as Melissande and Bibbie prepared to escort Eudora Telford down the pathway to her front gate. 'Tell her she's decided this business is so urgent that they've got to go over Sir Ralph's head to his superior, Sir Alec.'

Reg sniffed. 'Tell her yourself. I'm not your social secretary, sunshine.'

'How can I?' he demanded in an urgent undertone. 'I'm just a factotum, aren't I? Please, Reg. Hurry.'

'Blimey,' she said, and ruffled her feathers. 'What would you do without me, that's what I want to know.'

And she launched herself into air, towards Melissande.

'Good question,' said Monk, watching Reg land on Melissande, making enough fuss for three birds twice her size. 'You ever think about that? About not having her around?'

Gerald felt a cold shiver run through him. 'No. Not if I can help it. Now shut up and look obsequious. Their Royal Highnesses approach.'

CHAPTER TWENTY-THREE

When Gerald returned to the noisy, bustling Wycliffe R&D laboratory complex, every wizard stopped what he was doing: stopped talking, experimenting, surreptitiously eating, clandestinely drinking, sweeping, scrubbing, filing and skiving off ... and stared at him.

It was like walking into a wall of silence.

'Um,' he said carefully. 'Hello, chaps.'

Robert Methven broke the hostile stillness, pushing his way through the collection of wizards. 'What the hell are you doing here, Dunwoody? You're supposed to be ...' His face twisted. '*On leave.*'

He'd worked out his cover story during the taxi ride from Eudora Telford's bungalow. 'Ah, well, Mister Methven, I know. And I am. But I've come to do a favour for Mister Haythwaite. He asked me especially.'

Robert Methven looked down his nose. 'Really? Mister Haythwaite asked you for a favour? That's odd. *I* heard you nearly got him killed last night. *Again.*'

A mutter of comments ran through the watching wizards. Keeping a cautious eye on them, Gerald manufactured a suitably shocked expression. 'What? Oh, no. That's not right, Mister Methven. Who told you that?'

'Mister Wycliffe,' said Robert Methven. 'Are you calling him a liar?'

Well . . . damn. He looked past Methven, down to the far end of the lab complex towards Ambrose's office. Its door was closed. 'A liar? Oh, no, Mister Methven. Not at all. Either Mister Wycliffe — ah — misunderstood what Mister Haythwaite said, or else he's teasing. Yes. I'm sure he's just teasing. Perhaps if you asked him to step out of his office for a moment, we could —'

'Mister Wycliffe isn't here,' said Robert Methven. 'In Mister Haythwaite's absence, *I* am in charge of this facility until Mister Wycliffe's return.'

Oh. Well, it could be worse. 'I see,' he said humbly. 'In that case, Mister Methven, I'm sure you'll have no trouble letting me into Mister Haythwaite's office, just for a few moments? You see, when I visited Mister Haythwaite this morning he asked me to stop by and fetch something for him. It might be a bit uncomfortable if I have to say I couldn't perform this small errand for him because Mister Methven wouldn't let me.'

Around the laboratory, the other wizards were gradually, grudgingly, returning to work. Robert Methven made a strangled sound in his throat, clearly torn between doing down the accident-prone, unpopular Third Grader and not getting on the bad side of the Wycliffe's senior thaumaturgist. Just like Sir Alec, Errol cast a long shadow. Trying not to look as though he cared very much one way or another, Gerald shoved his hands in his pockets and crossed his fingers. Because if Methven decided to be an idiot about this, life was about to get very, very complicated . . .

'*Fine,*' Methven grunted, and jerked his head towards Errol's office. 'Go on, then, Dunnywood. But make it quick. You're a bloody jinx, you are. You're thaumaturgical quicksand, and the sooner you're out of here the better I'll like it.' He grimaced.

'Truscott's must have taken leave of their senses, sending you here.'

'Yes, Mister Methven,' he said, backing away. 'Thank you, Mister Methven. I'll be as quick as I can, I promise, Mister Methven. You won't even know I'm around, you'll see.'

With a withering stare of utter contempt, Robert Methven turned on his heel and stalked away. Acutely aware that he was still being surreptitiously stared at by his former colleagues, Gerald hid his relief, showing only the kind of servile gratitude expected of a Third Grader, and headed for Errol's office before Robert Methven changed his mind. Passing the Mark VI lab, he noticed it was warded shut, with a big red warning poster pasted onto the explosion-buckled door. Its forbidding black lettering read: *No Admittance, by strict order of the Ottosland Department of Thaumaturgy.*

Well. Sir Alec wasn't messing about, was he?

Easing Errol's office door closed, but not latched, he took a moment to breathe deeply, subduing nerves, and let his gaze roam around the room. It was immaculately tidy, which was a help. On the desk a blotter, a crystal ball, a telephone, an ink pot, a selection of pens and pencils and some drawing instruments: compass, slide rule, thaumic protractor and an etheretic plumb-bob. Beside the desk was an oversized filing cabinet, designed to house Errol's top-secret airship and thaumic engine designs.

But before he explored that likely target for proof of theft, he took a moment to get the feel of the office's etheretic ambience. Rather like a strong perfume, thaumic signatures lingered, sometimes for weeks, if their inherent strength was impressive enough. And the black market wizard who'd designed the hexes Permelia — or whoever was behind the thefts — had used to steal Errol's work was no weakling Third Grader, that much he knew for certain.

He may be a genius but he's a bloody menace, too. I wonder if Sir Alec will let me hunt him down when this is over? Unless of course it was Rottlezinder. In which case . . .

It was a possibility that hadn't occurred to him. But it would make a kind of twisted sense . . . as well as provide more proof against Permelia.

Slowly, carefully, holding his breath in case he inadvertently set off one of the laboratory's etheretic sensors, Gerald unfurled his *potentia* and let it taste the air.

Yes. There was Errol, sharp as snow on the wind, a bitter, biting essence of power. No warmth in his thaumic signature at all. Muddying all around it, the faint scents of other wizards who'd been summoned to his presence over the past week or two. Robert Methven, in particular. His *potentia* was tinged with anxiety . . . which wasn't surprising. Being Errol's direct underling would make anyone sweat.

Frowning lightly, Gerald pushed a little harder. There had to be a trace of the black market wizard in here. A hint of him . . . a suggestion . . . a shadow . . .

Yes. There it was. Subtle. Elusive. A *potentia* he'd never encountered before — which meant not Haf Rottlezinder. Damn. Nor did it belong to any of Wycliffe's R&D wizards. He fished the fake diamonds out of his pocket, closed his fist around them and inhaled. Yes. There it was again. The same sour etheretic aftertaste. Powerful. Very powerful.

Raised voices in the lab beyond the office had him jumping. He leapt back to the door to see what was going on, but it was only another argument between Second Graders Spinkniz and Nye. Idiots. All those two had in common were a lab bench and a bad temper.

So he wasn't unmasked. But he really had to get moving, before his precarious situation here deteriorated further. Time to check out Errol's precious airship designs.

He risked one last check of the lab complex. Spinkniz and Nye had lapsed into sullen silence, and no-one at all was looking his way. Not even Japhet Morgan, who'd been a sort of, kind of, friend. A fellow sufferer in Third Grade adversity, anyway. Wasn't that supposed to count for something?

Apparently not.

So, Wycliffe's wizards were busily at work and Robert Methven was nowhere in sight. Hopefully he was up to his eyeballs in an experiment and had forgotten about the appalling Gerald Dunwoody.

Easing back from the door, Gerald turned and headed for Errol's filing cabinet. Used one of his newly acquired incants to unhex it, slid the top draw open, pulled out the first sheaf of blueprints and ran his fingers lightly across them. No. No. No. No. *Yes.* The same thaumic signature as he'd felt in the fake diamonds, almost too faint to detect. He triggered a recording incant, recited the design code number, then checked the last two designs.

Nothing.

Putting those designs back, he pulled out the next file's worth. No. No. Yes. Yes. No. No.

Another pile. Yes. Yes. Yes. Yes. No.

And another. No. No. No. No.

Errol had certainly been busy. Six new airship designs, from small personal craft to enormous public carriers. And no less than *three* new engine designs, all building on the innovations he was trying out in the Ambrose Mark VI.

Blimey. If Errol managed to get even half of these to work, public transport would be revolutionised. Even if the portal network survived, and thrived, there was still a lot of potential in the designs.

Of course … there was even more potential for creating a truly formidable and terrifying military fleet.

Gerald swallowed. With designs like this in the hands of war-hungry Jandria, the world would be in mortal danger. The reminder was nasty: after the harmless fluffiness of Eudora Telford, a prick in the side with a smooth, cold knife.

This isn't a game, Dunwoody. You're a janitor. Get the job done.

Heart thudding just a little bit faster, he pulled out the last set of Errol's drawings, and was amazed all over again to see the ideas that had sprung from Errol's fertile imagination. Pillock or not, Haythwaite had enormous talent. So had the thief plundered these, too? No. No. Yes. Yes. Yes. Yes. And this time the thaumic signature was practically *buzzing*. However Permelia Wycliffe had done it — and he was convinced Ambrose's sister was behind this, no matter how far-fetched the idea — whatever copying incant or thaumic gizmo she'd managed to get made for her, it had been used on these drawings within the last twelve to fourteen hours. Which absolutely tied in with the period between his and Errol's journey to South Ott, and their subsequent return.

Things weren't looking too good for Ambrose's sister.

He loaded the recording incant into one of Errol's pencils and shoved it deep in his inside coat pocket for safekeeping. Then he crossed to the desk and stared at the crystal ball. A pity he didn't know Errol's password. Of course he could probably smash through it but that would likely set off the lab's alarms. So — time to use Sir Alec's very private phone number again.

'*Mister Dunwoody. How nice to hear from you at last.*'

Oh, ouch. Sir Alec's tone was so sharp it was a wonder there wasn't blood dripping from his ear. 'Sir Alec, I don't have long. I'm sorry. Is Monk there?'

'*Yes.*'

'And Miss Eudora Telford?'

'*Yes. Where are you, Mister Dunwoody?*'

'In Errol's office. I've found the link between the stolen plans and the fake gemstones — um, do you know about the —'

'*Yes, Mister Dunwoody. I have been apprised of recent developments.*'

And, making a wild guess, Sir Alec wasn't thrilled. *Bugger.* 'Oh. Good. Well, sir, everything ties together. The plans, the gemstones and Permelia Wyc—'

'Mister Dunwoody, what are you doing?' demanded a horrified voice.

Gerald spun round, swallowing a curse. *Now? You had to choose now to see if we could be friends?* 'Oh — Japhet — ah — I was just —'

'Mister Methven! Mister Methven!' shouted Japhet Morgan, backing out of the office. 'You were right! Gerald Dunwoody *is* up to no good! He's in here using Mister Haythwaite's telephone!'

Gerald strangled a groan. '*Damn,*' he said, and put the receiver back to his ear. 'Sorry, Sir Alec. Things are about to get a little bit awkward. If you don't mind, I'll call you back.'

And he hung up before he learned whether Sir Alec agreed with that plan or not.

A moment later, Robert Methven stormed into Errol's office. '*Right,* Dunwoody, you snivelling incompetent *toad*! What the *hell* do you think you're doing?'

Melissande stood in front of Miss Petterly's desk and let the foaming waves of vitriol wash over her, unchecked. According to the clock on the office wall, Miss Petterly had been haranguing her for twenty minutes without a breath, and furthermore showed no sign whatsoever of running out of invective any time soon.

Silly cow. I could have caught up on half the work I've missed by now if she'd just shut up and let me get to my cubicle.

Behind her she could feel the avid, straining curiosity of all the other Wycliffe gels, who never failed to be entertained by someone else's misfortune. Even the office boy had stopped trundling his squeaky-wheeled cart up and down the aisles between the horrible grey cubicles.

Behind Miss Petterly, in Permelia Wycliffe's office, Permelia and her brother Ambrose were once again at odds. In fact, they were so much at odds that Permelia hadn't closed her blinds properly. She could see bits of them railing at each other. The partially unshrouded glass and the depth of their mutual anger meant it was much easier this time to work out what they were fighting over ... although Miss Petterly's shrill shrieking did make eavesdropping that tad more difficult.

I hope Reg is hanging upside down outside the window again.

'— dereliction of duty that is *quite* insupportable in a Wycliffe gel!' said Miss Petterly. '*You*, Miss Carstairs, represent *everything* that is wrong with the young women of today! Flighty! Thoughtless! Concerned with nothing but your own pleasures! If you knew the vicissitudes faced by the women who came before you, Miss Carstairs! Women like myself who had to fight tooth and nail for the right to employment outside the domestic sphere! We battled and we struggled and we —'

Yes, I'm sure it was a trial. Try fighting tooth and nail with a dragon some time, you ridiculous woman.

And then, as Miss Petterly continued to rant, she felt a twist of guilt. Actually, that wasn't fair. Even in modern Ottosland there were barriers to break down. Prejudices to overcome. Women like Miss Petterly — as unpleasant as she was — had helped to make it possible for her and Bibbie to open Witches Inc., live outside the confines of the family, drive a car, wear trousers ...

Well. Get stared at while wearing trousers, but also not get arrested. That's progress — of a sort.

With difficulty she tuned out Miss Petterly's scolding and tried to focus on Permelia and Ambrose.

'— don't know what you're talking about,' he was saying. 'That old biddy? Why would I —'

Old biddy? Were they talking about Eudora Telford?

'— to call me, or come and see me, and she's vanished!' shouted Permelia. '*Vanished*, Ambrose! After going to see that dreadful wizard *you* —'

'*Miss Carstairs!*' said Miss Petterly, and banged her fist on the desk. 'Are you paying *attention* to me?'

Oh, how much did she want to say no. But instead she nodded, hoping her expression was suitably chastened. 'Oh yes, Miss Petterly. I've heard every word, Miss Petterly.'

'I find that hard to believe, Miss Carstairs!' retorted Miss Petterly. 'You have a singularly vacant look upon your face!'

Inside Permelia's office, the telephone rang. Permelia whirled away from her brother and snatched up the receiver. '*What?*'

'*Miss Carstairs!*' gasped Miss Petterly. 'How dare you? How dare you stand there and *ignore* me, gel!'

Melissande shot her an impatient look, abruptly tired of the charade. 'Oh do shut *up*, you wittering old bat! I'm trying to hear what's going on with Permelia and Ambrose!'

Especially since Permelia's busy incriminating the pair of them. So kind of her. I must remember to say thanks.

From the office's grim grey cubicles came loud, astonished gasps at her outright rebellion. And then the muffled sound of much merriment, repressed.

Miss Petterly looked like she was about faint. 'I beg — I beg — I *beg* your *pardon?*'

'Too late,' said Melissande, and stared through the office blinds. Now Ambrose was on the phone and he didn't look happy. He growled something into the receiver and slammed it back in its cradle, then marched to the office door and flung it open.

'My mind is made up, Permelia!' he snarled, pausing to glare back at his sister. 'I wanted to sack him last night but *you* overruled me. Well I'm tired of you overruling me, you interfering scold. *I* am the head of this family *and* this company, and *I* will decide who remains in its employ. This time Gerald Dunwoody *stays* sacked! And furthermore — I'm having him *arrested*!'

As he thudded his way past Miss Petterly's desk and through the outer office towards the door, Permelia — looking anything but self-controlled and haughty — tottered out after him.

'Ambrose, no! Ambrose, wait! Ambrose, please, listen, you don't know what you're doing!' Ignoring the astonished Miss Petterly she hurried after her enraged brother, pausing only to add, 'Miss Cadwallader? Your services have proven most unsatisfactory. Consider your contract summarily terminated. I expect my retainer to be refunded immediately. *Ambrose*!'

And she continued after her brother, hurling epithets and pleas. *Blimey*.

Melissande looked into Permelia's office, saw that Reg was indeed hanging upside down outside the window and in fact appeared to be in a spot of bother. So she shoved past Miss Petterly and into the office, rescued Reg, plonked the gasping bird on her shoulder and ran out again in pursuit of the battling Wycliffes.

Every gel in the office was on her feet and staring.

'Miss Carstairs! Miss Carstairs!' Miss Petterly screamed.

'Not Carstairs! *Cadwallader*!' Melissande shouted back, then looked around the office. 'Of Witches Inc., Ottosland's premier witching locum agency. No task too small, discretion guaranteed. And if I were you, gels, I'd start looking for different employment! Wycliffe's is about to go down in flames!'

Leaving a hubbub behind her she ran down the stairs and out to reception, where Bibbie — who'd insisted on coming to

Wycliffe's with her in the dubious guise of a young gel looking for work — was failing spectacularly to look plain and rustic and eminently employable.

'What's going on?' she said, leaping to her feet.

Ignoring shocked Miss Fisher, Melissande grabbed her by one blue muslin sleeve and tugged her towards the door. 'I don't know, exactly, but it sounds like Gerald's in trouble. Come on, we've got to get to him, quickly, before this whole case goes kablooey in our faces.'

They hustled out of the administration building and onto the path leading to the Research and Development block. Reg immediately launched herself into the air and flapped ahead.

The main door to the laboratory complex stood uncharacteristically open. Inside, Ambrose Wycliffe was shouting. As Reg glided into the building, staying high to avoid detection, Melissande grabbed Bibbie's arm again then pressed a finger to her lips.

'Not a sound, all right?' she breathed. 'Tiptoe and hold your breath! With any luck they won't notice us. Especially if Ambrose keeps on bellowing like that.'

Bibbie nodded vigorously, and they crept their way into the Wycliffe Airship Company's raging thaumic heart.

All of Ambrose's wizards were gathered in a nervous, ragged circle, as though they had a wild animal trapped and weren't precisely sure what to do with it. Gerald, very tense, was staring at Ambrose Wycliffe, who stood inside the ragged circle with him. And Ambrose Wycliffe, scarlet-faced and practically frothing at the mouth, very nearly demented with fury, looked in danger of having a stroke. Permelia hovered behind her brother, her panicked gaze darting from Ambrose to Gerald and back again.

'— since you got here, Dunwoody!' Ambrose's meaty hands were clenched to fists. He looked like he wanted to pummel

Gerald to a bloody pulp. 'At first I thought it was just Truscott's, slipping up, but do you know what I think now, sir? I think you're an *imposter*. I think you're a *spy*! I think you've been sent here to destroy my company!'

'Ah — no, Mister Wycliffe, that's not true,' said Gerald, as an ugly murmuring ran through the circle of wizards. 'I *was* sent here by Truscott's, remember? You were short a Third Grade wizard, *I'm* a Third Grade wizard, so they —'

'Poppycock!' shouted Ambrose. 'You're a *spy*, I *know* it. Who sent you? Was it Boswell? Is Boswell trying to resurrect his business again? Well, you can tell him from me he's an *idiot*! Wycliffe's buried Boswell once and we'll bury him again. We'll dance on his inferior company's grave a second time. A third time! As many times as it takes, I can promise you that!'

Gerald raised placating hands. Melissande couldn't tell if he'd noticed her and Bibbie, still as mice inside the laboratory complex door, or Reg, perched high above the spectacle on one of the light-fittings ... but if he had, he gave absolutely no sign of it.

Oh, Saint Snodgrass preserve us. Please don't let this go kablooey.

'Mister Wycliffe,' he said, his voice so meek and subservient, sounding nothing like the man who'd defeated a dragon, 'I'm terribly sorry, but I think there's been a dreadful mistake.'

Ambrose took a threatening step forward. 'My oath there's been a mistake! You set foot in my lab, Dunwoody, *that* was a mistake. Your *first* mistake. And *then* you started sabotaging my airships. Well, Mister Incompetent Third Grade wizard, we don't take too kindly to sabotage around here. *Especially* sabotage that lands our head designer in hospital and puts our brand-new flagship Ambrose Mark VI prototype on the scrap heap — *twice*.'

More ugly murmuring. The staring wizards tightened their ranks.

'Bloody hell,' muttered Bibbie. 'This is getting ugly. Any second now there's going to be real trouble.'

Alarmed, Melissande stared at her. 'Why? What's happening?'

'Can't you feel it?' said Bibbie. 'They're stirring up the ether.'

She sighed. '*Bibbie* —'

'Oh. Sorry.' Bibbie pulled a face. 'Mel, this lot aren't the best bunch of wizards I've ever come across but they've got more than enough juice to do Gerald a mischief. They're getting angry, and he's thaumaturgically outnumbered.'

'Yes, but they can't hurt him, Bibbie. He's — he's *Gerald*.'

'Not here, he isn't,' Bibbie muttered. 'He's nobody here, remember? And he can't afford to show his true colours either. This was supposed to be a watching brief, remember?'

Oh. So it was. Which meant what ... that he'd just stand there and let a bunch of wizards led by a portal saboteur — *and Ambrose has the hide to complain about industrial sabotage?* — rough him up?

Well, that's wrong. And silly. I'm certainly not going to stand here and watch these noddies hurt the man who saved my kingdom.

She looked up to see Reg wildly waving one wing. It wasn't hard to translate the body language: *Don't just stand there, ducky! Do something!*

Gerald, still with his hands lifted, was warily eyeing his erstwhile colleagues. Turning back to Ambrose he cleared his throat. 'Um — please, Mister Wycliffe, you really must believe me. I'm not a spy. Not for Boswell's, or anyone else. This is a rather unfortunate misunderstanding, that's all. And I'm sure it could be cleared up very easily if we could go somewhere quiet to discuss things. Say, into your office? Just you and me? Employer to employee? I think we have a lot to talk about.'

'*No*,' said Permelia Wycliffe, stepping forward. Hectic spots of colour burned in her pale, sunken cheeks. 'Ambrose, don't listen to him. I'm sorry, I was wrong and you were right. He's a menace. Some kind of — of imposter. A danger to everything you and I have been working towards. If you listen to him, Ambrose, Wycliffe's will be destroyed.'

Melissande swallowed a curse. 'Damn. I don't know how, but she's onto Gerald.'

'What?' said Bibbie, startled. 'How can she be? And how can you tell?'

'I don't know, but look at her face. She knows Gerald knows there's something going on. And *he* knows she knows he knows. Look at *his* face.'

'Oh,' whispered Bibbie. 'Rats, Mel. I think you're right. What are we going to do? We can't let Gerald's true identity be revealed and we can't let the Wycliffes get away with their crimes!'

'You can say that again,' she said grimly. 'All right. Here goes nothing. Bibbie, stay back. Consider yourself my last resort.'

And before Bibbie could stop her, she leapt into the fray. 'Excuse me! Excuse me, can I have everyone's attention? Excuse me, excuse me. Sir, *if* you don't mind, get *out* of my way.'

Startled, Wycliffe's wizards parted to let her through into the centre of their circle. Acutely aware of Gerald's consternation, and Bibbie's, of Reg still semaphoring wildly above her head, of all the wizards staring as though she were some kind of never-before-seen exotic creature, she halted before Ambrose Wycliffe and planted her hands on her hips.

'You're making a very big mistake, Mister Wycliffe. Things are already looking shaky for you. I strongly suggest you go no further in accusing an innocent man.'

As Ambrose Wycliffe gobbled at her, incoherent, Permelia Wycliffe recovered her wits.

'Miss *Cadwallader*! I don't know what you think you're doing but I thought I made myself perfectly clear: your sojourn at Wycliffe's is *ended*. You have *failed* to discharge the task with which you were assigned and your dubious services are no longer required!'

She pinned Permelia with a haughty glare. 'It's true I failed to find your biscuit thief, Permelia. But that's not the same as saying I failed to uncover a crime. In fact I uncovered several crimes in your company, and none of them had anything to do with *this* dolt.'

'What?' said Gerald. His voice and expression were outraged, but the tiniest gleam of appreciation lurked deep in his good eye. 'I'm not a dolt, Miss. And I'm sorry, but who are you? I thought you said your name was Carstars.'

Acutely aware of the other Wycliffe wizards, who were goggling in rapt, attentive silence, Melissande turned on him. 'Are you deaf as well as incompetent, sir? I am Miss Cadwallader. And you *are* a dolt. Errol Haythwaite has signed an affidavit to that very effect. Errol Haythwaite has lodged a formal complaint against you with the Department of Thaumaturgy, citing gross incompetence and — and — a stultifying lack of any thaumaturgical talent whatsoever. He wants your certification revoked. So I advise you to be quiet. You're in enough trouble as it is.'

And that should be sufficient to reduce Gerald to insignificance. Now for the Wycliffes. Gosh, I hope that mysterious Sir Alec's sending us loads of help . . .

As the watching wizards muttered and swallowed derisive laughter and poked each other with their elbows, Ambrose gaped at his disconcerted sister. 'This is one of your *gels*, Permelia. Isn't this one of your *gels*? She *looks* like one of your gels. She's dressed like an undertaker so she *must* be one of your gels. What is one your *gels* doing in my laboratory? You *know* they're not supposed to set foot over my threshold!'

'Miss Cadwallader is *not* one my *gels*, Ambrose!' Permelia retorted. 'She, like your Third Grade wizard there, was a *mistake*.

One I shall make her pay for, I promise. Now I suggest we throw both of them off the premises and —'

'Not so fast, Permelia,' said Melissande. 'I haven't finished with you.' She flicked a glance at Gerald, who tightened his lips at her and twitched one finger, ever so slightly.

What does that mean? Does that mean stop? Or does it mean keeping going, stall them, help is definitely on the way?

Taking a deep, shaky breath, she chose Door B.

CHAPTER TWENTY-FOUR

'I beg your pardon?' Permelia gasped. 'How *dare* you take that tone with me?'

Melissande bared her teeth in a fierce smile. 'I'll be the pot if you'll be the kettle, Permelia. How dare *you* steal Errol Haythwaite's airship designs and sell them to a foreign power?'

The spectating circle of wizards gasped. Ambrose Wycliffe made a choked, strangled sound. Permelia stepped back a pace, her face drained dead white, her eyes glittering with terror.

'You're mad, you silly woman. I don't know what you're talking about.'

'Oh come on, ducky,' she retorted, scathing. 'Give up the act. It's not like you're fooling anyone, you know.'

'Permelia,' croaked Ambrose Wycliffe. His florid face had paled to pink, and his extravagant ginger whiskers trembled. 'Permelia, what is this gel talking about?'

'Oh, do *listen* for once in your life, Ambrose!' snapped Permelia. 'I have no idea. The woman is deranged. Call the police. I want to see her thrown in prison.'

Melissande turned on him. 'Yes, that's a good idea, Ambrose. Call the police. I'm sure they'll be very interested to hear all about your sister's treason.'

'You — you *hussy*!' Permelia hissed. 'Just you hold your meddlesome tongue. Nobody's interested in what you have to say.'

'I am,' said Ambrose, some of the florid colour flooding back to his face. 'I'm *very* interested. How do you know she's been stealing Errol's designs? What do you have to do with any of this? Who sent you here, Miss — Miss — *gel*?'

Gel? *Again*? Melissande gritted her teeth. *I wonder what the legal fine print says about justifiable grievous bodily harm?* 'Who sent me here, Ambrose? If you really want to know, Errol Haythwaite sent me. In — in a strange, serendipitous coincidence, just as your sister hired me to unmask her office thief, Errol Haythwaite approached my agency to — to — help him discover who was stealing his work. He knew it had to be somebody at Wycliffe's, for only somebody at Wycliffe's had access to his office. And so I began my clandestine investigation and it led me down many a torturous path ... right to your sister's door, Ambrose. She's been stealing my client's airship designs for months and passing them along to — to —' Out of the corner of her eye she caught Gerald's tiny shake of his head. Oh. So no spilling the beans on who the foreign power was. 'To someone I am not at liberty to reveal,' she finished grandly.

'It's a *lie*!' cried Permelia. 'Not a *word* of it is true. I haven't stolen anything. Go to Mister Haythwaite's office, check through his designs. See if any are missing! I have no doubt every last one of them is there!'

Melissande flicked Gerald another glance. He rubbed his nose, disguising a nod.

Bugger. So if Permelia had stolen the designs — but they were still in Errol's office —

'Ah — yes —' she said. 'Well. I can explain that.'

'Then explain it,' said Ambrose, his voice a dangerous growl. 'Or I *will* have you and this buffoon thrown off the premises! And then thrown into prison for good measure!'

Oh. Dear. Bugger. Um ...

'She can't explain it!' cried Permelia, triumphant. 'Her outrageous claim is a tissue of lies from beginning to end, a deliberate attempt to smear me because she couldn't succeed in finding one tawdry biscuit thief! She can't explain it, I tell you, and so —'

'Maybe Miss Cadwallader can't,' said Bibbie, strolling into the centre of the circle. She was holding a large, rolled-up sheet of paper. 'But *I* can, Miss Wycliffe. Or should I say, *Permelia*?'

Melissande stared, horrified. *Bibbie, what are you doing?* She looked at Gerald, who raised an eyebrow, the closest he dared come to a shrug.

Oh, how wonderful. We're at the mercy of Mad Miss Markham.

All the Wycliffe wizards were gaping at Bibbie as though she were a celestial vision. And, really, since it was Bibbie, they weren't too far off the mark. She was looking particularly beautiful this morning, wearing a shade of blue that exactly matched her sparkling eyes. Danger and mayhem appeared to agree with her.

A pity they're so smitten they can't see she's actually a beautiful sword.

Ambrose Wycliffe cleared his throat, his chest swelling. A leering light gleamed in his eyes. 'Well. Good gracious. And who might this charming young gel be, eh? Got a name, have you, m'dear? Come, come, don't be shy.'

Melissande swallowed a groan. *Oh, lord. Any second now he's going to try and pinch her cheek … and she's going to pitch him through the nearest window.*

Bibbie looked Ambrose up and down with distaste, as though he were something unfortunate Boris had dragged in and left on the privy carpet.

'I am Miss Cadwallader's associate,' she said coldly. 'My name's not important. What's important, *Ambrose* —' She unrolled the rolled-up paper with a snap. ' — is that this is one of our client Mister Haythwaite's airship designs, and it's positively *stinking* of black market thaumaturgy.'

The leering light in Ambrose's eyes died. 'And how would you know?' he demanded. 'You're a *gel*.'

'Not quite, Ambrose,' said mercurial Bibbie, this time with a dazzling smile. Several of the watching wizards loosened their ties. 'I'm sorry, did I forget to mention I'm a witch?'

Ambrose's expression congealed. 'Oh. I see. But still. A *gel*.'

Sighing, Bibbie turned her back on Ambrose and held out the unrolled airship blueprint to one of the wide-eyed, watching wizards. 'You. You're a moderately powerful First Grader, aren't you? What's your name?'

'Methven, Miss,' the wizard said huskily. 'Robert Methven.'

Bibbie nearly knocked him unconscious with another smile. 'Well then, Robert, take a look at this. *I* think it's been tampered with.' She wrinkled her nose, delightfully. '*Robert*. Isn't that just a lovely name? Robert, I think someone's used a black market thaumaturgical device to take a copy of this drawing. I can still feel its thaumaturgical vibrations on the paper. Can't you?'

Dazed, Robert Methven took the outstretched plan and inspected it. A shadow of doubt raced across his stunned face. 'Yes. Yes, I can.'

'And funnily enough,' said Bibbie, reaching into the reticule dangling from her left wrist, 'the vibration matches — *exactly*, I might add — the thaumic vibrations that can be felt in these.'

And she held up the black leather pouch full of fake gemstones.

Melissande looked at Permelia, whose drawn face now glistened with sweat. Then she let her gaze slide over to Gerald. He dropped one eyelid in a brief, reassuring wink, and let his lips twitch once in what might've been a sort of smile.

'Robert,' said Bibbie, and tossed him the pouch. 'What do

you think? Am I right? By the way, be careful with that. In my line of work we call it *evidence.*

Robert Methven was clearly now Bibbie's adoring slave. The other wizards were glaring at him, pettishly jealous. He tucked the airship blueprint under his arm and carefully tipped the contents of the pouch into his hand. His watching colleagues gasped as the glittering stream of fake gemstones poured from the leather bag in an intoxicating stream of false promises and lies.

Robert Methven closed his fingers round them, closed his eyes and concentrated. After a moment he looked at Bibbie, surprise and respect mingled.

'Yes, yes you're right again. It's the same thaumic signature.' He frowned. 'But I'm awfully sorry, I don't know whose it is.'

'Of course you don't, Robert,' said Bibbie, gently chiding. 'You're not a vile criminal. How could anyone expect you to know? But I'll bet Permelia knows.' She turned. '*Don't you, Permelia?*'

'Permelia?' said Ambrose, his voice almost unrecognisable. 'Permelia, what's the meaning of this? How can that *gel* have those gemstones? You said they were for Haf. To pay him off and make him go away. I didn't want to but *you* said —'

'Oh, Haf's gone away all right, Ambrose,' said Melissande, stepping forward. *Time to wrap this up, while Permelia and Ambrose are still off-balance.* 'Not to put too fine a point on it, he's dead. Got himself blown up last night. Didn't you listen to the wireless this morning? There was a big explosion in South Ott. An old, abandoned boot factory got blown to tiny bits — and Haf blew up with it.'

'What?' Permelia whispered. She sounded as awful as Ambrose. 'But — but —' Her gaze fell on the pouch of gemstones, still in Robert Methven's hand. 'I don't understand. How did you come by those?'

'Well,' she said, perfectly prepared to twist the knife in horrible Permelia, just for a moment, 'it's possible I took them from Eudora Telford's lifeless hand after she got blown up along with Haf Rottlezinder.'

Permelia gasped, staggering. 'No — no —'

'No?' Melissande smiled. 'Then perhaps I took them from her cold, lifeless hand after a brutal, cowardly thief assaulted her on the dark streets of South Ott.'

'I don't believe you,' whispered Permelia, her voice ragged. 'Eudora's not dead. She can't be dead.'

'Oh *please*, Permelia,' she said, and gave her scorn free rein. 'Do you honestly expect us to believe you *care* two hoots what happens to Eudora Telford? If you cared you never would've sent her out to do your dirty work, would you? You used that poor silly woman, Permelia, and now she's paid a heavy price.'

Oblivious to the wizards staring at her with shock and dawning disgust, ignoring Ambrose's rising ire, Permelia took one unbalanced step forward. 'No. No. I won't believe you,' she said, a thread of hysteria sounding in her voice. 'Eudora's not dead. This is a trick. You're trying to trick me.'

'If there's any tricking going on here, Permelia, *you're* the one doing it!' shouted Ambrose. 'And now look what's happened! You've ruined *everything*!'

'*I've* ruined everything? *I* have?' shrieked Permelia, rounding on him. 'How can you even suggest such a thing?'

'Easily!' he snapped. 'If you'd done a better job of running the office you wouldn't have hired a petty thief and you'd not have had to invite this — this interfering Cadwallader *gel* into our midst! And if you'd minded your own business and let *me* worry about the company we'd be back on the road to solvency by now!'

'The company *is* my business!' said Permelia, hands clenched into unladylike fists. The stern, haughty president of the Baking and Pastry Guild was nowhere to be seen. 'I'm its last hope of survival, Ambrose!'

He laughed. '*You?*'

'Yes, *me!*' Permelia panted. 'Am *I* the one who's run Wycliffe's practically into receivership? Am *I* the one who's virtually bankrupted Father's legacy by insisting on all those ridiculous scooters and velocipedes and cut-rate cars that can't drive three miles without falling apart? Was that me? Were those *my* ideas, Ambrose?'

'No, they were *mine!*' he retorted, spittled with fury. 'And they were *good* ideas, Permelia, ideas that would have tided us over, but you'd never get behind them, you'd never let me spend the kind of money I needed to spend to make them work properly! Always bossing me, always throwing your weight around, just because you're two years older than me!'

'Ambrose, I am a *hundred* years older than you,' snarled Permelia. 'At least if we were counting time by common sense. Those stupid inferior vehicles were *never* going to work properly! Nor should they have. We do not truck with such inferior modes of transportation, you fool. This is the Wycliffe *Airship* Company! We sail through the skies, we don't grub along on the ground.'

'Yes! Yes! I know!' Ambrose retorted. 'You're not the only one who loves airships, Permelia! The cars and the velocipedes were to be a stopgap. Just a stopgap. I was doing *everything* in my power to save the company — and what were you doing? Getting in my way and — and — bleating about your stupid Golden Whisk and how to bake the perfect pumpkin scone!'

Permelia Wycliffe clutched at her ruthlessly styled hair, dislodging several jet-tipped hairpins. To Melissande it was clear that she and her brother were suddenly oblivious to their surroundings, oblivious to herself and Bibbie, and Gerald, to all the gaping, incredulous wizards. Were tumbled instead into some poisonous sibling nightmare where the rest of the world had simply ... ceased to exist.

The ragged circle of wizards was broken apart now. They were too stunned to do anything but watch their employer and his sister with dropped jaws and wide eyes. Bibbie and Reg were watching too, the pair of them reprehensibly entertained, and Gerald — Gerald —

Melissande saw that he'd ever-so-unobtrusively eased himself out of the way, to stand just far enough back so he might be nondescriptly overlooked.

Lurching forward, Permelia slapped her brother's face. 'I was not *bleating*, Ambrose, I was taking care of Father's legacy.'

'And so was I!' Ambrose shouted, clutching at his red-blotched cheek. 'A damned sight better than you ever have, my gel!'

'*How*, you fat buffoon?' Permelia taunted with shrivelling contempt. 'By digging through Father's old papers and finding the very worst possible wizard he'd ever refused to hire and then hiring him *yourself*? By paying him to wreck the portal system? Because nobody in the Government would *notice*? And you have the nerve to say you possess superior judgement, Ambrose? You don't possess the judgement of a *flea*!'

'Oh? Oh?' choked Ambrose Wycliffe. 'And I suppose your decision to pass company secrets to a foreign power demonstrates *your* superior reasoning skills?'

Permelia shoved him hard in the chest. 'I had to, Ambrose! You gave me no choice! It was only a matter of time before someone died in one of those portal *accidents*, you blithering *dunderhead*! I *had* to save the company from your imbecilic solution. It was my duty to Father!'

'But you haven't saved it, have you?' Ambrose demanded. 'Instead you've managed to get a man killed and implicate us in high treason to boot! They'll throw us in prison for the rest of our lives, Permelia. We'll never breathe free air again.' Seizing his sister's shoulders, he hauled her nose-to-nose with him. 'Was it worth it, sister? How much did your foreign friends pay you, eh? How much money will you never have the chance to spend?'

'*Fool*,' she spat at him. 'I didn't do it for *money*. I did it for the chance to take control of the company. The company that *always* should've been mine, that *would've* been mine, if Father hadn't been so stupidly short-sighted about *gels*. You're just like him, Ambrose. Narrow-minded and bigoted, puffed up with self-conceit. I *had* to stop you any way I could. And Manawa was only too *happy* to help me. She *understands* about women and power. We hatched the whole scheme between us. Let Wycliffe's go out of business, just another casualty of the thaumaturgic revolution, and in return for a few stupid airship drawings she'd arrange to buy the company — through a third party, of course — and then *you'd* be thrown out on the scrapheap where you belong and *I* would be installed as the new company director. *I* would see Wycliffe's attain its true potential! A task for which you are *eminently* unsuited!'

Ambrose let go of her and fell back, his mouth opening and closing with outraged disbelief. 'You're — you're *raving*, Permelia. You're utterly deranged! You stupid — stupid *gel*! If somehow you escape arrest I'm going to have you committed to an asylum! You stole Wycliffe's best airship designs and gave them to the wife of the —'

'*Don't say it!*' shouted Melissande, as Gerald's eyebrows shot up in alarm. 'In fact, don't either of you say another word! I think you've both said quite enough already!'

'I want her taken into custody!' cried Ambrose Wycliffe, spinning round. 'She's mad, I tell you, utterly *mad*! She should be locked away. I'll have her locked away. Just don't blame me, I had nothing to do with this! I had nothing to do with *anything*!

I'm an innocent man. This is all Permelia, the stupid gel. Father was right — women aren't to be trusted. *I'm* the victim here, I tell you!'

'Innocent, Ambrose? *Innocent*?' Permelia laughed wildly, a horrible, howling cackle. 'The only thing you're innocent of is having the smallest amount of entrepreneurial vision! You're a moron, an idiot, and you always have been! Put *me* in an *asylum*? I'll see you *dead* first!'

And then everything went horribly wrong.

With an infuriated roar, Ambrose whirled and grabbed Permelia around the throat and started choking, his already florid face suffused tomato-red. They overbalanced and fell sideways across the nearest laboratory bench. As Permelia coughed and gasped, and the watching wizards dithered like hens in a thunderstorm, Melissande turned to Bibbie.

'Come on, Bibs, don't just stand there! You're the genius witch, *do* something, quick!'

'Like what?' Bibbie retorted. 'I don't do martial thaumaturgy! And if I try I could blow them both up!'

Oh, how ridiculous. And Gerald wasn't any help either — *drat* his ludicrous Third Grade cover story! She rounded on Robert Methven. 'Then *you* do something, Mister Methven. You're a First Grade wizard, aren't you?'

'What? What?' said Robert Methven, appalled. '*Me* do something? But I can't! My specialty's aerodynamics!'

Melissande leapt to him and grabbed hold of his lab coat lapels. '*Really*? How's *this* then? *Thaumaturge those two apart or I'll kick you into bloody orbit!*'

But before Robert Methven obeyed her — or Gerald broke his cover — Ambrose let out a blood-chilling scream. Melissande spun round, one hand reaching for Bibbie, to see that Permelia had plunged one of her jet-tipped hairpins deep in her brother's throat. Even as she stared, horrified, Ambrose's face began to turn black, his plump cheeks swelling and splitting and dribbling green gore. She felt the air stall in her lungs. Felt her stomach heave, rebelling.

Lional ... Lional ... his beauty destroyed by the dragon's green venom ...

'Oh, Saint Snodgrass,' breathed Bibbie, on a sob. 'She's hexed him. That's a killing hex. Oh, *Mel*.'

Ambrose was dying, slowly and in shrieking pain. The corrupted flesh was peeling from his skull, revealing teeth and tongue and lidless eyes. The lab erupted into chaos, wizards running and shouting and throwing themselves under benches or onto the floor. Melissande grabbed Bibbie and dragged her out of Permelia's reach, then yelped as she felt a hand close on *her* arm.

'Relax, it's me,' Gerald muttered. 'You two stay here. I'll grab Permelia and hex her docile while nobody's looking.'

'No, no, Gerald, hex her from here,' she said. 'She might —'

'Can't,' he said briefly. 'Someone will notice. Besides, Melissande, look at her. It's over. She's done.'

Ambrose sprawled on his back, a bloated, black-faced, green-smeared corpse. Silent now, his suffering mercifully ended. Permelia was weeping, terrible, tearing sobs, bent double and swaying, a heartbeat from collapse. Her iron-grey hair had fallen out of its bun, tumbling over her face in lank disarray.

But when Gerald reached her and put his arm around her shoulders she erupted with a piercing screech of rage. And the next thing Melissande knew he was on his knees, Permelia's fingers tight in his hair, with his throat stretched taut and a jet-tipped hairpin sunk tip-deep in his flesh.

'Stay back!' said Permelia hoarsely. 'Stay back or he dies!' Her fingers tightened on the hairpin, and a trickle of blood seeped down Gerald's skin. 'One little push and it's all over. And if I see a single sign of thaumaturgy I will push, I will —'

On a howl of rage and in a flurry of feathers Reg dived from the ceiling like a bird possessed, all reaching talons and sharp, gaping beak.

'*Get your bloody hands off him, you harpy!*'

Startled, Permelia Wycliffe cried out and let go of Gerald and the hairpin to fling her hands desperately over her head. Reg set to with a vengeance, long beak stabbing, wings flailing and beating Permelia Wycliffe to her knees. When the woman was down, prone on the lab floor and crying for mercy, Reg spun in midair, her eyes alight with the flame of battle.

'Well don't just stand there gawping, you plonkers! Someone bloody sit on her before she tries to get up!'

Bibbie landed on Permelia so hard she nearly broke the woman's back.

'Gerald!' said Melissande and rushed to his side, dropping to her knees and trying to see the wound in his throat. 'Are you all right? Oh, you *are* an idiot! I *told* you to hex the bloody woman from a distance!'

Huffing and puffing, Reg landed on her shoulder. 'But he didn't listen, did he?' She shook her head and rattled her tail feathers. 'I don't know, sunshine. How many times do I have to tell you? *Never* underestimate a woman.'

Sitting up, Gerald accepted the hanky Melissande thrust into his hand and pressed it to the tiny dribbling puncture wound in his neck. 'Yeah,' he said. 'Especially a woman with feathers.' He kissed her beak. 'Thanks for that, Reg.'

'You're welcome,' she sniffed. 'Though perhaps after this you'll listen to me in the future.'

'Are you sure you're all right?' Melissande said anxiously. 'You're not going to turn black and green like an overripe banana?'

He reached for Permelia's discarded hairpin. 'No. This one's not hexed,' he said, inspecting it closely. 'She was bluffing. But whatever you do don't touch the one buried in Ambrose's throat. That was hexed all right …' He shuddered. 'I've never come across anything like it. Whoever it is supplying her — he's a devil.'

Bibbie shifted a little, making flattened Permelia groan. Staring at gruesomely dead Ambrose, she shrugged. 'That'll teach him to call his sister a *gel*.'

Gerald half-laughed. 'I'll be sure to remind Monk of that, next time I see him.' But his amusement didn't last long. 'Are you all right, Bibbie? That was a dreadful thing, how Ambrose died.'

'Oh. Yes,' said Bibbie, turning a pretty pink. 'Of course. I'm fine.'

'Are you sure?' he said, sounding anxious. 'It's all right if you're not, Bibbie, truly.'

Melissande swallowed a sigh. *Ask me if I'm all right, why don't you?* But he wouldn't. Of if he did, it'd only be an afterthought. Hadn't she already proven herself equal to any amount of ghastliness and bloodshed? She was Her Royal Highness Princess Melissande, and she didn't do soppy.

And anyway, Gerald's sweet on her. Anyone can see that.

'Hello,' said Reg, swivelling her head towards the lab door. 'Who's this come to spoil the party, then?'

They all looked to the doorway, where four newcomers were entering the lab complex.

'Damn,' said Gerald, and sighed. 'Reg, you'd better scarper. Quick. We don't want any awkward questions.'

Surprisingly, Reg didn't argue. Instead she took one look at Gerald's face then flapped her way out of the lab, through an open window at its far end.

Melissande stared at him. 'Friends of yours?'

He grimaced. 'Not … exactly. But they are from the Department.'

Around the laboratory complex the R&D wizards of Wycliffe's Airship Company were sheepishly getting back on their feet, or coming out of hiding from the labs, or generally pretending they *hadn't* all run about like hens in a thunderstorm at the height of the crisis.

As three of the four men from Gerald's mysterious Department started rounding up the witnesses, the fourth picked his way through the mayhem to join them. He was oldish and tired-looking, encased in a rumpled blue suit. His deep-set hazel eyes were unimpressed.

The first thing he did was check on Ambrose Wycliffe.

'He's dead,' said Bibbie, helpfully. 'In case you were wondering.'

Ignoring her, the man stared at Gerald. Gerald nodded. 'Dalby.'

Dalby's eyes narrowed. 'Nettleworth. Now. There's a car outside waiting.'

Melissande stiffened. 'Now hold on just a minute, Mister Dalby — or whoever you really are. I don't think I like your tone. *I* don't think you —'

'Don't, Mel,' said Gerald. 'It's all right. I'll be in touch, as soon as I can.' With a stifled groan he levered himself to his feet. 'Thanks, for everything.'

She watched him go, a tousled, lonely figure with a hanky pressed against the small wound in his neck. Then she turned on Mister Dalby from the Department.

'Look here, you,' she said, 'it's possible you don't know who I am, because I *never* talk about who I am, at least, not to say to people, "Do you know who I am?", but in this case I'm going to make an exception, because —'

'I know perfectly well who you are, Your Highness,' said Mister Dalby from the Department. 'Sir Alec's warned me all about you.' He flicked a glance at Bibbie, who'd clambered off Permelia and was straightening her skirt. '*And* you, Miss Markham.'

'Oh,' said Bibbie, and gave him her best smile. 'Did he? That's nice.'

But Mister Dalby from the Department was impervious to Bibbie's smile. He scowled. 'Nice? No. Not really. Have a seat, ladies. This could take a while.'

'Do you know,' said Bibbie, watching him walk away, 'I'm not entirely sure I like that man.'

'Oh, I'm sure,' said Melissande. 'I'm positive I don't like him.' She heaved a sigh. 'Are you really all right, Bibs? Gerald said it — that was a horrible thing to see.'

Bibbie looked away for a moment; there was the tiniest tremble in her bottom lip. Then she took a deep breath and nodded. 'Honestly, Mel, I'm fine,' she said, lifting her chin defiantly. 'Nobody said this job would be a bed of roses.'

True. But — 'Even so, Bibs,' she said gently. 'If you're not fine, that's — that's all right.'

'Melissande, I am *not* a shrinking violet,' Bibbie snapped. 'So you can stop fussing, thank you. Honestly, you sound just like Monk.'

Oh, lord. Monk. *He's going to be so upset.* 'Perhaps you should let me tell him about this, Bibs. You know — sort of soften the blow a bit before you regale him with all the gory details?'

Bibbie rolled her eyes. 'All right. Fine. If you think that'll help. But really, Mel, I'm not about to indulge in a fit of the vapours.'

No, clearly she wasn't. Clearly the redoubtable Antigone Markham's great-niece was made of the same stern stuff.

'Anyway, how are you?' added Bibbie. 'Speaking of incipient vapours …'

Melissande sighed, and looked down at Permelia's unfortunate brother. 'Well, I confess I'm a little rattled,' she said. 'But I'm better than Ambrose.'

'Or Permelia,' said Bibbie, and nudged the half-conscious woman with the toe of her shoe. 'Blimey. You know, I knew it was a mistake to get mixed up with the Baking and Pastry Guild. Didn't I tell you it was a mistake to get mixed up with the Baking and Pastry Guild?'

Melissande wrestled with the urge to punch her. 'No, Emmerabiblia. On the contrary, you did everything in your power to make *sure* we got mixed up with the Baking and Pastry Guild.'

Bibbie pulled a face. 'Oh yes. So I did. Well, let this be a lesson to you, Miss Cadwallader. *Never* get mixed up with the Ottosland Baking and Pastry Guild.'

Mister Dalby from the Department kept them waiting for nearly an hour while he and his … associates … talked to the Wycliffe R&D wizards, and did various thaumaturgical things with recording evidence at the scene, and saw that Ambrose Wycliffe was decently taken away, and that Permelia Wycliffe was also taken away, less decently. Eventually, though, he rejoined them at the lab bench where they were sitting.

'Right. That's it, then. You ladies can go.'

Melissande exchanged a look with Bibbie then frowned at him. 'I beg your pardon? We can what?'

'Go,' said Dalby. 'Depart. Leave. Be on your way.'

'But — don't you want to question us? I mean, we were here,' said Bibbie. 'We saw everything. We were *part* of it.'

'Someone from the Department will be in contact, I'm sure,' said Dalby.

'But —'

'Never mind, Bibbie,' said Melissande, and patted her arm. 'He's not important enough to interview us.' She gave Mister Dalby from the Department her best regally glittering stare. 'And what about Gerald? Mister Dunwoody?'

Blank-faced, Dalby looked at her. 'Who?'

'Oh, don't be stupid,' she sighed. 'You know very well who. And if Sir Alec did tell you about us, you know that we know too.'

Mister Dalby smiled. 'Sorry, ladies. You're not important enough to ask about him.' He nodded. 'Good day.'

They glared after him as he left. 'D'you know,' said Bibbie, 'I don't care if it is illegal. I'm going to find someone to teach me martial thaumaturgy and I'm going to track that man down and then I'm going to —'

'No, you're not,' said Melissande, suddenly exhausted.

'But —'

She raised a warning finger. 'Trust me, Bibbie, you're really *not*. Now come on. Let's get out of here.'

As they stood outside the lab complex, taking a moment to appreciate the fresh air and sunshine, Reg flapped down from a nearby tree.

'Girls,' she said, landing on Melissande's shoulder. 'We have to rescue Gerald. That government stooge Sir Alec is going to make his life hell for this.'

Melissande heaved another sigh. 'Yes. I know. Just let me go and fetch my reticule. It's still in the administration office. I'll call for a cab while I'm up there, and then we can go and straighten out this mess with Gerald. I'll meet you outside the door to reception.' She pointed down the left-hand path. 'That's the fastest way.'

'Excuse me?' said Reg, hopping across to Bibbie's shoulder. 'Do I need you to tell me how to find my way? Me, with my bird's-eye view of everything? No, I don't think I do, madam. Incidentally, just who was that short streak of misery that turned up earlier? I didn't like the look of him. Was he unkind to Gerald? I'll pluck out his bloody eyeballs and wear them for earrings if that bugger was mean to —'

'Now you're talking, Reg,' said Bibbie, with a wink. 'Come on. I'll tell you all about Mister Dalby while we're waiting for Mel. Hey —' They started off down the path. 'I don't suppose you know any good martial thaumaturgy ...'

So weary she could drop, Melissande defiantly undid the top two buttons of her hideous black Wycliffe blouse then made her way back to the administration block. Reception was deserted. Miss Fisher, sensible woman, must've read the writing on the wall. She climbed the stairs, pushed open the door into the office ... and saw that the gels, and Pip the office boy, had wisely taken her advice and scarpered.

Either that, or one of Mister Dalby's associates had stopped by to send them all home.

She took a moment to look around the deserted office. At the horrible grey cubicles and the narrow aisles and the never-ending piles of paperwork. And even though she'd been part of Gerald's investigation, an important part, even though she and Bibbie and Reg had helped avert not one, but two, major disasters, she was aware of a definite sense of melancholy. Because despite all that, she *hadn't* managed to solve the case she came here for in the first place: the Case of the Mystery Biscuit Pilferer.

Oh well. I don't suppose we can win them all.

She heard a sound, then, coming from Permelia Wycliffe's office. So someone was still here? As she moved forward to investigate she saw an enormous pile of cartons wearing a skirt walk out of the office — just as her own skirt pocket began to buzz.

What?

She clapped her hand to her side and felt the shape of Bibbie's thief-detector crystal. Felt its vibrations running through her fingers. She snatched the crystal out of her pocket, stared at it, then looked up.

'Hey! You! You there! Thief! *Stop!*'

With a startled cry the red-handed pilferer dropped the enormous pile of biscuit boxes.

Melissande gaped. 'Miss *Petterly*? It's *you*?'

Miss Petterly went white, then flushed bright red. 'What? What's me? What are you talking about? What are you doing here, Miss Carstairs — Cadwallader — whatever your name is? You've been terminated. I heard Miss Wycliffe say so herself.'

Melissande, shaking her head, sauntered across the office floor. 'I don't *believe* it,' she said. 'Miss Petterly, how *could* you?' Reaching the silent, mortified woman, she ran Bibbie's thief-detecting crystal over the woman from head to toe. The crystal flashed so fast it looked like it might explode.

She shoved it back in her skirt pocket, just to be on the safe side.

'How could I what? I don't know what you're talking about,' Miss Petterly blustered, her hunted gaze darting left and right. 'You shouldn't be in here. You're not wanted in here. You *never* belonged here. You were *never* a true Wycliffe gel.'

Melissande looked at the scattered cartons of biscuits. 'Well, no, Miss Petterly,' she said. 'I wasn't. Thank God. And clearly you aren't either. Not if being a true Wycliffe gel means you're also a *thief*.' She shook her head. 'You should know, Miss Petterly, that my name *is* Miss Cadwallader. I'm part of an agency called Witches Inc. We … investigate things, I suppose you could say. We solve mysteries. We uncover crimes. Miss Wycliffe hired us to discover the identity of the Wycliffe Airship Company pilferer. I will say this: I never once suspected *you*.' Then she sighed. 'At least not for long, and not for want of wanting it to be you. You did a very good job of hiding your tracks.'

'Of course I did,' Miss Petterly sneered. 'I am an extremely competent woman, Miss Car— Cadwallader.'

She shrugged. 'An extremely competent *con*woman, I'll grant you. Permelia didn't suspect you for a heartbeat.'

Incredibly, Miss Petterly preened herself a little. 'Yes, well, Miss Wycliffe trusted me *implicitly*.'

Horrible cow. 'Which was a big mistake, it seems,' she said. 'I don't understand, Miss Petterly. Why would you *do* this?'

Miss Petterly's pebbly eyes flushed pink around the rims, then slowly filled with tears. Her chin wobbled, and her lips. She said something, incoherently, her voice clogged with emotion.

'What?' said Melissande. 'I didn't quite catch that.'

'I *said*,' Miss Petterly gulped, 'she wouldn't approve my membership of the Baking and Pastry Guild. Permelia. *Miss Wycliffe*. She said — she said — she said my apple-and-walnut log wasn't — wasn't *up to snuff*. She let that — that *ridiculous* Eudora Telford join, kept her as a secretary, let her run around with her *everywhere*, but she wouldn't let *me* in. *Eudora Telford*. That — that — *bean*. Have you *tasted* her cooking? Her date scones sink ducks! I've *seen* it! They're a *disgrace*. She ought to be had up for cruelty to water fowl!'

That was sadly true. 'So, what — you decided to exact revenge by stealing Permelia's *biscuits*?'

'Not just biscuits,' said Miss Petterly, with a touch of watery pride. 'I took everything. The pencils, the pens *and* the erasers. And I always had *three* lumps of sugar in my tea when we're only supposed to have *one*.' Her chin wobbled again. 'And now I suppose you're going to arrest me.'

'Actually, I don't have the power of arrest,' said Melissande. 'My job was to tell Miss Wycliffe who the thief was and let her handle it from there. But that could prove to be a bit difficult now.'

'Something's happened, hasn't it?' said Miss Petterly.

'Yes. You could say that.'

Miss Petterly frowned. 'So … what now, Miss Car— Cadwallader?'

Melissande looked around the horrible office. 'Now, Miss

Petterly, if I were you, I'd take those cartons of biscuits and make myself scarce. I doubt very much if Miss Wycliffe will notice … and all in all — after four endless days in this place — I'd say you earned them. Now if you don't mind, I'm going to call myself a cab.'

And leaving Miss Petterly to stare at her, dumbfounded, she marched into Permelia Wycliffe's office to use the telephone.

CHAPTER TWENTY-FIVE

Sir Alec made him wait in an *interrogation* room. For *hours*.
Gerald didn't think it was funny.

But then he was too tired to have much of a sense of humour
left. If he wasn't so tired, he might have been ... nervous.
Apprehensive. Be feeling some concern about what must be his
uncertain future. After all, he had played fast and loose with the
rules on this, his very first official janitorial assignment. It had
been a watching brief, but instead of sedately watching he'd
been running around *doing*. And now there were two dead
bodies, an exploded boot factory and an entire labful of wizards
who'd heard things they doubtless were never meant to hear.
There was Errol, who now knew the truth about him. And
Eudora Telford, discreet as a goose.

There were Monk and Melissande and Emmerabiblia and
Reg.

True, there was also Permelia, but from what he could tell
she'd come more or less unhinged, so who knew how much use
she was going to be in foiling the Jandrians and their nefarious
plans?

That'll be a job for some other janitor. Maybe the one who's still in
Jandria, looking over his shoulder. Risking his life.

But that didn't answer what was going to happen to him,
now that he'd completed his first assignment — sort of. With a

lot of unauthorised assistance. And a great deal more fuss than he'd ever anticipated.

He tried to feel sorry that Ambrose was dead, and couldn't. That worried him a bit. Yes, Ambrose had been a criminal. Very nearly a murderer. And Haf Rottlezinder was dead because he'd worked with Ambrose. Although, really, Haf Rottlezinder had been bound to end up dead sooner or later. Haf Rottlezinder had lived that kind of life. But Ambrose hadn't been evil, not like that. He'd been selfish and misguided and driven to a desperate act. In a way, Ambrose Wycliffe was a man to be pitied.

Yes, he'd definitely be happier if he could feel sad about Ambrose.

I'm sure I'll feel sad when I'm not quite so tired.

One of the interrogation room's two doors opened, and Sir Alec walked in. 'Mister Dunwoody.'

Probably the polite thing to do would be to stand, because Sir Alec was a 'sir', after all, and older, and his superior, but he was just too damned tired for standing. Besides. He was sitting in an *interrogation* room, and really, honestly, he'd done nothing *wrong*.

Well. Nothing *illegal*.

'Sir Alec,' he said, and stayed where he was.

Sir Alec considered him for a moment, then quietly closed the interrogation room door. Crossed to the table. Sat down in the other chair. Clasped his hands in his lap and stared in silence with those cool, pale, unfathomable eyes. Gerald stared back, too tired to be intimidated.

'Well, Mister Dunwoody,' said Sir Alec at last. 'And what the bloody hell am I supposed to do with you?'

He shrugged. 'Pat me on the head and send me home for a good night's sleep?'

Sir Alec's cool eyes flared with unexpected temper. 'You think this is *funny*? You think this is a *joking* matter, Mister

Dunwoody? You think Department protocols, our secrecy, are things you need never be concerned with? You think the rules don't *apply* to you?'

He sat a little straighter. The interrogation room's air had taken on a nasty taste. In the invisible ether, fury was burning ... 'No, Sir Alec. Of course I don't.'

'Really?' said Sir Alec. 'Given the evidence at hand I find that hard to believe.'

'Sir Alec —'

'You will be *silent*, Mister Dunwoody. *I* am speaking,' snapped Sir Alec. 'It occurs to me, sir, that you, by virtue of your — unusual — status, feel you can flout all propriety with complete impunity. In short, Mister Dunwoody, you appear to be labouring under the impression that you are untouchable. Unstoppable. A law unto yourself. That your rogue thaumaturgic capabilities release you from the restrictions and obligations endured by other, *lesser* mortals. Well?'

He was so tired. And he wasn't in the mood for being scolded, like a child. Perhaps his methods had been unorthodox, perhaps it was true that in the end their victory owed more to Witches Inc. than Gerald Dunwoody — but did that really matter? Surely only the outcome was important. And the outcome had been good, this time.

He folded him arms, feeling reckless. Defiant. 'Oh. I can speak now, can I?'

Sir Alec placed his hands on the table and leaned forward. 'Do not attempt to cross swords with me, Mister Dunwoody. I am warning you: *do not.*'

Gerald met Sir Alec's pitiless gaze and held it ... but it was hard. On the inside, he was shaking. 'The answer to your question is no. I don't consider myself any of those things.'

'Do you recall,' said Sir Alec, sitting back again, 'what I said to you at our first meeting, in New Ottosland?'

'You said a lot of things, Sir Alec.' He swallowed. 'You said there were people who thought the world would be a better place if I ... didn't exist.'

Sir Alec's lips thinned. 'Essentially, yes. I did say that, though perhaps not quite as melodramatically. And you should know, Mister Dunwoody, that those people have not changed their opinion. And you should *also* know that recent events will do *nothing* to persuade them that their opinion is erroneous.'

Oh. Well. That could prove ... inconvenient, couldn't it? In which case perhaps antagonising Sir Alec wasn't the smartest of strategies. Perhaps the smart thing right now would be to keep the man on side.

'I'm sorry, Sir Alec,' he said, discarding all defensiveness. 'I never meant to cause the Department trouble.'

'I'm sure you didn't,' Sir Alec retorted, 'and yet trouble there is. The extent of Witches Inc.'s involvement — and Mister Markham's — in our business is causing no little excitement, Mister Dunwoody.'

Oh, lord. Monk. The girls. *No. Just no. I can't have them punished for being my friends.* 'Sir Alec, you have to know that without help from Monk and Her Highness and Miss Markham we would *never* —'

'I'm sorry,' said Sir Alec, eyebrows raised. 'Aren't you forgetting someone? I believe your list of extracurricular assistants is short one queen in a feathered headdress.'

Gerald felt some heat touch his face. 'Oh. Yes. Reg. Actually, Reg was a lifesaver.'

'Literally, as I understand it,' said Sir Alec. 'Mister Dalby is having some little trouble convincing the former R&D wizards at Wycliffe's that they did *not*, in actual fact, hear a bird scream: "*Get your bloody hands off him, you harpy.*"'

Gerald touched his fingers to the tiny pinprick in his throat. 'Is that what she said? I couldn't really hear her, I was too busy thinking a hexed hairpin was about to be plunged into my carotid artery.'

'*Mister Dunwoody —*'

'Look,' he said, as the stresses and strains of the past days caught up with him in one fell and blinding swoop. 'Sir Alec. You have to believe me, I never meant for it to happen like this, all right? Things just sort of — got away from me. I mean, it wasn't *my* fault the girls ended up at Wycliffe's at the same time I was there!'

'I never said it was, Mister Dunwoody.'

Encouraged, he plunged on. 'And I had *nothing* to do with them working for Permelia. But if you know the story already — if you've already bullied it out of Monk — or the girls — then you *know* it was bloody lucky they *were* there. Because if Reg hadn't overheard Errol and Kirkby-Hackett, if she hadn't overheard Permelia and Ambrose, if Melissande and Bibbie hadn't followed Eudora Telford all the way to South Ott, if Melissande hadn't been able to — to princess that foolish old lady into telling us the truth and giving us those fake gemstones and Permelia's note to Haf Rottlezinder — well, for starters you'd *still* be looking at Errol for this and you'd bloody well *wrong*, wouldn't you?'

Sir Alec's stare was unblinking. 'It's possible.'

It was more than bloody possible, but he didn't press the point. 'Well, then. As it stands the case is all wrapped up, the right people are arrested, and the day's been saved. Again. All right, maybe I *should've* been the one to save it — but I wasn't. And if that's embarrassed you or the Department, Sir Alec, then I'm very sorry. Really. I am.'

There was a long and uncomfortable silence. Then Sir Alec nodded, the merest, miserly tip of his head. 'I concede your points, Mister Dunwoody. All things considered, events have not fallen out ... unpleasantly. But you had no way of knowing that, did you? When you disobeyed my instructions? When you confided in Monk Markham? When you recklessly disregarded our most basic principles and involved two inexperienced young women in this case? And as for the bird —' His lips pinched thin again. 'To be frank, I don't know *what* to say about her.'

'Yes, well, Reg often has that effect on people, sir,' he murmured. 'If it's any consolation, you get used to it ... eventually.'

'Really?' said Sir Alec, so dry. 'How comforting.'

He swallowed. 'Sir ... what about Witches Inc? What is the Department going to do? And Monk? What are you going to do about him?'

'What we must, Mister Dunwoody,' said Sir Alec. Once again the air was full of icicles. 'Which is all I'm prepared to say on the matter.'

Have I ruined them? Has knowing me destroyed their lives? 'Sir Alec —'

'That's enough,' said Sir Alec sharply. 'The subject is closed, do I make myself clear?'

Miserable, he nodded. 'Yes, Sir Alec.' He cleared his throat. 'But — what about Errol? Since he's been cleared of treason, what —'

'Nor is Mister Haythwaite any of your concern,' said Sir Alec, still frosty. 'He has already been dealt with.'

Dealt with? *Dealt* with? What the hell did *that* mean? But one look at Sir Alec's face told him he wasn't going to get an answer to that question, so he didn't bother asking it aloud.

'And *you*, Mister Dunwoody,' Sir Alec added, still ice-cold, 'will under *no circumstances* make contact with him. *That* is an *absolute* directive — the ignoring of which will, I promise you, lead to a severe lack of future.'

Chilled to the marrow, Gerald nodded. 'Understood, Sir Alec. But what if he and I —'

'Rest assured, Mister Dunwoody,' said Sir Alec. 'Your paths are unlikely to cross again.'

And if that didn't sound sinister, he had no idea what did.

Abruptly, Sir Alec stood. 'Go home, Mister Dunwoody.'

'I'm sorry — what —' He stared. 'Go home?'

'Yes,' said Sir Alec. 'You are suspended, Mister Dunwoody. Pending further investigation into this case. Since you have contributed more than enough mayhem to the situation, your continued assistance will not be required.'

Feeling numb, Gerald pushed to his feet. 'Suspended,' he murmured. 'For how long?'

'Until I tell you otherwise, of course.' Sir Alec raised an eyebrow. 'I'm sorry. Did you think because the case was solved in our favour that there would be no repercussions? How terribly naïve of you. I will tell you a third time, but not for a fourth. *Go home,* Mister Dunwoody, and wait for my call.'

Gerald nodded. 'Yes, Sir Alec. Oh — my staff —'

'Is quite safe,' said Sir Alec. 'I think it can remain here, for the time being.'

In other words, they didn't trust him with it. *But it's mine. Not theirs.* Resentment curdled through his sluggish blood. 'I'm sorry, I don't think —'

Sir Alec's expression altered ... and he changed his mind about arguing any more.

'Right,' he muttered. 'Go home, Gerald.'

But at the interrogation room's door he hesitated, and turned back.

Sir Alec's glare was blighting. '*Yes*, Mister Dunwoody? What is it *now?*'

'I was just wondering, Sir Alec — do we know anything about the black market wizard Permelia Wycliffe went to? Has she given him up? Because that hexed hairpin she used to kill her brother ... that was a very nasty incant. The mind that dreamt it up — it has to be pretty bloody twisted.'

Shadows shifted deep in Sir Alec's guarded eyes. 'The matter is under investigation.'

He nodded. 'It's a problem, isn't it? Black market thaumaturgy. First that business with Millicent Grimwade — and now this. I didn't realise ...'

'Yes. It's a problem,' said Sir Alec curtly. 'But not *your* problem, Mister Dunwoody.'

In other words, bugger off. Get lost. You're not wanted around here.

'No, Sir Alec,' he said, subdued, and escaped while he still could.

On his way out of the Department's nondescript Nettleworth headquarters, he saw Dalby in an office off the ground floor corridor, banging typewriter keys as he made out his report. He hesitated in the open doorway, wanting to say something — say thank you —

— but the look Dalby gave him was so furiously unfriendly that he hurriedly retreated before the senior janitor surrendered to temptation and hexed him.

It wasn't until he stood outside the Department's headquarters, under a fading sky, that he realised he had no idea how he was going to get home.

And then he heard a honking car horn ... and saw Monk in his jalopy, parked a little way down the grey, dreary street.

So weary he felt like he was floating, he wandered along the pavement and got into the car. 'Oh, lord,' he said, looking at his friend. 'Not you too?'

'Yeah,' said Monk, his grin so sharkish and anarchic. 'Me too. Again.'

Bloody hell. 'I'm sorry,' he said, contrition choking his voice. 'I'm so sorry, Monk. I never meant —'

'I know you didn't,' said Monk, and fired up the jalopy. 'And anyway, it's not your fault. You didn't twist my arm, did you? You didn't threaten to turn me into a toad if I wouldn't help you. I did what I did with my eyes wide open, mate.'

'Well, yes, I know,' he said unhappily. 'But still, Monk, I —'

448 • K. E. Mills

'Hey,' said Monk, and pulled into the street. 'It could be worse, Gerald. At least they don't know about my interdimensional portal opener!' And he laughed, the crazy bugger, as though he didn't have a care in the world. 'So,' he added. 'The girls are back at my place. What do you say we pick up some Yok Tok take-away and have ourselves a bloody feast?'

Gerald laughed. He couldn't help it. 'Yeah. Okay. Why not?'

'Only you're paying, right?' said Monk. 'Because I've changed my mind. All of this *is* your bloody fault, Dunnywood!'

The knock on his closed office door came late, when all sane men were at home in bed. Of course, some would say that sanity was vastly overrated. Or at least not a requirement in his line of work. Perhaps it could even be considered a hinderment.

Certainly there are days, like this one, when insanity helps.

Sighing, he put down his pen and said, 'Come.'

'Alec,' said Ralph, and closed the door behind him. 'Burning the midnight oil, I see.'

'While you're out and about for a healthy constitutional?' he countered.

Ralph shrugged out of his overcoat, slung it over a low bookcase then dropped into the chair on the other side of the desk. 'What else?' he enquired, his hooded eyes sardonic.

'In Nettleworth?' He pushed away from his desk, crossed to his discreet drinks cabinet and poured them each a modest finger of malt whiskey. Then, after placing one glass in Ralph's outstretched hand, he shifted to his office's uncurtained window and rested his shoulder against the wall. Beyond the dusty glass, the night was clear and cold and pricked with distant stars. 'You must be desperate.'

'No more desperate than you,' said Ralph, eyeing his emptied glass appreciatively. 'You only break out the good stuff when you're feeling particularly pressed.'

'Control that bloody nephew of yours, Ralph, and I promise my nerves will be markedly less agitated.'

'If only I could control him, Alec,' said Ralph, with a sigh. 'But alas, it's years too late for that. I blame my brother, of course. Wolfgang has encouraged Monk's waywardness from the moment of his birth. I tried to tell him, but he never listens to me. Thank your lucky stars you're an only child, old boy. I promise you it makes for a far less complicated life.'

True. 'And is Wolfgang also responsible for your gifted, wayward niece?'

Ralph groaned. 'It's a tragedy we've done away with convents, that's all I can say. In the good old days I could've locked her behind high stone walls, comforted by the knowledge the world would remain safe from the gel. But instead ...'

Despite his weariness, and the burdens that made his neck ache, he smiled. 'Don't be too hard on Emmerabiblia, Ralph. Or on Monk.' He returned to his chair and sat down again, bones creaking. 'Without their assistance we might be having a very different conversation altogether.'

'Yes, well,' Ralph muttered. 'Be that as it may ... I'm still appalled that you've tripped over Monk *again*. And now his sister, too. You're more forgiving than I am, Alec.'

'Oh, I wouldn't say that,' he replied, still nursing his own drink. 'I've just had bigger fish to fry.'

Silence. Then Ralph let out a slow, heavy sigh. 'So. What are we going to do about him, Alec? I'm not ashamed to confess it: he scares me half to death.'

He raised an eyebrow. 'Only half, Ralph?'

Ralph put his emptied glass on the corner of the desk. 'I don't suppose there's a chance Dunwoody was exaggerating, is there? About how he got through Rottlezinder's wards?'

He shook his head, smiling gently. 'No. Gerald's failings are many, but self-aggrandisement's not one of them. And if it's any consolation, Ralph, I think he scares himself as much — if not more — than either of us.'

Ralph drummed restless fingers on one knee. 'And you think we should be satisfied with that? Trust in that to save us? Bad enough he's a rogue, Alec. But if he should *go* rogue — if he should succumb to the power of his *potentia* ...' Ralph shivered. 'Are you strong enough to stop him? I know I'm not.'

'And *I* know I'm not prepared to countenance drastic measures,' he replied. 'Gerald's young, and misguided, but there's no malice in him, Ralph. He's not a Lional of New Ottosland, or another Haf Rottlezinder. He's not even an Errol Haythwaite. He's the son of an honest hardworking tailor from an obscure rural backwater, and he's doing his best to make sense of this gift. This curse. This power he never asked for.'

Eyes narrowed, speculating, Ralph stared at him gravely. 'You like him, don't you?'

He shrugged. 'That's hardly relevant.'

'It's relevant if you're wrong about him, Alec,' Ralph retorted, leaning over the desk. 'It's relevant if one day he decides the rules really *don't* apply to him and we've let ourselves get so attached we're not able to do what must be done for the greater good.'

He snorted. 'You mean *me*, not *we*.'

'Yes. All right. You,' said Ralph, frowning, and sat back. 'He is in your Department, after all.'

He and Ralph had known each other a very long time. They shared memories and secrets and bitter regrets. A few small triumphs, to offset the many losses. Ralph Markham wasn't a ... comfortable ... man.

But then neither am I.

'That's right, Ralph,' he said quietly. 'He is in my Department. And until such time as Dunwoody's ... reassigned ... I'll be the one who decides what's done with him. All right?'

Ralph looked aside. 'Fine. Have it your way. I just hope you know what you're doing, Alec.'

So do I, Ralph. Believe me, so do I.

But he wasn't about to admit any doubts. Not even to this man, who in an odd way was his friend. 'There's no question Gerald exceeded his assignment mandate but I'm not entirely displeased with him, nevertheless. As first assignments go, the outcome could've been far less satisfactory.'

'True,' said Ralph grudgingly. 'But even so, we've got a mess on our hands, haven't we?'

A mess. Well, that was one way of putting it. Monk Markham. His sister. Princess Melissande. That bloody bird. And unpredictable, potentially lethal Gerald Dunwoody's stubborn friendship with all of them. The young wizard was right about one thing: together they'd solved this difficult case. Without Witches Inc., and Ralph's uncontrollable nephew cheering on the sidelines and playing at chauffeur, the government could well be looking at more wrecked portals ... or worse.

But even though Gerald's entanglement with his unlikely friends had proven useful this time, it also promised to be problematic in the future. Unless it could be turned to the Department's advantage, of course.

I could be wrong, but I have the sneaking suspicion that these friendships might be all that can keep Gerald on an even keel. Because if this portal business has taught us anything, it's taught us that we've not begun to plumb the depths of his abilities ... and we don't know what in time he'll become.

'So,' said Ralph. 'How are we going to clean the mess up, Alec?'

He smiled. 'Funny you should ask me that. Ralph, I've been thinking. And I believe I have a workable plan ...'

*　　*　　*

Suspension — exile — stretched out to ten days. Abandoning the dreadful bedsit, Gerald camped out with Monk. They amused themselves in Great-uncle Throgmorton's attic, mucking about with various dubious experiments, and every day drove to the Witches Inc. agency to have lunch with the girls.

Really, it was almost like a holiday. Except he didn't want a holiday, he wanted to get back to work.

'Don't be in such a rush, mate,' said Monk. 'Who knows when you'll get some time off again, once Sir Alec's put you back in harness?'

'*If* he puts me back in harness,' he replied, morose. 'Ten days and not a word either way, Monk. I just want to know what's going on. That's all.'

'Nothing's going on. This is just his way of slapping your wrist,' said Monk. 'You don't really think they'll throw you on the scrapheap, do you? Their very own tame rogue wizard?'

He supposed not. But knowing that didn't make the waiting any easier.

Lunchtime on the tenth day rolled around, and found him and Monk at Witches Inc., again. Reg brooded on her ram skull, Melissande slumped at her desk, he sprawled in the client armchair, Monk perched on Bibbie's desk, and Bibbie hovered outside the window on her flying dustbin lid. She and Monk were fighting a pitched battle with hexed paperclips.

According to Reg, the Witches Inc. phone hadn't rung for a week.

Sighing, Melissande let the *Times* fall onto her knees. Curled up on her lap, Boris hissed a complaint.

'So I was talking to Rupert last night,' she said to no-one in particular. 'He says Zazoor might have finally found himself a bride. Only Zazoor's not quite sure, because apparently the gods are being coy about it.'

Gerald smiled, half-heartedly. 'So what else is new?'

'Well, true ... but Rupes seems to think Zazoor's rather keen on this girl. And it is past time he settled down, after all.'

Reg stirred on her ram skull. 'Tell him to tell Sultan Hoity-toity I'm happy to stop by and have a word with the gods on his behalf. That old Shugat's probably past it, deaf as a post, I'll bet, and as an honorary ex-god myself I'm sure I could —'

'*No!*' everyone said loudly. 'Don't you even bloody think about it, Reg!'

Reg cracked open one eye. 'Yes, well, it was only a suggestion. I'm sure there's no need to deafen a woman. And anyway, why shouldn't I go on a little jaunt to Kallarap? It's not like anything's happening here.'

'It's not *fair*,' said Bibbie, as her paperclips fought to the death with Monk's. 'That bloody Eudora Telford. I mean, we save her life and *this* is how she repays us? By telling everyone in the Baking and Pastry Guild that *we* got Ambrose killed and sent Permelia *insane*?'

'Well ...' He shrugged. 'I suppose, when you think about it, she's not *entirely* wrong.'

'And look on the bright side,' said Reg. 'At least she's not heading off to New Ottosland to poison Rupert.'

'True,' said Melissande. 'Although —'

The agency door opened without warning, and Sir Alec walked in. If the sight of Bibbie bobbing outside the window on a dustbin lid perturbed him, he didn't show it.

Gerald sat up. *What's he doing here?* He exchanged a worried look with Monk, who'd turned pale.

'*So,*' Sir Alec said briskly, hands clasped behind his back. 'Listen carefully, ladies and gentlemen, as I explain to you how this arrangement is going to work. To all intents and purposes, Witches Inc. shall continue to operate as a legitimate thaumaturgical troubleshooting agency. In fact I anticipate that for most of the time, you shall be occupied with the kind of work you anticipated handling when you started the business. Of course, from this time forth most of that work will be filtered in to you from various avenues approved by my Department, and every job will be vetted for potential nefarious connections, but nevertheless the agency will, for the most part, be what it claims to be. Although the entire operating budget will be provided by the government and any revenue you generate shall be laid against expenses.'

Melissande, shocked, was staring with her mouth open. '*What*? I don't think so, Sir Alec. At least not without the proper consultation. You can't barge in here and —'

Sir Alec's smile was particularly wintry, even for him. 'Yes, I can, Your Highness. Or did you not realise you were interfering with an ongoing, highly classified government investigation?'

'*Interfering*?' said Reg. 'You cheeky bugger! We saved your Department's hide and you bloody well know it!'

Sir Alec ignored her. '*You*, Mister Dunwoody, shall be joining Witches Inc. as one of its employees. When not engaged on official Department business you'll keep yourself busy with any Third Grade wizard work that might cross the agency's desk. *You*, Mister Markham, will continue in your current position in Research and Development, but with secondment duties to my Department as and when I require your services. Miss Cadwallader, Miss Markham and Dulcetta —'

'I prefer Reg,' said Reg coldly. 'If it's all the same to you, sunshine.'

This time Sir Alec offered her a small bow. 'Very well … *Reg*. The three of you shall be considered auxiliary Department personnel, subject to the same official government restrictions and conditions as restrain Mister Dunwoody and Mister Markham.' He frowned. 'At least when it suits them to be restrained. In short, ladies, you are now *honorary janitors*, though I do strongly advise that you *not* let the title go to your heads.'

Her heart-stopping face framed in the open window, golden hair gleaming in the sun, blue eyes bright with unholy amusement, Bibbie bounced on her dustbin lid and laughed.

'How about that?' she crowed. 'What a *wonderful* idea!'

'You think so?' Melissande demanded. 'Well, *I* think it's — it's the most high-handed, autocratic, *bossy* —'

'I know!' said Bibbie. 'He sounds just like you — and Reg!'

As Melissande spluttered, Sir Alec continued. 'These new arrangements will commence immediately. Mister Markham, Mister Dunwoody, you will report to Nettleworth at nine o'clock tomorrow morning. Miss Cadwallader, Miss Markham and Reg, someone will be stopping by this office later today with papers for you to sign. Or, in your case, Reg, scratch. Then you too shall report to Nettleworth for further briefings.'

'Um,' said Gerald, not daring to look at Melissande. 'Wasn't there something you wanted to add, Sir Alec?'

Sir Alec frowned. 'No. I don't think so. I think I've been quite clear.'

'No, no, I think there was something else,' he said. 'Something about — I don't know — asking if we're *interested*?'

'I'm sorry,' said Sir Alec, one pale brown eyebrow lifting. 'Did you not hear what I said to Miss Cadwallader? This is — as you'd say — most definitely a done deal. Ladies and gentlemen, this is what happens when you solve a highly delicate and dangerous secret mission.' He smiled, unamused. 'You get given another one.'

'But — but —' said Melissande. 'Rupert — he's not going to like me getting involved with —'

Sir Alec considered her. 'Actually, Your Highness, His Majesty has already been informed. He asked me tell you, from him, *"Have fun"*.'

'Oh,' said Melissande faintly. Stunned, she patted Boris on the head. 'I see. Well. Gosh. Did he really?'

'Yes,' said Sir Alec, then added, 'Your family has also been informed, Miss Markham.'

'And did they give you a message for me?' asked Bibbie brightly.

'No,' said Sir Alec. 'But I've got one. *Get off that dustbin lid. It's time to grow up.*'

As the agency door clicked closed behind him they all looked at each other, lost for words.

Well. Almost lost for words.

Comfortable on her ram skull, Reg let out a sudden cackle. 'Well, boys and girls, you know what they say. If you can't beat 'em, join 'em. Bloody hell! What's next?'

Acknowledgements

This writer is only as good as the people who tell her the truth about the quality of the current work in progress. I continue to be blessed by Glenda Larke, Mary Webber and Elaine Shipp, who never pull their punches and make sure I'm doing the best that I can. If I fall short, blame me. They did their best.

Tim Holman, a true gentleman of publishing, for his ongoing support.

Samantha Smith, for all her wonderful PR efforts.

The production and design team, who lavish so much care on Orbit's books.

Britain's fantasy readers, who are so willing to embrace this wordy colonial.

The readers, who keep coming back for more.

Britain's wonderful booksellers, especially the team at Waterstones, without whom I'd be lost.

extras

www.orbitbooks.net

about the author

K. E. Mills is a pseudonym for Karen Miller, who was born in Vancouver, Canada, and came to Australia with her family when she was two. Apart from a three-year stint in the UK after graduating from university with a BA in Communications, she's lived in and around Sydney ever since. She started writing stories while still in primary school, where she fell in love with speculative fiction after reading *The Lion, The Witch and the Wardrobe*. Over the years she's held down a wide variety of jobs, including: customer service with DHL London, stud groom in Buckingham, England, PR officer for Ku-ring-gai Council, lecturer at Mount Druitt TAFE, publishing production assistant with McGraw Hill Australia and owner/manager of her own spec fic/mystery bookshop, Phantasia, at Penrith. She's written, directed and acted in local theatre, had a play professionally produced in New Zealand and contributed various articles as a freelance journalist to equestrian and media magazines. For more information visit www.karenmiller.net

Find out more about K. E. Mills and other Orbit authors by registering for the free monthly newsletter at www.orbitbooks.net

if you enjoyed
WITCHES INCORPORATED
look out for
MAY CONTAIN TRACES
OF MAGIC
by
Tom Holt

He was losing her, he could tell. The polite smile was still there, but the eyes were glazing over, the mind was drifting away. Right, he thought.

'Or there's the new BB27Ks,' he said, increasing the volume just a trifle. 'I think they'd do really well for you. Ever since we brought them out, it's been phenomenal.'

He'd got her back, just for a moment. 'I read about them,' she said; just enough enthusiasm to dirty a microscope slide, but that was something like a ninety per cent improvement. 'How are they going?'

'Brilliant,' he said, 'absolutely brilliant. Doing very nicely. Everywhere I go, people keep telling me they're just flying off the shelves.'

Immediately, he knew he'd said the wrong thing; her mouth tightened, her eyes narrowed a little. No idea why. 'In fact, we're doing a special . . .' he started to say, but a flicker of movement behind her head snagged his attention and he dried up. On the top row of the shelf unit facing him, a cardboard box had just sprouted wings.

Sod it, he thought. The NM66.

'Um,' he said, as the box stretched, preened its light grey feathers and made a soft cheeping noise. The shopkeeper looked round, swore and grabbed at it, but it was too late. The box spread its wings, hopped off the shelf and glided lazily, just out of reach of the shopkeeper's flailing hands, over their heads, out through the open door into the street.

She looked at him.

'We're working on that,' he said sheepishly. 'Bit of a snarl-up with quality control, but they promise me the next batch . . .'

'Fifteen of them,' she said bitterly. 'In just one week.'

'It's the mating season,' he mumbled. 'But they've completely redesigned the DNA sequence, and that'll sort it, no problem. Meanwhile, if you'll just do us a returns note for the, um, escaped stock, we'll get that straightened out for you, and . . .'

He ran out of words. The expression on her face was quite clear: forget it, don't bother, save your breath. But that wasn't his way. He sucked in a little air, and said brightly, 'So, shall I put you down for three dozen of the BB27K, for starters? We're offering special display materials, dumpbins, special promotional . . .'

'No, thanks,' she said.

Oh, he thought. Right, fine. 'Well, I guess that's about it for today, then. Thanks ever so much for seeing me, and I'll be back again first week in June. Meanwhile, if there's anything I can help you with . . .'

It was like pouring water into sand. He was used to it, but that didn't make it fun. And it'd be nice, just once, if he got a chance to end a sentence with something other than three dots. He smiled, closed the lid of his briefcase, thanked her once again for her time and left the shop.

It was raining outside, needless to say, as though tears for the miserable fate of all salesmen everywhere were rolling down heaven's face. One of these days, he thought, I'll get a proper job, in an office, and I won't have to do this any more. One of these days.

He looked up, and saw the stray NM66 perched on top of a nearby traffic light. Stupid bloody things, he thought as the box, now distinctly damp, cooed mildly at him; not enough sense to stay out of the rain, it'll get all soggy and fall to bits if it's not careful.

He walked back to his car, which winked its indicators at him as he thumbed the plastic key thing. At least someone's pleased to see me, he thought.

Before he drove off, he filled in the order form. That didn't take long. No BB27Ks, no GP19s, he'd been stone-cold certain he'd be able to shift a couple of outers of YJ42s but no dice. Just a couple of trays of AA1s and the inevitable repeat order for DW6 . . .

That made him frown, as it always did. DW6: one of the firm's biggest sellers, but in seven years he'd yet to meet anybody who knew what the stupid stuff was actually *for*. It was, by any criteria, the weirdest, most totally improbable concept he'd come across (and in this business, that was saying a lot). None of the reps knew what it was supposed to do, the buyers hadn't got a clue, the shop managers and sales assistants didn't know; but *the customers bought it*, by the bucketful, by the skipload, so—

Never mind, he told himself firmly as he switched on the SatNav and waited for it to warm up. A mystery it might be, but at least he could shift it; three hearty cheers for small mercies. There were some months (and this might well prove to be one of them, the way things were going) when the only thing that stood between him and an excitingly challenging change in career direction was DW6.

Even so.

SatNav flickered into brightly backlit life, and he touched the nail of his index finger to the screen. The colours swirled, and it said—

(It said; *she* said –)

– SatNav said, 'Your route is being calculated; please wait,' and for a moment he forgot about snotty shop managers and flying cardboard boxes and his monthly target and perversely inexplicable megaselling DW6, because there was something about its voice, her voice, that was so wonderfully soothing and reassuring; like she understood him, like she cared—

He frowned. They'd warned him about that, of course. He glanced at the little screen, as the picture swung wildly through the *x* axis and settled itself. Straight on out of town until he hit the main A666, then take the second exit. Fine.

Not much traffic at this time of day. He'd warned them about the NM66, of course, told them till he was blue in the face and would they listen? Fat chance. He'd told them that it was just a matter of time before an escaped pair started breeding, and then the brown stuff'd hit the swiftly whirring blades all right: tabloid headlines, billion-dollar lawsuits, the boing-boing noise of rolling heads in the deep-pile-carpeted corridors of corporate power. He sighed. They lived in a world of their own in Kettering.

He turned the radio on, but it was some phone-in, so he fished about in the glove compartment for a CD. Now there (he thought, as he scrabbled one-handed through the plastic cases) was another bloody mystery, because a third of the stuff in there was garbage he'd never have bought in a million years, a third he couldn't even recognise, and of the remaining third that he was prepared to acknowledge as his own, the one thing he actually wanted to find was always missing. White Stripes; no, not today. Very Best of James Blunt – contradiction in terms. He looked up just in time to avoid smashing into the back of a lorry, and grabbed something at random.

It turned out to be a home-made job, no label or writing on it, so presumably one of Karen's compilation CDs – no idea how they came to end up in his glove compartment; another mystery. He stuck it in anyway, and it turned out not to be too bad after all, though of course he had to keep the volume right down so he could hear SatNav—

'After three hundred yards,' SatNav said, 'turn left.'

He realised he was smiling, and frowned instead. So what, she had, *it* had a nice voice: bright, warm, friendly, ever so slightly sexy but— All right, so *what*? Obviously they'd chosen a voice that was carefully designed to appeal to the tired, stressed-out male driver, and they were good at their jobs, and they'd succeeded. There was absolutely nothing wrong with that, nothing odd or sinister or strange about it, and if he'd rather listen to her – it – than to the Proclaimers or the miserable sods on the radio, that was perfectly all right, nothing whatsoever to worry about. Even so, he turned the CD player up just a little bit, and self-consciously tapped out the beat on the steering wheel with his fingers.

I worry too much, he thought; and when there's too much or too little to worry about, I worry about worrying. Maybe I should be worried about that, too. Or maybe I should just get a bloody grip, and concentrate on getting through the next call without screwing up too monumentally badly.

'At the next junction,' SatNav said, 'turn left.'

'What? Oh, yes,' he muttered, and dabbed at the indicator stalk. 'Thanks.'

'You're welcome.'

Now then, he thought. Next call was Stetchkin & Sons: old-established family firm, conservative, the archetypal no-call-for-that-round-here outfit, which meant he was going to have to come up with something pretty stunningly amazing if he was going to offload any BB27Ks on them. He rehearsed the standard pitch in his mind. No chance. Come on, he told himself reproachfully, you're a salesman, you can do this—

'I can,' he said aloud, like they'd told him to on his Innovation & Assertiveness Awareness Day (complete waste of time, except for the spring rolls at lunchtime). 'I can. There's no such word as can't.'

It sounded even sillier than usual, and he grinned. Yes, he thought, but just for the hell of it, like it's some kind of bet I'm having with myself; if only to see the look on old Mr Stetchkin's face when he realises he's just placed an order for three dozen of something he didn't know he wanted. I *can* do this—

'Yes,' he said. 'Can't I, SatNav?'

'Of course you can.'

He frowned, changed down to overtake a cyclist, and said, 'Yes, well, it's easy for you to say. You've never met old Mr Stetchkin.'

'Tell me about him.'

He grinned, and turned off the CD player. 'Oh God,

where do I begin? Right, then, for a start he's seventy if he's a day, bald with little bits of white fluff over his ears like cotton wool, stupid little tufty white beard—'

'He sounds rather sweet, actually.'

Bitter laugh. 'I don't think so,' he said. 'He's one of those miserable, nit-picking types, never satisfied, nothing's ever right, won't ever listen to what you've got to say, reckons he knows it all, you really wouldn't—'

'After three hundred yards,' SatNav interrupted, 'turn right. And perhaps,' she went on, 'if he's been in the business for a long time and he's still going, maybe he does know it all. Or at least quite a lot of it.'

He was going to laugh derisively, but he didn't. 'It's a good business, Stetchkins,' he said thoughtfully. 'They've always done well, even in the recession. There's not many that can say that.'

'Now turn right,' SatNav said. 'So perhaps Mr Stetchkin's got good reason to think he knows it all.'

'Maybe.'

'I'd have thought someone like that would be quite proud of his experience.'

He frowned. 'Go on.'

'Oh, I was just thinking, after all those years in the trade, he must have heard every pitch there is, over and over again, till he's sick of hearing them all. People trying really hard to sell him things, I mean.'

'I suppose so,' he said. 'But that's not helping me, is it?'

'After six hundred yards, take the second exit. If I was Mr Stetchkin,' SatNav said, 'I wouldn't want some young rep coming into my shop and trying to shove some new product up my nose, telling me how wonderful it is. No, if there's a new line I might be interested in, I'd want to look at it carefully, see if it's any good and make my own decision. Don't you think?'

'Fine,' he replied huffily. 'That's me out of a job, then.'

'Not at all. Your job is to bring the merchandise to the customers' attention.'

'That's one way of looking at it,' he said sarcastically. 'Only I wouldn't last very long if all I . . .'

'Take the second exit.'

'What? Oh, shit, right.'

'Personally,' SatNav went on, 'if it was me, I'd start off just taking down the reorders, let him do all the talking to begin with, and then I'd say something like—'

'Like?'

'I'm thinking, please wait. Something like, "I don't know if you've got a moment, Mr Stetchkin, but I'd quite like your opinion of this new line we're bringing out"; and then you hand it to him and take a step back, and don't say anything until he's finished looking at it—'

'That's not bad,' Mr Stetchkin said.

Oink, he thought. 'You think it's OK?' he said.

Mr Stetchkin nodded. 'It's quite good,' he said. 'Neat. Well thought out. Good value for money.'

He frowned, like she'd told him to, and tried to sound slightly worried. 'You don't think the packaging's a bit, well, loud—?'

Mr Stetchkin shook his head. 'No, not really. Nice bright colours, catches the eye.'

'But isn't it a bit on the dear side? For what it is, I mean.'

Mr Stetchkin thought about that for a moment. 'I don't think so,' he said. 'Customers know they get what they pay for. If it was any cheaper, it'd send the wrong message. You wouldn't expect to get anything like this worth having for nine ninety-nine.'

'That's true,' he said, as though reluctantly conceding the

point. 'And you think the way it folds up at the back is all right? I was a little concerned people might think it's a bit, well, fiddly.'

Mr Stetchkin gave him a patronising smile. 'Hardly,' he said. 'Look, I can do it with one hand, see?' And he folded it up easily, as though he'd been practising for a week. 'No, I have to say, I really like this – What did you say the code was?'

He made a show of looking at his book. 'BB27K,' he said.

'Yes, thank you.' Mr Stetchkin handed him back the sample, and nodded. 'I'll take ten dozen.'

'I *think* we may be able to – Just let me check.' He looked back at the book and saw that it was upside down. Luckily, Mr Stetchkin hadn't noticed. 'Yes, we can let you have ten dozen, just about. Usual rate?'

Mr Stetchkin nodded again, and for a moment the shop seemed to flicker, because Mr Stetchkin *always* screwed you to the floor over discounts. 'Now then,' Mr Stetchkin went on, 'I'd like another six dozen of the DW6, and this time, tell them I don't want to find any of them with the seals broken, I think I may have mentioned this before—'

'It was amazing,' he said. 'Ten dozen. He took ten dozen, and—'

'At the end of the road, turn left.'

'Yes, I *know*, I've been here before. Now all I've got to do is shift three dozen more and I've made my target, and I'm pretty sure I can get rid of two dozen on the Valmet brothers, which just leaves one, and I'm home free.'

'That's marvellous. I knew you could do it.'

He was grinning again. But, he thought, why the hell not? Nobody else would've said that to him. 'I reckon we've done a good day's work today,' he said. 'You and me.'

No reply; but that was fair enough, it was a straight stretch of road. He sat back in his seat and tapped the wheel a few times, beating out the rhythm from one of the tracks he'd played earlier; catchy tune, he wondered who it was by.

'Excuse me.'

'Mm?'

'Only,' she said, 'I was wondering.'

'Yes?'

'This BB—'

'BB27K?'

'That's it, yes. Only . . .' Brief hesitation, like she was about to take a slight liberty. 'What is it? I mean, what does it actually do?'

He smiled. 'It's the latest thing,' he said. 'Kettering's mad about it, really pushing it. Hence the bloody enormous target.'

'Yes, but—'

His smile widened. 'It's a portable folding parking space,' he said. 'It comes in a little plastic wallet, and you take it out and unfold it and lay it down on the road, and it expands into a space big enough to take anything up to a small minibus. When you're ready to leave, you just pick it up and put it away and off you go. Even works on double yellows. I'm going to see if I can nick one for myself, it'll make my life so much—'

'That's a really good idea,' she said.

'Invented by Professor Cornelius Van Spee of Leiden,' he recited, 'a by-product of research into—'

'Wasn't he the one who went mad and tried to blow up the planet?'

He shrugged. 'Search me,' he replied. 'I just sell them. Or try to,' he added. 'And, thanks to you . . .'

'Not at all,' she said. 'You were the one who made the sale. I just—'

'Should I be turning right here?'

'What? Oh, yes, sorry.'

'No problem,' he said, turning the wheel. 'And then it's right at the crossroads, isn't it?'

'Yes. I mean, at the end of the road, turn right. Sorry.'

'That's OK.' He slid the gear lever into fourth. 'What were you telling me just now about Professor Van Spee?'

'Well,' SatNav replied, 'if he's the one I'm thinking of, he tried to create a pocket universe. There was a lot of trouble about it, at the time.'

He frowned. 'That's no big deal,' he said. 'I mean, we do those: the JH88C. Get away from it all in a world of your own for only two-nine-nine ninety-nine. We sell a lot of them.'

'Yes,' she said. 'But this one actually *worked*.'

'Ah.' He thought for a moment, then said, 'Hang on, though. The JH88C works. Any rate, I've never had any sent back, so they must be all right.'

Slight pause; then she said, 'The JH88C creates an inter-dimensional bubble capable of supporting one adult human for up to forty-eight hours at a time, while the inbuilt matter/energy transfiguration unit allows limited holographic imaging for a strictly limited range of pre-programmed fantasy activities. Van Spee's version was permanent, and you could do anything you liked in there.'

'Really?' He raised his eyebrows. 'Cool.'

'Cool,' she agreed, 'except that it did all sorts of horrible things to the real world. But he didn't care about that. Not a nice man.'

'Obviously.' He thought for a moment, then said, 'You know a lot about it—'

'For a SatNav, you mean?' She didn't say it nastily or anything, but he got the message. 'I don't just do quickest-way-from-A-to-B, you know.'

'That's for sure,' he said. 'You know, I went to this launch meeting about the JH88C, and they told us all about it and the points we should be stressing to customers and all that, but they didn't say anything about interdimensional bubbles or blowing up planets.'

'Didn't want to overload you with stuff you didn't need to know, presumably.'

'I guess so.' Pause; thought. 'But *you* know—'

'After six hundred yards, take the first exit.'

So he did; and a sociopath in a Daf sixteen-wheeler tried to carve him up on the inside, which provoked him into the use of intemperate language, and after that he'd forgotten what they'd been talking about; and soon afterwards they turned into Frobisher Way, and she said, 'You have now arrived at your destination,' and he parked the car and went in to the office.

'Oh, it's you,' said Julie on reception. 'You're late.'

'Am I?'

She nodded. 'He's waiting for you,' she said. 'In the small interview room.'

'Ah,' he said. 'Lucky me.'

As he trudged slowly through the industrial Axminster, he ran through a short list of possibilities. Get rid of the most unlikely ones first: he's pleased with me, he wants to give me a pay rise, he wants to promote me. Yes indeed; and the pig now boarding at gate number six is the 17:09 scheduled flight to Mogadishu. Rather more probable: he's pissed off at me, he's really pissed off at me, he's really seriously pissed off at me—

He knocked on the door, waited for the familiar grunt, and went in. At the far end of the room, his huge pink face reflected in the highly polished table top, sat Mr Burnoz, area manager; not a pleasant sight, but not so bad if you're expecting it. Opposite him was some scraggy kid in glasses.

'You wanted to see me, Mr—'

'Come in, sit down.' Mr Burnoz turned his head and smiled at the scraggy kid. Female, he noted, more than a passing resemblance to a weasel. 'Angela, I'd like you to meet Chris Popham, one of our sales reps. Chris, this is Angela –' some surname he didn't catch '– who's joining us for a month as part of her degree course.' Burnoz smiled hugely, as if he was trying to catch the sun in his teeth. 'Angela's taking advantage of our sponsored graduate-intake programme. Ultimately we're hoping she'll be joining us at Kettering, meanwhile we're giving her this opportunity to get some front-line hands-on experience in basic marketing.'

A chill sensation, like a column of frozen ants climbing up his leg. 'That's great,' Chris said through a fixed smile. 'How do I—?'

'We thought it'd be a really good idea if Angela sat in with you while you do your rounds for the next six weeks,' said Mr Burnoz, cheerful as a game-show host, oblivious as an ice-breaker grinding through permafrost. 'You can show her what it's really like in the trenches, so to speak, the raw, bloody cut and thrust of modern marketing. Not something you can get a feel of from books or sitting in front of a computer screen, I'm sure you'll agree. I know Angela's really looking forward to it.'

In which case, Chris thought, never under any circumstances play poker with this child for money, since she clearly guards her emotions like a dragon on a pile of gold.

'Absolutely,' he heard himself croak. 'Great idea.'

'Splendid,' said Mr Burnoz, as the scraggy kid shifted her head a fraction to the left and gave him a look that would've separated paint. 'In that case, why don't you pick her up outside the building here at, what, let's say six-fifteen tomorrow morning, and you can take it from there.'

Chris hoped he'd managed not to let the pain show in his face. 'All right, then,' he said. 'I'll look forward to it.'

The raw, bloody cut and thrust of modern marketing. That was, he told himself as he slouched back across the pure-wool tundra, one way of describing it. But offloading a trainee – and not just a trainee: a graduate trainee, a graduate bloody trainee who hadn't even graduated yet, a *kid* – on him was a refinement of cruelty he wouldn't have thought anybody, even Mr Burnoz, was capable of. It was heartless, it was vicious, savage, inhuman and unnatural; furthermore, he was at least ninety-nine-point-nine-eight per cent sure that Mr Burnoz hadn't meant it that way. Far from it. Somebody – Kettering, presumably – had sent Mr Burnoz a memo saying *offload this skinny kid on one of your reps*, and Mr Burnoz had chosen him at random, or because he'd seen his name on a report or an expenses claim at some point recently, and had recalled it when faced with the chore of placing the trainee . . . Arguably, that was worse. Which would you rather be: the martyr on the lonely gallows, or the hedgehog squashed flat by the artic whose driver hadn't even seen you?

Back into reception, where Julie – she was married, and every time she mentioned her husband Chris couldn't help thinking of those birds in Africa who live by picking shreds of meat out of the jaws of crocodiles – handed him a sheaf of yellow While You Were Out notes, which he stuffed into his briefcase without looking at them. A *trainee*, he muttered to himself as he splashed through puddles in the car park, a sodding *kid*. And six-fifteen in the bloody morning.

He'd started the car and let in the clutch before he remembered; and then he felt a little better. Today was Wednesday, Karen's evening class, which meant . . . He smiled, eased the car into gently purring motion, and drove gracefully home, stopping to let other people go at junctions.

There was a note on the kitchen table: *no food*. Chris acknowledged it with a slight nod. Sometimes, though rarely, Karen cooked. He didn't hold it against her; he guessed it was something she felt she had to do now and again, and it was probably just as well that she got it out of her system, rather than bottling it up and getting some sort of a complex. Nonetheless, in their house the definition of good food was like the proverbial definition of good news. He'd get a burger instead, or a kebab. Things were looking up.

Chris changed quickly, lynching his suit on a wire hanger and pulling on a pair of jeans, transferred his wallet, phone and keys to his civilian jacket, checked the mercifully mute answering machine and lunged back out again, walking quickly without actually running, as if escaping from a PoW camp. A glance at his watch told him he was cutting it fine, for which he had Mr Burnoz and the skinny teenager to thank. As he turned the corner by the pillar box, he realised that he was rehearsing an opening line in his head. He wondered about that, just briefly, but so-whatted away the tender shoots of guilt. My evening off, he told himself. I deserve it.

She'd got there first; she always did. She'd bagged a table – not too close to the door, the bar or the toilets – and bought the drinks. She always did it, and he'd never once commented on it. Furthermore, she always smiled when she saw him. He couldn't think of anybody else who did that.

(But that's OK, Chris told himself, his inner voice just a touch nervous inside his head. That's the difference between a permanent might-as-well-be-married girlfriend and a, well, a *friend*. A friend is someone who likes you.)

'Sorry I'm late,' he said, dropping into his seat. 'Held up at the office. Don't ask. No,' he added, as his fingers closed around the cool, damp body of the glass, 'Ask. I need to whine at somebody.'

'Fine,' she said. 'Whine away.'

So he whined: Mr Burnoz (she knew all about him by now), the trainee, six-fifteen in the morning. She nodded at just the right times, precisely the right tempo and degree of spinal flex, the murmurs and tongue-clicks interpolated at exactly the right moments. All fake, of course; but somehow, that didn't spoil it. Quite the reverse, in fact. Chris knew perfectly well that if her boss called her in and assigned her a trainee to babysit for six weeks, she'd accept the assignment as an interesting and worthwhile challenge, and by the time the six weeks were up the trainee would scuttle back to college with a renewed sense of purpose, and quite likely they'd send each other Christmas cards for the rest of their lives. So of course she didn't understand why he was ranting about the bitter injustice of it all, but nevertheless she was pretending to, and that was really very kind—

'Anyway,' he said (rant over; and yes, he felt a whole lot better now), 'that's quite enough of that.'

'Yes,' she replied, with a very slight nod of her head. 'So, how's Karen? I haven't heard from her for ages.'

'Oh, same as usual.' He was frowning, for some reason. 'Still doing the evening classes. And working late.'

She absorbed the information without any show of opinion. It was a special talent of hers. 'She always was a busy bee,' she added. 'I remember her in our A-level year—'

'You can't talk,' Chris felt constrained to point out. 'You were worse.'

She nodded. 'Still am,' she said. 'All work and no play makes Jill a senior executive officer and deputy head of department. Of course,' she added, 'it helps if you enjoy what you do.'

He frowned a little. 'Quite,' he said. 'Killed anything interesting lately?'

'As a matter of fact, yes. We had a level-three infestation just outside Faversham, and it was my turn. Bloody Robinson tried to gazump me, but I insisted. Two of them,' she went on, fiddling with the rim of her glass. 'A nesting pair.'

In spite of himself Chris was impressed. 'They're supposed to be particularly nasty, aren't they?'

Nod. 'We eventually got them cornered in the toilets of a sort of Happy Eater place – me, Derek and old George Ruffer – he's supposed to be semi-retired now but he still turns out when we're short-staffed. They had to cone off two lanes of the motorway. Got them in the end, though.'

'Rather you than me,' Chris said, with genuine feeling. 'I really don't know how you can do that,' he went on. 'I mean, quite apart from the danger. I just can't get my head around how you go about it. Mentally, I mean. You wake up, coffee and cereal, what shall I wear to work today, seat on the train if you're lucky, and then, ten minutes after you've clocked in you're out there with a suitcase full of weapons fighting the forces of primeval darkness. I don't think I could face it, really.'

Jill shrugged. 'It's interesting,' she said. 'Also useful, you've got to admit.'

'Dirty job but someone's got to do it?' Chris pulled a face. 'Come on,' he said, 'that's not the real reason.'

'Very true.' She smiled. 'The real reason is, if I stick at it for another three years—'

'And manage not to get killed or horribly mauled—'

'Yes, quite. If I stick at it three more years, I'm practically guaranteed the next junior secretaryship when one crops up, which otherwise I wouldn't have a hope in hell of being considered for until I'm at least forty. And after that—'

Chris pulled another face, and Jill laughed again. 'Well, I'm sorry, that's just how I am,' she said. 'I like being ambitious, it keeps things interesting. I know it doesn't suit you, and that's fine. I guess I'm just not a rut person. And if it means having to kill a few demons now and again, there's worse ways of making a living. Accountancy. Insurance. Anything with children.'

'Or selling,' he said. 'Now there's a dead-end career if you like.'

'Quite.' Jill grinned. 'Look at you, for example. Seven years of devoted service, and they land you with a trainee. Give me a nice, straightforward demon any time.'

Chris realised he was scowling, but made no effort to stop. 'Ah well,' he said. 'I didn't go to university, so what can I expect?'

She didn't react; she never did. But Chris felt something click into place between them, separating them, and (as always) wished he hadn't said it. Meanwhile, she was looking at him, and he could read the message as clearly as though she had a ticker-tape machine on her forehead. *It's not just because she's a trainee*, he read, *it's because she's a graduate trainee. Can't forgive her for that, can you?* He shrugged, and she knew him well enough to accept it as a retraction, a reset to zero, as though the U-word hadn't been said out loud that evening.

'Changing the subject,' he said briskly (and a slight glow in Jill's eyes meant she approved), 'there's something I've been meaning to ask you, since you know all about the business and everything.'

'I do,' she said. 'Go on.'

So he told her all about the DW6 mystery; but he hadn't got very far when she stopped him.

'How do you mean,' Jill said, looking uncharacteristically blank, 'powdered water?'

Chris looked at her. 'You're kidding me, right?'

But she wasn't, because she didn't do that sort of thing. He paused, while the world went all to pieces and slowly re-formed around him. 'Are you seriously telling me you've never heard of—?'

Jill frowned. 'Come to that,' she replied, 'are you seriously telling me there's such a thing as powdered water?'

'Apparently.' Chris shrugged. 'At least, it's this sort of very fine grey powder, like a kind of mixture of talc and soot. It comes in a plastic tub with a kidproof lid, you can have the one-kilo size or the five-hundred—'

'Powdered *water*?'

'That's what it says on the label,' he replied, ever so slightly defensively. 'Mind you, I've never actually seen it in action, so to speak. But—'

Jill was focusing on him. He knew that look. It was lucky she didn't wear glasses, or she'd burn holes in things. 'It's a gag thing, surely. Like pet rocks and bottled LA smog, novelty Christmas gifts for sad people.'

Chris shook his head. 'I don't think so,' he replied. 'We don't do stuff like that.'

Now Jill raised her eyebrows; not a good sign. Two gym mistresses and a maths teacher had needed counselling, back in Year Ten. 'Does it say on it how you're supposed to use it? I mean, are there instructions on the tub?'

Another headshake. 'All it says is, *instant powdered water, just add . . .*'

Pause. She was thinking. 'Just add?'

'And then three dots,' he told her. 'Just add dot dot dot. Oh, and there's a lot of legal stuff: *for use as a water substitute only, may contain traces of*—'

'Just add.' Jill's thoughtful frown had escalated into a scowl. 'That's silly,' she said.

'Yes.' His turn to frown. 'Really, haven't you heard of it? I thought you knew all about – well, trade stuff. Magic artefacts and their properties. Didn't you do a—?'

'A course, yes,' Jill said. 'In my second year at Loughborough. And yes, we did everything, you name it, from mandrake roots to elixirs of eternal youth.' A thought struck her; Chris could see the ripples of impact in the lines appearing on her forehead. 'Is it a fairly recent thing?' she asked. 'Only I suppose it could be a recent invention, hence not covered in the course.'

Shrug. 'Don't think so,' he replied. 'I get the impression from customers that they've been ordering it from us for years.'

'Powdered water, for crying out loud.' Now he'd done it; a question to which Jill didn't know the answer. She hated those. 'And you've no idea what the people who buy it use it for?'

'That's what I wanted to ask you.' Now he was starting to feel guilty. She took things seriously. Something like this could spoil her whole day. 'I wish I hadn't asked you now. Only I was sure you'd—'

'No, that's fine.' She sounded like she was having trouble remembering he was there. 'I'll ask around at work,' she said, making an effort to break free of the mystery. 'Someone's bound to have . . . And you sell a lot of this stuff?'

'Hundreds of kilos,' Chris replied. 'One of our best lines. Most of the places I go've got a standing order.'

'Oh. Oh well. As soon as I've found out about it, I'll tell you. Just add,' Jill repeated, the frown coming back and changing her face into one he hardly recognised. 'Just add what, though? And why bother? I mean, it's not as though water's all that hard to come by in this country. For export, yes, I could see the point. But when all you've got to do is turn on a tap—'

This could go on all night, Chris realised, and it wasn't the way he wanted to spend his evening off. If he wanted tension and one-sided conversations, he could talk to Karen— 'Anyway,' he said, a little louder than he'd meant to, 'how's everything with you? Apart from work, I mean,' he added quickly.

'What? Oh, fine.'

'Heard from any of the others lately?'

He was on firm ground there. Jill had taken on herself the duty of collating and distributing detailed updates on every-body in their year, and needless to say, she did it very well. 'Paul's still with the BBC, of course, he's producing garden-ing programmes now. Amelia's transferred from the Tank Corps to Signals. Sara got deported from Bolivia for raising awareness about something or other; she's being very smug about that. Colin's still on the run, there was a sighting in Leeds about six weeks ago, they assume he's trying to leave the country on a false passport—'

Fine. Ten minutes or so later, the difficulty had evapo-rated, though Chris knew it hadn't really gone away. Rather, Jill had filed and stored it, and sooner or later an answer would be forthcoming. He noted with approval that at no point had she said, 'Well, why the hell don't *you* ask someone, it's your stupid firm that makes the stupid stuff,' or words to that effect. She understood perfectly why that simply wasn't an option; though of course, if she was a sales rep for JWW Retail, it'd have been the first thing she'd have done. As for that cursory *What? Oh, fine*, he was prepared to take it at face value; not because he wasn't interested. Quite the opposite. One of these days, he'd get an answer to that question that he knew he wasn't going to like. The longer that particular experience could be postponed, the better.

They chatted aimlessly for a while after that, and Chris

managed to keep the conversation away from any more danger areas, though it was touch and go a few times; the nastiest moment was when Jill started complaining about how she'd been putting on weight again (and, since she'd raised the subject, it was perfectly true; but he knew it didn't signify, since she had one of those Stock Exchange metabolisms – massive gains one week, huge losses the next – and so long as she kept two sets of clothes, one in size zero and the other in extra-large, he couldn't see how it could possibly matter to a rational human being ... In the event, he deflected her away from all that by asking her about the demon-hunting business; it wasn't something he liked being told about, but it was better than a detailed analysis of her latest diet.

'We really need to find out how they're getting through,' Jill was saying. 'Until we know a lot more about that, it's really just guesswork and how quickly we can react once an infestation's been reported to us. There's theories, of course, but none of them seem to hold up once you try applying them in practice. For example, there was this article in *New Thaumaturgical Quarterly* about quantum fluctuations in the Earth's metadimensional field—'

'Is that right?' Chris said hopelessly. 'I didn't even know we had a—'

'Which,' Jill ground on, 'may give rise to anomalous crossfield events which the demons could've evolved to exploit, sort of like cracks, or bubbles. But it's all a bit vague and theoretical, if you ask me. I still prefer the hypothesis put forward by Kanamoto and Van Spee in 1846, which seeks to explain demon incursions in terms of artificially induced Otherspace interfaces, presupposing a negatively charged ionic curtain existing somewhere in the D6 void—'

In other words, white noise, which Chris had long since

learned to tune out; it was soothing, when you were sitting in a pleasant pub holding a full glass, and basically he just liked hearing the sound of her voice: eager, earnest, clever, friendly, safe; not asking him to understand, let alone agree or form an opinion. It wasn't like when Karen talked at him, when there was always a very real threat that there'd be a test afterwards, or a sudden silence which he was supposed to fill with exactly the right form of sympathetic reassurance. Most of all, he liked being talked at by Jill because she never ever talked about Us; though the downside of that was that there wasn't an Us for them to talk about. But, he felt sure, even if there had been (if only −), she'd never have dreamed of talking about it. He couldn't imagine her doing such a thing. To the best of his knowledge, in all the years he'd known her she'd never been half of any kind of an Us. She belonged to too many people, he supposed, too many friends all relying on her to listen and understand. A greater Us, of which she was the coordinator and historian. For a moment he felt a stab of jealousy, but it didn't take long for it to pass.

Closing time swooped down too soon; Chris said good-night and walked home. It was only as he unlocked the door, shoving the thing he'd been carrying in his right hand under his arm so he could get out his keys, that he realised he'd picked up her bag by mistake. Ever since he'd known Jill, she'd always had a carrier bag; Tesco or Safeway in the early days, upgraded to M&S once she left school and started earning; these days, now that she was affluent and successful, it'd be something black or burgundy with gold lettering on it, but still a plastic carrier, her trade mark. What she carried in her carriers had always been something of a mystery, since she packed her vital instruments − purse, phone, glamour-repair kit and the like − in a conventional handbag, usually of great elegance and splendour. But she also had the knack of frustrating curiosity without even seeming to try; the carrier always came to rest between her feet, or wedged between her thigh and the side of the chair, safe from surreptitious investigation. But not, apparently, this time.

Chris paused, standing in the hall by the cheap Ikea phone table, and tried to reconstruct the sequence of events. Jill had stood up; the carrier had been in her hand, but she'd rested it on the table while she'd put on her coat; he'd picked it up to give it to her, but then she'd dropped her handbag, and by the time she'd retrieved that they'd been talking about something – Izzy Bowden's divorce, he recalled – and then someone had nearly barged into them and they'd been preoccupied with taking evasive action; and they'd walked out of the pub together, and *he'd still been holding the carrier—*

Chris went into the kitchen and sat down. A square of spilt milk on the worktop told him that Karen was home – she had an unfortunate tendency to attack cardboard milk cartons with wild enthusiasm and knives, which meant milk went everywhere when she poured – but he couldn't hear her crashing about and she hadn't called out when he opened the door, so presumably she'd already gone to bed. He put the carrier bag down on the kitchen table and looked at it, torn apart by opposing forces of extraordinary power.

On the one hand: anybody who took advantage of an honest mistake to go snooping about in other people's private carrier bags was obviously lower than a basement, and even the thought of doing such a thing made Chris shudder. The honourable course of action would be to seal the top with parcel tape and quickly leave a message on her answerphone to say he'd got it. On the other hand—

As the debate raged inside him, Chris examined the outside of the bag. It was dark navy blue, with *Shotwell & Hogue* ·tten on it in curly gold italics. He knew them, of course.

They were on his patch; good customers, in fact they'd taken a dozen BB27Ks purely on his unsupported recommendation. Somehow, that tipped the balance (he had absolutely no idea why). Feeling like someone robbing his child's piggy bank to get money for drugs, he gently opened the bag and peered inside.

Something of an anticlimax. Inside the bag Chris saw a paperback book (something by Alan Titchmarsh entirely unrelated to gardening), a packet of plain digestive biscuits, a baseball cap with the letters DS on the front and a pair of black patent shoes. He frowned, feeling let down and betrayed as well as guilty. It was a bit much, he felt, to have sold his soul and forfeited his honour for this collection of old tat.

The phone rang. Chris let go of the bag and lunged back into the hall, to shut the stupid thing up before it woke Karen.

'Chris?' It was Jill.

He scowled. 'Yes, I've got it,' he said. 'Your blasted bag. And before you ask,' he added, 'no, I haven't looked inside it. It must've been when you were putting on your coat, I suppose I—'

'That's OK,' Jill said; and it wasn't just his imagination, she did sound relieved. 'I was just worried I'd left it in the pub, that's all. Look, is there any chance you can drop it round at my place on your way tomorrow morning? Only—'

'Sorry,' Chris said, 'not really. I've got to pick up that bloody trainee at six-fifteen, remember. Which reminds me,' he added. 'Must remember to set the alarm.'

'You could leave it in the porch,' Jill said. 'Or ring the bell and I'll pop down.'

Chris felt his eyebrow hitch. 'At half past five in the morning?'

'I'll be up, I expect,' she replied, in a voice he couldn't immediately analyse. A pause; then, 'It's just that strictly speaking we're not supposed to take confidential stuff out of the office, and the new manager gets quite stressy about that sort of thing. I don't want to give him an excuse to have a go at me.'

'Fine, no problem,' Chris replied, as he thought: Confidential stuff? Would that be the top secret paperback or the For-Your-Feet-Only slingbacks? 'I'll drop it off, then.'

'Thanks.' Again, the relief. 'Just ring the bell, don't wait for me. Sorry to have bothered you.'

As Chris returned to the kitchen to pick up the bag and put it in the hall where he wouldn't forget it, the criminal urge came back. After all, Jill wouldn't know if he took just one more peek, and somehow the fact that she'd lied (confidential stuff, mustn't leave the office; yeah, right) made it seem tantalisingly easy. This time, though, he fought it back, and that made him feel rather proud – she'd lied, he'd resisted temptation, so he'd managed to fight his way back to the moral high ground, which is always nice. He turned off the lights and went to bed.

The blue Shotwell & Hogue carrier bag waited until it was quite safe – the humans were making loud respiratory noises, indicating deep sleep – then stirred, its thin plastic fabric shivering like the shell of a hatching egg. If anybody had been there to see, he'd have had a frustrating time of it, because as the bag shivered it sucked in darkness from the surrounding shadows, a useful trick well known to its kind. When it felt dark enough to be safe, it shook itself like a dog and stood up, the plastic stretching and moulding itself into a new shape: humanoid but short, bow-legged, crouching. It took a step forward, leaving the cap, the shoes, the book and the empty ̲̲̲̲it wrapper (it had been peckish) lying on the carpet.

Treading carefully, it stepped over them and walked silently through the hall into the kitchen, following the human's scent trail. It found nothing of great interest there, though it did pause to lap up the few drops of spilt milk, and went on into the sitting room, where it rubbed itself against the television screen, happily absorbing the static electricity, pulled out the plug and licked the brass prongs. A few sights and smells there, but nothing it could really use; the good stuff had faded, dried up so that it tasted dusty and bitter, all the nourishment desiccated out of it. A pity: if it had been there a week earlier it could've had a feast. It yawned and stretched; then, taking extra care not to make a sound, it gently nudged open the bedroom door and peered round it, to stare at the two humans asleep in the dark.

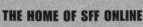